SUSPICION'S FIRE

MARI CARR

LILA DUBOIS

For Karen, because she thrived.

For American Airlines, because their accidental destruction of Lila's laptop inspired us to drink gin at 9 am and rage-plot with darker elements than normal. After drunken plotting, rather than scrap everything, we looked at one another and decided to keep the plot and write a dark romance. On that note, please read the author note.

AUTHOR NOTE AND TRIGGER WARNING

Suspicion's Fire is a dark romance. This is the first book in the series to which we're giving the "dark" label. The story contains depictions of human trafficking and rape.

If you would still like to read the story, you can skip chapters 16 and 17, but be aware that the end of the book deals with the aftermath of the events depicted in those chapters.

CHAPTER ONE

Emiliano Ortiz glanced across the courtyard and smiled as he watched his bride conversing with her mother and several other guests, flutes of champagne and small plates of canapes in their hands. She appeared to be telling an entertaining story as the people surrounding her leaned closer, smiling and laughing.

After the ceremony, the wedding party had adjourned to their rooms for a brief respite while guests enjoyed light refreshments, and the staff had set up the courtyard for the cocktail hour and the small ballroom for the seven-course dinner.

Emiliano had remained in his tuxedo, but his new wife had changed out of her wedding dress—a stunning white lace gown that had taken his breath away when he'd first seen her—into an equally eye-catching evening gown, the deep red silk bringing out the dark auburn highlights in her hair.

Among the other women, Gabriella Torres stood out. Not because of her beauty—though she was truly gorgeous—but because of her presence. Gabriella seemed to command the room, her poise, her wit, her intelligence radiating from her, drawing others in, making them want to bask in her glow.

His wedding day had loomed large in his mind ever since joining the Masters' Admiralty, recruited into membership by the previous admiral of Castile, Ricardo Garcia, a decade earlier.

Emiliano had initially been shocked to learn of the centuries' old secret society that operated in the background of much of Europe. The Masters' Admiralty existed in the shadows, influencing not only governments but also advances in science, medicine, and the arts. They recruited the best and the brightest, their membership roster filled with people all dedicated to the idea of making the world a better place.

He'd been honored and astounded when invited to join their ranks, unconcerned about one rather unconventional membership requirement.

He'd agreed to be placed in an arranged marriage.

A marriage between not two but three people.

"She's beautiful."

Emiliano turned and nodded slightly as Vicente Coval—his new husband—stepped next to him.

"She is indeed," Emiliano agreed.

Admiral Santiago De Leon had performed their marriage ceremony only hours ago. A powerful man, Santiago's title of admiral had nothing to do with the Navy and everything to do with ruling a portion of Europe's oldest secret society. De Leon hadn't been the admiral—territory leader—for long, and had only come to power after the previous admiral was killed by a sniper in England.

De Leon was also the person who had arranged Emiliano's marriage, selecting his spouses for him. A month ago, Emiliano went to a dinner party at the admiral's home. De Leon and his two wives, Valery and Carmen, frequently hosted parties, so

Emiliano hadn't thought much about the invitation at the time.

Then Santiago had pulled him, Vicente, and Gabriella aside, asking them to join him in his study for a drink. Pouring each of them a glass of brandy, he'd announced that he was placing them in a trinity and that the marriage ceremony should take place in one month's time, which would allow them time to get to know each other and set their affairs in order. He'd then proposed a toast—to their future and their happiness—as if he hadn't just upended all of their well-ordered lives.

The rest of that night had been a blur as Emiliano studied the two people he was expected to spend the rest of his life with. Gabriella, a legacy of the Masters' Admiralty—and therefore raised within the society—had appeared better prepared for the announcement. She had offered both him and Vicente a warm kiss on the cheek, telling them she looked forward to getting to know them.

Emiliano had followed her example, smiling genially, letting excitement take precedence. He'd looked at the upcoming nuptials as an adventure, as a new chapter beginning, and the admiral had certainly placed him in an auspicious trinity.

Vicente had reacted differently. He held a very dangerous and powerful position in the society as the security minister—working immediately under the admiral himself—and had been harder to read, his face revealing nothing of his feelings. It wasn't until Emiliano looked into the other man's eyes that he saw a flash of anger, a split second of emotion that was quickly hidden away once more by an unreadable mask.

Even today during the wedding ceremony, Vicente had been locked down tighter than a drum, the stoic man revealing nothing of his feelings, either through expression or tone. Emiliano wasn't sure what to make of him, his new husband.

It was unusual for Emiliano to struggle to connect with someone at least on some basic level. He prided himself on his ability to not only read people but to find a way to relate to them, to set them at ease. His mother insisted it was that skill that enabled him to find success—as a lawyer and as a politician.

Emiliano lifted his glass of champagne. "To our future happiness," he said, hoping to find some way to draw Vicente out of his shell.

They tapped glasses, Vicente acknowledging the toast with little more than a nod of the head, before turning once more to study their shared bride.

Emiliano regretted not making more of an effort to get to know his future spouses since the dinner party. However, circumstances had not been on their side, as the last four weeks flew by in a flurry of activities.

Gabriella was an heiress and a philanthropist, her parents—two fathers and a mother—billionaire business magnates who had amassed their great wealth in the world of fashion. By sheer force of will and with a shit-ton of money, Gabriella's mother, Genevieve Torres, had managed to organize the wedding and this reception in record time.

By necessity, the wedding party was small—though at over a hundred people, it seemed decent sized to Emiliano. The guests were all successful, brilliant men and women from Spain, Portugal, and France, all fellow members of the Masters' Admiralty, from the territory of Castile—which encompassed Spain and Portugal—and the territory of France, which included parts of Belgium, as well as France. The territories of the Masters' Admiralty had borders and names that predated the modern geo-political map.

Gabriella's family had offered their Barcelona estate for both the ceremony and reception. The enormous stately mansion—twenty-plus bedrooms strong—had lush, classically Spanish courtyards and also boasted rolling green lawns, countless outbuildings, statuary, fountains, and an impressive view of the ocean.

Emiliano had been knee-deep in work this past month because the Spanish Parliament was still in session, so he hadn't had much to do with the reception planning.

"It's an elegant party," Emiliano said, taking yet another shot at somehow drawing Vicente into conversation. "Quite a guest list. And this house..." He gestured to the mansion, still struggling to take in the sheer luxuriousness of the place.

Unlike Gabriella, Emiliano hadn't grown up wealthy and powerful. He was the son of a single mother, who'd worked two jobs to support their small family of three—Mom, him, and his older brother, Gael. Emiliano had honored her sacrifices for them by dedicating himself to his career path, graduating top of his class in school, working hard to pay his own way through university and then law school. Everything he'd achieved in his life had been through blood, sweat, and tears.

Vicente's gaze seemed to move over the entire area, and it occurred to Emiliano the man wasn't looking at the people or the house, rather the perimeter of the property. "Elegant, yes. Defensible, no."

Defensible? "I hadn't considered that."

Vicente finally looked at him, and Emiliano realized that this time, he wasn't imagining the cold, distant look in his husband's eyes. "A man in your position should pay more attention. You have enemies."

Enemies was a strong word. Obviously, it wasn't unusual for him to come up against a rival or disgruntled constituent, and as such, he was usually very aware of his surroundings. However, he wasn't looking for *enemies* today.

"Of course I'm concerned with security, but this is a wedding, Vicente. A time for celebration, not fear."

Vicente raised a brow. "Nothing bad ever happened at a wedding?"

Emiliano stiffened and resisted the urge to snap at the other man. The Morral affair in 1906 had been an attempted regicide with a bomb in a bouquet. King Alfonso XIII had survived, but now Emiliano was eyeing the flowers suspiciously.

Every conversation with Vicente this past month—and there had been precious few—had felt steeped in landmines. No matter how hard he tried, Emiliano couldn't seem to find any topic that would engage Vicente for more than a few awkward moments before an uneasy silence descended again. He wasn't sure if it was due to Vicente's personality or his position—chief assassin of a secret society probably wasn't a job that made someone chatty.

Emiliano had patience to spare, learning long ago that cooler heads and calmer voices always rang out louder than impassioned voices raised in anger. He tried to swallow down his frustration over his inability to make a connection with this man whom he was expected to share his future, his wife, and...his bed.

Before he could figure out how to proceed, the photographer approached them. "It's time for the fountain pictures."

Emiliano nodded, certain that the low growl that emanated from Vicente hadn't been missed by the photographer, who shot his husband a wary look. They'd already posed for countless photos and according to the "down to the minute" itinerary the wedding planner had shared with them yesterday, they were now going to take pictures on the wide lawn, in front of a stately fountain. In addition to these photographs, there would be three more photo sessions at specific times and places throughout the remainder of the evening.

He and Vicente followed the photographer, and he watched as Gabriella, summoned by the wedding planner, made her way over to them. She gave them a warm smile, which Emiliano returned.

Emiliano offered his arm to help Gabriella walk across the lawn in her delicate-looking heels. The feel of her fingers on his arm had him thinking about their honeymoon, which started tomorrow.

The photographer posed them, placing Gabriella in between himself and Vicente. Emiliano hoped Gabriella couldn't feel his hand trembling as he laid it on her back or the way he jumped when Vicente's fingers brushed his.

They posed, smiled, and then the world exploded.

IT WAS NOT an ideal start to a marriage, and that was before the bomb.

Vicente leaned down to look over the shoulder of one of the people working in the study that had been quickly set up as operational headquarters for the bombing investigation.

"Go," Santiago insisted.

Vicente looked at his admiral. Santiago De Leon was unrumpled, his tuxedo shirt still pristine white. The bowtie that hung loose around his neck seemed more a fashion statement than a sign of exhaustion or stress.

Beside him, Natalia Perez, vice admiral of the territory of Castile, had a silvery emergency blanket wrapped around her shoulders. Her velvet wrap was undoubtedly still draped over the cocktail table she'd been standing beside. That table, along with most of the others, was a tumbled, broken mess, hunks of wood amid the scattering of glass, porcelain, and other debris. The damage at the courtyard cocktail hour had been from the post-blast panic, not the bomb.

"Admiral," Vicente started. "I'm needed here."

"Trust my people," Natalia interjected. "And your own."

He looked at Santiago, then back to Natalia. These people were not his friends, but they were his allies, his compatriots. Together, the three of them were the ruling triad of the territory of Castile.

Vicente wanted to argue. He wanted to be here for the investigation. Technically, it was Natalia's purview—she oversaw the *caballeros*, who served as the territory's law enforcement. Every *caballero* was smart, honorable, and a good person to have at one's back in a fight. His own people, the security officers, walked a darker path. If the *caballeros* were law and justice, the security officers were the monsters in the dark. They did what the *caballeros* could not and would not.

Someone had blown up his wedding reception. He didn't want them captured and questioned. He wanted them shot on sight, with the first shot being to the knee.

"Vicente." This time Santiago sank a bit of authority into the word, an order and a warning in one.

Vicente ground his teeth, but he knew Santiago was right. "Yes, Admiral."

As much as he would prefer to focus on the bomb rather than his marriage, he wasn't needed here. Santiago and Natalia and the *caballeros*, both those who'd been here as guests and those who'd been called in, could handle the investigation. And given that the investigation would include questioning three of his security officers who'd been the active event security, it was arguably better that he wasn't here.

All those sound reasons didn't change the fact that he would rather be here than in the safe house where the *caballeros* had stashed his husband and wife.

His husband and wife.

Vicente nodded to the others and turned on his heel. Javier, one of the *caballeros* who'd been here as a guest, escorted Vicente to a black town car. Unlike Santiago, Javier looked like a man who'd survived a bomb. His tux jacket was gone, there was a rip in the knee of his pants, and his once-white shirt was gray with dust and sprinkled liberally with blood. There was no obvious wound, which meant the blood was someone else's.

It was a short fifteen-minute drive to the safe house, though it would have been shorter if Javier hadn't taken precautionary measures and doubled back several times.

All too soon, the car pulled to a stop. Vicente got out. He tugged on his shirt, which was untucked and dirty, though not as bad as Javier's.

The door to the safe house opened as he approached. Alejandro, another *caballero*, filled the doorway. He glanced from Vicente to Javier and back. Then, with a nod, he stepped back, allowing Vicente in.

"You can go," Vicente told him. There was no foyer, no welcoming entrance, only a long hall that stretched almost to the back of the building.

"I will stay to guard—"

"You are needed there more than you are here."

Alejandro hesitated. "I will send one of the security officers."

"I've already called Xiomara." She was one of his newer security officers, recruited after he lost three people in a bombing in Bucharest.

"I will stay until—"

Vicente cut off Alejandro. "Do you think I am incapable of protecting them, *caballero*?"

Alejandro stiffened. "Of course not, sir."

"Then please, do not insult me. I may be old, but I am not infirm, and the house itself is a fortress." Vicente gestured to the hall, which was a cleverly designed security measure. Anyone who made it through the front door would find themselves in a killing field, thanks to transom windows above the steel doors that lined the hallway. Each room off the hall had a sturdy piece of furniture near the door that could be used to give a gunman inside the height needed to use the window as a modern-day arrow slit.

"Very well, sir." Alejandro nodded his head once, then slipped out.

Vicente bolted the front door, then used the keypad to activate the security system. There was a muffled *thunk* as a second bolt, hidden in the threshold, shot up into the steel door.

"You're not old," a feminine voice said.

Vicente rolled his shoulders and tipped his head to the side to pop his neck before turning.

Gabriella Torres stood at the far end of the long hall. He was surprised to see that she still wore her cocktail dress. It had not fared well. The silk was dirty and torn, her hair was loose around her shoulders. She was beautiful, undeniably so. It was a classic Spanish beauty, with strong cheekbones, full lips, and deep, rich brown eyes. Her disheveled appearance did nothing to lessen her presence. She was the kind of woman who drew attention when she walked into a room, and not just because she was stunning.

He slipped one hand into his pocket. "I am not that young."

Gabriella arched a brow. "True. You are not."

Behind her there came a strangled sound. Emiliano stepped into the hall, placing a hand on her shoulder. His lips were twitching, but he'd managed to stop from outright laughing.

His new husband's coloring was as dark as Gabriella's, though without the auburn highlights. Emiliano's hair was cut in a conservative, short style that made him look like a lawyer or politician. He was both.

Standing there, they looked like a couple. A dirty, disheveled couple but a couple nonetheless.

Emiliano and Gabriella, they...matched.

"Any news?" Emiliano asked.

"Not yet." Vicente started down the hall. "We've confirmed there were no major injuries."

"My family, are they somewhere safe?" Gabriella asked.

"Yes."

Emiliano nodded tightly, and Vicente wondered if the younger man was sorry he couldn't invite his family to attend. Vicente's family hadn't been among the guests either. Neither he nor Emiliano were legacies. Their families wouldn't have understood the trinity marriage and couldn't know about the Masters' Admiralty.

Someday, perhaps someday soon, Emiliano and Gabriella would marry publicly, and that wedding Emiliano's mother and brother could attend. Vicente knew all about his spouses— Santiago had given him their files the night he announced they were to be married.

The three of them hadn't discussed that yet, that Emiliano and Gabriella would be publicly and legally married. There hadn't been time, but it was the logical course of action.

Vicente walked down the hall, and Emiliano and Gabriella retreated into the room they'd emerged from.

The small living space was elegantly furnished with wide, comfortable chairs, hassocks, and a small fireplace. The fireplace was electric—a chimney would have been a security risk —and the drapes were decorative rather than functional, as there were no windows in the room or anywhere on the ground floor.

Gabriella went to a chair, perching on the edge, dirty, ripped silk splayed out on the floor around her. "Any information, clues as to who planted the bomb?"

Emiliano took a seat in the chair beside her, elbows braced on his knees, hands clasped.

"No, but we will find them, and the would-be assassin will be punished," Vicente said.

"Assassin?" Emiliano looked up. "You think this was an assassination attempt?"

"Bombs kill." Vicente peered down at the other man. "Did you hit your head?"

"I'm not stupid. I mean, do you think the bomb was meant to kill one specific person, or maybe two or three specific people?"

That statement hung heavy in the air.

"If there's no evidence at the scene, we could work backwards." Gabriella tapped her fingers on her knee. "We identify who the bomb was meant to kill and find the villain that way."

Vicente opened his mouth, closed it, then shook his head. Taking a moment to gather himself, he sat in the third chair, stretching out his legs. One knee, the one he'd fallen forward on, was throbbing. "The *caballeros* will handle the investigation."

"They'll need to talk to us, then." Emiliano tapped the heels of his hands together, his brows furrowed in thought.

"Possibly, but for now we should..." Vicente wasn't quite sure how he wanted to end that sentence.

His hesitation gave Gabriella the opportunity to fill in the blank. "Go on our honeymoon? Pretend nothing has happened?" She made a dismissive noise, waving one hand in the air.

"At this time, it's best that we stay in Barcelona and not go to your family's home in Palma de Mallorca." Vicente ignored her tone.

"I figured the honeymoon plans were dead," Emiliano said grimly.

Gabriella looked back and forth between the men. "When are the *caballeros* coming to talk to us? What should we be doing now?"

"Nothing," Vicente assured her.

"Vicente, it is ludicrous for us to not talk about what happened." Emiliano's calm, modulated tone was the perfect accompaniment to his reasonable words.

"There's no need." Vicente was not used to having his authority challenged, and he was fighting down his irritation.

"We almost died tonight," Gabriella added. "Someone tried to kill us."

Vicente had forgotten that most people found that objectionable. "If you need to rest—"

"I do not need to rest. I need you, *husband*," her tone was overly saccharine for that word, "to be honest."

"I haven't lied to you." Lies of omission implied that everyone deserved information, and there were times when that wasn't the case. Times like now.

"Maybe not," Emiliano said. "But you are treating us like we are fools."

Vicente started to get up. "If you two wish to talk about it—"

"You're the security minister. You stayed there while *caballeros* put us in a car and brought us here. You know more about what happened than we do, and you are talking to us," Gabriella snapped.

Vicente hadn't wanted this marriage yet. Originally, he simply hadn't wanted to be married at all—he was devoted to his position and the safety of every member of the territory, but he knew that marriage wasn't something he could avoid, given the requirements of the society.

However, the truth remained that there wasn't time and space in his life for one person, let alone two, and that wasn't fair to his spouses. He'd explained all of this to Santiago, and he'd thought Santiago was in agreement in terms of holding off on placing him in a trinity for another year or even more. At least, he'd believed that until the night of the dinner party.

Perhaps Santiago had an undiagnosed sadistic streak that led him to give Vicente spouses who were strong-willed, intelligent, and fierce. The kind of people who didn't let shadows linger or leave secrets unspoken.

All Vicente had were shadows and secrets.

"I'm sorry you feel this way." Vicente looked from Gabriella to Emiliano, their gazes locked.

My husband.

The words, the idea, took root, suddenly real in a way they hadn't been in the lead up to today.

"That bomb was meant to kill one of us," Emiliano said.

Vicente cursed in the quiet of his head, keeping his expression neutral. "The bomb may have been meant to—"

"Why are you trying so hard to pretend what he said isn't true? To make us stop talking about it?" Gabriella narrowed her eyes. "Perhaps you already know who did it and—"

"Enough!" Vicente surged to his feet. He turned his back to them, running a hand through his hair. It was long enough to brush his cheekbones, and unlike his spouses' hair, his was more gray than brown. He'd started going gray when he was in his early thirties—Emiliano's age—and at forty-four, even his beard would be gray if he let it grow out.

His past lovers had assured him he was sexy, that the color of his hair only enhanced his stern demeanor. He wondered if his spouses agreed, or if they thought he was simply old.

Vicente turned to face them. "Very well." He went to the fireplace, leaning against the mantel. "The schedule for the wedding was not secret—multiple people had it. Anyone who read it knew we would be taking photos by that fountain at that specific time."

Emiliano and Gabriella were both silent, but her expression had softened from accusatory to focused. Emiliano had the same neutral expression he'd had before. It was a lawyer's face, able to dissect any information without showing a reaction.

"There is nothing I can do to apologize," Vicente said in a low voice. "No way to make right what could have happened to you."

"It is not your fault there was a bomb. I, we, are not blaming you for this." Gabriella glanced at Emiliano, who nodded in agreement.

"But you should." Vicente smiled at them, but it felt tight and grim. "The bomb was most likely placed by the Bellator Dei in an effort to kill me. I am the reason you almost died."

The words hung heavy in the air. This was why he hadn't wanted to talk about this. He hadn't wanted to tell them how much danger they were in being married to him. They would have to know, but he'd wanted...wanted to wait. Wait until he knew the danger had passed, the enemy dealt with.

Gabriella and Emiliano looked at each other and then back to Vicente. It was Emiliano who asked, "What are the Bellator Dei?"

CHAPTER TWO

Gabriella resisted the urge to rub her bare arms. It was cold in the safe house. Her dress was perfect for a lovely outdoor cocktail hour in a heated courtyard, followed by an indoor, formal meal where each course's expertly paired wine would warm her. It was less ideal for an overly air-conditioned room.

Some of her shivering might be from shock. She'd almost died. *They'd* almost died.

She knew the instant she gave any indication she was cold, one of the men would offer to find her a blanket or sweater, or maybe even give her their shirts if they were feeling gallant. The damp, singed suit jackets were long since gone, shed in the aftermath of the explosion.

She looked between her husbands, considering the two very different men.

Emiliano was classically handsome, which he minimized with a conservative haircut and clothes that fit well but weren't tailored to show off the breadth of his shoulders. She'd recognized him that night at the De Leons' party, even before they'd been pulled into the admiral's office. Prosecutor turned politician, he was known for his aggressive stance on crime and corruption. Rather than prosecuting individual citizens, he focused on corporations, which had given him a reputation as a bit of a *bandolero*—the romanticized version from popular TV —who fought injustice and robbed from the rich.

Vicente actually looked the part of the *bandolero*, especially at the moment with his torn shirt and dirt-streaked face— dashing and dangerous. She knew him by reputation but had no reason to have interacted with the territory security minister.

Though technically she shouldn't have been told specifics about the organization until she was herself a member, she'd grown up on stories of the honorable *caballeros* and clever finance ministers. The security officers and their dangerous leader, the security minister, were subjects of darker stories, told not by parents trying to pass on their values but by older children impressing their friends with the grim stories of assassins and spies.

Now she was married to the security minister, and despite the marriage being only hours old, they'd almost died and were having their first fight.

These were the men she was going to spend her life with, whom she would come to love, and with whom she'd share her hopes and fears. She wanted them to know her, all of her, as she would know them. Apparently, Vicente was going to be difficult when it came to communication and sharing information.

Gabriella was aware of her own privilege. When the men looked at her, she knew what they saw—the heiress to generations of wealth and power. A woman blessed with facial features and a body type people found beautiful. She didn't need to work, so she used all she had and all that she was to bring attention to social and political issues in Africa that Europe would otherwise happily ignore.

And she was a legacy member of Europe's oldest and most powerful secret society.

Given all that, she was used to being well informed. If she wanted to know something, needed a piece of information, she could usually get it.

But when Vicente mentioned the Bellator Dei, she had no idea what he was talking about. And that...scared her.

"Who are the Bellator Dei?" Emiliano asked again.

Vicente returned to his chair and sat down, legs stretched out in front of him. She was sure he intended to look relaxed, but she saw the exhaustion in the lines of his body and the tightness around his eyes.

"An old enemy," Vicente said after a long pause.

"That is all you're going to say?" Gabriella fought to keep her tone level. She'd almost died tonight, she was worried about her family, and damn it, she was freezing. The urge to rage at Vicente, to shake some information out of him, was nearly over-powering. Her mother could pull off passionate anger, could seamlessly switch from tirade to cool and aloof, and everyone respected her. The times when Gabriella gave in to the urge to raise her voice and throw something, she got a pat on the head or a gentle admonition to not throw a tantrum, which only enraged her further.

The moment she realized she'd be marrying two men, she'd promised herself she'd be elegant and poised when she inter-acted with her new husbands. It took a powerful woman to hold her own against two equally powerful men, and if she let herself *be* herself...they might not respect her the way Gabriel-la's own fathers respected her mother.

Vicente studied her, and his gaze flicked briefly to her arms.

Surely he couldn't see the gooseflesh that covered her arms from across the room.

"The Bellator Dei are a religious sect. They believe the Masters' Admiralty way of life, in particular that the ménage marriage, is evil, and we need to be stopped."

"Why have we never heard of them?" Emiliano demanded.

"Because there was no indication they had a presence in Spain or Portugal. Both traditionally, and since their resurgence, they have operated primarily in Rome."

"The city or the territory?" she asked.

"Territory."

The territories of the Masters' Admiralty had been drawn and named long before the current geo-political alignments. The society's territory of Rome was far bigger than the city and encompassed all of Italy and Greece, as well as sections of Slovenia, Croatia, and Albania.

"What about the situation makes you think it was them?" she asked.

"Their preferred weapon is a bomb."

"Wait." Gabriella sat up straighter. "The admiral of Rome's villa was bombed not long ago. Was that the Bellator Dei?"

"That information wasn't made public," Vicente said with a frown.

"We are not the public," she countered. "We are members, too."

Vicente shrugged, a negligent gesture that seemed to almost indicate he didn't see the difference.

Gabriella bit back a sharp reply and looked at Emiliano. Their gazes met, and his lips curved in a small, almost rueful smile. She felt a jolt of emotion—attraction, certainly, but also a little romantic thrill. This handsome, noble man was her husband.

She was going to ride that handsome face and damn, she was looking forward to that.

Probably better to act a little reserved the first time they had sex. Men could be put off by a woman who was too comfortable with her own sexuality and knew what she liked. That lesson she'd learned the hard way with past lovers. Just one more thing about herself to conceal and restrain.

Gabriella closed her eyes, the weariness she'd been fighting breaking free and briefly swamping her.

Be what they expected, but make it clear she was not a dilettante heiress. Be open and emotionally honest with them while also locking down any extreme emotions so they didn't dismiss her as hysterical. Be ready and willing for double penetration but don't talk about sitting on their faces.

She'd known marriage was going to be exhausting, and that was before someone tried to blow them up. The last of the adrenaline that had flooded her bloodstream in the aftermath of the attack was fading.

"Gabriella—"

Emiliano's tone was gentle, and the instant she heard it, she opened her eyes and interrupted him before he could call out her moment of weakness by saying she should get some rest.

"You say the bomb means it was Bellator Dei." She focused on Vicente. "But the Bellator Dei have not attacked anyone in Castile before tonight. Why now? Why us?"

Vicente considered her. "Not us. Me."

Arrogant fuck.

She wanted to slap him—not hard, not to hurt him. Just enough to shock him, maybe goad him into an aggressive, angry kiss. Then Emiliano would come up and demand to get in on the action and...

The desire for sex was a normal, healthy reaction to a near-death experience. She sat back, hoping that would keep them from noting the flush that she could feel spreading from her chest up to her cheeks. A flush that had nothing to do with embarrassment.

"You helped Rome try to catch them?" Emiliano asked.

"No."

"Then why do you assume it's you they're after?" Gabriella demanded. "The members within Castile know your name, but isn't your identity kept confidential outside of that?"

"It is."

"Then why would you think you are the target?" Gabriella raised a brow. "It was my family's house. Emiliano is a politician. Everyone hates politicians." She smiled at him to show she was teasing.

"Not everyone." Emiliano tried to look wounded, but his lips twitched. "My mother likes me."

Gabriella laughed, and to her shock, Vicente grinned, a genuine smile that showed off his straight white teeth.

"It is possible," Vicente conceded. "But as they showed in Rome, they are looking to destabilize us by attacking leadership."

"Did they think our admiral would be by the fountain?" Emiliano asked.

"They may have wanted to target him but were unable to plant the bomb in a location where they knew he would be," Vicente said. "The bomb was in the fountain, and the fountain was the only place we planned to take photos on the grounds."

"All our other photos were taken in one of the rooms or interior courtyards." Gabriella grimaced. "And they knew right where we'd be and when, thanks to the event schedule."

"Precisely."

"I'd like to point out that none of us actually died. We're

not even that badly injured." Emiliano tapped his hands together. "So maybe it wasn't an assassination attempt."

"The extra water saved us," Vicente said.

It took Gabriella a moment to understand. Once she did, she swallowed hard, realizing how close they'd come to not surviving.

"Extra water?" Emiliano asked.

"It's a working theory."

"Vicente, please explain." Emiliano had switched back to a lawyer voice, but there was impatience threaded through his tone.

"The bomb hasn't been analyzed yet, but..." Vicente seemed to struggle with something. Maybe he was deciding if he should answer Emiliano's request for more information.

Gabriella's patience ran out. "My mother had the groundskeepers overfill the fountain this morning so the secondary spouts could be turned on. Normally they aren't used." She held up a hand. "That's the extra water you're talking about, isn't it?"

Vicente nodded. "That was a last-minute decision and not listed on any itineraries or planning documents. We believe the bomb was engineered based on the volume of water normally in the fountain. The additional water muffled the blast."

For a moment, she was back in that place, just before the blast went off. They'd been standing with their backs to the fountain. Gabriella had been trying not to think too hard about the fact that they were touching her simultaneously while also maintaining the perfect smile and holding her pose.

Then she'd been thrown forward. It had been so forceful and quick, it felt like a giant had slapped her back, sending her sprawling on the blessedly soft grass. At the same time, there had been a quick burst of sound, more felt than heard, followed by an intense ringing in her ears.

"The bomb was in the bottom of the fountain pool?" Emiliano clarified.

"Camouflaged against one of the underwater light casings."

"I assume there are surveillance tapes, that the estate has security?" Emiliano was looking at Gabriella, but it was Vicente who answered.

"Yes, but it could have been planted any time in the past three weeks, since invitations for the reception were sent."

"Two weeks," Gabriella countered. "Two weeks ago was when we met with the photographer to plan the photos and set the schedule. Before that, they would have had no way of knowing we would be anywhere near that fountain."

Vicente froze, then reached into his pocket. He pulled out a phone and sent a quick message.

Gabriella waited for him to say something, to acknowledge the information she'd given him, but when he was done, he silently tucked his phone back into his pocket.

Gilipollas.

Dumbass.

"How did they get the reception schedule?" Emiliano asked. "Are we sure this bomb wasn't meant as a distraction from a larger threat? Perhaps the fact that we weren't more seriously hurt was by design."

"We're already considering those questions. The *caballeros* and my security officers will handle this."

"One of us was the target. We have the right to know what's going on in the investigation," Gabriella insisted.

Vicente shrugged, an awkward movement since he was slouched in the chair. "I'll provide details when the threat has been dealt with."

Fuck that.

Gabriella surged to her feet but managed to check herself. Rather than race across the room and give Vicente a little slap, she raised her chin. "No. You will not wait until you or one of your assassins has done their work. We have the right to—"

"You have no rights when it comes to what I do." Vicente's words were cold and almost cruel—a slap far more shocking than anything physical.

"Your investigation has to do with me. With us. We have a right to know." She gestured to Emiliano and then back to herself. "And you should want to tell us, *husband.*"

Vicente's jaw clenched. Slowly, he gripped the arms of the chair and used that hold to pull himself up from a slouch, until he was sitting upright. It was like watching a snake coil before the strike.

Gabriella held perfectly still, angry. Twin strands of fear and dark arousal slithered through her. She met and held Vicente's gaze. His eyes should be as black as a snake's, but they weren't. They were softer than that, coffee-colored, but with tiny flecks of gold that seemed to shimmer when caught just right by the light.

"Resurgence." Emiliano's cool, crisp word shattered the tension between them. He stood, but it was a casual gesture. He tapped his fingers on his thigh, clearly a habitual movement, then turned, sliding past her, his arm just barely brushing her front. He went to a slim sideboard, opening each drawer in turn, looking inside before closing it.

She watched him, trying to decide if she was pissed or appreciative that he'd stepped between her and Vicente. She didn't need to be rescued, but perhaps she did need to be stopped from doing or saying something she couldn't come back from.

Emiliano went to a small chest. "You said these Bellator Dei are an old enemy." He opened the lid, smiling as he grabbed a blanket. "How old? What caused the resurgence?

Why..." His voice trailed off as he noticed the stash of guns and ammunition that had been concealed under the blanket.

Gabriella stood on her toes to get a better look. She knew this was a safe house, but seeing the weapons made that fact more real.

Emiliano let the lid drop with a thunk. He gingerly shook out the blanket, but when no weapons fell out, he brought it over to Gabriella, wrapping it around her shoulders. She braced to defend herself, to insist she wasn't cold, to make sure that Vicente didn't use this as an excuse to bow out of this conversation.

Emiliano gave her upper arms a gentle squeeze, then walked back to his chair and took a seat. Vicente watched the other man, then his gaze flicked to her for a moment. He was frowning, but it seemed introspective, and a second later he switched his attention back to Emiliano.

"The Bellator Dei haven't been a problem since early in the last century," Vicente said. "And they were deliberately resurrected." He held up a hand even as she opened her mouth. "But that's a story for another time. We are all tired, and soon the adrenaline will wear off. We are going to hurt. Here, and here." Vicente touched his knees and one elbow.

The grass had kept them from getting scraped or cut, but once he said it, the throbbing she'd been able to ignore made itself known.

"There is a task force hunting the Bellator Dei," Vicente continued. It was good he was finally talking, but it was clear he was measuring each word. Unexpectedly, he flipped from Castellano to English for the next bit. "The Masters Protection Force, MPF."

"Masters Protection Force," Emiliano repeated, his accent thick as he stumbled a little over the English words.

"England named it." Vicente shrugged. "And since the Americans are helping us..."

"The Trinity Masters?" Gabriella sank down to sit in the chair, stunned as much as tired. "We have a joint task force with the Americans?"

"The who? Wait, is there a Masters' Admiralty territory in America?"

Vicente looked at her, then gestured with a finger for her to go on.

"There's a secret society in America. Modeled on ours, of course—including the trinity marriages—but it is not as established. One of my grandfathers used to talk about it, but he spoke of it like it was a made-up story. Then, when the Masters' Admiralty reestablished contact several years ago, my family reevaluated those old stories."

"The existence of the Trinity Masters isn't a secret," Vicente conceded. "But it is not a well-known piece of information."

"So this task force, the Masters Protection Force—ah, yes, I see, the word master is in both—are hunting the Bellator Dei?" Emiliano asked.

"Tonight's bombing was...unexpected," Vicente said. "Not as effective as their past attacks, but the MPF has weakened them."

"Are you part of the task force?" Gabriella asked.

"No, but Rodrigo, one of my officers, is."

"So really it isn't just our *caballeros* who will be solving this crime," Gabriella said. "It's the MPF."

"Yes."

"And you wouldn't have told us any of this if I, we, hadn't pushed you for information."

Vicente ran a hand through his hair, but when he looked at

her, his expression was cold and resolute. "No, I would not have."

"We're your spouses," Emiliano said slowly. "We need to work together."

"No," Vicente countered. "We need to be allies. We need to form an alliance that will strengthen our society. You two will marry legally, live together as man and wife. We can arrange connecting homes, or perhaps we will wait until you have a child and I will visit regularly under the guise of godfather. It is neither safe nor necessary for you two to know more than you already do about my position and my work."

His cold arrogance was breathtaking. He'd planned their marriage, and their lives, without any input from her or Emiliano. Their marriage was hours old, and he was already carving a fissure between himself and them, making sure they knew their place and that he had little to no part of the life he'd so casually planned for them, not with them.

For a stunned moment, all Gabriella could do was stare at him. Shock kept any one emotion from taking hold. Anger, embarrassment, dismay, all were equal possibilities, jockeying for position.

It was Emiliano who broke the silence. He rose silently to his feet, his posture stiff, his jaw clenched, his hand curled into a fist so tight that his knuckles showed white. Emiliano was angry. No, not just angry. He was enraged. Yet somehow, when he spoke, his voice was low, even, the emotion present in his expression shockingly absent in his tone.

"This conversation ends here, before you say any more things you'll regret."

Vicente stiffened.

Emiliano turned to her. "Gabriella, may I escort you to a room?"

She rose, holding the blanket closed around her with one hand, and then slid the other around Emiliano's forearm.

Together they walked out of the lounge and through another door, which took them to the stairs.

It wasn't until she was safely in her bedroom and alone that Gabriella let herself fall apart. She limped into the bathroom, whimpering in pain, but she didn't let the tears fall until she was in the shower, where the warm water could wash them away.

CHAPTER THREE

Emiliano stared at the ceiling, the room blindingly bright as the sun streamed through the lone thick-paned window that he suspected was constructed of bulletproof glass. A quick glance at the time on his phone revealed it was six a.m. He'd retired to his bedroom shortly after one, only managing five hours of sleep. Despite that, it was a good sleep and he felt mentally refreshed, for which he was grateful. He would need a clear head for whatever today threw his direction.

In hindsight, he should have pulled the curtains prior to climbing into bed last night, but his thoughts had been consumed by too many other things.

Primarily the fact that he was married to virtual strangers, he was supposed to be on his honeymoon but was instead sleeping alone in a safe house, and...most importantly...he'd come terrifyingly close to dying.

His new husband's revelations about the Bellator Dei had been as shocking as Vicente's immediate declaration that yesterday's bomb had in fact been someone's attempt to assassinate him. Emiliano hadn't had time in the past month to truly consider exactly how dangerous the security minister's life was and how those external threats would endanger him...and Gabriella as well.

Gabriella.

The more time Emiliano spent in her presence, the more impressed—and attracted—he became. And there had been a couple times last night when he'd thought that attraction might be shared. His cock twitched at the idea. He tried to batten down those needs for now, as nothing could come of them. Or perhaps nothing should come of them.

Too much was still up in the air. Their fight last night had been impressive and disheartening as Vicente drew a clear, deep divide between them. Sex was probably the last thing on his spouses' minds.

More's the pity.

Regardless of his own unease over events at the wedding reception, his desire for Gabriella was real. And growing.

If only the same could be said of Vicente.

He closed his eyes, trying to will his concerns away, but the damn light streaming in was too bright.

To hell with it.

He wasn't going back to sleep.

He threw his legs over the edge of the bed and stretched, wincing slightly. He looked at the dark bruises on his forearms and knees, evidence of the powerful impact from the blast that threw him forward onto the grass. Even now, when he allowed himself to think of that moment, he could appreciate just how damn lucky he was to be alive. How lucky they all were.

Rising gingerly, he walked over to his suitcase and rifled through it in search of something to wear to breakfast. All of their luggage had been retrieved and delivered by a *caballero* a few hours after their arrival at the safe house last night. Tossing aside the shorts and swim trunks he'd packed for what was supposed to be a relaxing honeymoon basking in the sunshine on the white beaches of Palma de Mallorca, he found a comfortable pair of lounge pants and a soft cotton T-shirt. He left on the clean boxer briefs he'd donned after his shower and before going to bed, pulled on the rest of the clothing, and left the room in search of the kitchen.

They'd missed dinner, something he hadn't considered last night. Now, his empty stomach was protesting. Perhaps he could find something in the refrigerator to sate his hunger until they decided their next move. He wasn't looking forward to remaining in limbo, hiding out in this safe house for days on end.

Walking downstairs, he was met by the smell of coffee as soon as he reached the first floor, and he instantly felt more optimistic about the day.

There was coffee.

All would be well.

He paused at the doorway, the sound of the espresso machine covering his arrival. He took a moment to...well...brace himself. Emiliano had hoped when he'd smelled the coffee, he'd find Gabriella.

Instead, it was Vicente standing at the counter watching the last of the strong, bitter espresso pour into a cup.

"Do you want coffee?" Vicente asked gruffly, not turning around. Given his tone, his new husband's mood had not improved since yesterday.

"Yes. Please." Emiliano entered the room and joined Vicente by the counter.

"Espresso?" Vicente twisted the porta-filter free and banged the used grounds into a garbage can.

"Americano. Thank you."

Vicente nodded, and Emiliano was pleasantly surprised

that his new husband didn't comment on him wanting a little water in his espresso.

Emiliano watched silently as Vicente deftly and efficiently ground more beans, added them to the port head, and worked the expensive machine. He idly wondered who'd outfitted the safe house and was more than a little amused that a good espresso machine was considered necessary for safety.

Vicente added hot water to the cup before passing it over. Emiliano accepted it with a nod of thanks, and then they took their coffee to the contemporary glass-topped kitchen table and sat down.

Emiliano willed the caffeine to work its way through his system. It was too early in the morning to try to maneuver his way through a conversation with Vicente, which would require too much effort on his part to get the man talking.

Mercifully, he was saved from having to make the attempt when he heard footsteps coming down the stairs. Emiliano looked up just as Gabriella walked into the kitchen, her hair pulled up in a messy bun on top of her head. She was obviously wearing what she'd slept in, the loose cotton pajama pants and tank top rumpled, her face free of makeup.

Despite the fact she'd just rolled out of bed, she still looked lovely...and while her sleepwear was more practical than sexy, his desire for her was undeniable.

"Coffee," she said, sounding a bit like a zombie, as she made a beeline for the machine. "Is there condensed milk?"

He and Vicente exchanged a glance, and Emiliano could swear he'd actually seen a split second of amusement on the other man's face when Gabriella started to loudly open and close cupboards looking for a can of condensed milk so she could make a *café bombón*. They both stood, Emiliano going to help her look through cupboards, while Vicente got the milk from the fridge, setting it and a metal steaming pitcher by the machine. By the time he and Gabriella gave up the search, Vicente had added a small bowl of sugar packets to the supplies he'd gathered.

"May I?" he asked.

Gabriella nodded, her hair bouncing. "*Con leche*, please. Not too hot."

The sounds of grinder and steam wand kept everyone silent until Vicente was done, and he brought her coffee—along with sugar packets and a spoon—over to the table.

Gabriella added two sugar packets to her drink as she spoke. "How did the two of you sleep?"

"Well." Vicente was a man of few words who made very good espresso. His gaze was not on her but rather the curtains above the sink. As with the room yesterday, there wasn't actually a window, since they were on the first floor. Vicente's attention switched to the doorway, and then after a measured pause, to his phone, which he'd set on the table.

Emiliano suspected Vicente was "on duty," even at this ungodly hour, ascertaining if the room was secure, safe. How exhausting must it be to always be on the alert? Emiliano craned his neck to peek at Vicente's phone. It showed the feed from a security camera, probably one mounted near the front door.

"I slept quite well," Emiliano said. "Which is surprising, all things considered. Not enough but well."

Gabriella gave him a tired smile that made it apparent her night had not been as restful. "I can't seem to stop playing it over in my mind." She didn't bother to indicate what *it* was. She didn't need to. She'd clearly been shaken up by the bomb and rightfully so. After all, the bomb had been planted right outside her family home. Yesterday could have ended much, much worse than it had.

Emiliano reached over and placed his hand on top of hers where it rested on the table. "It's the same for me."

Her grateful smile told him she appreciated his attempt to comfort her.

He gave her fingers a gentle squeeze before forcing himself to let go. "Perhaps when all is said and done, we can hold another party with our family and friends to celebrate our nuptials."

Vicente's quiet but heavy sigh was all they needed to know exactly what their husband thought of that idea.

Gabriella grinned. "Not a fan of parties, Vicente?"

Vicente shook his head. "Too many variables."

"That's why you hire a party planner...or if you're into self-flagellation, you could always ask my mother to help," she teased.

Emiliano chuckled, having witnessed Gabriella's mother in action these past few days as she organized the finishing touches for their wedding with a take-no-prisoners tenacity.

"I meant security variables." Vicente paused, and with a visible effort made himself relax and add, "The color scheme also had too many variables."

Vicente was making an effort. Emiliano resisted the urge to pat him in approval.

"Don't worry," Gabriella reassured Vicente. "We'll have a big party for our first anniversary and keep the color scheme simple. For now, I am content to simply spend time with you both. We haven't had much of an opportunity to talk before. Except about the wedding...and the bomb."

Ever since the admiral had announced they would be a trinity, Emiliano's days had been a whirlwind of activity, split between time spent in Parliament and wedding planning. He and Vicente had both made the three-hour train ride to Barcelona from Madrid twice to meet with Gabriella, her mother, and the wedding planner to discuss the details of the event. Though in truth, he'd contributed little to the decision-making, allowing Gabriella—or more accurately, her mother—to choose the menu, colors, and flowers. Vicente's contributions had been limited to questions regarding security, the layout of the house and courtyard, staffing, and similar.

This morning was only the second time the three of them had been alone together. And Emiliano didn't count last night, as they'd all been shell-shocked—literally—and too overwhelmed by the events of the day to acknowledge that, for better or worse, until death they did part, they were now wed.

While he was tempted to ask more questions about the investigation and the Bellator Dei, he decided this time could be better spent trying to get to know his spouses.

"We haven't had an opportunity to get to know one another, have we?" Emiliano said. "Why don't you tell us about your philanthropic work, Gabriella? I know about the case, that it was dismissed."

Gabriella's fingers tightened on her cup, but he couldn't tell if it was from rage or nervousness.

"I know you're not—"

Vicente cut him off. "A criminal case?" He looked Gabriella up and down, as if seeing her again.

"Guess," Gabriella said.

"What?" Vicente looked nonplussed. "You don't have a criminal record."

"You ran security checks on us?" Emiliano asked.

Vicente only raised a brow.

"This probably didn't make my file because it didn't go anywhere." Gabriella also arched a brow. "I want you to guess what kind of criminal I am."

Emiliano drank the last of his coffee and settled back, ready to be entertained.

Vicente picked up his phone, but Gabriella slapped his hand. "No cheating. Guess."

Gabriella wasn't going to let this go.

From the set of Vicente's mouth, he'd realized that fact too. He ran a hand through his salt-and-pepper hair, pausing to think before saying, "Assault."

"Assault?" Gabriella stiffened. "I haven't lost my temper or—"

"You're a beautiful woman." Vicente shook his head. "You are...more than just beautiful. You are..." He looked at Emiliano, as if for help.

"Regal," Emiliano supplied, his voice gone husky. "You have a presence, a power that people feel when you walk into the room."

"I have no doubt you face harassment, perhaps more," Vicente said quietly. "And I hope any man who dared touch you against your will was repaid with violence that spoke to his feeble mind."

Emiliano stared, open-mouthed, at Vicente. Gabriella was doing the same. It was the longest and most eloquent sentence he'd heard the other man utter.

"I..." Gabriella reached out, tentatively touching the back of Vicente's hand. "Thank you, Vicente, you..." She twisted to look at Emiliano while keeping her hand on Vicente. "*Bandolero*, yes?"

"*Bandolero*! That's it. I was trying to figure out what he reminded me of."

Gabriella grinned. "I'm glad you see it too. Though you're a bit of one too."

"You two think I'm a highwayman?" Vicente asked.

"No, I think you look and sound like a dashing *bandolero*. Dangerous, romantic. Emiliano attacks the rich and powerful. So really, I married a pair of *bandoleros*."

Vicente did a slow blink.

Gabriella sat back, releasing Vicente's hand as she did. "It is almost disappointing to tell you that I'm a suspected human trafficker. I'm currently under investigation by the Moroccan government."

Vicente's eyes widened. "You...you're... What?"

"She does philanthropic work," Emiliano said, not bothering to hide his amusement at Vicente's shock. Then he turned to Gabriella. "How much danger are you in when you're there?"

Gabriella looked at him, a tremulous smile curving her lips. "When people hear that I do philanthropic work, they assume I host fundraisers and dinners. But you know?"

"The first time the charges were brought up, I was still a prosecutor. The idea of trying Gabriella Torres for human trafficking crimes made all of us break out in a cold sweat. It was obvious to most of us what they were doing."

Gabriella grinned. "I wish they had gone through with it. The amount of attention I could have brought to the issues..." She switched to looking at Vicente. "I work with migrants fleeing Africa for Europe. Mostly religious minorities who have been persecuted. Moroccans, and those passing through Morocco, on their way to Spain. I value life over politicized immigration laws, so what I do isn't always technically legal. They tried to stop me by saying I was profiting, taking money to help people cross."

"They tried to say you were doing it for the money?" Emiliano grinned. "That I hadn't heard."

"It wasn't until after the first time I was arrested that the authorities realized I have resources most don't. I live simply when in Morocco."

"Explain, please," Vicente requested. Actually, it was really more of an order.

"What I do is mostly legal, and what is less than legal, well, I've always been able to get out of the charges or pay fines. I angered people, both in Morocco and here in Spain. They decided to stop me by charging me with human trafficking. A far more serious crime."

"The Spanish authorities did this?" Vicente looked incredulous.

"That's the expression I made when I heard about it," Emiliano added. "I have no idea what the prosecutor was thinking."

"The charges were dropped here in Spain. Technically the case is still pending in Morocco," she said. "I guess you didn't check for active, open cases in North Africa."

"I did not." Vicente looked troubled that he hadn't known all this. He shook his head, as if forcing himself to put that aside. "You are more the *bandolero* than I am."

That made her laugh. After that, they lapsed into a companionable silence, as the other two sipped their coffee and Emiliano debated making another cup. He didn't want to get up though, didn't want to ruin this moment of quiet closeness and sharing.

"You grew up in Barcelona?" Emiliano asked Gabriella. He winced internally, as it was a rather inane question.

She nodded. "Yes. In the house where we were married yesterday."

Emiliano took another sip of his coffee. "It must have been nice, living so close to the sea."

"It was. The view never fails to take my breath away, no matter how many times I've seen it. Although, the sunsets in Morocco are equally stunning. It feels as if the sky reflects the land—mirror images in hue, the colors unlike anything I've seen before, the perfect blend of burnt orange and garnet." Gabriella's memory provoked a smile, then she leaned a bit closer to him as she rested her elbow on the table, her chin in her palm.

The new position gave him a glimpse of the top curves of her breasts above the neckline of her tank top, and his body reacted to it instantly.

His response to her didn't surprise him. His desire had awakened the night the admiral declared they would be married.

What he didn't expect, however, was the obvious attraction on Vicente's face. He was looking at Gabriella more intently this morning, as if discovering something he hadn't previously seen before. It made sense. On the surface, Gabriella appeared to be nothing more than a rich heiress. Something that clearly couldn't be further from the truth, given her work in Morocco.

"Enough about me," Gabriella said. "Where did you grow up, Emiliano?"

"Seville."

"Oh, I love Seville. Such a wonderful mix of old and new architecture."

"You've spent time there?" Emiliano asked.

She nodded. "My family and I traveled there to attend the *Feria de Abril* once when I was young. I was enthralled by the spectacle of it all, the costumes, the dancers, and parades. And the food! It was such a wonderful place, and I've often wanted to return. Is your family still there?"

Emiliano nodded, mentally comparing the mansion of Gabriella's youth to the home he'd grown up in on the outskirts of the city. He, his mother, and brother had shared a two-bedroom flat on the fourth floor of an apartment building with no lift. "My mother is still there, though my brother's work has taken him to Huelva."

"Is he a lawyer as well?" she asked.

"No. He works for a mining company."

"And now you live and work in Madrid," she said.

"I do."

"How about you, Vicente? Where are you from originally?" Gabriella asked, turning her attention to Vicente, attempting to draw him into the conversation.

"I have always lived in Madrid," he replied. "Though I traveled a great deal when I was in the military and when I served the territory as a security officer."

Emiliano took a moment to process that. As the security minister, Vicente was part of the territory's leadership trinity, a position that he had imagined involved sitting behind a desk, analyzing and assessing threats. It made sense that once, he'd been one of the shadowy, dangerous security officers, but the reality of that struck him now. He was married to a man who had operated outside the purview of the law, who had most likely killed people to keep the Masters' Admiralty's secrets.

"I suspect you've seen some interesting places," Emiliano said.

Vicente nodded, though he didn't elaborate. "I have. Since taking over as minister, the majority of my time is spent at headquarters, while my officers do what is necessary and what the *caballero* cannot."

He'd definitely killed people. No trial, no due process. Emiliano had to process that later, but for now, talking about where they'd grown up brought another thought.

"I have to admit that given mine and Vicente's work, I had assumed we would live in Madrid. I realize now that's something we should discuss." Emiliano was suddenly sorry the three of them hadn't set aside a bit of time prior to the wedding to make some of the bigger life decisions. Though the idea of where they would live no longer felt like the more pressing issue, given Vicente's comments last night.

Emiliano had never considered his trinity wouldn't truly live as one. In truth, it was something he'd looked forward to, that caveat of membership more appealing than he'd admitted to himself.

The son of a single mom who worked long hours and who was frequently gone, he'd found himself drawn to the idea that his children could grow up in a home with three parents. Three times the love. Three times the attention. Always someone there for them. He wanted that for them.

His childhood had been quite lonely. He and his brother, Gael, hadn't been particularly close—their personalities and interests too dissimilar for them to make a genuine connection. Their last conversation, just a few weeks ago, had quickly dissolved into a tense, volatile argument, one that still upset him every time he thought of it...one that made him genuinely feel that he no longer had a brother.

Last night, Emiliano had grown more and more furious as he'd listened to Vicente very calmly write himself out of their marriage, speaking in that arrogant tone of his as if everything he said was a fact and not open for debate.

Emiliano hadn't made it where he was in life by standing aside and letting others make decisions for him, nor had he ever allowed anyone to tell him how to think or behave. He charted his own path, set his own goals, formed his own opinions, and he steered his own goddamn ship.

He'd held his tongue, refusing to force the issue because his emotions had been riding too close to the surface ever since that bomb had exploded.

No.

That wasn't the main reason he'd cut the conversation short. It had been Gabriella's face. Her mask had slipped for a moment and he'd seen the genuine hurt in her eyes.

"I need to live in Madrid," Vicente said, his gaze steady on Emiliano's face. The wise man was treading more lightly this morning, considering the way their conversation had ended the night before.

Gabriella looked at Emiliano. "I suspect the same is true for you, correct? After all, Parliament is in Madrid."

"I prefer to live in Madrid, though I do keep an apartment in Seville as well. Nothing has been decided, Gabriella," Emiliano said, wanting to reassure her that she had an equal voice in this marriage. They all had an equal voice despite what Vicente might think.

Gabriella took a sip of her espresso. "I travel a great deal, so I split my time between my own suite at my parents' house and a tiny flat in Cadiz. While I will no doubt keep my flat, as it is convenient for my work in Morocco, it makes sense for me to be the one to move."

"Then it's settled," Vicente said. "We will live in Madrid."

Emiliano noticed he didn't say anything about them living *together* in Madrid.

"Look at that," Gabriella said. "Our first decision as a married trinity. So...how about we make another stride toward solidifying things?"

Emiliano held his breath, anticipating that Gabriella would call Vicente out for his comments last night about how they'd live their lives.

So he was floored when she rose from the table and said, "I think it's time for the honeymoon to truly begin."

CHAPTER FOUR

———————————

Gabriella grinned as Vicente rose from the table without a moment's hesitation, reaching out to grasp her hand in his.

"Another thing we agree on," Vicente said, his voice suddenly husky, deep. Sexy as sin.

Gabriella had felt an almost instant emotional attraction to Emiliano. However, her desire for Vicente had been a slower burn, based entirely on his *bandolero* look. Even that had been nearly extinguished completely last night when he heavy-handedly tried to dictate how their marriage would work.

"I didn't like sleeping alone last night," Emiliano confessed, rising as well, placing his hand on her lower back. She loved the feeling of their hands on her, the possessiveness in their touch. She'd played this moment out in her mind ever since the admiral told her that these men were hers.

The three of them climbed the stairs together, the anticipation almost palpable.

Vicente guided them to the largest upstairs room. Much like the room she'd slept in last night, this one was well furnished in the same utilitarian style as the rest of the house. There was a door that opened to a private en suite bathroom with a walk-in shower, a closet, a three-drawer bureau, and a tall, oversized California king taking up most of the room.

She assumed no one had slept in it until she saw Vicente's suitcase in the corner and the remains of his dress shirt in the garbage.

She smiled as she noted the perfectly made bed, no doubt sporting hospital corners. She would have bet her entire inheritance that Vicente kept his home immaculate, and the state of this room proved her right. She wondered what he would have thought if they'd gone to her room instead, and he'd seen her cocktail dress laying on the floor and her unkempt bed with wrinkled sheets that revealed just how much she'd tossed and turned, unable to stop thinking about the fact her husbands were sleeping just down the hall.

She hadn't expected to spend the first night of her marriage alone. And like Emiliano, she hadn't liked it.

Today—right now—they were going to make up for that lost time.

"Take off your shirt," she said to Emiliano, her impatience getting the better of her. She wanted to see both of them naked, and she intended to watch every second of their disrobing.

Emiliano glanced toward Vicente, and Gabriella sensed the slightest amount of hesitation on his part. She'd believed they'd made inroads—small ones—toward coming together as a trinity over their espressos. Perhaps Emiliano hadn't felt the same.

The two men stared at each other in a silent standoff that ended when Emiliano reached for the bottom of his T-shirt and tugged it over his head.

Gabriella didn't bother to shield her obvious appreciation. Emiliano was no stranger to the gym. His tanned chest was bare, with washboard abs she could bounce a quarter on. She was tempted to step closer, to run her hands—and her tongue—all over his gorgeous chest.

But first...

Twisting to face Vicente, she lifted her hand, waving it regally. "Your turn."

Vicente's eyes narrowed briefly, just long enough to let her know he wasn't one-hundred percent on board with her calling the shots. Her first impression of him had whispered "dominant" and it stood to reason. Vicente was the leader of the security officers, a position that commanded respect, that demanded he rule with an iron fist.

Obviously, he was used to being in control. And while she had no problem taking the submissive role from time to time—D/s being only one of the kinks she enjoyed—a role was all it would be, her playing a part, because there wasn't a truly submissive bone in her body. She took pleasure from being the bottom...and the top.

Something Vicente would have to understand, accept.

Rather than back down at the sight of his haughty glare, she tilted her head in an arrogant fashion, offering him a look he should recognize from his own reflection in the mirror. It basically screamed "get on with it."

Gabriella waited, holding her breath. She'd played this moment out over and over last night until her arousal had reached its feverish peak.

She was equal parts surprised and—yes—disappointed when he reached behind his head and pulled his own T-shirt off one-handed. Fighting him for control would have been just as hot as having him obey her command.

Her gaze slid down his body. Like Emiliano, Vicente was built. Ripped was probably a more accurate term. He had referred to himself as an old man last night, but none of that was present in his physique. The only thing that indicated the slightest bit of age was the light smattering of salt-and-pepper hair on his chest. Her fingers itched to pet it to see if it was coarse or soft.

Vicente, the devil, wasn't as compliant as he pretended. He lifted one brow as he repeated her hand gesture, his expression pure dare. She'd let her appreciation of their bodies distract her briefly, but it was apparent her husband expected tit for tat in this peekaboo undressing game.

Never one to give in easily, she shot Vicente a sensuous smile before ignoring his unspoken request, turning, and walking over to Emiliano. Reaching up, she wrapped her arms around his shoulders, drawing him down for a kiss.

Emiliano had been the most passive thus far. Though perhaps that was the wrong word. He'd been the most patient. It hadn't taken Gabriella long to size up her husbands over the course of this past month.

Vicente was stoic, strong, commanding, with an air about him that said "don't fuck with me," while Emiliano exuded a different, quieter kind of strength. She didn't mistake that introspectiveness as disinterest. Rather, Emiliano seemed to be the kind of man who was always observing and taking notes in his mind for later reflection. He was the type who thought before he acted, weighing all the facts before forming an opinion, good attributes for a politician.

Of course, her husbands' personalities combined with hers proved that theirs would be an interesting, if somewhat combustible, marriage.

Because she was much more emotional. One of her fathers had proclaimed on countless occasions that she tended to "lead with her heart, her head typically several miles behind." Her other father always softened those words, declaring it was her passion that made her so good at the philanthropic work she did.

Now, however, Emiliano's patience vanished as he took possession of her lips, kissing her with a hungry—almost wild—fervor that had her head spinning. His tongue touched hers, the bitterness of his espresso mixing with the sweetness of her own breath.

After a minute or so, she pulled back, simply to suck in some much-needed air and to try to gather her wits.

"Need more," he murmured against her lips. "So beautiful. So fucking beautiful." Emiliano drew her close again, deepening the kiss. It was heady, sexy, wonderful. While their association had been short thus far, Gabriella didn't doubt for a second that she was going to fall head over heels for this man.

Her husband.

Hers.

She startled briefly when she felt Vicente's hands on her waist, his chest brushing her back. She'd initiated the kiss with Emiliano, purposely moving away from Vicente, in the manner of waving a red flag at a bull.

Vicente had dictated their future last night with an arrogance that had enraged and hurt her. So she'd decided to taunt him by offering Emiliano the first kiss, hoping her actions would show him just how wrong he was to write himself out of this relationship.

They were a trinity, and by God, there would be two men in her bed each and every night. Gabriella fully intended to refuse his asinine plan.

She gasped slightly when Vicente's teeth bit into her earlobe, his words puffing over her ear. "Cutting me out, wife?"

"You already did that," she said, silently cursing her breathlessness as her head fell to the left, Vicente's lips traveling along the side of her neck.

"Not from this."

"Stop," Emiliano said when she stiffened, her anger beginning to pique. He ran the back of his knuckles along her cheek in a gentle, soothing way. "We're not bringing that discussion in here."

Emiliano had halted this same conversation last night as well, and to be honest, at the time she'd been grateful for the reprieve.

Right now though...

Emiliano cupped her cheek in his hand, forcing her to hold his gaze. "There will be time to talk. After. Right now, I want to be with you." Then, much to her surprise, he looked over her shoulder at Vicente. "And with you. My wife. And *my husband,*" he stressed the last, speaking with a conviction that dared Vicente to refute that title.

"I am your husband." Vicente had never denied the existence of their marriage or who they were to each other.

No.

What he'd denied them was a chance to live their lives together as a true trinity.

However, neither man seemed too keen on talking about any of that right now, and given the racing of her heart and the undeniable wetness between her legs, she didn't have a problem with that. There was a day of reckoning coming.

But today wasn't that day.

Vicente gripped the bottom of her tank top and pulled it over her head. His large, rough hands were on her breasts in an instant, cupping, squeezing the flesh before seeking out her nipples with his fingers, pinching them with a delicious roughness that had her rising up on her toes.

"Yes," she hissed when Emiliano lowered his head, sucking one of her taut nipples into his mouth as Vicente held her breasts up for him. It was the first time the two men had worked together on anything. And she had absolutely zero complaints about this joint effort.

Emiliano's hands rested on her waist, his fingers tightening when she moaned, the result of his deep suction. It was painful yet perfectly pleasurable.

As Emiliano sucked on her nipples, Vicente continued to pay homage to the side of her neck and the sensitive spot just behind her ear, using those erogenous zones to drive her mad. Especially when he shifted closer, his erection pressing against her ass.

"Your pants," she said, oh so ready to move them on to the next part. Emiliano released her nipple with a soft pop, lifting his head when her hands fell to the waistband of his lounge pants, intent on stripping them off him.

He took a short step away from her, taking over the task, shoving the pants off as well as his boxer briefs. His erection was long and thick and ready.

By moving back, Emiliano ensured that not only could she see him clearly, but Vicente could as well.

Gabriella was curious about her husbands' sexual preferences in the bedroom. Bisexuality was common in the Masters' Admiralty, but it wasn't a requirement. Emiliano stood before them with a quiet confidence, clearly unfazed about his nudity in front of another man.

Vicente stepped next to Gabriella, the two of them now side by side. Gabriella glanced in Vicente's direction and saw the naked appreciation in his hungry eyes as he looked at their husband.

She was no stranger to threesomes. As a member of the Masters' Admiralty, she would have been a fool to enter into her marriage unprepared for sex with multiple partners.

However, her past experiences had all been limited to a man and a woman. If Gabriella had had her choice, she would have preferred her marriage to be the same dynamic, as she enjoyed sex with other women, loved the softness of their skin, the feeling of long nails drawing pictures over her body, the tangy taste of female arousal.

This was her first time with two men, and the idea that Vicente and Emiliano might fuck each other, as well as her, was a bigger turn-on than she could have imagined.

Closing the distance, Gabriella reached out and closed her hand over Emiliano's cock, stroking it several times before releasing him to turn back to Vicente.

"Your turn," she said, gesturing to his pants.

This time, Vicente didn't hesitate, didn't call her to task for her demands. He shed his pants, revealing he'd been going commando all morning.

Like Emiliano, his dick was rock hard, the slightest sheen of precum on the tip. Gabriella licked her lips, torn between sucking him into her mouth or demanding that Emiliano do it so that she could watch. Both options were far too tempting.

Before she could do either, she felt Emiliano's hands grasping the waist of her pants. She shifted her hips, helping him slide the material—and her lace panties—down.

She felt the weight of their eyes on her body, their obvious and matching looks of admiration potent.

"Lie down. On your back," Vicente commanded her, attempting to grab the reins.

She smiled as she shook her head. "No." She waved her hand toward the bed. "Go sit on the bed with your back against the headboard."

Vicente's reluctance returned, and she wondered if she'd pushed him too far. If his dominant streak would rear its head, demanding control. She welcomed the challenge, but Emiliano stepped between them, clearly choosing his side when he said, "Do as she says."

Vicente, shockingly, listened. Climbing to the center of the bed, he sat up, reclining against the headboard with a relaxed yet regal pose. He looked like a king on his throne. He might be following her commands, but his posture let her know without words that he was choosing which ones he would obey.

Gabriella followed him onto the mattress, crawling over his outstretched legs, her breasts sliding along his thighs until her face was inches from his. She closed the distance, stealing her first true kiss from Vicente.

He allowed her a few moments to play, her kisses soft, exploratory, more tease than temptation. When she drew her tongue along his lower lip, his patience snapped and he gripped her cheeks in his strong hands, taking control of the kiss. Their tongues touched, stroked, and she whimpered softly when he nipped her lower lip, just hard enough to sting.

She loved her sex with a rough edge, something Vicente seemed to understand. He turned her head this way and that, keeping her close every time she started to pull away, refusing to release her. She fucking loved it.

These men—these kisses—had every part of her body tingling, clenching, aroused. She couldn't recall ever wanting anyone more.

Their kiss ended when the bed shifted and she felt Emiliano's hand brush her bare ass, the soft touch causing her to shiver. She looked over her shoulder at him as she wiggled it, an invitation she hoped he'd understand.

Emiliano winked as he lifted his hand and brought it down hard, the silence in the room disrupted by the sharp slap.

Gabriella tilted her hips, lifting her ass higher.

"Do that again," Vicente said, his voice gruff.

Emiliano graced the other ass cheek with a firm slap and she moaned with delight, the sound growing louder when Vicente pulled the band from her hair and grasped a handful, which he used to turn her face back toward his.

He resumed their kiss as Emiliano planted a dozen more

hard smacks to her ass. She could feel the heat building, felt the way it turned inward. She was hot. So damn hot. The intensity of this moment had been ripped right from her naughtiest fantasies.

She broke the kiss when Emiliano slid his fingers through the slit between her legs, quietly cursing when he discovered her wet heat.

"*Joder*," he murmured reverently, speaking the very word she'd been thinking when he touched her clit.

Fuck.

This was all so fucking good.

After that, words became unnecessary as the three of them gave into their baser desires, lust consuming them.

Emiliano bent over, drawing his tongue along the same path his fingers had just traveled before placing soft kisses on her sore ass.

Gabriella followed his lead, lowering her own head to Vicente's cock, taking the head into her mouth, loving the way he grunted, his fingers tightening their grip around her long tresses.

She loved giving blow jobs, loved holding a man's pleasure in her hands, driving them wild with her mouth, her hands, her hot breath. It made her feel powerful, knowing she could drive a man like Vicente out of his mind with lust. Gripping the base of his thick cock, she took him deeper into her mouth, lifting her eyes just in time to see Vicente close his, his head falling back against the headboard in undeniable bliss.

Her concentration was distracted several times by Emiliano, who seemed determined to assert his own authority over her pleasure. He continued to stroke her clit with wicked, knowing fingers as he fucked her pussy with his clever tongue.

She moaned deeply, the sound reverberating against Vicente's cock.

"*Mierda*," he grunted. "Gabriella."

She loved the sound of her name on his lips, the way it sounded almost like a prayer. She increased her pace, sucking harder as she fucked him with her mouth and her hand.

Emiliano, observant bastard, followed suit, determined she would suffer—ha-ha, as if—the same orgasmic fate as Vicente.

She only had a split second of warning when Vicente gripped the sides of her head, holding her still as he came down her throat with a roar. Her gaze was locked on his face and she watched as he fell apart.

Mercifully, Emiliano took pity on her, lifting his head, granting her reprieve. She could only assume he wanted to see their husband as he climaxed as well. They all had so much to learn about each other. Then she smiled, suddenly feeling as if a lifetime with these men wouldn't be enough.

It was far too early to feel that way. She was practical enough to admit that. But she'd grown up in the world of the Masters' Admiralty, something that had clearly impacted her view of love. For her, it didn't seem odd at all to offer her heart to two strangers because she'd seen the true beauty of trinity marriages, standing witness to the genuine love and affection her parents shared. She believed deeply in the rightness of the trinity and she was so grateful to be here...with Emiliano and Vicente, right at the start of something that could be truly miraculous and wonderful.

When she released Vicente, his eyelids lifted, his expression almost peaceful, a look she suspected was rare on this man's face. Then his gaze traveled over her shoulder to Emiliano.

"Take her. Make it good," he murmured.

Emiliano grasped her hips, pulling her toward him. She only had a moment to prepare before the head of his cock breached her opening and he thrust deep, fast, hard.

Gabriella gasped, her body clenching around him, her orgasm too close.

"Emiliano, please," she begged, foolishly pretending she was asking for mercy, even though she pushed back against him, adding more force to his relentless thrusting.

"Come for me, *tesoro*," Emiliano said. "I'm there too."

His words—that sweet term of affection—as well as his rough claiming proved to be her undoing. Her orgasm struck hard and fast, her back arching with the impact. Emiliano hadn't lied about his own state, his climax coming right on the heels of hers.

She shuddered as she tried to find a way down from the amazing high.

"Incredible."

She opened her eyes when she heard Vicente's deep voice. He remained in exactly the same place she'd put him, his back against the headboard, ensuring he'd had the perfect view of her face and Emiliano's.

She gave him a soft smile, her happiness escaping.

This.

This was how she'd imagined her honeymoon.

She opened her mouth to say so, but before she could speak, they were distracted by a buzzing sound from across the room.

VICENTE FROWNED, tempted for a moment to ignore his phone. Unfortunately, his position didn't allow him the luxury of placing his cell on silent. And given the fact they were in a safe house instead of on their honeymoon because of him... well...he needed to set things right, to put them back on the right track, one that would ensure Gabriella and Emiliano's safety.

The moment De Leon had told him he was to marry them, Vicente began charting out a course that would allow him to obey his admiral, to honor his vow to the society, while still managing to do the job he'd been hired to do.

When he'd first met Gabriella and Emiliano, he'd thought it would be easy to maintain a life separate from them. What he hadn't expected was to like them so much. He begrudgingly admitted to himself that his plans for their future would be easier if he maintained some level of distance, but watching Gabriella kiss Emiliano, knowing her intention was to show him exactly what a life spent on the outside would look like, had sparked feelings he didn't want to acknowledge.

Desire. Jealousy. Need.

He had to put those things on the back burner. There was no place for any of those emotions in his life.

"I have to take the call," he said.

Gabriella, whom he was still caged beneath, lifted her upper body until she was kneeling. Emiliano wrapped his arms around her, securing her back to his chest. She leaned her head back against their husband's shoulder, the two of them already so comfortable with each other, so at ease.

Rising, he crossed to the bureau and looked at the phone screen.

Rodrigo was calling. Vicente glanced at the bed, picked up the phone, then stepped out of the room before answering the call.

"You have news?" he said instead of hello.

Rodrigo could be both eloquent and loquacious, particularly when he was seducing an interesting woman, but he responded in kind. "It wasn't the Bellator Dei."

Vicente froze, shock tightening every muscle. "Explain."

"The Italian defector from the Bellator Dei, Luca, looked at it. Nothing about the bomb construction matches their signature or their assembly style."

"They may have..." Vicente heard himself and stopped. He knew better than to argue. If Rodrigo was calling him with this information, he'd already considered every angle, asked every question.

"Not Bellator Dei," Vicente said.

"No, sir." Rodrigo hesitated a moment. "Which means—"

"Which means that if the bomb was an attempted assassination..." A small sound had him turning. Gabriella and Emiliano stood in the door, watching and listening. "It could have been meant for any one of us."

"We're running threat assessments," Rodrigo said. "But we need names."

"I'll get them." Vicente ended the call.

They stood in cool, tight silence. Emiliano put his arm around Gabriella's bare shoulders. Neither of them had bothered to dress.

Vicente wanted to go to them, wanted to bring them into his embrace, but he was the security minister. That duty came before anything else—they needed him to protect them more than they needed comforting touches.

"What do we do?" Emiliano asked.

"We find and neutralize the threat."

"Or identify the perpetrator and take them to the authorities," Emiliano countered.

What the fuck had Admiral De Leon been thinking to pair him with a man who believed the law was enough to handle the world's evil? Eventually, Emiliano would grow to hate him, hate what he represented and what he did. Another reason that Vicente's place in this trinity had to be in the shadows, supporting them from the darkness, where he'd lived for so long, while they lived as husband and wife.

"We find the bomber first," Vicente said. His gaze swept over them. "Which means I need to know everything."

"What do you mean, 'know everything'?" Emiliano demanded.

"An assassination attempt was made." Vicente put a little bite in his tone, and they both stiffened in reaction. "So tell me, husband, wife...who wants you dead?"

CHAPTER FIVE

B y unspoken agreement, they dressed and went downstairs before having this conversation. Vicente was first down, so he went to the kitchen, preparing a coffee for each of them, based on their preferences from that morning. It was late in the day for coffee, but he felt they all needed it, and it was possible that it would be a very long night.

Once he'd made and gathered everything, he put it all on a tray.

It felt very...domestic.

Really, it was about efficiency. He couldn't carry three things at once, hence the tray. He walked into the lounge where Gabriella and Emiliano—now dressed and without the post-sex rumpled look he'd so enjoyed—looked up at him. Their attention flickered to the tray and there were differing degrees of surprise evident in their expressions. Vicente realized that no matter what internal justifications he used, this *was* a very domestic moment. They were his spouses and he was caring for them in this small way.

It was his right to care for them but his duty to protect them. Protecting them would, should, always come first.

He set down the tray and passed them each their coffee, including two sugar packets and a small spoon on the saucer of Gabriella's.

"From sex to murder to coffee," she murmured.

"And our marriage is less than thirty hours old." Emiliano's lips twitched.

Vicente took a seat and then a few sips. "That this isn't the Bellator Dei is a problem."

Gabriella set aside her saucer, holding her coffee cup in one hand. "I believe I mentioned yesterday that you should include us in the investigation."

Vicente refused to take that bait. "Yesterday, there was no reason to involve you."

"Don't do that," Emiliano said. "Don't pull back."

Vicente was startled by the vehemence in his voice. He looked at Emiliano for several beats. Then they both looked away, sipped their coffee in silence, and as impatient as Vicente was to further the investigation by generating a list of names, he found he didn't want to ruin the mood further.

"Someone wants one of us dead." Gabriella looked up.

"We're sure one of us was the target?" Emiliano asked. "It could be all of us. You said the Bellator Dei had moral objections to the trinity marriage. Maybe there's someone else with similar motives."

"How would they know it was a wedding?" Gabriella countered. "The ceremony was private, and we never referred to the reception as a wedding reception. My mother and I were very careful about that. I believe my fathers even had a cover story ready about starting a nonprofit and the three of us being on the board."

"We'll explore all options," Vicente assured them.

"*We* meaning you and the security officers and *caballeros*." Gabriella's words were accusatory, but her tone was softer than expected.

"Yes." Vicente resisted the urge to soften his own words. "Just because we are married doesn't mean you now have access to the details of territory investigations."

"I think I, we," she pointed at Emiliano, "had and have a right to know not because we're now married to the security minister, but because *we were the ones who almost got blown up*." Gabriella didn't quite yell the final words, but it was close.

Vicente watched as she caught herself, visibly forcing herself to calm down. He hated the cool mask that slipped over her features, preferring the passionate woman she'd only given them glimpses of so far.

The silence hung heavy, and Vicente waited. He realized he was waiting for Emiliano to step in and say something, but the other man was silent. He ran a hand through his hair, then said, "It's possible that the bomb was meant for another guest, but the perpetrator was unable to access an interior location or pinpoint where anyone else would be."

The point of the bomb could have been to create chaos and then take out the real target in the aftermath. That was a sound theory, except for the fact that no one had gone missing or been seriously injured. It was possible that their tight security protocols—which had gotten everyone indoors and secured relatively quickly, despite the panic—had thwarted that.

Gabriella sat back and crossed her legs, the loose, wide-legged pants she wore riding up to reveal one very pretty ankle. "The bomb was timed to go off while we were there taking pictures. No one was scheduled to take photos with us, though I had considered asking my parents to take some more formal photos with us, instead of just the shots we did with them and the admiral after the ceremony."

"Your parents are one of the things I want to talk about." Vicente sat forward. "Do they have any enemies? Anyone who threatened them recently?"

"Are my parents in danger?" Gabriella uncrossed her legs, sitting forward so she was perched on the edge of the chair.

"It's a possibility, but they have their personal security and my people are doing regular sweeps."

"You think Gabriella was the target? Hurt her to hurt her parents?" Emiliano looked thoughtful.

"It's possible. The attack took place on her parents' property, and that might not be coincidental."

"Business rivals, possibly. I mean, the high fashion world is dramatic and cutthroat, but trying to blow someone up is not... fashionable." Gabriella shook her head slowly. "If it had been poison..."

"The admiral is speaking with your parents now," Vicente said. "There may be things you don't know about them. Secrets or fears they haven't shared."

"My parents..." Gabriella hugged herself, and Emiliano reached out to squeeze her knee.

"They weren't scheduled to be in the photos by the fountain," Emiliano pointed out. "I don't think it was them."

"Nor do I, though I have people talking to them, investigating that angle. Your parents are safe, as are you," Vicente reassured her. "But it's unrealistic for us to live like this for longer than a few days."

"We were only supposed to be in Palma de Mallorca for three days. I cannot take off more time than that," Emiliano said. "Not with Parliament in session."

"If we can identify the assailant, it will only be a matter of hours for us to neutralize the threat."

"Unless they went on the run or are in hiding," Emiliano countered.

Vicente would never tell them what kind of information and weapons he had access to. Normal people were terrified when they realized privacy was a fairy tale, and that it was shockingly easy to kill and get away with it if one didn't mind getting one's hands dirty.

"I wonder...I mean, I didn't think...that the Moroccan government wanted to kill me," Gabriella said. "Stop me, yes. But if they kill me, they make me a martyr, and my family would raise hell."

Vicente considered the direction of her thoughts, played it out in his mind. "It is possible the Spanish government is behind it, though they have less motive."

"Our government does not kill its own citizens," Emiliano said hotly.

Vicente snorted in amusement, then cleared his throat when he realized Emiliano was serious. "Of course."

"It could be one of the anti-migrant extremist groups," Gabriella said. "I've received some threats from them, but they are not the sort of people who take real action. They simply sit around and blame immigrants for their own inadequacy."

"Vicente, are you telling me that you have knowledge of government officials ordering the assassination of private citizens?" Emiliano sounded like a senator, all righteous justice and an expectation that his question would be answered.

Vicente looked at him, raised one brow, and then switched his attention back to Gabriella. "Do you still have the letters?"

"I gave them to my parents' head of security. I wouldn't let them give me a guard, but when I started getting that kind of mail, I went to them. I'm not stupid."

Vicente pulled out his phone and sent a quick text to Rodrigo, who was at the Torres' house.

"Anyone you interacted with personally?" Vicente asked

her. "The escalation from threats to real violence is rare, and less common than popular media makes it seem."

Gabriella started to shake her head but stopped. She crossed her arms, propping them on her knees. Her hair hung forward, hiding her face. Her body language was both protective and defensive.

"Gabriella?" He considered her. "An ex? Were you seeing someone before De Leon announced our marriage?"

"No. I've always been responsible. Made sure the people I was with knew it wasn't long term."

Vicente nodded, but it was clear she'd thought of something. "Tell me what you're thinking." He put some power into the words, using the same voice and tone he would to make soldiers pay attention.

"I...I need a minute."

"We don't have a minute."

"Leave her alone, Vicente." Emiliano rose from his chair, stepping in front of Gabriella, blocking Vicente's view of her.

"I don't need you to protect me," Gabriella said from behind Emiliano.

"I'm not protecting you." Emiliano's jaw was tight, the words coming out from between his clenched teeth. "I'm giving Vicente a moment to reconsider how he speaks to you."

Vicente felt his own temper, usually tightly controlled, rise. "Whatever secrets you've kept, you *will* share them. Now."

"And you will do the same? You'll tell us your secrets?" Emiliano scoffed. "No, of course you won't. You'll—"

"My secrets aren't just mine," Vicente countered.

"You expect us to bare our souls and—"

"I destroyed the lives of twenty-three people." Gabriella's quiet words cut through the room.

Vicente's heart clenched at the agony laced through her voice.

Emiliano turned. "Gabriella, you—"

"Don't tell me I'm not responsible when you haven't heard the story."

When she looked up, Emiliano stiffened, then returned to his chair.

The silence was tight, anticipatory.

"When I first started working with refugee and migrant communities, I was just doing education and resource brokering. Talking them through the process and helping people get access to the resources, usually legal aid, that they needed.

"After a few years of that, I realized their chances of success were much better if they were already in Spain, and, by that point, I was disillusioned. So I started to help more directly."

She looked at Emiliano and smiled. "In a technical, if not exactly legal sense, that's when I became a human trafficker."

"The legal standard is that you need to charge, or otherwise make money, for it to count as human trafficking."

"Well, I didn't make money, but I did move people. Mostly by chartering ships. I paid for their passage. Sometimes I'd go with them. If we were stopped, I'd talk to the Civil Guard."

"What happened?" Vicente asked.

"The Moroccan government cleared out a bidonville. So many people needed help. Not all wanted to leave the country and I did what I could to help them, but there were more than a few who decided since they'd been pushed out anyway, that now was the time to try for a better life in Europe.

"I had two boats I used regularly. Two captains I trusted. But there were just so many, and they needed to get out immediately, not in a few weeks—I always had the boats wait a few weeks after making a run. Sending them on back-to-back trips like a ferry guaranteed the second time they'd be stopped.

"So I chartered a different boat. One with a captain I knew and had met but hadn't worked with before. He assured me he could do it. Assured me it would be okay. I was so young and arrogant. I thought my money, my name, the fact that I had the moral high ground meant I was untouchable. That I could do no wrong."

She paused and pressed her fingers against the inner corners of her eyes. When she dropped her hands, he could see the wet streaks on her cheeks.

"The captain left from Rabat, but he didn't go to Spain. He turned back, toward Essaouira, where he was met by the Civil Guard. He turned over everyone on that boat to the authorities. The ten adults went to detention centers, and the thirteen children were put into orphanages."

"It was not your fault," Emiliano said instantly.

"Wasn't it? I didn't look hard enough. Didn't see that the captain had a history of discrimination against the Sahrawi. All the people I put on his boat were Sahrawi, and he happily took my money, then the bounty the authorities offered. Those people trusted me."

"Gabriella—" Emiliano was half out of his chair, ready to go comfort her.

Vicente rose and walked to his husband's chair, putting a hand on his shoulder and forcing Emiliano down. "Are they all still in prison?" Vicente asked Gabriella.

"The adults? Yes. The cases are open, but I think they're purposefully losing our paperwork. The stalling has gotten worse since they weren't able to make a case against me for human trafficking."

"It sounds like these people wouldn't have the resources, especially from inside prison, to attack you."

"No, not them, but they had other family. Most of the people on the boat were parents with younger children. I was able to get the children out of the orphanages and turned over to grandparents or other relatives, most of whom were too old or unwilling to migrate. They were—rightly—enraged. I had promised their children and grandchildren safe passage, and instead their adult children went to jail and their grandchildren spent months in state-run care before I could get them out."

It was unlikely the bombing was related to the situation she'd just described, but Vicente didn't say that out loud. She'd just bared her soul, shared a shameful secret, and he would honor that.

"Can you get me names?" Vicente asked.

Without a word, Gabriella took her phone from her pocket and started tapping. A moment later, his own phone pinged, and when he checked the email, it wasn't just a list of names but copies of court filings.

"Thank you." Vicente hesitated, knowing he should say more, should acknowledge the magnitude of what she'd just shared, but he didn't quite know how. Before he made a conscious decision to do it, he squeezed Emiliano's shoulder.

When the other man twisted and looked up at him, Vicente cleared his throat and jerked his chin at Gabriella.

Emiliano raised an eyebrow, but after a moment—and a faintly amused shake of his head—turned back to Gabriella.

"Gabriella, listen to me. What happened was not your fault. You were betrayed by the captain, and you're fighting a bureaucracy that has the law on its side and time to burn."

"I should have done better, been better."

"Fine, let's play it out... Are you better now?"

"Better at smuggling people?" She smiled, though it was shaky. "Absolutely."

"And are you still fighting for these people?"

"Of course. Always. And I have contingencies in place if I am incarcerated, to make sure their cases remain a priority for the Moroccan law firms I use."

Vicente snorted. "You won't be incarcerated."

Gabriella raised her chin. "You don't believe me when I tell you that I'm considered a serious criminal by—"

"No. I mean that if anyone were to take you, I would find you." Vicente spoke simple truth.

Gabriella's mouth formed a little "o," her bottom lip looking soft and bite-able.

"You'd break me out of prison?" She was trying to make it a joke, to play off what he'd said.

"Yes." That was all he needed to say because it was the truth.

"I think...I think you could, would, do that." Gabriella let out a watery laugh. "And I don't know why that makes me feel better, but it does." She covered her face with her hands and let out a little sob.

When Emiliano rose from his chair and went to comfort her, he dragged Vicente along with him. Emiliano perched on the edge of the chair and pulled Gabriella into his arms, murmuring soft, comforting words.

Vicente knelt in front of them, and for a moment he felt like a knight, a guardian kneeling before a king and queen, pledging his life to protect them. But he was no knight, literally, since he was not one of the *caballero*, and figuratively, since he was not the type to fight great battles while wielding a sword of justice from atop a white horse.

No, he was the man who slipped out of the shadows, slit a throat, and melted back into the darkness before the arterial spray hit the ceiling.

But for a moment, with them, he could pretend.

Vicente put a hand on each of their legs, squeezing gently. First Gabriella, and then Emiliano reached out, laying one of their hands atop his. He laced their fingers together, held fast.

He wasn't sure if a long time passed, or if, for him, time

simply slowed in that moment. But when Emiliano sat up, easing Gabriella away from his chest, things felt different.

"I...I have a name for you," he said.

"I'm sure you have a long list of people who have threatened you," Gabriella said. "You're a politician, and you had to have people who threatened you when you were a prosecutor."

"Yes, of course, and the CNI have a list. But this name wouldn't be on there. This one is...personal."

Vicente pushed to his feet. "The name?"

"Gael Ortiz. My brother."

CHAPTER SIX

"Your brother?" Gabriella asked, her eyes wide.

Emiliano sighed heavily, suddenly feeling exhausted. He'd been torn over saying Gael's name ever since Vicente demanded to know who would want to kill them. His brother might not like him, might even hate him, but he would have never thought his brother would want to kill him...except it had been a bomb, and it hadn't actually killed him.

If it were only him in danger, Emiliano would have remained silent. He *had* remained silent, his silence driven by family loyalty...and guilt.

The bomb could have killed Vicente and Gabriella. It was that realization, that fear, that led him to speak his fears aloud now.

"My brother and I have had a somewhat contentious relationship since we were teenagers."

Vicente's brow furrowed. "I'd say more than somewhat if you believe he's trying to kill you."

"But the bomb wasn't lethal. No one died," Emiliano reminded them.

"Because of the extra water," Gabriella reminded him.

He was still trying to rationalize. To minimize what Gael might have done. "Gael and I were raised by a single mother, our father leaving her just two weeks after I was born. Gael was only two years old, so neither of us remember him at all. We grew up without a male influence and our mother worked two, sometimes three jobs to support the family. So I suppose you could say we basically raised each other."

Gabriella reached out and placed her hand on his knee, sympathy in her gaze. He lifted her hand and kissed her palm.

"It wasn't a bad childhood, Gabriella. My mother was a kind, loving woman, who always tried to do her best for us. I wouldn't be who I am without her influence."

"I'm glad."

"Why do you think your brother is trying to kill you, Emiliano?" Vicente asked, his impatience predictable. It seemed to be Vicente's permanent state.

"Unlike me, Gael struggled in school. He was a poor student, often getting kicked out of class for his behavior. He was the definition of lazy. He hated homework, housework, and anything else with the word *work* in it."

"And you?" Gabriella asked.

"I liked school. Took the advanced classes, studied hard."

"Let me guess, you graduated top of your class."

Emiliano grinned. "Well, I don't like to brag..."

She laughed, and he was grateful to her for bringing some levity to what was a painful conversation for him.

Vicente huffed but said nothing. Emiliano paused for just a moment to collect his thoughts before speaking.

"When we were teenagers, my brother found a new group of friends, a rough crowd of guys who were a couple years older than him. All of a sudden, he wasn't just getting kicked out of class, he was skipping school completely, drinking cheap liquor, smoking pot, stealing stuff from convenience stores. He was eighteen and I was sixteen at the time."

"Emiliano," Vicente said, but Emiliano held up his hand, well aware of what his husband's complaint was going to be.

"There is a point to all of this, Vicente. I just...wanted you both to understand...why..."

"Why..." Gabriella prompted.

"I did something stupid. My brother and I were fire and gasoline, our personalities very different. Gael was his own worst enemy, never able to get out of his own way. Always impulsive with a hair-trigger temper, while I was held up as the model student, the model son."

"You said you did something stupid," Gabriella prompted.

"One day, I asked if I could hang out with him. I thought maybe it would help our relationship if I stopped acting like the perfect kid and just acted like a regular teenager."

"What did being a regular teenager look like to you?" Vicente asked.

"Skipping school with Gael, hanging out with him and his friends. I was determined to fit in. No matter what. So I drank the liquor, smoked the pot, stood lookout while they lifted cigarettes from the market, and then I even smoked those with them. By late afternoon, I was drunk and stoned for the first time ever and acting like a jackass. I think Gael was regretting letting me tag along by that point."

Gabriella laughed softly. "I would have liked to have seen that."

Emiliano wished he shared her mirth, but even after so many years, he found it impossible to laugh about that day. "I started mouthing off to one of Gael's friends like an idiot. The guy was just as drunk as me. He got pissed off and took a swing.

I hit back, then grabbed the guy's arm when he tried to retaliate. I heard a crunch, and Gael heard it too. He stepped in and punched the guy, really hard. Then...he just kept hitting him until he knocked him out. Someone called the police. The second we heard sirens, Gael shoved me out the back door and told me to get the hell out of there. He and I both knew I'd broken the guy's arm. I was up for a scholarship, my school record spotless. If I'd been arrested for assault, even as a minor...I would have lost all of that. My whole future destroyed."

"What happened?" Gabriella asked.

"I resisted, tried to stay, knew I needed to own up to what I'd done, but Gael kept pushing me, yelling at me to go the fuck home, telling me he'd take care of it. If I'd been thinking clearly...if I hadn't been under the influence of...too many things..."

"You went home," Vicente said.

Emiliano nodded. "A couple hours later, my mom got a call from the police station. They'd arrested Gael for assault. The guy I hurt had been too trashed to remember who'd done it. So Gael took the blame. He was tried and sentenced to two years in prison. My brother went to jail because of what I'd done."

"He hurt the guy too," Gabriella said. "It wasn't just you. For God's sake, he beat the man until he was unconscious."

Vicente looked impatient.

"What is it?" Emiliano demanded.

"Your brother hates you enough to want you dead?"

"I..." He wasn't sure how to answer that.

"This all happened years ago, Emiliano," Vicente went on. "Well over a decade. Why now? Why a bomb?"

"It was hard for Gael when he got out of jail. He had a record. It made it difficult for him to find a job. His anger, his resentment toward me started the day he was sentenced, and it's grown every year since then. Gael blames me. And he's not wrong. If I hadn't run my mouth, hadn't picked that fight, if I'd stepped forward and told the truth. I'd been a kid and scared and..."

Gabriella shook her head. "Emiliano, you can't—"

"My brother works in a mine, remember? He works with explosives."

"Ah." Vicente seemed more interested. "How many other attempts has he made on your life?"

"None."

Vicente closed his eyes and pinched the bridge of his nose. "Then why now?"

"Recently, he asked me for money. Again. I said no. For the first time."

"Why did he need money?" Gabriella asked.

"He's gotten control of his anger, but now his vice is gambling. I've paid for rehab, staged interventions with my mother, but for years, whenever he needed help, I gave him the money to pay off his debts.

"Two weeks ago, he came to me again. Needed twenty thousand euro. But this was after we'd met. I knew we were getting married. When it was just my money I was throwing away, I was willing. But it wasn't fair, to either of you, for me to bring my brother's debts into our marriage. I knew someday I'd have to cut him off, so this last time when he asked, I said no."

"Did you tell him why?" Vicente demanded.

"I told him I'd met someone." Emiliano held up a hand to stop either of them from talking. "I didn't say anything about there being two people, or the wedding event, or even if I was talking about a man or a woman. But when he asked me why I wouldn't help him after everything he'd done for me—that was the phrase he always used to guilt me—I was too much of a coward to tell him it was past time I stopped. Instead, I said I met someone."

"Emiliano," Gabriella said. "Look at me."

He stared into her eyes, filled with understanding, and felt somehow better.

"You were sixteen."

He tried to let those words sink in, but he still struggled.

"You were a kid, desperate to make a connection with a beloved older brother. People make mistakes, and no one is perfect, least of all a drunk teenager. You can't keep holding yourself accountable for this. Because the fact is, your brother brought you into a dangerous situation with drugs and alcohol. And he didn't break up the fight. He escalated it, made it so much worse."

"Blaming others for your own bad choices is a defense mechanism for the weak," Vicente added.

Emiliano bit back an instinctive defense of his brother. Vicente's words were harsh, but they weren't wrong.

Gabriella agreed. "Your brother needs to own up to his part in what happened. And he has no right to blame you for the gambling. That's all on him."

Emiliano let their words sink in.

"And if he did plant that bomb," Vicente said, his dark voice rife with warning. "He, and he alone, will pay for it. I'll make sure of that."

Before Emiliano could reply to that, could even figure out what the hell to say about it, Gabriella rose and took his hand, pulling him up so that she could wrap him in her embrace. He held her close, pressing a soft kiss on the top of her head, grateful for her comfort and wishing he didn't need it.

For so many years, he'd pushed the memories associated with Gael down deep so that he wasn't consumed by the guilt.

Vicente watched them intently, not seeking to join them.

Emiliano wondered how long Vicente would insist on remaining apart. There had been moments—brief ones—where Emiliano felt as if Vicente's resolve was weakening.

Given the emotional revelations of the past hour or so, Emiliano needed his partners—both of them.

"I think we should return to the bedroom," Emiliano said, his gaze locked with Vicente's. He suspected his husband would reject the idea, insisting that they continue slicing open these wounds, allowing the pain to bleed all over the floor.

Instead, Vicente held out his hand. "I agree. Come."

Gabriella's arms loosened around him and she turned, taking the hand Vicente proffered, then grasping Emiliano's with the other.

The three of them returned to the room they'd vacated just a short time ago. Emiliano couldn't believe how different he felt as they reentered it. He'd never talked to anyone about the day Gael was arrested.

It had been hard to admit to his spouses that he had ultimately made his brother's current situation even more difficult. By paying his debts, he'd enabled Gael's addiction rather than forcing his brother to be accountable for his vices. By bailing him out, he'd ensured the cycle would continue.

Gabriella turned and walked toward the bed backwards, facing him and Vicente. With each step, she slowly stripped off her clothing, first her tank top, then her lounge pants, and finally her panties. Sitting on the edge of the mattress, she crooked her finger at them. She was sex incarnate and Emiliano found her absolutely irresistible.

The saying "confession is good for the soul" never felt truer. After sharing his secret shame regarding his brother, Emiliano felt a thousand pounds lighter.

He stripped off his T-shirt, Vicente following suit. Neither of them wasted any time accepting Gabriella's sensual invitation.

This morning, she'd taken control, directed the play. He'd gone along with it, interested in watching the power exchange between her and Vicente.

He wasn't new to threesome relationships, nor sex with a man. The moment he'd been recruited to the Masters' Admiralty, he'd sought out all different kinds of sex, determined—as always—to excel, to be, as Gabriella pointed out, the top of the class.

While Vicente had relinquished the power to her this morning, something had shifted in the man and Emiliano suspected this time would be different. Ever since discovering the assassination attempt hadn't been directed at him, Vicente's attitude toward them had changed.

Emiliano sensed Vicente's resolve to remain on the outside of their marriage weakening. Or perhaps that was wishful thinking on his part.

Vicente shed his pants, losing no time in pushing Gabriella down on the bed. He climbed over her, kissing her roughly, their tongues stroking, their breathing accelerating.

Emiliano circled the bed, sitting on the opposite side where there was more room. Gabriella and Vicente broke the kiss when his weight shifted the bed, but he shook his head.

"No. Continue," he said. "I want to watch you."

He'd had sex with their beautiful wife this morning. Vicente had not.

This interlude would give him a chance to indulge his voyeuristic tendencies.

His spouses resumed their kiss, deepening, expanding on it with exploring hands. Gabriella stroked Vicente's thick cock, provoking a deep, guttural groan.

Vicente moved away after several minutes, dismissing

Gabriella's mew of disapproval. She attempted to draw him back down, but Vicente grasped her wrists, pulling them away.

"Hold her hands over her head," he commanded Emiliano.

Emiliano quickly shifted, moving to the spot above Gabriella's head. She didn't resist as Emiliano pressed her hands tight to the mattress. Instead, she closed her eyes, trembling with arousal.

Vicente slowly retreated down her body, not stopping until his mouth was only an inch or two from her pussy. He pushed her legs farther apart to accommodate his broad shoulders, then closed the distance, stealing his first taste.

Gabriella's graceful neck arched in obvious pleasure when Vicente's tongue stroked her clit.

"Beautiful," Emiliano murmured, his voice drawing her attention. She opened her eyes, her gaze locked with his.

Emiliano watched Gabriella's eyes lose focus as Vicente drew her closer to orgasm. Her hips began to shift, to lift, seeking out more of Vicente's ministrations.

Vicente's fingers tightened on her thighs, holding her in place, while Emiliano retained his grip on her wrists. While she struggled for freedom, Emiliano could tell it was not because she was upset by the bondage, but rather because she was seeking her climax, too impatient to wait.

Vicente played her body with skill, pushing her to the edge time and time again before pulling away just seconds before she came. Soon, Gabriella was panting heavily and cursing loudly, much to Emiliano's and—given the slight upturn of his lips—Vicente's amusement.

"*Gilipollas! Joderme!*" she cried.

Emiliano chuckled as she called them both dumbasses before demanding they fuck her. It had become clear to Emiliano that Vicente wasn't merely playing with her, he was getting back a bit of his own for this morning, for the way Gabriella refused to relinquish the reins.

Vicente finally granted her reprieve, sucking on her clit as he thrust three fingers inside her. Gabriella splintered beneath him, and Emiliano was certain he could watch her come every single day for the rest of his life and never get tired of the sight.

Her cheeks were flushed, her chest rising and falling rapidly, drawing his gaze to her perfect breasts. He released her hands so that he could cup them. Vicente observed him for only a moment or two before moving upwards once more.

Gabriella's long, thick lashes fluttered several times as she slowly came back to earth. When she did, she gave them both a soft, sated smile.

Vicente reached down, gripping his dick, placing the head of it at her opening. He slid inside slowly, not stopping until he was buried deep. Then he lifted his head to look at Emiliano.

Emiliano couldn't resist the urge to solidify exactly where he stood on their bedroom play. He leaned forward to lay claim to Vicente's lips in a scorching kiss. He felt Gabriella's eyes on them, watching them. He could taste her on Vicente's lips.

It was one of the most moving, most powerful moments of his life.

They broke the kiss after several moments, Emiliano kneeling above Gabriella's head, his position giving him a bird's-eye view of his lovers, his spouses, as they made love for the first time.

Vicente began to thrust, his movements slow at first, before building speed, depth. Gabriella, a vocal lover, cried out "yes!" several times before begging Vicente to take her even harder.

Despite her earlier orgasm, Gabriella came quickly, her body trembling as she yelled Vicente's name. He offered her no reprieve, continuing to pound inside her, looking like a man possessed.

A few minutes later, he was there...coming loudly, his body jerking, his eyes squeezed tightly shut.

"*Mierda*," he murmured when the pleasure began to wane. Neither he nor Gabriella moved for several moments.

Not until Emiliano said, "Perfect."

Vicente opened his eyes, looking years younger as a grin covered his face. Then he and Gabriella seemed to realize that while they'd found their pleasure, Emiliano was still rock hard and hurting.

"Lean back," Gabriella murmured. "The way Vicente did this morning."

Emiliano quickly shifted into the position she requested. Unlike his lovers, he had no problem handing over control or following commands...in the bedroom. Given the number of decisions he had to make on any given day, it was a relief to be able to shed those responsibilities, to put himself into their oh-so-capable hands.

He groaned when Vicente grasped his dick in a firm grip. There was no hesitance, no reticence in the way Vicente touched him. It seemed he and his husband shared similar sexual appetites.

Gabriella bent her head, teasing the opening of his dick, tasting the precum there, as Vicente began to stroke him.

Emiliano blew out a harsh breath when Gabriella drew him inside her hot mouth, the suction tight, almost painful.

"God," he said on a gasp, his hands flying to Gabriella's head, his fists closing over her long tresses.

He leaned his head back against the headboard and closed his eyes, losing himself in the sheer magic of this moment. His lovers worked together—Vicente using his hand, Gabriella her mouth—driving him ever closer to his own climax.

He was just there—so fucking close—when Gabriella

released him with a soft pop. His eyes flew open just in time to see Vicente lowering his head.

"*Dios*," he breathed when his husband took him deep into his mouth, the head of his cock brushing the back of Vicente's throat.

Emiliano was hanging on by a thread, but desperate not to come, not to give up the sheer bliss.

Gabriella, however, was his undoing. As Vicente sucked him, she reached lower, cupping his balls, playing with them for only a few seconds before pressing the tip of her finger into his anus.

Emiliano's climax erupted without warning as he came in Vicente's mouth. He swallowed it all, then released him, moving away as Gabriella used her tongue to lick every single stray drop.

Emiliano didn't have the strength to move, chuckling hoarsely as Gabriella and Vicente each claimed one side of him, lying on their backs. He reached out, clasping hands with both of them, feeling for the first time in his life that he was where he was truly meant to be.

CHAPTER SEVEN

He let them sleep.

They'd roused early afternoon and spent a lazy day in bed, sharing a very late lunch—or possibly an early dinner—each of them carefully avoiding sensitive subjects, talking only about mundane things, like well-loved books, favorite vacation spots, and even the weather, before returning to the bedroom. When they'd climbed into bed again last night, none of them had sought to do more than merely kiss, exploring each other's bodies, and getting to know each other physically, while emotions and plans for the future were firmly set on the back burner.

Vicente slid quietly from the bed, his hands gliding over limbs and soft skin, caressing them, shifting the blankets enough to let cold air into the cocoon of heat they'd created. Emiliano mumbled something, eyes opening but not focused. Vicente gave him a little nudge, rolling him toward Gabriella. Emiliano gathered her in his arms even as his eyes closed and he slid back into the cool darkness of sleep. Vicente tucked the covers around them.

Vicente had cat napped for several hours, but the middle of the night was when bad things happened. Either bad things he had to deal with or bad things he'd put in motion. Either way, it meant he rarely slept through the night, instead favoring a bifurcated sleep routine where he was awake for several hours in the middle of the night.

Once out of the bedroom, he rolled his shoulders, then tipped his head to the side, gently pulling it to stretch his neck. He'd fallen asleep in an odd position, and his body was reminding him that he was not as young or limber as he once was.

Gabriella and Emiliano made him feel young, even though he had a decade on both of them. They certainly inspired him to the point that he had the stamina of a younger man.

He let himself into a small workroom. It had once been an interior closet that was now soundproofed and had both a secure landline phone as well as a closed-network computer system. Settling into the office chair, he picked up the tablet he'd stashed there earlier and started going through the reports and updates on the bombing that had come in since he'd stepped away to do his husbandly duty.

That thought made him smile, even as he skimmed through pages of notes and documents about death and rage.

Hours passed, and his internal clock said it was near dawn when the security system dinged, a small beep that indicated an interior sensor had been tripped. He checked the internal camera feeds, displayed on one of the closed-system monitors, just in time to see Gabriella open the bedroom door and stick her head out into the hall. She held a shirt over her bare chest with one hand, but the naked curve of her shoulder and the side of her breast were visible and enticing. He would delete all this footage once they were gone. No one but he and Emiliano should see their luscious wife's nakedness.

Setting aside the tablet, he rose, slipping out into the hall in time to catch Gabriella's attention as she was closing the door.

"Vicente." She swung the door open, and the relief in her voice morphed with her next words. "Don't just disappear like that," she snapped.

"Were you worried about me?"

"Of course."

He'd been teasing when he asked the question, but her response made his chest tight, his fingers tremble. She was his wife by Masters' Admiralty law, and his lover by mutual choice. She *would* care if he disappeared. There were plenty of people in his life who would *notice* if he was gone, but they wouldn't cry for him the way he thought Gabriella might.

Emiliano appeared behind her, one arm sliding around her middle. He dropped a sleepy kiss on her head, then glanced up, smiling at Vicente. He wondered if Emiliano would weep if he died, or if he would charge out into the danger, demanding justice and answers.

As Vicente closed in on them, Gabriella held up her hand. "Stop."

He froze, his eyes sweeping the floor, the walls, then skittering up her body. "What did you hear?" Whatever the danger was, wherever it came from, he would protect them.

"Hear?" Gabriella arched a brow.

"He thinks you saw or heard something dangerous," Emiliano murmured to her.

"What? I thought this was a safe house?" She twisted, the shirt...his shirt...flaring out for a moment so he caught a glimpse of her soft stomach before the fabric fluttered back into place.

"Why did you tell me to stop?" Vicente needed to focus before her nakedness, and the sight of Emiliano's hands on her, made him forget himself.

"If you come any closer, we're going to end up back in that

bed," Gabriella said. "And as sexy as you both are...I'm hungry."

Emiliano grinned, disappearing into the room. A moment later, the bathroom door closed.

"We ate dinner very early last night."

"I thought that was a late lunch," Gabriella teased.

Vicente glanced at his watch, then leaned so he could see into the bedroom. Around the heavy curtains, there was the faintest glimmer of gray pre-dawn light. "Nothing will be open this early."

"I can make breakfast," Gabriella said. "And Emiliano said he can cook too."

Vicente nodded, but when she raised her brows, he cleared his throat. "I saw some nice jam in a cupboard."

"Toast, an egg, good jam, and your excellent coffee. A perfect meal."

Vicente smiled as she turned into the bedroom, gathering up her scattered clothes and then slipping down the hall to her room to shower and change into something clean.

Vicente turned for the stairs. By the time his spouses joined him, he had toast made and coffee for each of them. They drank their coffee and ate a slice of toast each, before Emiliano went to the stove and made a second breakfast course of fried potatoes with chorizo, olives, and plenty of pepper.

When the plates were cleared and the conversation—which had been pleasant and light, focused on their favorite foods—died down, the silence grew heavy.

It was Emiliano who sat forward, clearing his throat before he spoke. "Is there any news?"

"They've isolated the day they believe the bomb was placed." He could stop there. That gave them all the information they needed for what came next. Yet he found himself hesitating, wanting to share with them, precisely because they were both so intelligent and insightful. And because it felt... nice...to open up to them.

He wasn't a fool. He wouldn't, couldn't, tell them his secrets, but he could share this little thing with them.

Vicente cleared his throat and walked them through the information that he'd gotten from reports that came in while they were talking and fucking. "The angle of the camera doesn't offer a clear image of the bottom of the fountain, so there is no way to compare before and after to see if there's a change in the outline of the machinery, but on the day in question, several vehicles, most of which had logos for gardening companies, parked near the fountain. One of the vans had a simple stylized tree logo, no name, and an image search revealed that the logo is a free stock image. Tracing the logo isn't an efficient lead, as it was downloaded hundreds of thousands of times just in the last month."

"Could you isolate it by downloads in or around Barcelona?" Emiliano shook his head at his own question. "No, because they might have driven in from somewhere else or spoofed the IP address."

Vicente nodded in agreement.

"What day was it?" Gabriella asked.

Vicente gave her the date, but he was looking at Emiliano when he added, "Your brother has an alibi."

Emiliano's shoulders drooped in clear relief. "I knew it probably wasn't him, but..."

Gabriella reached out and took his hand in one of hers. "But it's good to know for sure."

"It is."

"And none of the incarcerated family members from your list have entered Europe anytime in the last month," Vicente told Gabriella. "The *caballeros* are still working on tracing alibis, but given the ease with which the 'gardener' moved, it suggests a younger man or larger woman, which also rules out anyone on your list, as they're all older." He leaned back in his chair. "We've also run financials on them, and there were no transactions indicative of someone hiring an assassin, though, of course, it could have been cash."

"Those people don't have that kind of money," she murmured.

"That was our assumption too," Vicente said.

"So my list of enemies is looking improbable. I guess it always was improbable." Gabriella breathed out, long and slow, as if exhaling the stress.

"Yes."

"What about facial recognition?" she asked. "Can't you identify the fake gardener that way?"

"He wore a bandana and a cap, and kept his back to the estate."

"So he knew the camera was there?"

"Or guessed that if there was a camera, that's where it would be."

His spouses both took a moment to process what he'd told them.

Gabriella laced her fingers together, leaning back in her chair and bringing one leg up, hands cupping her knee. "If it wasn't one of our enemies, then it was someone from your list."

Vicente nodded. "Yes, either a personal enemy or a professional one."

"A professional enemy...you mean like an enemy of the Masters' Admiralty? I thought it wasn't the Bellator Dei."

"They are not our only enemy, only the most likely."

Silence descended again, both of them watching him. Vicente rose and gathered their cups, taking them to the sink before turning to grab milk so he could start on fresh coffees.

"Vicente!" Gabriella sounded exasperated.

He turned.

"Well?" she demanded.

"Well, what?"

"Aren't you going to tell us who your enemies are?" She waved one hand in the air, smiling a little.

Damn it. He knew that they were going to be upset, so he'd hoped to just avoid this conversation. He took the milk to the espresso machine, pouring some into the little pitcher that he'd already washed out after the previous use.

"Vicente." Emiliano's voice was sharp, a demand couched inside a name.

He slid the pitcher in place under the wand, then paused. He could start the machine, let the hiss of steam fill the silence. But that was a cowardly move.

Instead, he faced them, leaning back against the counter. "No."

"That's it. Just 'no'?"

"You asked if I was going to tell you who my enemies are. No, I am not."

"What the fuck?" Emiliano demanded, instantly pissed. "We bared our goddamned souls to you."

"My information is too dangerous."

"You can't hide behind that." Gabriella was on her feet. "We get it. There are things you can't tell us. We're not asking you to make us security officers."

"I'm not hiding. I'm stating facts."

"That's bullshit. You just said 'personal or professional'." Emiliano had mastered his anger and was speaking with cool, clipped words, as if Vicente were a criminal on the witness stand. "That means there are individuals who want you dead for personal reasons."

"Semantics will not make me tell you."

"Very well. No names," Emiliano countered. "You don't have to give us names, but you have to tell us the stories."

"No," Vicente said simply. "I don't."

"Whoever it is who wants to kill you almost killed *us*. We have the right to know why we almost died."

"You have the right to be protected. To be safe. I will protect you." That was all that mattered. All that he really had to offer them.

Gabriella let out a harsh, barking laugh. "You have no intention of being part of this marriage, do you?"

Before he could stop himself, Vicente took a half step forward. "You're my wife." He glanced at Emiliano. "My husband."

"Then be intimate with us. Not just naked, physical intimacy. I told you both something I am so deeply ashamed of that sometimes I can't sleep because if I do, I know I'll see their faces. Sharing that story...that's intimacy. What Emiliano told us, about his brother...that was painful for him too."

Vicente felt trapped because they weren't wrong. If he were someone else, he would. But he'd lived too long in the shadows, and he knew that if he were to confess his sins, they wouldn't offer him comfort and reassurance.

"You decided that Emiliano and I would get publicly married. You decided that we would live together while you would live somewhere else. *You* decided."

When Gabriella paused to take a breath that vibrated with the force of her anger, Emiliano jumped in. "You made decisions that weren't yours to make."

"I made logical—"

"No. You had one foot out the door before this even began." Gabriella threw out an arm, gesturing toward the front of the house. "You have the whole time. I thought maybe what we had, earlier..."

"You don't want to be married," Emiliano snarled. "It's been clear every time you looked at us. Since the moment we met, you were planning a way to obey the admiral without actually having to be a husband."

Vicente heard the hurt beneath the words and it made him feel sick.

"Please—" he started.

"Please what? Please be a good little husband and wife and do what you say? Please stop asking questions? Stop expecting you to be our husband?" Gabriella slid up to him and there were tears on her lashes, but he didn't know if they were of sadness or anger. "How often are you planning to join us in bed? Once a week? No, too much. Once a month?"

She let out that same sharp, barking laugh that was anything but mirthful. "You'll sneak in, fuck us, and then be gone by morning." Her smile was brittle. "We're not your spouses, just an easy lay."

Damn her. Damn her for not seeing that all he wanted was for them to be safe. They were good and courageous. He was fairly certain that at this point in his life, he was evil, destined for Hell. An immoral act done for moral reasons was still immoral, and the things he'd done to protect his admiral and his territory fell all along the spectrum of immorality.

His throat tight, Vicente tried again. "Please—"

"Please spread my legs? Lie back so you can fuck and leave? Please get on my knees for Emiliano so you can watch as he—"

"Gabriella." Emiliano wrapped his arms around her, pulling her back.

She jerked in his hold, struggling for only a moment, before she stilled, a calm mask dropping over her features. Gone was the open, passionate woman, replaced by the elegant, controlled creature she'd been in the aftermath of the attack.

"Finish what you were going to say," Emiliano demanded of Vicente.

Vicente tore his eyes from his wife to his husband.

"Please...what?" Emiliano prompted.

"Please accept...accept that this is all I have to offer," Vicente said softly. The words felt ripped from his soul. They'd wanted him to bare his soul, well, this was it. He was begging them to take him as he was, to accept him despite the shadows in which he hid the most damaged and dangerous parts of himself.

Emiliano looked up and met his gaze. For a moment, Vicente thought it would be all right. Thought that the other man understood him.

A cruel smile twisted Emiliano's lips. "No."

Vicente rocked back, as if the single word had been a blow.

"No," Emiliano repeated. "No, we won't accept that."

Gabriella's eyes widened, and she twisted in Emiliano's arms, trying to see his face. Emiliano laced his hand through her hair and dropped his mouth to hers, taking her lips in a hard, rough kiss. She stiffened in his arms, and Vicente's shock at the rejection was subsumed by his own anger.

Taking two quick steps across the kitchen, Vicente grabbed Emiliano by the neck, squeezing hard enough to put pressure on his carotid arteries. Emiliano released Gabriella, both hands coming up to grab Vicente's wrist.

"Stop!" Gabriella gasped.

"Never touch her in anger," Vicente snarled.

"You're strangling him." Gabriella shoved between them.

Vicente let go, let her push him away, backing him up until he hit the refrigerator. He looked down at her, saw some soft emotion in her gaze. He reached for her hair, but she backed up.

"Did I hurt you, Gabriella?" Emiliano studiously ignored Vicente. "I'm sorry, I just—"

"Wanted to use me as a way to punish him?"

Emiliano winced. "Maybe that is why. I didn't consciously..." The anger seemed to drain out of him. He held out a hand, offering it to her. "May I?"

The tense lines of her body relaxed, and Gabriella placed her hand in his, letting Emiliano draw her into his arms. As she leaned into Emiliano, Gabriella looked over and met Vicente's gaze. He didn't know what emotion he saw in her eyes, but he knew he not just wanted but *needed* to be with them, to be a part of their embrace.

Vicente went to them, and as Gabriella rose on her toes to kiss Emiliano, Vicente wrapped his arms around both of them, cradling them as they embraced each other. This was what he'd imagined. These two together, but he was there too, protecting them.

For one perfect moment, as Emiliano's lips feathered over Gabriella's, he thought their trinity would thrive, that the relationship he'd envisioned would work, because they'd understand what he already knew—that it had to be this way for them, with him on the outside but still there.

Then Emiliano's hand rose and shoved Vicente back.

He wasn't ready for it, and he stumbled.

Emiliano broke the kiss, twisting to face Vicente. "Don't touch me."

Vicente felt his own anger rise. Anger was far easier to deal with than grief or heartbreak. "You can't manipulate me by withholding sex."

"Both of you need to..." Gabriella looked back and forth between them, and something passed over her face. "I changed my mind. Don't calm down."

"What?" Emiliano demanded.

She pointed from Emiliano to Vicente. "You don't want to fuck him, or for him to fuck you." Then she pointed from Vicente, back at herself and Emiliano. "You're happy to fuck us but don't want to be in any kind of real relationship." Her words were blunt, cold. "Everyone's angry, hurting. The smart thing to do would be to walk away for a few hours." Slowly, she reached for the hem of her shirt. "But we're not going to do that." She pulled her top up and off, then shimmied out of her pants. "Strip, boys. We're going to hate-fuck."

CHAPTER EIGHT

This was either a terrible idea or her best idea.

One second became two as she stood in the kitchen in her underwear. By the third second, soul-crushing humiliation started to take hold. This was what happened when she let her emotions get away from her, when she let insane passion take the reins.

It was Vicente who stepped forward, his gaze steady and focused, like that of a jungle cat locked on prey.

Emiliano stayed in place.

"Sex helped us get close to each other," she said. "Then we started talking and fucked it up."

Vicente's lips twitched in a small, sexy smile that made her heartbeat stutter and then start up again, faster than before.

"And you think hate-fucking will fix what we just broke?" Emiliano's voice was quiet, and she could hear the hurt in it. She wondered if Vicente could hear it too. Wondered if he'd figured out, as she had, that Emiliano was the kind of person who would love deeply and eternally, and that he hoped for the same in return.

"No, I think hate-fucking will give us an outlet for all this anger." She would look ridiculously stupid if she put her clothes back on again, so she put a hand on her hip, tucking the tips of two fingers under the waistband of her underwear. Vicente's gaze followed her hand.

"I'm not fucking him," Emiliano snarled. "I get what you're trying to do, Gabriella, but I just...can't."

She doubted he knew what she was trying to do. He was probably attributing her actions to altruistic motives. After all, they didn't really know each other yet. They'd had sex, shared a few secrets, but in so many ways that mattered, they were strangers. If the bomb hadn't gone off, if they'd had a normal honeymoon, they probably would have begun their married life discussing less emotionally devastating things than who might want them dead.

Vicente touched the notch at the top of her breast bone, just under the hollow of her throat. It took her by surprise—she'd been focused on Emiliano—and she jumped in reaction. Vicente's dark eyes moved down her face to her breasts. "I do not hate you, Gabriella."

"Well, I'm starting to hate you," she countered. It was a lie. What she felt for him was not hate. She hated his rejection. Wished it didn't hurt so much.

"And you want me to fuck you?" Vicente's brows rose. "In spite of that?"

Hot, heavy need slid through her, stripping away inhibitions, making it dangerously easy for her to say what she wanted. "Not in spite of. Because of."

"That's..."

"Perverted? Perverse?" A voice in the back of her mind was begging her to shut up, but the voice wasn't strong enough to override the dark, self-destructive desire that had prompted her to start taking off clothes.

The truth was she was hurting, emotionally. And not just from Vicente's insistence on standing apart. Emiliano didn't see it, but he'd done his share of damage too. He'd laid down ultimatums that forced her into the middle, drawn lines in the sand that destroyed any slim hope of them finding happiness as a trinity.

All that had fed on itself, like a star collapsing before going supernova. Her inhibitions and sense of self-preservation were burned up in the cold fire, leaving her wanting.

Wanting her internal pain to be matched by external sensation.

Wanting hands to grip her so tight they left bruises.

Wanting to be not just fucked but used.

Wanting to have a physical stimulus that would make her cry from pleasure or pain. And those tears would be a secret release. No one would ever know which tears were physical agony and which were emotional anguish.

Vicente's gaze searched her face, and then his hand slid up, circling her neck. He gripped her as he had Emiliano, but his hold was light.

"Harder," she demanded.

Vicente's lids lowered, hiding his expression for a moment. Then his fingers tightened around her neck, squeezing just enough that she felt blood pounding in her ears, and her mouth fell open as she panted out each breath.

Vicente watched her, cold and stern.

In that moment, the fact that he was older became important, when it hadn't been before.

"I don't want you to just fuck me," she breathed. "I want you to punish me, Daddy."

Vicente jerked her forward. His lips brushed her temple, cheek, ear. "Have you been a bad girl?"

Heat flooded her body, and her nipples were tight inside

her bra. When she shifted her weight from foot to foot, rocking her hips, she could feel how wet her pussy was.

Vicente's hand slid around her neck, until his thumb was under her jaw, the tips of his fingers tangled in the hair at the nape of her neck. He pressed up, thumb digging into the soft skin and forcing her head up and back. Back, back, until she was looking at the ceiling, her throat exposed.

She couldn't talk, and she wasn't sure if it was because of the stress position of her neck, or because she was so aroused, she simply didn't have the capacity to say anything.

Vicente's lips slid down the long line of her throat, then across her shoulder. He caught the strap of her bra in his teeth, used his mouth to draw it down and off so it dangled near her elbow.

"A very bad girl," Vicente murmured, lips retracing their path. "Bad enough for a real spanking?"

She jerked, her hands, which had fallen lax at her sides, reaching for him. Emiliano had spanked her a little. She was pretty sure if Vicente spanked her, she wouldn't be able to sit comfortably for a few days.

He knocked her hands away. "No. You don't touch me. I touch you. Because you're mine, aren't you, *muñequita?*"

Hands gripped her hips from behind. A tight part of her that had been waiting, waiting, relaxed as Emiliano joined them. She knew he liked to watch, but she wanted more. Maybe it was cruel of her to drag him into her perversion.

Fingers dug into her, eight little points of bright pain that made her shiver, and then she was jerked back, away from Vicente.

Emiliano banded one arm around her waist, the other coming up and across her front, his forearm between her breasts, his hand resting on the upper swell of one tit. She arched, rising up on her toes in an effort to rub her nipple against his fingers. He tightened his hold on her waist, forcing her to still.

"You don't have to do this," he murmured into her hair.

"What do you think I'm doing?" Her words came out on little panting breaths. The way he held her—tight, possessive—did nothing to cool her desire. And the way Vicente was looking at her, at them...

"You're initiating sex because we connect when we're fucking. You're giving us a way to be intimate despite the...anger."

The way he said that last word made her think it was almost something else. Something like "hurt." For a moment, arousal dimmed, subsumed by a need to comfort Emiliano. To hold him and assure him that she too was hurt by the way Vicente was holding back.

"You're either blind or stupid, *carajito*," Vicente said.

Emiliano's whole body tightened, his hold on her restricting enough that for a moment, she couldn't breathe. It was delicious.

Emiliano was far from a little boy, but Vicente's insult reinforced the age-gap quasi role-play she and Vicente had started. Gabriella's arousal came surging back.

Impatient, she grabbed Emiliano's wrist and dragged his hand to cover her breast, arching into his palm with a little moan of pleasure.

"Gabriella wants rougher, dirtier sex than we've given her," Vicente said. "She wants it to hurt, just enough."

"If she wants S&M, there is a safe way to do that, and this isn't it."

Gabriella licked her lips, which felt full and hot. She wanted her lips on their flesh, wanted them to stop talking and start doing. She could say that, could wade into the conversation, but part of her enjoyed them talking about her as if she weren't there. Outside of this very specific situation, she would never have allowed it, but listening to her husbands debate the best way to fuck her was pushing all kinds of buttons.

"Life isn't safe, and this isn't S&M." Vicente reached for his belt. "At least, not yet."

Gabriella moaned as Vicente whipped his belt from his pant loops, doubled it so he held the buckle and tail in one hand. He raised his arm and brought the belt down on the counter. The vicious crack of sound made both her and Emiliano jump.

Emiliano made a noise that sounded like frustration, or maybe that was the sound of him giving in to the messy, dirty, emotionally dangerous situation she'd initiated.

Emiliano gripped the center of her bra and yanked it down, exposing her breasts. The straps were tangled around her arms, the barest hint of restraint.

He grabbed one breast, squeezing so hard that the flesh plumped between his fingers. She hoped she'd have bruises in the morning. The other hand delved into her panties, fingers rough and fumbling as he forced her pussy lips apart. One finger glanced over her clit and she yelped—she was so turned on that the sensation was almost painful.

He withdrew, and she took a breath to protest, to tell him that he hadn't hurt her, but she didn't get the chance. Emiliano's hand covered her pussy on the outside of her underwear. He began forcing the fabric between the lips of her sex, the material molding to her clit and inner labia. The elastic edges pulled her open, lewdly spreading her pussy. She looked down, past her bare breasts, to the apex of her thighs. The electric-blue satin was tucked up tight inside her, the pink, wet lips of her sex spread and protruding on either side. The fabric was darker where wet, the obvious sign of exactly how turned on she was making her cheeks heat.

Emiliano scraped a nail over her cloth-covered clit and she

jerked, nearly breaking free of his hold. Sharp shards of pleasure pierced her, and when he did it a second time, she yelped.

"If you want me to be rougher, I will," Emiliano murmured. "I'll hurt you, and then I'll soothe you, take care of you."

"Touch me," she pleaded. "Both of you."

Vicente had been watching, his interest clear, thanks to his very evident erection, but now he closed the space, reaching for them.

Emiliano held out a hand, halting him. "No. You...I don't want you to touch me."

Pain flitted across Vicente's features, but then the hard, stern mask was back in place. "You want her in the middle."

"I'm going to fuck my wife," Emiliano countered. "I don't give a fuck what *you* do."

Vicente inclined his head, his arms loose at his side, the belt still dangling from one hand. He even took a step back, as if he were going to do nothing but watch.

Emiliano released her, his hands sliding between their bodies so he could unfasten his pants.

Vicente struck, his relaxed manner a ruse. One moment, she had her back to Emiliano, the next, his hand was gripping her elbow and she stumbled forward, fetching up against Vicente's chest. She raised her face to look at him, lips parted in surprise. His hand tangled in her hair, tight enough to pull, to make her scalp prickle with delicious pain.

"My bad girl," he murmured.

"Are you going to punish me?" she whispered.

He tugged on her hair, making her moan. "I should make you beg, but I don't want to wait." Vicente spun her, the kitchen swirling around her. He bent her over the table.

She planted her hands on the tabletop but he forced her down, until her breasts grazed the cold wood. His hand on her back was relentless, not letting up until her ass was high in the air, her breasts, shoulders, and cheek against the table.

Vicente kicked her ankles apart, slid his leg between hers, the contrast of his fully clothed body versus her mostly naked form wicked and delightful.

His thigh brushed against hers as he shifted to the side. She knew what that meant, knew what was coming, but the first swat of his hand on her ass made her jump. The slap of flesh on flesh was loud.

Oh yes, he spanked harder than Emiliano did.

In the echoing silence that followed, she heard Emiliano's harsh breath.

For a moment she worried, worried that she was losing the husband who wanted to actually be a husband to her. Vicente had understood what she needed, what she was looking for right now. Emiliano hadn't lied when he said he was ready and willing for anything, but she worried she'd also shocked him, either with her desires or with the fact that she was willing to let anger toward Vicente push them into physical intimacy, when it was clear that what they needed was to talk to one another, no matter how difficult the conversation.

Another spank. A third, back on the first cheek, striking the same spot so that she whimpered and pushed up on her toes.

Emiliano stepped up beside the table, his hand sliding into her hair, far gentler than Vicente's had been. He bent, meeting and holding her gaze. "Tell me you want this."

"I need it," she breathed. "I need you, both of you, to use me. Fuck me. Make it so I can't think or worry or grieve anymore."

Emiliano's eyes tightened, and she knew he understood. Understood that the anger that had pushed them to this place was covering up the grief she hadn't fully acknowledged. She was in mourning for the trinity marriage she'd always envisioned. Grieving its loss because Vicente had made it very clear he would protect them but not be married to them, not in the way they were meant to be. She wouldn't know the kind of relationship or love her parents had. She would love and be loved by a good man, and for most people, Emiliano would have been more than enough.

But she grieved, and now Emiliano understood.

His lashes lowered, his mouth twisted for a moment in an expression that made her heart clench even as she moaned in response to another swat on her bottom.

When Emiliano looked up, his gaze skittered past her face, sliding up her naked back. She couldn't see Vicente's expression, but something passed between the men, and whatever it was caused Vicente's spanks to increase in both force and frequency.

Her ass was starting to really hurt now. The heavy slaps caused heat to spread through her backside, and she was leaning into the table, the edge of it pressing hard against her thighs as she strained away. Emiliano disappeared from her field of view. There were soft noises as he moved around the kitchen, and then something thumped down on the table by her waist.

She twisted, eyes going wide when she saw the wooden spoon and bottle of olive oil.

"Emiliano—"

He stopped her words with the simple act of forcing two fingers into her mouth. "Suck," he commanded.

She obeyed, making wet, sloppy sounds. She kept sucking as Emiliano fisted a hand in her hair and lifted her. She braced her palms on the table, locking her elbows, while behind her Vicente continued the spanking.

Emiliano took his hand from her mouth and ripped at his pants, shoving them down and off but not bothering to remove his shirt or boxers. Then he was climbing onto the table, kneeling between her hands. He sat back on his heels, yanking her head down. He forced her face against the front of his boxers. Frantic, needing to have him in her, she rubbed her face, her mouth, over him, until she managed to free his cock, which jutted out of the front of his boxers.

Then he was guiding her lips to the head of his dick, giving her only a moment to run her tongue around him. He was already wet, salty on her tongue. He forced her head down onto his cock. It was rough and angry, without the care and control he'd shown previously. He was using her, fucking her face.

She'd been so caught up in getting his cock in her mouth, she hadn't noticed that Vicente had stopped spanking. She noticed when he started again, because this time it wasn't his hand but the spoon Emiliano had brought over. Emiliano was too angry with their husband to let Vicente touch him, but he had no problem collaborating with the other man on ways to use and abuse her.

The head of the wooden spoon cracked against her ass, low down, near her sit spot. Gabriella shrieked around Emiliano's cock. He rewarded her by yanking her head down even as he thrust up, the head of his cock hitting the back of her throat.

Another strike from the spoon, and tears formed on Gabriella's lashes. Her arms trembled, and she dropped onto her elbows. It changed the angle of her neck and face enough that the head of Emiliano's cock entered her throat. She fought the urge to gag, even as fresh pain laced through her from yet another strike of the wooden spoon.

"Damn you," Emiliano growled. "Damn both of you."

Tears spilled down her cheeks. She swallowed around Emiliano's cock, felt him shudder in reaction to the constriction of her throat. Behind her, Vicente threw the spoon away. It hit the wall, then clattered to the floor. Then his hands were on her ass, ripping her panties down her thighs. The feeling of the wet fabric peeling away from her clit was almost enough to bring her to orgasm. Almost.

When he slid his cock into her pussy, when he fucked her at the same time Emiliano railed her mouth, that would do it. That would give her the push she needed.

She'd forgotten about the oil. Forgotten what that might mean. Slick fingers slid between the cheeks of her abused ass, spreading the creamy, cool olive oil over her anus. She stiffened, shaking her head as much as she was able with Emiliano's cock in her mouth.

"Make a fist if you don't want it," Vicente barked.

Gabriella closed her eyes, at war with herself, fresh tears slipping over her cheeks. Carefully, deliberately, she put her palms flat on the table, spreading her fingers wide.

Vicente grunted, a sound of stern approval that made her tremble. Then his finger was sliding inside her, forcing her open. The pain of the intrusion mingled with the pain of her spanking. It would have been agony if not tempered by the molten heat of need and arousal.

Emiliano bent over her, sliding his hands between her body and the table to grab her breasts. He pinched her nipples, then leaned back, pulling mercilessly on her tits.

The first quiver of her orgasm shook her, as Vicente added a second finger to her ass. It burned as he stretched her, spread her. She started to bob her head on Emiliano's cock. She was past the point of thinking, of caring how carnal and wanton this was. Of how debased and degraded she must look. They were giving her what she needed, the kind of physical, rough sex she so rarely dared to ask for.

"Spread your legs. Bend your knees," Vicente demanded.

She did but not fast enough. He forced her feet apart, pressed his own knee against the back of hers so it bent and gave. Then his fingers were gone from her ass, and the feeling of them being removed was pure pleasure. She swayed, taking Emiliano's cock deeper into her mouth as she went forward, offering her ass and pussy to Vicente as she rocked back.

Vicente's thumbs dug into her ass, spreading her wide. Then the blunt head of his cock was there, at her entrance. She tightened, partially on instinct, partially out of a desire to feel Vicente force his way into her.

He seemed to realize what she was doing and squeezed her ass, the shock of pain from her abused butt making her tense and then relax. It was in that moment that he thrust, the head of his cock spearing into her. The pain-laced pleasure from all those nerve endings merged with the other physical sensations —her throbbing, well-spanked bottom. Her stretched, pinched nipples. Her aching jaw.

That was almost enough to make her come. Almost.

Then Vicente slid in deeper, only to withdraw. In tandem, Emiliano released one breast and lifted her head off his cock.

For a moment they were all still, each of them breathing hard.

Blood returned to the recently released nipple, and Gabriella whimpered in need. As if that was the signal they'd been waiting for, both men moved, taking her, fucking her with angry, relentless intensity. Emiliano grabbed her head in both hands, releasing the other nipple in the process. Vicente grabbed her ass, spreading her cheeks wide, and shoved his thick cock into her with a brutal thrust, just as Emiliano forced her head down on his cock.

The orgasm ripped through her, so intense, it wasn't really pleasure but a release. The tension, both physical and emotional, shredded, and her body shook in reaction. The pleasure was there, in the tightening of her lower abdomen, in the fluttering of her anus around Vicente's cock, and her frantic swallowing of Emiliano's dick. She pulled them with her, each man becoming brutal and selfish for the few moments it took them to reach climax, her mouth and ass pounded ruthlessly.

Then it was over, and they were pulling out of her. Gabriella let them care for her, not really paying attention to what they were doing but rather accepting the softness of their hands, even as she gave herself over to tears. By the time her sobs of pleasure, pain, anger, grief, and a dozen other emotions had quieted, they had her wrapped in a blanket. Despite Emiliano's insistence that he didn't want Vicente to touch him, the men were seated together on a small couch in the other downstairs lounge, with her draped across both their laps. Her head was on Vicente's shoulder, while Emiliano had his hands under the blanket, gently massaging her calves and feet until sleep claimed her.

CHAPTER NINE

"**I**'m leaving."

Emiliano looked up from the mystery novel he'd packed, expecting to read it on a sandy beach at his honeymoon, not holed up in some safe house.

Vicente was standing at the doorway to the living room. A full day had passed since the "hate sex." Nothing had been resolved. Not truly. After the intensity of the—God, the only word he could think of was *scene*, they'd cuddled Gabriella until she fell asleep, then carried her up to her bedroom and tucked her in. He and Vicente had stared at each other for a long, tense moment, then both headed to their own rooms for the night.

Today had been an experiment in avoidance. Rather than continue the same argument, the three of them had essentially retreated, circling around each other without saying much of anything.

He hadn't known exactly what to say after yesterday's encounter in the kitchen. He'd tried to broach the subject several times with Gabriella, but every time, the words got stuck in his throat. The entire interlude had left him feeling shaken—not in a bad way but in a *what the fuck just happened and can we do it again* way.

He'd indulged in more than his fair share of kinky fantasies in the past, but nothing had ever come fucking close to that—it had been rage, insanity, greed, misery.

Freedom. Bliss.

His emotions when it came to his spouses were all over the place, settling nowhere.

"Leaving?" Gabriella asked Vicente, glancing up from her phone. She'd been playing one of those mindless game apps ever since dinner. She'd ordered a whole lasagna from a local Italian restaurant earlier—the officer on guard outside had gone to pick it up—and put it in the oven to keep warm, each of them cutting a piece whenever they were hungry. Which meant they'd all taken turns eating alone at the kitchen table.

Sitting at the kitchen table had brought up plenty of memories, and as such, Emiliano didn't recall eating or tasting the food.

Tired of having only himself for company, Emiliano had joined Gabriella here an hour or so ago, the two of them sharing opposite ends of the couch as well as a bottle of red wine. He'd opened his book to read, then teased her about Candy Crush. She claimed it helped her relax, allowed her to think.

Vicente had alternated between his room and the security office on the second floor most of the day. Emiliano assumed the times he was in his room, he was resting. The man's sleep patterns were grueling, as he catnapped off and on so that he could work during the wee hours of night.

Vicente was standing in the doorway, his jacket on, keys in his hand. "I need to leave."

Emiliano swallowed deeply, trying—and failing—to control

his anger. He was typically a man who never lost his cool, but Vicente tested him...greatly.

"So we're back to this," Emiliano said.

"If I'm the target, my presence could be putting you in danger," Vicente said.

"We're in a safe house. Your safe house," Emiliano countered.

"And you will be safe here." Vicente was stiff, formal.

"*Gilipollas*," Gabriella muttered under her breath, shaking her head in disbelief.

Emiliano couldn't disagree with her assessment of their spouse. Vicente continued to prove himself a dumbass time after time.

Vicente's resigned expression told them he'd been anticipating their anger. But the stiffness in his posture—and the suitcase by his side—also said he was resolved.

He *was* leaving.

Gabriella put her phone down as she rose. "Where are you going?"

"It's best if you don't know."

Gabriella threw her head back, her eyes closing as if she was praying to some higher power for patience. Or perhaps for lightning to strike Vicente down.

"That's not a good enough answer," she insisted.

"It's all I can give you. I...I need you to understand. As long as I'm with you, your lives are in danger."

"Tell us why," Emiliano insisted.

"I won't do that."

Emiliano rose as well. "Fine. If you've determined that the bomb was meant for you and you're leaving, there's no reason for us to stay either. I've had enough of this place, and our honeymoon is almost over."

"No," Vicente said, raising his hand before they could walk

out of the living room. "Neither of you is permitted to leave. It's possible that the bomber will have identified you two as potential pressure points."

"Pressure points?" Gabriella demanded. "Ah, you mean that we're a liability because we'd make good hostages?"

"Hurting you would hurt me," Vicente said quietly. "The bomb was left at our wedding reception. There's a good chance whoever placed it knows who you are...what you are...to me."

Gabriella barked out a mirthless laugh. "Clearly we are nothing to you."

"Don't, Gabriella," Vicente implored. "Please."

"We can't stay here indefinitely," Emiliano said. "I need to return to work."

"It's not safe."

"*Joder!*" Emiliano said, running his hand through his hair in frustration. "You know very little about us if you think you can make that proclamation and have it stick. You can't expect the two of us to hide out here from a faceless, nameless enemy with no explanations, no information, for God knows how long. Neither Gabriella nor myself is wired that way."

"I can—and do—expect that. The investigation is ongoing, not only into my enemies, but we're also looking at threats you've received as a senator, and threats to the Torres family."

"Ah, so now that we want to go, you're going to make up reasons one of us might be the target?" Gabriella asked.

"No. The *caballeros* are conducting a thorough investigation."

"And you think that's a waste of time." Gabriella's smile was cold. "You're only mentioning it to manipulate us into staying where you want us to be."

Emiliano stepped in front of Vicente, who held his ground when Emiliano spit out, "You don't dictate how I live my life."

"You are a member of the Masters' Admiralty, in the territory I have sworn to protect. If you won't listen to me as your husband, then you *will* listen to me as your security minister."

Emiliano had a lot of things he wanted to say to that, but Gabriella's soft sound of distress had him turning toward her. Her eyes were filled with angry tears.

How many times would Vicente continue to toss them aside?

How could he not see—not understand—how badly he was hurting her? Them?

"Vicente," she said, swallowing heavily. "Stay."

It was a heartfelt request, Gabriella swallowing her pride to issue it. He recalled the way she'd reached out to Vicente yesterday, the way he'd seemed to understand her darker needs long before Emiliano had.

Emiliano's respect, his admiration for her, grew more with each passing day. She was passionate, determined, a fighter from the word go. She refused to give up on them, on what they could have.

Vicente put his keys in the pocket of his jacket and side-stepped Emiliano so that he could go to their wife. Emiliano didn't stand in his way, hoping—praying—that perhaps this time, Vicente would do the right thing.

Vicente looked as if he were going to embrace her but dropped his arms before actually touching her. Instead, he leaned in and placed a tender kiss on her forehead. "I wish there was some way I could make you understand."

"Try," Emiliano demanded. "We aren't asking you to talk about your job. I understand that. There will be things I won't be able to tell the two of you about my job. I understand that," he repeated the words, hoping to make Vicente hear him.

Emiliano had their attention, and he thought for a moment he saw a shift in Vicente. Then the older man shook his head. Emiliano was fairly sure they were fighting a lifetime habit of keeping secrets, and there may be nothing they could say to make Vicente open up and let them in.

"Anything I tell you could put you in danger," Vicente continued. "Nothing matters more to me than making sure you are safe." He took a breath, his head bowed. "Please let me protect you."

"You're not giving us a chance," Gabriella whispered.

Vicente shook his head. "Better that you're safe and...hate me."

Gabriella's eyes widened at the word hate, and the tension ratcheted up. For a moment, it seemed that they would repeat the experience in the kitchen, but Vicente turned away from her, looking at Emiliano.

Emiliano could see the stress in Vicente's face and he recognized the plea in his eyes, silently begging him to understand.

Emiliano couldn't offer him any reassurance. Because while he thought he understood Vicente's point of view, crafted as a result of a lifetime of doing the dirty work for the territory, that didn't negate the fact that they were married now, and that had to mean something.

"If you're right," Emiliano said, in a last-ditch effort to make this work, "and telling us anything about your past would put us in danger, then don't tell us. We'll learn to accept that."

Gabriella opened her mouth as if to protest, but when he shook his head at her, a small gesture, she stilled, then nodded, protest left unsaid.

Vicente glanced back and forth between them, a look that was either surprise or hope coloring his features.

"We'll accept that...but you have to stay. Stay with us."

"Yes." Gabriella touched Vicente's shoulder. "Stay with us here, now. Let your officers and the *caballeros* figure it out. And after this, when it's over...stay with us then too. Be our husband in truth."

"Stay with you..." Vicente looked between them.

For a moment, Emiliano thought they'd won him over, that Vicente would stay. But the spark of hope that he saw in the other man's eyes faded and died, his expression cold and reserved. The man standing before them wasn't Vicente, their husband. This was Vicente Coval, security minister of Castile.

Vicente crossed the room and picked up his suitcase. Gabriella made a small noise of shock and distress. She'd still thought there was a chance.

Vicente looked back over his shoulder. "Better that you are alive to hate me," he said once again. He left the house without a word of goodbye.

Gabriella sank back down onto the couch. "Looks like the honeymoon is over." It would have been a valiant attempt at humor if her voice hadn't wavered at the end.

Emiliano went to her, knelt on the floor at her feet. "It's been a rocky start, hasn't it?"

She gave him a sad laugh. "I suppose we should cut ourselves a small break. After all, we were strangers a month ago, and a bomb nearly killed us three hours after we said our wedding vows. Talk about obstacles."

Emiliano chuckled. "Why don't we get some sleep? We can figure out where to go from here tomorrow."

She nodded and took the hand he offered, the two of them rising, making their way to the stairs. When they reached the top, they paused, both looking at what had been Vicente's room, now empty.

"I don't want to be alone anymore," Gabriella admitted, her words telling him how she felt about being tucked in without them last night. He'd been so tempted to join her in bed, but then Vicente might have joined, and Emiliano's pride, his anger at the time, wouldn't let him share that place with his aloof husband.

Emiliano was tired of being alone too. He led her to his bedroom. The two of them undressed, Emiliano leaving on his boxers, while Gabriella helped herself to one of the clean T-shirts in his suitcase. They crawled beneath the covers together.

He wrapped his arm around her shoulders, tucking her against his chest, but neither of them sought more than that, not even a good-night kiss.

It felt strange to be in bed with just the two of them. They'd either slept alone or as a trinity.

Without Vicente there...

It felt wrong.

"Good night, Gabriella," Emiliano whispered.

"Good night."

EMILIANO BLINKED SEVERAL TIMES, trying to focus, the room dim despite the open curtains. It was early, just after dawn, and he wondered what had woken him from a sound sleep.

Gabriella shifted, her ass brushing against his crotch, his dick thickening in response, and he suddenly understood.

He was spooning her, their bodies naturally adjusting to each other as they slept. One of his hands was wrapped around her, cupping her breast above the T-shirt she'd worn to bed.

He could tell from her deep, even breathing that she was still asleep and had no idea the impact she was having on his body.

Unable to resist, he lightly squeezed the breast he was holding, seeking out her nipple with his fingertips. It tightened beneath his touch and Gabriella moved again, her ass pressing back against him more firmly.

He stifled a groan. She felt so good in his arms, and he considered pulling her panties to the side, shoving down his boxers, and continuing the honeymoon as a party of two rather than three.

However, the reminder that Vicente had left them last night—driven out by his inexorable sense of duty—weighed heavily on Emiliano's chest.

Gabriella had the right of it last night. They were three people who'd been tossed headfirst into an untenable situation. It seemed incredible to him to realize they hadn't even been married a full week yet. Considering they'd been essentially strangers, it stood to reason that all of them would be struggling to find their footing, their place in this trinity.

But they'd never do that if Vicente insisted on keeping his distance...and he'd been planning to do that even before they found out that the motive for the bombing was most likely linked to his past.

Emiliano had been emotionally wrung out the last few days, so he'd responded badly yesterday. Today...he felt better able to handle things.

When Gabriella wriggled a third time, he realized she was now awake and teasing him.

"Good morning, wife," he murmured, kissing the side of her neck.

"Mmmm." Gabriella purred happily, stretching slightly, encouraging him to tighten his grip on her breast. "It's early," she mused sleepily.

"It is." He pushed his erection against her ass.

She laughed breathily. "Someone is wide awake."

"Natural reaction to waking up with a sexy woman in your arms."

Gabriella arched her back slightly, adding more pressure to their clothed, doggy-style dry humping.

He slipped his hand beneath her shirt, wanting to stroke her soft skin, to tease her taut nipples. Recalling her penchant for rough play, he pinched her nipple with more force than he would normally use.

Gabriella moaned in pleasure, rubbing her ass back and forth along his crotch in a way that drove him wild.

"Gabriella. Beautiful Gabriella," he said, his hand drifting lower, his fingers slipping beneath the elastic of her panties.

She gasped when he stroked her clit, discovering he wasn't the only one who'd woken up aroused. He dragged his fingers through her slick heat, circling the opening to her body.

"Our honeymoon is over," she whispered.

Though he knew it wasn't her intention, that word was the equivalent of having cold water dumped on them.

"He should be here," Emiliano said, pulling his hand out of her panties when she shifted from her side to her back, looking at him sadly. "He's acted like a high-handed, self-sacrificing prick, but..."

"But we're supposed to be a trinity. We've spent the last few days fighting to pull him into this marriage. And...I can't accept that..."

"You can't accept that he won't be a part of this." He blew out a long, slow breath, as his body rejected what his head was telling him was right. "I haven't accepted that yet either. I'm trying, but..."

"It would be wrong to continue the honeymoon without him." Gabriella sighed. "I can't give up yet. I...I want him to be with us. Truly with us. Emiliano, do you—"

"I want the same. Dammit. It would be easier if I didn't." He ran the back of his hand along her soft cheek. "However, despite Vicente's presence or absence, I think it would benefit both of us to take a small step away as well. The past few days have been...an emotional roller coaster."

Gabriella grinned. "That's putting it lightly."

"We've come at each other like live wires, shifting between

sex, making love, and flat-out fucking. A breather might be in order. A chance to let our emotions catch up?"

She nodded. "I think that's a good idea."

"So, more sleep?" he asked. "Or breakfast?"

"I don't think I can sleep anymore," she said.

"Me either."

Neither of them made any move to get out of bed or say more, each soaking up those last vestiges of lazy, comforting warmth beneath the duvet.

"Are you still angry at him for leaving?" Gabriella asked after several minutes.

Emiliano shrugged. "Not really. Although I am pissed off at him for one thing."

"What's that?"

"He's left us here to fend for ourselves on the coffee."

His joke had the desired effect as Gabriella giggled, rolling out of bed. She looked adorable in his T-shirt and her panties, and he decided there was another reason he was mad at Vicente. Until their husband got his shit together, Emiliano was going to suffer from an acute case of blue balls.

He grabbed a pair of lounge pants, gingerly pulling them on over his still-thick cock, which either hadn't gotten the word that sex was off the table or refused to accept it. He eschewed the shirt and took her hand, the two of them drifting downstairs to the kitchen.

They worked together to figure out the espresso machine, begrudgingly admitting that Vicente's coffee was better.

"So, what now?" Gabriella asked once they settled down together at the kitchen table with their cups.

"I need to work," Emiliano said.

Gabriella sighed. "What do you think the chances are that the security officers standing guard outside will let us return to our homes?"

Emiliano reached out and grasped her hand. "Home. Singular."

She smiled and amended her comment. "Our home... though we better decide what and where that is."

He rubbed his neck wearily. "I'm sure Vicente left orders that we're not allowed to leave. Regardless, I had to take some last-minute days off and away from a tricky bit of legislation I'm working on. My mafia law. Time is not a luxury I can afford at the moment."

"The mafia?" Gabriella's curiosity was clearly piqued.

"There's a bill I'm working to get passed through Parliament to crack down on the Italians and Russians who've opened up shop in Spain. There are too many drugs being trafficked through our ports."

"You're going to take down the mafia...with a law?" Her brows rose and her lips twisted with a suppressed smile. "I'm fairly certain we already have laws..."

"Ha-ha." He slapped the side of her butt, and his cock twitched when she moaned.

"Don't do that," she whispered. "If we're holding off until Vicente is back..."

"I should bend you over a chair and spank you." He reached for her, and she pulled away. "Punish you for making my cock this hard when we can't do anything about it."

"You have a hand," she snarked, but her gaze was on his dick. "And a spanking is foreplay, not punishment."

"The punishment will be that after the spanking...nothing happens."

"Oh, that's cruel," she breathed.

Emiliano stood and pulled her up, herding her back until she hit the wall. Caging her in his arms, he leaned down to kiss her and...stopped.

She sighed and rested her head on his shoulder. "I...want him here. With us."

Emiliano backed up and turned away so he didn't have to see her looking cute and sexy with that hot look in her eyes. "Bills, laws, paperwork," he said aloud. His work in the Senate was boring enough to be a boner-killer.

"Can you work from here?" Gabriella asked.

He nodded, turning now that he had himself under control. "If I had my laptop and my files, yes. For at least a few more days, I suppose."

"So there's today's game plan." Gabriella pulled out her cell phone. "Let's call Vicente." She dialed Vicente's number and put him on speaker.

"Gabriella," Vicente said when he answered.

Emiliano was relieved he'd picked up, part of him worried Vicente would avoid their calls.

"We're going to Madrid today," Gabriella said.

"No."

Emiliano counted to ten in his head before speaking. "I didn't intend to be away from work beyond today, and I have several pieces of senate business that cannot wait. I need my laptop and files. We'll retrieve those, then return here."

Vicente was quiet for several moments, long enough that Emiliano feared they were about to have another fight. Because he wasn't taking no for an answer. He'd compromised on everything thus far. This time, it was Vicente's turn to bend.

Finally, Vicente said, "I will make the arrangements. I'm sending a car and a security detail. You will get everything you need and then return to the safe house."

"Very well." Emiliano felt ridiculously pleased as they disconnected the call. It was only a small concession on Vicente's part, but for some reason, it felt like a victory. Now, they just had to wear him down on the bigger things.

Their future happiness depended on it.

VICENTE HUNG UP THE PHONE, his fingers trembling. The sound of their voices had affected him far more than it should have. He hadn't wanted to get married because he knew he'd be a bad husband.

He'd been right. He *was* a bad husband. He'd hurt them without meaning to. Some of what they'd asked of him, he would never be able to give them.

Sharing traumatic stories from his past would not bond them through intimacy. It would give them concrete reasons to fear and hate him.

Even thinking the word "hate" brought back memories of the kitchen sex. The way they'd come together physically, reading and responding to one another's needs, even when they were fighting, had been nothing short of incredible.

Emiliano had claimed they could get past his necessary silence, as long as he promised to be their husband in truth. For a moment, Vicente had considered it, but only for a moment. He would always have enemies, would always live and work in the shadows. They didn't want that. They might say they did, but only because they didn't really know what it would mean to have him around as a full-time husband.

Better to keep his distance, both to protect them and to protect himself. The past several days had shown him that his own heart needed protecting. He'd anticipated the physical attraction. The emotional connection, the desire to be loved by them...that was unexpected and unacceptable.

Vicente put his phone back into his pocket and plucked a fresh glove out of the small box. The one he'd stripped off before answering was in a red garbage bag at his feet, destined for the incinerator once he was done.

The sooner he learned who'd wanted him dead, the sooner Emiliano and Gabriella would be safe. He couldn't live with them, couldn't love them, but he could protect them.

Shifting his attention to the stainless steel table, he picked up a pre-filled syringe. When he turned, plucking the cap from the syringe, the man bound to a stainless steel chair started to scream through the gag. Vicente let the man see, let fear start to do his work. He smiled, knowing it was a cold, cruel expression, then reached out and flicked off the lights.

The concrete holding cell under the territory headquarters in Madrid was sound- and lightproof. With the lights off, they were in stygian darkness. Vicente pulled down the night-vision goggles, which allowed him to see, thanks to hidden red-light bulbs that were invisible to the naked eye.

There'd been a time he'd been more direct with breaking people. Physical assaults, torture tactics that the Geneva Convention frowned on, but which, despite popular opinion, yielded results. He'd stopped assassinations and terrorist bombings, found serial killers' victims while still alive.

Now he favored a more psychological approach. Darkness and fear of the unknown were just as effective.

"You said you wanted me dead. Did you plant the bomb?"

The man shook his head, mumbling into the gag.

"I don't believe you."

Barefoot, Vicente walked across the floor, watching his victim thrash in the chair. Vicente pushed away all thoughts of his spouses. His hand shot out, the needle sliding into the man's upper arm. The suspect started to scream, a high, keening sound.

He waited several moments, then pulled the man's gag out.

"Did you plant the bomb?"

The man started to mumble denials, insisting he was innocent. It was laughable, since he was a paid assassin who'd made the mistake of accepting a contract to kill a judge who just happened to be a member. Vicente had shown him the error of his ways, then paid the man to find out the identity of his client. He'd later heard that the assassin had vowed revenge on Vicente, which had brought him to the top of the bombing suspect list once the Bellator Dei was eliminated.

Vicente jabbed the needle back into his arm, and the man screamed.

This was why Vicente could never be with them. Emiliano and Gabriella had no place here, in the terrible darkness that was his home.

CHAPTER TEN

It was both awkward and intimate to wander through Emiliano's home. She'd shared so much with him, in such a short time, it was strange to realize that until this moment, she hadn't known things about him like his favorite brand of milk.

"Enjoying yourself?" Emiliano called out as she closed his refrigerator door.

"Yes, thank you." She leaned back until she could see through the doorway between the kitchen and dining room. The dining room had a large table and a matching sideboard, both well-made, heavy wood pieces. The craftsmanship was obscured by papers, folders, books, two printers, and a scattering of odds and ends. Emiliano was using his dining table as a desk—the matching chairs were shoved against a wall, and an ugly, modern desk chair was pulled up along one of the long sides. The sideboard was where his two printers and the base to a cordless phone were set up, the cords running down over the front rather than tucked behind.

Her husband was standing beside his chair, going through a stack of file folders, slipping some into a large attaché case, while others went back into a black file box with a lock on it, which he'd pulled out of one of the sideboard's compartments.

"If we decide to live here, this room will be the first I redecorate."

Emiliano frowned in mock dismay. "You don't like my office."

"Is that what this is? How silly of me. The dining room furniture had me thinking it was a dining room."

She circled the table to stand beside him, having finished her exploration of his home. He closed the largest of the files, which had the word "corruption" scrawled across the front of it, and tucked it into his case.

"That's everything I need." He looked at his makeshift desk, then at her, and when he did, his lips quirked in a smile that promised things. Sexy things.

Gabriella leaned into him, loving the way his arm slid around her waist, over her hip, and down to her ass. She may never have been in his house before, but they were not strangers.

"If that's everything..." a female voice said from near the door.

Gabriella let her head drop against Emiliano's shoulder. His silent laugh vibrated through her.

Yurena was a tall, willowy woman. Nothing about her screamed "dangerous" or "deadly." That's probably what made her such a good security officer. She and a man named Thiago had escorted them from Barcelona to Madrid in an armored limo. Thiago wasn't a member of the Masters' Admiralty, but he was employed by *Seguretat Rodeleros*, secretly owned by the society. All security officers were company employees, which gave them a cover story for their activities on behalf of the society, but not all company employees were society members.

Because Thiago wasn't a member, and because Yurena had insisted they keep the privacy screen down, she and Emiliano hadn't talked about Vicente on the drive from Barcelona.

Thiago had stayed with the car—parking in central Madrid was a nightmare even for the ubiquitous Mini Coupes, never mind a limo, but Yurena had accompanied them inside.

And now Yurena was going to make them get back in the limo and not avail themselves of Emiliano's table. Or his bed. Not that they would have done anything, but it would have been fun to tease Emiliano.

"Why do we have to rush back to Barcelona?" Gabriella asked as she stepped away from Emiliano, giving him space to finish up. "Why don't we go to a safe house here in Madrid?"

If they were here, they'd be in the same city as Vicente. It would be easier to...

Easier to trick him into coming to see them? He was their husband; they shouldn't have to manipulate him into spending time with them.

It wasn't anger she felt when she thought about Vicente, not anymore. It was an aching sadness because she thought she'd figured out the root issue of what he was doing when he separated himself from them. It wasn't that he didn't want them. He didn't think he deserved to be loved.

"The Madrid safe house is not suitable," Yurena said.

"Not suitable?" Gabriella raised a brow. "That sounds..."

"Ominous." Emiliano hoisted his case, hooking the strap over his shoulder.

Yurena said nothing.

Gabriella had left her purse in the limo—she wasn't even sure why she'd brought it. Their phones had been confiscated, and they'd been given burner phones but told not to use them unless it was an emergency. With nothing better to do with her hands, she slid one along Emiliano's back, under the hem of his casual jacket, and tucked her fingers into his back pocket, cupping his ass.

He slanted a glance her way, and she smiled as they walked through the living room to the front door. Yurena made them pause. She slipped out first, then opened the door a moment later, motioning them to step out. The limo was double-parked, taking up half the street. Angry drivers zoomed around, honking, but Thiago, standing by the driver's door, seemed unperturbed.

They walked across the landing towards the warm-toned stone steps, her fingers in Emiliano's back pocket, Yurena behind them.

It was because she was behind them that Yurena died.

Gabriella heard the rapid thud of running footsteps, the scratching sound of shoes on stone. Unused to violence, her brain didn't immediately process that she was in danger. It wasn't until she heard a strangled sound, and felt the splash of hot liquid hitting the back of her bare arm, that fear flooded her.

Out in the street, Thiago was yelling, a gun in his hand that hadn't been there a moment before. He motioned to them, but she didn't understand the words through the sound of blood pounding in her ears. Even as part of her was demanding she run for the limo, Gabriella turned, her hand sliding away from Emiliano.

The man wore black, including a balaclava. Yurena was pulled back against his chest, his arm around her waist, trapping her own arms to her sides. His face was alongside hers, and it was almost like they were lovers.

But the knife in his free hand was coated in blood. Yurena's throat was cut, ear to ear, the slice so deep that her head had fallen back against the man's shoulder, allowing arterial spray to spurt from her neck. Her heart was still beating, and a fresh spray of bright-red blood shot out.

Even as fear bit her, part of Gabriella's mind refused to accept what she was seeing.

A second man—holding a gun in one hand—dashed toward them. He'd been hiding in the narrow space between Emiliano's house and the one beside it. Behind them a car door opened, and she heard Thiago shouting. Gunshots rang out, the sound painfully loud.

Thiago wasn't shouting any longer.

Time had slowed, from that first moment she heard footsteps to now. In the next second, it sped up, and everything else happened fast.

The man who'd killed Yurena dropped her, her body folding in on itself. The hand not holding the knife reached for Gabriella.

Emiliano threw himself at the man—bold, courageous, and stupid—even as Gabriella jerked back, stumbling down the last few steps onto the footpath.

The second man grabbed Emiliano, hauling him off the man with the knife. Emiliano struggled, but the second man slid his arms under Emiliano's and laced his hands behind Emiliano's neck. The hold forced Emiliano's arms out to the side, his chin to his chest.

The first man had fallen when Emiliano tackled him. Now he pushed to his feet. Rolling his shoulders, he walked toward Emiliano.

The first man pulled back his fist. Gabriella screamed, then reversed course back up the stairs. The black-clad man punched Emiliano in the stomach, and even from several meters away, Gabriella heard the breath leave Emiliano's body.

They were going to kill him. Emiliano was the target.

Those thoughts flew through her mind, important but useless. She turned to Thiago, seeking help, but the man was gone and she remembered the gunshots.

A third man, wearing the same black balaclava as the other two, was behind her. One of the cars parked on the street, and partially blocked in by the limo, had an open rear door. There was blood dripping from the man's fingers onto the sidewalk.

Gabriella dove for the limo, veering to the side to stay out of the third assailant's grasp. She needed a phone. A weapon. Something.

Think, think. Be smart.

It was the middle of the day, and they were on a public street. Someone had probably already called the authorities, which meant help was on the way. Still, she needed a weapon, a way to defend Emiliano until the police got here.

She reached the limo just as the third assailant caught up with her.

His hand in her hair yanked her back, and she screamed at the burning, tearing pain. He flung her backwards and she hit the ground, landing half on the footpath, half in the road between two parked cars.

Adrenaline had her up on her feet, but she wasn't fast enough. He caught her again, but this time she whirled to fight, her fist connecting with his head. It was a glancing blow along his ear rather than breaking his nose.

He shoved her, hard, and she tumbled back, this time landing on the stone steps. Agony shot through her upper arm, hip, and knee where they'd impacted. Up on the landing, the knife-wielding assailant was continuing to beat Emiliano while the gunman held him immobile. She watched in breathless horror as fists slammed into Emiliano's face, chest, stomach.

Her assailant grabbed her by the throat, his fingers pinching down, cutting off both blood and oxygen. She kicked out, aiming for his balls, but it wasn't the man's first fight. He shifted his hips to the side, her foot glancing off his thigh. She punched and kicked, fighting him with everything she had.

It wasn't enough.

Her attacker backed up, but only to grab her ankles. He yanked her down onto the footpath, and she curled her chin to her chest, protecting her head from smacking against the steps.

Other hands grabbed her wrists, yanking her arms up and back. She screamed—again—as they lifted her, her body hanging between them. One of them said something, but she didn't understand, the words familiar but wrong. A small part of her brain processed that she didn't understand because they weren't speaking Castellano.

The man holding her ankles dropped them, her heels cracking against the sidewalk. Lightning strikes of pain radiated up her legs, stealing her breath. The man holding her wrists hauled her up, wrapping an arm around her neck, his elbow just under her chin. The other arm went across her waist. She was trapped, could barely breathe.

There were people out now—looking out windows, at least one person in a car with a phone to his ear. It was daytime. There were people, witnesses. That should have made her safe.

But none of the witnesses got involved. No one tried to stop them from hauling her to one of the cars parked on the curb, the car the third man had been hiding in. The man holding her climbed into the backseat, pulling her with him. She glanced back to the house, blinking through the tears of terror and pain. She saw Emiliano hanging limp in one man's arms, blood dripping from his face.

The other assailant jumped into the driver's seat, yelling something.

The man holding Emiliano tucked what looked like an envelope into his shirt, then shoved him aside. Even from inside the car, she heard the crack when Emiliano's head hit stone. She screamed, a high, thin sound, choked off as the man's arm tightened around her neck.

Then the last of the attackers was sprinting down the steps, leaping into the car. He closed his door and the car pulled away from the curb, swerving around the front of the limo, then the stopped car in the street, the driver watching with horror, phone still to his ear.

Her captor released her only to flip her over, facedown on his lap. She sucked in air, then released it as a terrified sob. He slapped her ass, laughed. A different kind of fear skittered through her.

Then a sharp pain in her butt, followed by a burn. A needle.

She struggled, trying to yank her hands free from his grip. She'd throw herself out, better to break bones and scrape up skin than be in this car.

She fought him, sobbing, as they laughed, the car flying through the streets of Madrid.

Then the drug took hold, and Gabriella's struggles weakened, her sobs slowing to whimpers. As the darkness closed in around her, her last thought was for her husbands. Hoping Emiliano was alive...and trusting Vicente would find her.

Maybe not in time, but he would find her.

"WHY ARE YOU STILL HERE? You should be looking for her! I've answered all your questions and I've told you, I don't know who attacked me."

Vicente stood in the hallway for a moment, taking in the frustration and panic, the weariness, the pain in Emiliano's voice. It had taken Vicente most of the drive across the city to the hospital to find his own bearings.

His assessment had been incorrect.

He'd failed them. Failed them both.

A shuffling of feet captured his attention, and he watched as two members of the *Policía Municipal* moved to the doorway of Emiliano's hospital room.

Ordinarily, the CNI would step in after an attack on a senator, providing protection while investigating the crime. However, the Minister of Defense was a member of the Masters' Admiralty. After a call from the admiral, she'd stepped back, allowing Vicente to take the lead on the investigation, promising assistance from the CNI if needed. There were two secret service agents stationed at the end of the hallway.

Their presence was necessary, because it was what the police would expect, and it would be a delicate balancing act, making sure that appearances were maintained while leading the investigation.

"Please let us know if there is anything else you remember," an officer said on his way out.

Vicente waited until the police passed before entering the room. Emiliano was sitting on the edge of the bed, attempting to rise. Given the deep, measured way he was breathing, it was clear he was trying to fight through the pain to do so.

"They'll keep you overnight."

Emiliano turned at the sound of Vicente's voice, sinking back onto the bed. "They took Gabriella." The sheer desolation in Emiliano's tone was almost Vicente's undoing.

"I will find her." The moment Vicente had gotten word that police had been called to Emiliano's address, he'd known something terrible had happened. He'd stayed calm, even as he headed for the door, calling in to the *Seguretat Rodeleros* comm center in time to learn that Yurena had missed her last check-in.

Halfway to Emiliano's house, one of the other security officers had called to reroute him to the hospital and read him the police reports that were coming in. He'd even played Vicente one of the emergency calls—a man's voice, shaky with horror, describing the attack—Yurena's throat slit, the shootout between the assailants and Thiago, two men beating Emiliano before they all escaped, dragging Gabriella into the car with them.

Yurena was dead. Emiliano was injured. Gabriella was gone.

By the time he walked into the hospital, he'd already ordered a camera trace on the car. The digital tracking team at *Seguretat Rodeleros* was one of the best in the country. They'd access public and private security cameras, from traffic to ATM cams, and track the vehicle Gabriella had been taken in.

The cold, cynical part of him knew it wouldn't be that easy. This had been a targeted attack, which meant the assailants would have charted their escape, would have taken pains to ensure they couldn't be followed or traced.

Vicente took a deep breath. "I thought...I thought my enemies would come after me. I should have protected her, and you, better. I'm sorry, Emiliano."

Emiliano looked up, an expression of surprise on his face.

Did his husband think him so cold, so distant that he wouldn't care? He hated thinking he'd let things digress so quickly, so badly. "I swear to you, I will find her. And when I do...the people who took her will pay."

Vicente didn't bother to shield his words or hide his intentions, despite the fact he and Emiliano had very different approaches to public safety and law enforcement.

Emiliano started to shake his head but stopped, wincing and rubbing his temple. Vicente had accessed the hospital computer to read the emergency room report on Emiliano's injuries. In addition to countless contusions, several cuts that required stitches, three bruised ribs, and a concussion. All of his injuries combined were enough that the hospital wanted to keep him overnight for observation.

"No, Vicente. It was my fault. Not yours. The bomb...it was meant to be a warning. To me."

Vicente tilted his head, confused. "You told the *policia*—"

"I couldn't tell them. Didn't know if I could trust them."

"Trust them?"

"I know who took her. We need to get her back. Now." He watched as Emiliano tried once more to rise but was overwhelmed by a wave of dizziness, causing him to gasp in pain and clutch his temple. "*Joder*." Despite the obvious pain, Emiliano continued to try to rise.

Vicente walked to Emiliano, placing what he hoped was a calming hand on his husband's shoulder. "Stop. Sit. Who has Gabriella?"

Emiliano swallowed deeply, looking not only pale but somewhat green. His pain was clearly making him nauseous. "The Mafia."

Vicente looked at Emiliano, concerned his head injuries were more serious than the doctors believed. "No," he said at last. "You must be mista—"

"Sicilian mafia. Camorra, to be exact," Emiliano said. "The accent was Italian, and they spoke Italian to one another.

"The bomb was meant for me. A warning from the mafia to stop my work against them. There had been no previous threats, I swear that to you. Prior to the wedding...God...there had been nothing. I didn't realize... It didn't even occur to me that I was on their radar, though...it should have."

Vicente hated the pain in Emiliano's voice, the way he became more upset with each word. There was no missing the guilt Emiliano felt over putting them all in danger. It was consuming him in a way that wasn't productive.

"I'm sorry. I never—"

Vicente cupped Emiliano's face in his hands, forcing him to stop talking and to look at him. The desolation he saw on his husband's face nearly crushed him. Vicente gave him a quick, hard kiss that did exactly what he'd hoped. It shocked Emiliano enough to draw him out of his dark thoughts.

He and Emiliano had only kissed that one time, that second night when Vicente and Gabriella had given their husband a blow job together. Since then, the only thing they'd traded had been barbs and angry words.

"Don't," Emiliano said, though there was no heat behind the word.

"Focus. Start at the beginning. Why would the Camorra want to harm you?"

"Because I'm in the process of writing a bill that targets the different criminal organizations who have set up shop in Spain. We need to pass a mafia association law like the one in Italy because corruption and organized crime are running rampant in our country, and our legal system is sadly lacking—the laws inefficient and too lenient. Did you know that legally, we have to try members of, say, the Camorra the same way we would burglars?"

Vicente shook his head. "I did not." Of course, he didn't bother to add that he'd never been overly concerned with the legal system. In his mind, it wasn't effective, offering too many undeserving assholes impunity for their wrongdoings. By the time people came to his attention, they were past the point of being worthy of a judge and jury.

"The word mafia doesn't even exist in Castellano," Emiliano continued. "Not in the law books. So we can't have anti-mafia prosecutors like those in Italy. And yet, there are pages and pages of investigative files mentioning the Cosa Nostra, the Bratva, the 'Ndrangheta, the Camorra."

"And you believe they're targeting you?" Vicente asked.

Emiliano nodded. "It's my bill. I've taken the lead on writing it and I've been working hard to get it on the agenda in this current session. We need these laws in place now. Not three, five, ten years from now. The Russians and Italians are moving drugs from Latin America through our ports, and if that wasn't a big enough injury, they then launder their dirty money here as well."

For the first time, Vicente could see why Emiliano was such a successful politician. He spoke with passion, conviction, and intelligence. He couldn't imagine there was any law Emiliano wouldn't manage to get passed with his persuasiveness, his intensity, his unyielding desire to do what was right.

"This law that you're proposing. It's that powerful?"

"Yes." Emiliano ran his hand through his hair. "It's modeled after what Italy has done, and it was successful there. It's one of the reasons the mafia is so active here in Spain. Italy's laws forced these organizations to relocate. And here we were, all but opening our arms to welcome them. My law basically rewrites the book on how we fight corruption in Spain, because corruption laws target the structure of the mafia, and how they do business. It will have stricter penalties, mafia-specific task forces. These organizations have had free rein for too long. This would definitely make it much more difficult for them to traffic drugs, launder money. It would place a spotlight on things they've managed to hide in the dark for too long. I should have..."

"Have they lodged any threats toward you prior to this? Contacted you?"

Emiliano shook his head. "No. Nothing. If there had been... I would have..." He ran his finger over one of the bandages on his forearm. There was another on his wrist. Emiliano was struggling to finish his thoughts, though Vicente wasn't sure if it was caused by the concussion or his elevated level of anxiety. Regardless, he needed him to remain focused. Vicente needed information. As much as Emiliano could provide.

"You said Sicilian. Why?"

"One of them whispered something just before he threw me down. He told me not to fuck with Camorra."

Emiliano's hand trembled as he reached under the pillow of his hospital bed. "*Joder.* I should have given you...my head is fuzzy. There is this. One of the attackers slid it into my pocket just before they escaped. I...it..."

Vicente looked at the envelope, smeared with Emiliano's blood, then reached into his pocket, pulling out gloves.

"You walk around with gloves in your pocket?"

Vicente ignored him as he slapped them on, then gingerly took the envelope, carefully, at the corners. He withdrew the note inside with the same level of care.

Vicente frowned as he read it, his blood turning cold.

KILL THE BILL, and we'll give her back.

EMILIANO PICKED at the bandage around his wrist. "I've been thinking about that note since they grabbed her. Without my support, there would be no one pushing the bill through Parliament. I proposed it, researched it, wrote it, and spearheaded a committee. Actually, I'm still working on it, refining parts of it. I know it inside and out. If I withdraw it, I'm not sure any of my fellow colleagues would care to take it over.

There's still a lot of work to be done. But if I were to be killed by the mafia, I'd be made a martyr. The media would have a field day with it, sensationalize it, make it a cause the entire Senate will get behind."

"So you believe the bomb was a warning, not an assassination attempt," Vicente said. "An ineffective warning, since we didn't know it was aimed at you, or why they were threatening you."

"Yes."

"They've escalated, and now Gabriella is a hostage."

"It's my fault."

Vicente gripped Emiliano's shoulder. "Assigning blame is useless. I need a copy of that bill and as much research as you've gathered on the different criminal organizations. I will have the CNI check for any threats that they've intercepted."

"Get me out of this damn hospital, Vicente."

"You have a concussion."

"A mild one. And I don't give a shit."

Vicente considered pushing the issue, fighting Emiliano on it, but he knew if the shoe was on the other foot, if he was the one with the injuries, he'd burn the entire hospital down to get out.

"We will return to my home," Vicente said. "When we get there, you will rest, that is nonnegotiable. Concussions are dangerous, and I can see you are in pain. You won't be any good to Gabriella if you're dead from a brain bleed."

It spoke to the level of pain Emiliano was in that he didn't argue. "I will lay down, but you'll wake me the moment you learn anything."

"My people, my officers...remaining officers...are tracking the vehicle. They are good at their job. The moment they find her location, we'll make a plan to retrieve her."

"I'm killing the bill," Emiliano said.

Vicente nodded. He and Emiliano were on the same page. "Good. Let's go back to my place and plan our course of action."

He reached out to help Emiliano stand, and then, despite all anger lingering in the background, all the things left unsettled between them, he pulled him into his arms for a strong embrace. "We are going to find our wife."

CHAPTER ELEVEN

Gabriella was bruised, scraped, and sore from the fight she'd waged, trying to escape. Her scalp was tender from where she'd been yanked away from the limo, both heels were bruised, and her right ankle was swollen, though she couldn't exactly recall when she'd twisted it.

She had been unceremoniously thrown into this room...no, cell was a more accurate term, by one of the men who'd kidnapped her, though she couldn't begin to guess how long ago that had been. Was it still the same day? The middle of the night? She hated feeling so disoriented.

Her head was fuzzy from whatever they'd injected her with. She'd started to wake up while they were still driving, but she had been too groggy to notice anything. The fresh wave of fear when they'd put a blindfold on her and hauled her out of the car hadn't been as muted by the drug as she would have hoped.

The windowless cell was like something out of a horror movie. Cold concrete served as the floor, the cinder block walls dank and musty. The only furniture in the room—if she could call it furniture—was a dirty mattress with stains she didn't want to try to identify and a bucket, which she assumed was meant to serve as her toilet.

After they'd locked her in, it had taken her a full ten minutes to stop shivering in fear, standing in the corner in a blind terror, unable to focus on anything, the edges of her vision hazy. The drugs in her system left her foggy enough that she'd dropped down onto the mattress, allowing the sedative to take over. She'd been using sleep as an escape since then, dozing on and off for hours, without allowing herself to fully wake.

Now, however, her wits were returning, sleep no longer an option as panic and terror crept back in. She wished to go back to the previous state as she looked around the cell, the reality of her situation sinking in. If she survived, this place would haunt her dreams for years to come.

If she survived…

The thought of dying terrified her as much as this place.

She wasn't exactly sure where she was, but it was obviously some sort of cellar or basement that had either served as a prison at some point in time or had been fashioned into one now. Because there wasn't a door on her narrow cell but rather bars. Forcing her feet forward, she looked through the tight bars. All she could see was a narrow hallway, the opposite wall just that, a concrete wall, covered with cracked, chipped paint, and what she feared was mold. Her head wouldn't fit through the bars so her range of vision was pitifully short, allowing her to only see a few meters of that horrible hallway with no idea of how long it was or what lay at the end.

For a moment, she considered screaming, but that impulse passed quickly. She was underground and surrounded by concrete and cinder blocks. At most, all she could expect to accomplish from that was to either annoy or call back the horrible men in the balaclavas, the men who'd taken her.

And beaten Emiliano.

The memory of that pulled an anguished sob from her.

"*Het is oke,*" a female voice said from somewhere down the hallway to her right.

"What? Who's there?" Gabriella asked, her heart racing in fear. She'd thought herself alone, and that had felt safe. Was this woman one of her captors?

The response came in halting Castellano, the speaker clearly adapting to Gabriella's words. "*Buurman...uh...vecina.*"

While Gabriella assumed the word was meant to be humorous, the voice delivering them was wooden.

"Neighbor?" Gabriella whispered, rubbing her temple, wincing at the dull, thudding ache behind her eyes. Perhaps remnants of the drug were still in her system. Or perhaps she'd slept too much. Either way, she still felt a bit slow-witted, sluggish. And horribly nauseous. Her gaze drifted to the bucket. She was grateful her stomach was empty.

Her neighbor continued in halting but understandable Castellano. "I saw them carry you in here. I'm in the cell next to yours."

"Oh," Gabriella said. "I...I don't feel very good."

"The drugs wear off after several hours, but the side effects remain longer. You'll have a sore head for the next day or so."

"They drugged you too?"

"*Ja.*"

Gabriella was struggling to determine the woman's accent, her affirmative response providing a clue, though not a great one. *Ja* meant yes in many languages.

"How long have you..." Gabriella swallowed, not certain she wanted an answer to the question racing through her mind.

"How long have I been here?" The woman asked the question for her.

"Yes."

"In truth, I have no idea. Time...it passes strangely down here. Without windows, it's impossible to know when one day has ended and the next has begun. Meals are served sporadically and they're always the same thing—stale bread, cheese, a bottle of water."

"Are we the only ones down here?"

"No. There are two other women, farther down the hall, but they only speak Russian. That is a language I do not know. They...they stopped talking to each other a couple of days ago."

"They stopped talking?"

"No more fight in their voices, no more terror, no more tears. I suspect the hope is gone and they are now trying to make peace with their fates."

Gabriella didn't have the courage to ask what that fate might be.

"You speak Castellano well," Gabriella said.

"I have studied several languages—French, English, Spanish, German, though my native language is Dutch."

"I'm also fluent in French and English." Gabriella could hardly call herself a Torres, the name synonymous for high fashion, and not speak those languages. She was no stranger to Paris or New York.

"Oh, then we can talk to each other in this language," the woman said in English. The tone of absolute delight in her voice actually had Gabriella smiling for a second.

"Can I ask you something?" the woman asked.

"Of course."

"Where are we?"

Gabriella reared back, the question one she hadn't expected. "Madrid, I think. Or somewhere close." Though she couldn't be certain of that. She'd been unconscious for most of the drive and blindfolded once she began to come to. For all she knew, they'd driven for hours.

"Ah. I knew it was far."

Gabriella was confused for a moment, then enlightenment dawned. "Where were you when...?"

"Belgium. I was taken from my home, drugged like you. When I awoke, I..." The woman paused, and it was the first time Gabriella heard any tinge of emotion in her voice. When she continued, there was no mistaking the fear behind her words. "I was locked in a small box, tight, in the fetal position. I was in a vehicle, we were moving. It was many hours. Too many hours."

Gabriella struggled to breathe as she imagined herself transported that way, the claustrophobia, the sheer terror. "I'm sorry."

"*Ja*," the woman said sadly. "*Ja*."

"What is your name?" Gabriella asked. While she was still terrified, having someone to talk to, someone in the same position, who knew what they were facing, helped more than she would have realized.

"Talya."

"I'm Gabriella."

"I hope you won't take this the wrong way, Gabriella. Because while I'm very sorry you are here, I'm also very glad you are here."

Gabriella's eyes filled with tears she tried to blink away. She couldn't—wouldn't—cry. If she started, she feared she'd never stop. "I understand," she whispered. "I feel the same.

"Do you know..." Gabriella wasn't certain how to word her question because Talya's presence confused her. Originally, she'd thought she had been taken because of Emiliano, but he was left behind. Which left only one answer that made sense. She was the only daughter of billionaires. She'd had a target on her back since birth, ripe fruit for the picking by criminals looking to make money through kidnapping and ransom.

However, knowing Talya and two other women were imprisoned here as well didn't make sense. "Do you know what they plan to do to us?"

Talya didn't respond for several long moments; so long, Gabriella wondered if she'd understood the question or hadn't heard her.

Finally, Talya said, "I only know what they have done to me. I... Are you certain you wish to hear this?"

Well...that was ominous and scary as fuck.

Did she?

Yes, she decided. Forewarned was forearmed.

"I do."

"The men who took me...they are demanding something of me. Something I will not give them."

"You're a hostage."

"I am, but...it is more than that. These men...they are true evil. Violent, with no regard for human life. What they ask from me..."

Talya stopped speaking. Gabriella was curious about what the woman had that they wanted. Was she from a wealthy family like Gabriella?

"What do they want?"

"I have created something they want. Something that would be deadly in the wrong hands."

Gabriella started to ask what, but Talya continued talking.

"When I first woke up, they kept me in the box, shook it violently, said they were going to bury me alive. I cried, begged them to release me. I think they thought I was going to give in, so they dumped me out of the box. When I still refused to talk, they beat me, threatened to rape me, if I didn't give them what they wanted."

"Did you give it to them?"

Talya was quiet for a long time, and it occurred to Gabriella that this conversation had brought up some unwanted, painful memories for the woman.

"No," Talya replied at last. Her voice was smaller when she added, "Not yet."

Gabriella didn't press for more because she could hear the shame, the fear in Talya's voice, and she understood it. Understood how difficult it would be to hold on to her principles, her beliefs in the face of ongoing pain, torture...rape.

Talya struck her as a strong woman, but everyone had a breaking point. She prayed Talya wouldn't be forced to discover hers down here.

They fell silent for a little while. Gabriella lost in her thoughts, trying to make sense of what was happening.

The men had come to Emiliano's house, and she'd assumed they were there to attack him...but they'd kidnapped *her*. Kidnapped her because she was with Emiliano? Or had they kidnapped her and beaten Emiliano as a way to get to Vicente? Or was it what she'd suspected when she first woke up—that this was a kidnapping for ransom, and even now her parents were filling a bag full of cash? That had always been a possibility in her life, more so when she was a child than now as an adult. Or so she'd thought.

After a long time, Talya said, "I only tell you this because I do not know the reason you are here. If you are being held hostage for a specific purpose...there is a chance they may ask you to make the same decision. Their fists hurt, but it is their threats that do the most harm. I thought you should know so you are prepared."

Gabriella suspected she would not be offered a decision. Her fate was in the hands of Emiliano, Vicente, or her parents.

She hated feeling helpless. Hated being afraid.

Though she was terrified and cold and desperate to get out of here, Gabriella never doubted for a moment that Vicente and

Emiliano—God, please let him be okay—were tearing the world apart looking for her.

"Talya," she said. "Is...is there someone looking for you?"

Talya whispered, "I don't know."

EMILIANO JERKED AWAKE, a cold sweat on his brow. It took him a few moments to figure out where he was, then a second or two longer to remember why his heart was racing so fast.

He'd made a call last night, the moment they'd arrived here from the hospital, and killed the bill. A foolish, naive part of him had hoped that would be an instant fix, that he'd wake up to discover Gabriella magically returned to them.

But she was still gone.

His attention was distracted by Vicente, seated in the chair across from him working with his laptop on his lap. It was almost as if his husband had positioned himself so he could work and keep an eye on him.

Vicente lowered his feet. "How are you feeling?"

"Fine," Emiliano said gruffly, though he was a million kilometers away from fine.

Vicente read the words as a lie and pressed on. "How is your head?"

This time, Emiliano paused and really considered the question. The throbbing when he'd left the hospital had been unbearable, blinding white lights flashing behind his eyes, a sharp shooting pain in his temple that felt as if someone was jamming an icepick directly into his brain. That was gone. Now, what remained was a dull ache, still annoying but definitely manageable.

"Better. How long was I asleep?"

Vicente glanced at his watch. "A few hours. Not enough," he said sternly, but Emiliano ignored him.

"What time is it?"

"Nearly dawn."

Emiliano saw the weariness—no, the utter exhaustion—on Vicente's face. It was clear that while Emiliano had been sleeping off the pain, Vicente had been working tirelessly to find Gabriella.

He forced himself to ask the question he already knew the answer to. "Have you..."

Vicente shook his head. "No. My officers, and *Seguretat Rodeleros*, are working on this round the clock. Emiliano, when we returned here...after you fell asleep, I went through your attaché case. I wanted the information on the legislation so I could study it."

Emiliano nodded, wondering about Vicente's hesitance. Did he think he'd be angry about him going through his bag? There was nothing Emiliano wouldn't give Vicente if it would help find Gabriella. "That's fine."

"When you returned home, did you also retrieve your mail?"

Confused, Emiliano nodded. "Yes, but I didn't have time to open it. I threw it in my case, intending to look at it when we returned to the safe house."

"There was a letter."

Emiliano tilted his head, confused.

"A letter from the people who planted the bomb."

Emiliano rose from the couch, the quick action unwise as he was besieged by a wave of dizziness. He hated feeling so helpless, hated that a concussion could bring him so low at a time when he needed his strength, his wits.

"Sit down." Vicente's deep voice made it clear he would make Emiliano obey that command.

He sank back onto the couch. "Show me the letter."

"I sent it to a forensics lab. But I took a photo." Vicente tapped on his laptop, then turned the computer screen toward Emiliano, who leaned forward. The image was of a typed letter, though "letter" was a grandiose word when it was only two sentences.

THAT WAS A WARNING, Senator.
Kill the corruption bill.

"MY GOD," Emiliano murmured, his stomach clenching. "It *was* me."

"They escalated to the attack because they believed you ignored the first message. The bomb." Vicente turned his laptop around, head bent as he went back to work. Without looking up, he said, "We will find her, Emiliano."

Vicente had done nothing but offer words of encouragement since coming to him in the hospital. He spoke reassuringly, with a determination that Emiliano was supposed to find comforting. He didn't. Gabriella had been kidnapped because of him. It was all his fault.

Because of the bill.

And because he hadn't been strong enough to defend her, to save her.

He couldn't stop replaying the attack, couldn't stop himself from turning around to see the man in the balaclava. Only in his mind, it wasn't Yurena whose throat had been cut. It was Gabriella.

He rubbed his eyes hard, fighting not to shed the tears threatening to fall.

"Do you think they'll hurt her?" It physically hurt him to ask that question, but that fear wouldn't leave him alone.

"No," Vicente said with a strength that almost dared Emiliano to disagree with him. "You've given them what they want."

"Yes, but—"

"Either they return her to us, unharmed, and then I find them and kill them, or I find them first, take her back, and then kill them."

The Emiliano he'd been yesterday would have rejected the idea of killing, would have insisted on operating within the lines of the law, allowing the justice system to do its job. Today...he wanted that vengeance.

"She's alive, Emiliano, and she will be alive when I find her. Do you trust me?"

Emiliano nodded, but gently, in deference to his head.

Vicente studied him for a moment. "You're the white knight, husband. You believe in justice. The world needs your light. Just as it needs men like me, the ones who can see in the dark. I am the monster hiding in the shadows."

Emiliano looked at Vicente, into the dark depths of his eyes, and he believed every word.

"I will find the men who took her," Vicente finished. "And I will destroy them."

This wasn't the first time Vicente had alluded to such things. At the safe house, Emiliano got a sense he said them as a way of holding him and Gabriella at a distance. He'd meant them to be a warning.

Right now, Vicente offered those same words as a way of soothing Emiliano's fears, and it was working.

"*We* will find them," Emiliano repeated, correcting the pronoun. Then he considered the second part of Vicente's vow. Emiliano had always believed in the law, believed in the justice system. But that was before he'd seen a woman's life snuffed out with a single slash of a blade. Before he'd heard Gabriella's screams, felt her dragged away from him, helpless to help her. No amount of justice could make any of that right.

That was when he felt it. The shift inside him, his eyes opened to something he'd never allowed himself to see. The foundation on which he'd always stood, resolute and sure, was crumbling beneath his feet.

"And *we* will destroy them," Emiliano added.

Vicente didn't respond for a moment, and when he did, it was with just one small nod of his head.

More progress.

Emiliano noticed his phone laying on the coffee table. The security officers had taken his and Gabriella's phones before driving them to Madrid. Someone must have retrieved and delivered their things from the safe house in Barcelona while he was sleeping.

Obviously, Vicente placed it there. Was anticipating a call.

"No contact yet?" Emiliano asked.

Vicente shook his head. "No. Rest some more."

"Have you slept at all?"

"I have to prepare."

"Prepare?"

"The admiral has requested a briefing and ops meeting for this afternoon."

Emiliano sat up straighter. "I'm going."

Vicente sighed. "I know. I had hoped to persuade you to remain here, to rest. But I'd sooner stop the tide." Vicente put his laptop on the coffee table and rose. Emiliano stood as well. "Come. We'll both rest. Just for a couple of hours." He gestured toward the stairs.

The two of them climbed to the second floor. Emiliano recalled the great pleasure Gabriella had taken in snooping around his space, while he hadn't had the energy, strength, or interest to look around Vicente's home.

When they reached the top, Vicente said, "There is a guest room down the hall to the left or my bedroom is...here."

Emiliano turned away from the guest room and walked to Vicente's room. The two of them stripped down to their boxer briefs before climbing beneath the covers. They didn't touch or talk. It wasn't necessary.

Just lying next to his husband, being close to him, was enough.

CHAPTER TWELVE

Castile was about to go to war.

They met in a heavily secured and private room in the territory headquarters. Emiliano was there, his eyes wide as he looked at the wall of monitors, the spiky black soundproofing on the ceiling, and the rack of weapons. Two stainless steel tables created a long counter down the middle of the room. Normally it was used to pack and check weapons, but today it was a conference table, the black folding chairs serviceable but not comfortable for the people at the meeting.

All the chairs were on one side, facing the wall of monitors, with Emiliano at the end closest to the door. Normally the position closest to the door was the most dangerous, but here, in Vicente's black-ops command center within the already fortress-like headquarters, he wanted Emiliano close to the door in case the other man needed to be escorted out, either because he needed more medical attention, or if what they were about to discuss was emotionally too much for him to handle. Guilt was riding the young senator, and what this briefing and ops meeting was about would only make it worse.

Plus, Emiliano was still in pain, and a concussion—mild or otherwise—was nothing to be trifled with. Vicente's medical training was all battlefield and necessity, but he'd been doing a basic neurological exam every few hours, checking Emiliano's hearing, vision, and balance. There were private medical facilities Vicente would send Emiliano to if needed, even if he had to handcuff his husband to the bed and hire guards to make sure he stayed there.

Vicente was standing on the opposite side of the table from the chairs, the screens at his back. They waited in a silence that was deceptively calm. Everyone here but Emiliano knew how to force themselves to relax before battle.

Rodrigo, his most senior security officer, slipped in, nodding to Vicente, who returned the gesture.

The Masters' Admiralty had been fighting a shadowy war of late, first with a villain who called himself the Mastermind and then with the Bellator Dei. Every time they chopped a head off the Hydra, two more grew back.

In the past eighteen months, their society had seen too much bloodshed at the hands of people who would stop at nothing to see the Masters' Admiralty crumble. Vicente's people had suffered heavy losses. Three of his officers had died, two killed by a sniper, the third in a bombing.

Now Yurena was dead. She'd been one of the new officers brought in to replace previous losses. A skilled intelligence asset—a very nice way of saying a retired spy—her strength had been in information gathering and people manipulation, not brute hand-to-hand combat. He'd been sure that guarding Emiliano and Gabriella was a low-to-no-risk assignment, except possibly from Gabriella herself, who had a glorious temper when she let herself reveal it.

He hadn't grieved for Yurena yet. There wasn't time. Later,

however, he would grieve for her as he had for Penny, Jordano, and David.

Rodrigo sat down in the remaining empty chair, between Xiomara and Javier. Xiomara was a security officer, as Rodrigo was, while Javier was one of the *caballeros*. The admiral and vice admiral were the other attendees, Santiago and Natalia seated farthest from the door. Alejandro, another *caballero*, was stationed outside the door. He was a redundancy, given all the levels of security necessary to bypass in order to penetrate this deep into the Castile headquarters, which, from the outside, was a Vienna Secession-style building, with crisp, angular lines and gold architectural details.

Vicente took his hand from his pocket and stepped to the side. Balancing a small tablet on one hand, he tapped the screen with the other.

Locking down all his emotions, he began the briefing. "Yesterday at 15:43, three assailants attacked the home of Emiliano Ortiz."

Emiliano made a sound that was either suppressed rage or horror as he looked at the screen. The video now playing had been taken by one of the bystanders who'd called emergency services.

The witness had started taking video after Yurena was already dead, but they watched Thiago, arms extended on the roof of the limo, head tucked low, taking aim. He fired, and one of the three black-clad and masked assailants jerked, but another raised a gun. The bullet hit Thiago just above one eye, though that wasn't visible on screen. What they did see was the man's head jerk, the gun falling from his hand as his body folded down on itself, before sprawling in the road. He'd died almost instantly.

The shocked scream of the witness was ear-piercing through the speakers. Everyone flinched, and Vicente turned the volume down. He let it play all the way through twice, though he knew almost everyone in the room had seen the video already. They watched Gabriella and Emiliano fight. Watched as Emiliano was held and beaten, Gabriella grabbed and hauled into the car.

When he finally turned it off, there were tears in Emiliano's eyes. He'd turned his head to the door, and Vicente was the only one who could see the wet tracks on his cheeks.

Vicente walked in front of the screens again, drawing everyone's attention, giving Emiliano time to gather himself.

"The vehicle was reported stolen yesterday morning and found abandoned in a long-term parking facility at Madrid Barajas Airport." Vicente clicked, and behind him another video played. This time it was security camera footage from the parking facility showing the kidnappers' vehicle pulling into the lot. "We're tracking all vehicles that left the facility after 16:00 yesterday, but so far there are no solid leads."

"They will have changed cars and plates since then," Xiomara pointed out.

Vicente nodded. "Tracking the vehicle is not our primary investigative focus."

Rodrigo sat forward, one forearm braced on the metal table. "Show us the notes?"

Vicente tapped again, bringing up the scanned images of the two notes Emiliano had received. The originals were at a private forensic lab, which was running every test anyone could think of. In reality, the results would most likely only help them confirm the identity of the men who'd taken her, after other investigative avenues had provided the names.

"Senator Emiliano Ortiz received this note in the mail the day after the bombing." Vicente turned to gesture to the image on the left. Typed on a plain sheet of printer paper, it had been folded in fourths to fit inside a wedding-invitation sized envelope, and the creases from the folds showed on the paper.

THAT WAS A WARNING, Senator.

Kill the corruption bill.

"DO we know how they got his home address to deliver the letter?" Javier asked.

"No," Vicente answered. "CNI is doing an information leak assessment."

"Why bomb the wedding, and not his home?" Xiomara asked.

Emiliano cleared his throat. "All my packages are held and inspected at a Correos facility. It's not just me, it's the same for all members of Parliament. If there'd been a package on my steps, I wouldn't have touched it."

"They not only have his address, they know about government security measures," Xiomara observed.

Vicente picked up the briefing once more.

"The attack and kidnapping was an escalation in reaction to Emiliano's perceived disregard for the warning."

Emiliano made a pained noise. Guilt ripped at Vicente. He'd put them all in the safe house, ensuring that Emiliano hadn't received the message.

It wouldn't have mattered.

That cold, reasonable voice was the part of him that was dispassionately assessing and planning.

"The attackers knew enough about Emiliano's schedule to know that he would be at a party on the Torres family estate but did not know he was taking vacation afterwards and wasn't due back in Madrid for several days."

"How many people knew about your plans?" the admiral asked Emiliano.

"My staff—that's only a few people—knew about the vacation, but there was a committee meeting scheduled the day of the wedding, and I told multiple people I wouldn't be at the meeting because I was going to be in Barcelona attending an event hosted by the Torreses."

"Gossip-worthy information," the vice admiral observed. "So it's possible they knew about the party far enough in advance to plan the bombing but didn't have access to his calendar to know about the vacation time."

Rodrigo shook his head. "If they knew where he lived, they could have been watching and realized he wasn't there to get the mail. Why escalate without giving him a chance to respond to the bomb threat?"

"First, maybe they weren't watching." Rodrigo nodded as if conceding the point. "But also, the bomb's impact wasn't as large as anticipated." Vicente clicked, bringing up a picture of the bomb fragments laid out on a sterile white sheet. "Further investigation indicates that the bomb was probably never meant to kill but was meant to do more damage than it did. Emiliano, Gabriella, myself, the wedding planner, and photographer were close to the fountain, and none of us required medical attention, only a few bandages. The rest of the damage was due to panic."

Xiomara, Rodrigo, and Javier all grimaced. A panicked crowd could be the most dangerous part of any major incident, and each of them had firsthand experience with that, thanks to backgrounds in law enforcement, military, and security.

"Additionally," Vicente went on, "the cover story we used— that the explosion was an accident—may have pushed them to escalate because, again, the bombing didn't have the effect or get the attention they wanted."

Vicente clicked back to the notes, this time gesturing to the one on the right.

"This is the message they left during the kidnapping." Unlike the first piece of paper, this one had reddish-brown smudges on the corners. Dried blood, from where Emiliano had opened it. Rather than a printed note, this one was handwritten—scrawled on the back of a utility bill. The bill was addressed to the owner of the stolen car, and the envelope it had been in was the return envelope addressed to Madrid's electricity provider.

"Kidnapping Gabriella was a crime of opportunity." Vicente knew his voice had gone cold and hard. If he let himself think about what Gabriella might be living through right now...

KILL THE BILL, and we'll give her back.

"WE BELIEVE they began watching Emiliano's residence the morning of the attack, saw him and Gabriella arrive together, with their security detail, and decided to kidnap her to ensure Emiliano's compliance. Whatever their original intent, her presence changed that."

"Any contact besides the notes?" the admiral asked.

"No. Not yet, but I did what they asked," Emiliano said. "As soon as I could, I notified my office, told my staff to stop working on the bill, and to pull it from the list of legislation being considered. I did everything I could to kill it."

"And that information is public?" Javier asked.

Emiliano nodded. "It is, but it's...it's just a footnote at the end of the articles about the kidnapping."

Gabriella's kidnapping was dominating the news not only

in Spain but in much of Europe, due in part to her family name, but also because of the graphic footage of the kidnapping. The fact that she'd been kidnapped when she was with Emiliano had also linked Gabriella and Emiliano together romantically, with most news organizations at least obliquely referring to their "secret" relationship. Very few of the articles mentioned that Emiliano was planning to step back from his senatorial duties, which included drafting and spearheading an anti-corruption bill. Only one report specifically stated he'd dropped the bill from consideration.

"I need to resign," Emiliano insisted. "If they think I'll bring the bill back once they release her…"

"It's more likely that they want you to stay in your position. They'll want a senator they can control," Xiomara said.

Vicente had always appreciated her honesty. Right now, it was not helpful.

"You mean they'll keep her? Forever? No, no—" Emiliano looked ready to bolt, to run through the streets of Madrid screaming her name.

Vicente sympathized with the urge.

He swept a gaze over the room, taking in each person, silencing them with a look.

"It is possible they are planning to hold her longer. It's possible, now that Emiliano has complied once, that they will want more from him."

"There's been no ransom demand?" Xiomara asked. "She's a high-value individual."

"No ransom demands, but we have K&R specialists with her parents," Natalia said. As vice admiral, she was in charge of the *caballero*. Providing kidnap and recovery expertise to the Torres family was her realm of responsibility, and if they needed to stage a rescue, under normal circumstances that too might be a job for the *caballero*.

What happened to the kidnappers after? Well...the basement chamber several floors below them was empty, but it had been washed and cleaned. It was ready for new occupants.

Rodrigo twisted to look down the table at Emiliano. "You've made an enemy of the Camorra."

It was the first time anyone had said the name aloud, instead using "they" and "them." Vicente hadn't even realized he was doing it until Rodrigo named the enemy. He ran a hand through his hair, realizing that he'd been avoiding referring to their current enemies as Camorra, or the mafia, because every time he did, he had to face exactly how slim Gabriella's chances of survival were.

Fear churned in his gut, and Vicente lifted his head, paying attention to the explanation Emiliano had been giving about the legislation he was sponsoring, how Italy had used anti-corruption legislation to force organized crime out of the country.

"The mafia is not above kidnapping for ransom," Rodrigo pointed out. "I think it's possible that they may try to extort her parents too."

"Is that why we don't have her back?" Emiliano's voice was raw.

Vicente could feel Emiliano's eyes on him. This information was all new to the senator. Vicente hadn't had time to share it with him before this meeting.

That was a lie. He could have made time. He hadn't read Emiliano in pre-briefing because he hadn't wanted the other man to worry any more than he already was.

Vicente focused on Rodrigo and Xiomara. They were his people. They were the ones he'd be ordering into certain danger. "We don't know what their plan is, which is why we are not going to wait for them to release her."

Everyone nodded, agreeing with a statement that, on its

surface, was insane. Even with the resources of the Masters' Admiralty, taking on the Camorra was nearly suicidal.

Vicente tapped the tablet screen again, and images of four men appeared. "Thanks to Xiomara, we have the National Intelligence Center's files on the strongest mafia families in Europe, including the names of who the CNI believes are the Camorra's top people in Spain."

The photos were arranged in a hierarchy, with one photo in the top row, one directly under that, and two in the bottom row, spaced equally under the center photo.

He started at the bottom. "Borja Labrador and Denis Carnicero. Both native Spaniards. Their criminal records started when they were teens. About five years ago, all criminal activity stopped." Vicente paused, lips quirking in a cold smile. "What actually happened is they stopped getting caught because the Camorra recruited them and taught them to be smart. If you were to ask them, they would say they work in client relations, a nice way of saying they shake down businesses for money while offering protection and special favors."

Vicente pointed to the middle photo. "This is Rufino Nori. Italian father, Spanish mother. He grew up in Spain, but after school spent extensive time in Italy with his father's people. He is the top Camorra agent in Spain. It's most likely that he decided Emiliano needed to be stopped and planned the bombing. The impulse kidnapping may have been on his orders, or it could have been initiated by Denis." Vicente keyed up a still from the kidnapping video. "Denis matches the height and body type of one of the kidnappers."

"What is Camorra's business in Spain?" Santiago asked. "I mean that literally. How are they making their money?"

"Drugs and human trafficking," Xiomara replied quietly. "Specifically club and designer drugs, and sex trafficking. High-end sex trafficking—Eastern European and North

African women trafficked to work as 'escorts' in casinos and on yachts all along the Mediterranean. From there, some are being trafficked to the Americas and Middle East for auction."

"Auction? You mean..." Emiliano shook his head. "I didn't know about that." His small sound of pain tore at Vicente's heart. Emiliano was worried what these monsters were doing to Gabriella...and he had a right to be worried.

"It's not the bulk of business because it's high risk," Xiomara said. "And some of the women auctioned off are believed to be Camorra agents, who report information on their wealthy 'owners' back to the families."

Emiliano closed his eyes, his lips moving silently. He was praying.

Vicente's heart broke, but he ignored that to continue the briefing. "I've ordered real-time surveillance on a list of properties owned by these three." He pointed to the photos of Borja, Denis, and Rufino. "We're also working on suspected properties and checking recent real estate sales within a hundred-kilometer radius of Madrid. Priority targets are anywhere that we think they've kept or housed the women they're trafficking. Those properties are more likely to have facilities they could adapt to use as a temporary prison."

Emiliano shoved up from his chair, turning his back to the room. His grief and fear were almost palpable.

In the tight silence, Santiago said, "Any and every resource we have is yours, Vicente, until she's home."

"Thank you, Admiral."

"I'm speaking with the fleet admiral after this, to brief him on the situation. He called when the international news of her kidnapping broke and offered assistance. If we need something from the fleet admiral, or the other territories, ask." That was a heavy promise, because unsaid but understood was that

Santiago was willing to make threats and/or promises that might be problematic down the road.

Vicente locked down his relief that territory politics weren't something they had to worry about, as well as his own fear for their wife, before turning back to the board.

"Rufino Nori reports to Armani Capello, the don of this family." Vicente pointed at the top photo without looking at it. "Armani lives in northern Italy, in Genoa, but he has property in Sicily as well. Word on the street is Armani is looking to increase his territory. He has a very long, very powerful reach. He's been a person of interest both in Italy and internationally —some of our information on him comes from Interpol. He's never been charged."

Javier, a man of few words, whistled in acknowledgement of how much power Armani had.

Vicente glanced over his shoulder at the image of the leader of the Camorra and paused, forgetting what he was about to say. He frowned, glanced at Rodrigo, then looked back at the picture.

Xiomara and the admiral were also frowning at Rodrigo.

Santiago cleared his throat. "Is it just me, or does Rodrigo look like Armani Capello?"

Vicente lifted the tablet, pulling up another image of Armani. Clearly taken from a distance, this image showed him standing on a sun-drenched patio, holding a phone to his ear.

Xiomara nudged Rodrigo.

"What?" Rodrigo demanded.

"Go stand by the picture."

Rodrigo made a face that said he doubted Xiomara's sanity.

Santiago cleared his throat. "Rodrigo, would you stand up?"

Rodrigo stiffened, looked around. His gaze shot to Vicente. Vicente nodded at him.

Finally, Rodrigo stood, circling the tables to stand beside the bank of screens. Vicente brought up the room lights a bit.

Rodrigo kept his hair long on top, his close-trimmed beard and "anchor" mustache a few shades darker than his gold-streaked brown hair. He was striking and had more than once adopted an identity as a model or actor for various ops. His eyes were deep brown, and his nose widened a little at the tip, an odd almost-flaw in a strong-jawed face.

Armani Capello's short hair was brown streaked with both sun-lightened gold and silver. He was clean-shaven, and his body was soft with age and a life of luxury.

He had dark eyes, a strong, square jaw, and a nose that widened a little at the tip.

Javier leaned forward, comparing Rodrigo to the image. He whistled again, a long, low tone.

"Can you use this, Vicente?" Natalia asked.

Vicente pursed his lips, thinking. Clean-shaven and with a haircut, Rodrigo would be a dead ringer for Armani. Maybe they could—

He cursed, a sharp, hard word as he remembered something. He looked at Rodrigo, saw the panic deep in his officer's eyes.

"Are you related to the Italian mafia?" Emiliano joked. He'd turned around, and the effort he was making to act normal was visible on his face. The joke was clearly a part of that.

Emiliano had no idea how powerful his question was.

Rodrigo stepped away from the wall, turning to look at the picture. The light from the screens bathed his face.

"I don't know," Rodrigo said quietly. "I have no idea who my biological father is."

CHAPTER THIRTEEN

Emiliano pushed the bowl of soup away, his appetite completely gone even though he'd eaten little over the past two days. His stomach still churned from all the information he'd learned at the briefing.

On a normal day, he would have been fascinated by what had seemed to be Vicente's lair within the territory headquarters. He would have asked countless questions about the technology, the process, the officers themselves. None of that had sparked even the slightest bit of interest today as he was inundated by exactly how much danger Gabriella was in.

It was one thing to imagine the worst. It was something else entirely to know the worst.

After the meeting, he and Vicente had returned here—with two *caballero* bodyguards—and his husband had heated up some lentil soup.

Emiliano had insisted he not bother on his account, but Vicente was determined to feed him. In the end, Emiliano had gotten up and tried to enhance their meal by tossing a salad and heating up some frozen rolls he'd found in the freezer. When he'd inquired about the fresh vegetables—given what he'd noticed of Vicente's limited cooking skills—his husband's only response had been that he lived on salads because he couldn't burn that.

"You need to eat something," Vicente said, gesturing to his untouched plate. "You will need your strength for the coming days. Rest, food...these things are as important as gathering information."

Emiliano suspected Vicente had a great deal of experience when it came to compartmentalizing his feelings. On a professional level, Emiliano could do the same, but today had been hard for him. Between the war council, the media circus surrounding Gabriella's kidnapping—his assistant had texted and emailed him no fewer than twenty times, overwhelmed by the deluge of questions and requests for interviews—and his injuries, he was running on empty.

The mafia bill was something he'd been very passionate about, but he hadn't hesitated for a moment when he killed it. Because what was happening now was personal. And there wasn't a snowball's chance in hell he'd manage to tuck his emotions away while Gabriella was...God only knew where, possibly enduring unspeakable things. All because of him.

His fault.

He rubbed his eyes, trying to block out the images he'd seen, the video footage of his beating, of Gabriella fighting to escape. He'd thought living through it had been horrible enough, but seeing it from a different perspective, forced to watch what Gabriella had been going through, with him helpless to save her, was soul-crushing.

"Emiliano," Vicente pressed, when he didn't reply or begin to eat, his voice uncharacteristically gentle.

"I was a picky eater when I was a little boy. My mother would try to coax me sweetly. Told me I would get sick and skinny. She always called me Emil during those times, kissing my forehead, telling me she wanted me to grow up to be big and strong." Emiliano hadn't thought about that in years, but there was something about Vicente's attempt at making him eat that felt the same. Like Vicente genuinely cared, just as his mother had.

Vicente grinned, something he did all too rarely. Emiliano never failed to be taken aback by how much younger he looked when he smiled.

"My mother called me Cente, but that was usually reserved for times when I was being a little devil and she was too angry to get my full name out."

"In that case, I'm surprised she ever used your full name," Emiliano joked.

Vicente picked a small corner off his roll and chucked it at Emiliano's head. The act was so playful and unexpected, Emiliano didn't know how to respond.

"I had forgotten about that. My mother died when I was fourteen, cancer," his husband said.

"I'm sorry," Emiliano said.

Vicente nodded his head, just once, the gesture one of unspoken thanks. "It was a long time ago."

"Do you suppose anyone ever called Gabriella 'Gabby'?" Emiliano asked in an attempt to pull them away from darker topics.

Vicente tilted his head, considering the nickname. "If they did, I suspect they did not do so a second time."

Emiliano chuckled and agreed. He couldn't picture their lovely wife responding to Gabby either. "Are you a legacy, Vicente?"

"No, I am not. I was recruited like you. Only Gabriella was raised within the Masters' Admiralty." Vicente took a sip of water. Emiliano glanced at his husband's bowl. It was empty, every bit of soup consumed. Vicente practiced what he preached.

Emiliano pulled his bowl closer and picked up his spoon, determined to follow suit. "I must admit, the ménage marriage requirement was a cause for concern when I was recruited."

"I suspect there are very few members who aren't legacies who didn't struggle to wrap their heads around that. It is...unusual."

"Perhaps I should say there was one part of that requirement that gave me reason to pause."

"Only one part?"

"I was raised by a single mother, as you know, so the idea of my children being raised by three appealed to me greatly."

Vicente ran his hand through his hair. "So you do hope for children?"

Emiliano recalled Vicente's assertion that he would serve as godfather to his and Gabriella's children. Those words had cut deeply. "I do."

Vicente seemed slightly bothered by that response, and Emiliano was tempted to ask the same question of him, praying that this time the answer would change. Ever since he'd shown up at the hospital, Vicente had been...different. More open, more honest, and at times, more vulnerable. The stoic warrior attitude he'd been wearing like armor since the night they'd met seemed to vanish when they were alone together.

However, witnessing Vicente in action today, Emiliano knew there was no other man he would ever want in his corner, and he didn't doubt that he would love his husband *and* his wife equally. It was that realization that had started this conversation.

"If you had no concerns about raising a family in a trinity, then what was it about the ménage marriage that bothered you, Emiliano?"

"As a legacy, Gabriella had been a witness to what it meant to be part of a trinity. She'd seen the inner workings of that type of marriage by watching her parents. Meanwhile, I'd had no experience with marriage at all, not even the conventional kind. Your parents...they were married?"

Vicente nodded. "Yes. Until my mother passed away. My father remarried when I was twenty. She's a very nice woman and they are happy together."

"I spent far too much of my childhood alone. I was concerned that perhaps I wasn't hardwired to share my life with anyone else. I worried that I'd be placed in a trinity and feel...overwhelmed, a fish out of water. What I hadn't expected—hadn't anticipated—was that I would feel so much for you and Gabriella so soon. The two of you have blindsided me, taken me unaware, snuck under my defenses."

Emiliano hadn't planned to reveal so much, but part of him felt as if he and Vicente were living on borrowed time. He, Vicente, and Gabriella had wasted the first days of their marriage, offering each other only angry words and hurt feelings. Well, that and some really good sex.

Gabriella had been the only one willing— No, that wasn't exactly right. She'd been the only one seeking ways to bring them together. She had come to their marriage with open arms, and while Emiliano had tried to do the same, he'd closed them in response to Vicente's rejection of their marriage. Unlike her, he'd stopped fighting *for* them, opting instead to simply fight.

What if they didn't get her back? The thought crushed him like a two-ton weight. He would spend every day of the rest of his life, buried alive under a mountain of self-recrimination and regret.

For the things he hadn't said, hadn't shared with her.

He couldn't do the same with Vicente. Even if his husband

slammed the door in his face again, he was going to speak what was written on his heart.

"I know we haven't known each other for long and yet…"

"You'd lay down your life for her," Vicente finished.

Emiliano shook his head. "I'd lay down my life for both of you. I should have fought harder." His voice grew thick, his throat tight as once again he saw the footage of the attack.

Vicente rose from the table, claiming the chair next to him rather than the one opposite. He scooted it closer, grasping Emiliano's hand and squeezing it firmly. "You could never have won that fight."

"I could have—"

Vicente's words were calm and cold. "You weren't a real threat to them, and that's the only reason they didn't hurt you more seriously."

"I'm guessing *you* would have been a threat," Emiliano said, aware the words were bitter.

"Yes," Vicente agreed. "And they most likely would have shot me or slit my throat."

Emiliano took a minute to process that.

"We're going to find her." Vicente had said those same words several times since the attack.

"We *have* to find her, Vicente. I've never considered myself a particularly romantic man and a concept like love at first sight has always felt ridiculous to me. Yet, when the admiral introduced us, when he said that you and Gabriella would be mine… something inside me changed."

Vicente didn't respond immediately; instead, he studied Emiliano's face for several moments. Emiliano imagined he could see a tornado of emotion swirling behind his husband's eyes and then, Vicente's mask fell away completely.

"I understand that feeling, Emil," Vicente said. Emiliano

grinned at his use of the shortened pet name. "I too have been changed."

"You have?" Emiliano was unable to shield the doubt in his tone. Too many times, he'd imagined Vicente softening, only to watch him double-down and fortify the walls again.

"I said some things," Vicente began, his words coming slowly as if he was thinking of each one, carefully choosing them as he spoke, "some hurtful things, at the safe house in regards to our marriage."

Emiliano nodded just once but didn't interrupt.

"I have dedicated my life to my work, first in the military, then as a security officer, now as the minister. I take that position, my role within the society, very seriously."

"I understand—" Emiliano started, but Vicente raised his hand to cut him off.

"I tried to warn you and Gabriella that my life is dangerous. *I* am dangerous."

"And that means you shouldn't get married?"

"Let me be more clear. I do what is needed. *Whatever* is needed, to protect the society."

"You consider the things you do immoral."

Vicente's expression was calm, as if they were talking about the weather. "An immoral thing done for a moral reason is still immoral. I do my job."

"Vicente—" Again, Emiliano was cut off.

"Yurena was good at her job too."

It was the first time Vicente had mentioned the security officer who'd lost her life trying to protect Emiliano and Gabriella.

"Were you close to her?" he asked.

Vicente shook his head. "Close is not a word I would use to describe my relationship with my officers. I am their leader, not their friend."

"Must be lonely."

"No," Vicente said sternly, lapsing for a moment, refusing to show any weakness. Emiliano watched as he forced himself to soften, to say more. "Sometimes," he admitted. "Though I suspect those lonely times are behind me, now that I have you and Gabriella. It is impossible to feel lonely when surrounded by the two of you. You bring so much life to every room you enter."

Emiliano sucked in a quiet, shocked breath. Surprised by Vicente's admission, but more so by the revelation that Vicente no longer seemed to be rejecting the idea of a true marriage.

Vicente rubbed his thumb over the top of Emiliano's hand, the soft stroke soothing. "Yurena was new to her position. Only serving as an officer for a few months. She is the fourth officer to die in the line of duty in the last year and a half. Each death...has been difficult, tearing away another piece of my soul. Sometimes I fear that I don't have much more of it left to lose."

Emiliano flipped his hand over, gripping Vicente's hard, wanting to refute his husband's words as much as he wanted to offer him support. Emiliano had been so wrapped up in his own guilt over Gabriella's abduction, he'd failed to see that Vicente was suffering the same feeling over Yurena's death.

"Yurena was looking forward to being placed in her trinity. She told me so in her interview. I remember thinking it was... odd. Misguided perhaps. For her to want both to be a security officer and to be married. The job is dangerous. Requires focus and, at times, long periods away from home. Yet, Yurena wanted both. Thought she could have both. I understand why now."

"You do?"

Vicente nodded. "We work in darkness, but we cannot live there. Not if we hope to retain our humanity, our sanity.

Yurena knew that, knew she would need partners waiting for her at home, who could drag her out of the shadows and into the light."

Emiliano shifted, moving toward Vicente so that he could kiss him. This kiss, like their first, lingered, full of passion and hunger. However, this time, there was something more. Affection...and a promise.

When they parted, Emiliano rested his forehead against Vicente's. "We won't let you get lost in the dark," he whispered.

"I am...frightened, Emiliano." His face was stark. "Terrified of losing Gabriella. Fear has no place in my world."

"I believe in you, Vicente. The man I saw today at headquarters—I'm not afraid of who he is or what he does. God, I've never been more impressed, more proud, more...comforted. Because that man? He's the only one I trust our beautiful, wonderful wife's life to."

Vicente leaned back, drawing in a deep breath, a ghost of a smile on his face. "She is beautiful, wonderful. She's also passionate and intelligent."

"She's got a hell of a temper when she lets go."

Vicente chuckled. "Does it make me a masochist if I say that's my favorite thing about her?"

"If it does, I'm one as well."

The two of them shared a laugh.

Vicente gripped the back of Emiliano's neck, drawing him closer. "For the first time in my life, I can feel the sunshine on my face. And I like it." He sealed those words with a quick, hard kiss.

Emiliano smiled when they parted. "Gabriella had your number right from the beginning. *Bandolero.*"

"I owe you—both of you—an apology."

"Let's get her back, and then you can apologize."

Vicente nodded. "You and I will find our way through this...with Gabriella at our side."

Emiliano wished Gabriella had been here with them for this conversation.

He wondered where she was. What she was going through. He could only imagine how terrified she must be.

If—no, when—they got her back, she was going to need them. Both of them. Because they both brought something different to the table.

To the bedroom.

"Vicente, when we find Gabriella, I fear..." He paused, trying to figure out how to word his concern.

"Fear?" Vicente prompted when he failed to finish his thought.

Emiliano recalled the way Gabriella had asked them to hate-fuck her at the safe house. Vicente had known exactly what she wanted, what she needed, while Emiliano had struggled with it. "She will have seen things, God, maybe experienced things that are going to change her. She will have seen that darkness you speak of, that you know firsthand. You will relate to her better than I can. You'll be better able to give her what she needs."

"There is nothing I won't give Gabriella. That I won't give you, Emiliano. I—we—will do what is needed to help our wife."

Emiliano wasn't quite satisfied that he'd gotten his message across, but before he could explain it better, Vicente's phone rang.

He picked it up. "Rodrigo."

He listened for only a moment before cursing under his breath. He disconnected the call without saying goodbye, then rose from the table.

"Vicente?" Emiliano said, following him out of the kitchen

and to the living room, where his husband turned on the television.

Emiliano's heart was in his throat, fear washing through him as he glanced at the screen, terrified of what he would see.

Surely if they'd found Gabriella, if...something horrible had happened to her, Vicente would tell him rather than have him find out from the media.

Vicente found a news station and crossed his arms, a deadly scowl on his face.

Emiliano began to breathe again when he realized the story wasn't an update about their kidnapped heiress.

That relief was short-lived when the broadcaster introduced one of his colleagues, Senator Juan Alonzo. The video cut to a section of a press conference.

It began with Senator Alonzo expressing his deepest sympathies for Emiliano and Gabriella's families. The asshole was using Emiliano's tragedy to put himself on TV.

On screen, Juan's face was concerned but approachable as he stood behind a podium. "Senator Ortiz needs time and space during this horrible event, but I will not let the things he, we, have worked for, be lost. Earlier today, Senator Ortiz withdrew the anti-corruption bill from the legislation schedule for this session. I am pledging to take over sponsorship of the bill. This important piece of crime legislation will not be lost."

"No," Emiliano breathed in horror. "He can't. He wouldn't...Juan wasn't even on the committee working on the bill," he finished stupidly.

Vicente was already on the phone, barking out orders.

On screen, there were a few questions, some posturing, and then the press conference ended.

Juan was going to resurrect the bill.

Juan had just killed Gabriella.

Emiliano surged to his feet. "They're going to kill her. We have to find her!"

He raced for the door. He wasn't thinking. He was reacting. Gabriella was out there somewhere, and now they would kill her because Emiliano hadn't done what they'd asked. He hadn't stopped the bill. The stupid legislation no one had wanted to work on was now Juan Alonzo's new project because playing savior was how Juan got his face on TV and kept getting reelected.

"Emiliano." Vicente gripped the back of his neck in a firm hold, forcing him to meet his gaze. "They're not going to kill her."

"But—"

"They are not going to kill her. Not tonight."

"You can't just will that to be true," Emiliano snarled.

Vicente was cold, controlled. "I'm not. They won't kill her tonight because that isn't what I would do."

Emiliano sucked in air.

"If they want the bill stopped, they have a new target."

"Good. I hope they kill Juan."

Vicente's brows rose, but he ignored the remark. "They are left with a hostage they can't leverage against you, but they still won't kill her."

"Ransom. They'll ransom her to her parents." Emiliano's relief made him light-headed.

Vicente hesitated a beat too long. "Yes."

"Don't do that," Emiliano snarked. "Tell me. Whatever it is you're thinking, tell me."

Vicente ran his free hand through his hair, looked away. "The media coverage of the kidnapping makes any sort of ransom exchange very dangerous."

"You mean dangerous for them."

"Yes. Kidnapping and ransom is safest when it's quiet. This isn't quiet."

"What are they going to do?" Emiliano asked through gritted teeth.

Vicente tightened his hold on the back of Emiliano's neck, and the pressure helped. Emiliano took a deep breath.

Vicente's expression was grim. "Gabriella is worth more alive than dead."

"YOU HAVE SEEN THE NEWS?"

Rufino had been expecting Armani Capello's call. Dreading it. Grabbing the Torres woman had been a mistake, one Denis and Borja would pay for. Especially since it didn't achieve the results they'd hoped for. The bill was going forward without Ortiz. It might even have more support now than it had before. Which meant they hadn't gotten what they wanted and now had a high-profile hostage on their hands, with half the country's law enforcement agencies looking for her. "I have."

"It is time to dispose of the woman. The risk to the organization is too great. She should never have been taken to begin with."

"I have a plan," Rufino said. The moment he'd seen Senator Alonzo's press conference, he'd known he would need to act fast to ditch the woman. Killing her would solve the problem, but Rufino still hoped to turn this mistake into money, a way to buy forgiveness for his men's mistake.

Ransoming her to her parents was too dangerous at the moment, but she was a beautiful woman, and her parents would still pay for her, even if she was damaged. "There's a way we can profit from this. The timing is fortuitous. As you know, there is an auction this week."

His words were met with silence, never a good thing with Armani. Rufino held his breath. His men had fucked up. *His* men. Which meant he had fucked up. He needed to salvage this, to make his way back into Armani's good graces, because those who found themselves on the boss' bad side always wound up in body bags or wearing cement shoes at the bottom of the Black Sea.

"If this fails, Rufino..." Armani said at last.

Rufino shuddered, quickly interjecting. "It won't. I will oversee it myself, will ensure the purchaser understands that—"

He didn't have a chance to finish.

"There is no second chance," Armani warned.

"I understand." Rufino was wasting his breath. Armani had already disconnected the call.

Fleet Admiral Eric Ericsson dropped his chin to his chest, breathing hard. His bench and free weights should have been smoking, considering how intense that workout had been.

Rolling his neck, he turned to take in the view. The wall of windows at the far end of his long, open-concept living space had a gorgeous panoramic view of the Atlantic. The sun was setting, a hazy, gold sweep of light behind the misty cloud cover that blanketed the northwestern part of the Isle of Man.

As his breathing slowed and his muscles stopped trembling from exertion, the itchy feeling of being trapped returned.

"Fuck."

Eric picked up a hoodie, tugging it on so he wouldn't get cold from the drying sweat, and wiped his damp face with the sleeve.

There were just under two thousand people in the Masters' Admiralty. Two thousand people who depended on him to lead them, make decisions for them, and above all, protect them.

He was good at protecting people, when that method of

protection involved shooting someone or taking a bullet himself. That was no longer an option for him. Since he'd come back to the Isle of Man after his "walkabout" to hunt a serial killer, the Spartan Guard had been watching him like a hawk. Multiple people had pointed out to him that the best way he could protect the Masters' Admiralty, and the nearly two thousand members, was to stay alive, stay on the Isle of Man, and be the fleet admiral.

The itchy feeling wasn't just because he was all but trapped on this island by a job he'd never wanted. That itch was the same uneasy sensation he used to get in those dark years when he was a mercenary, when something was about to go FUBAR.

He mixed a protein shake, ate some Swedish-style hardtack with butter. The hardtack made him think of Trina and Dahlia, his wives. He missed them, but thinking about them no longer made him feel guilty, and the grief had been muted by time.

He was contemplating a shower and the list of situations that needed his attention. Sophia was still catching him up on decisions she'd had to make while he was MIA. There was a Bellator Dei dossier update he wanted to go over a second time, a situation report on a kidnapping in Spain, a few less urgent reports about members who had issues, as well as some more academic reports the librarians had put together months ago, but he hadn't had a chance to read. The small thinktank group had been disbanded after Josephine's murder, the former members all turning to focus on their own marriages or new positions within the society.

Thinking of Josephine reminded him that he needed to go to Dublin and check up on Colum.

Now the itchy feeling, that tingle at the back of his neck, was worry. Colum had taken his sister's death badly. It didn't help that, as the Archivist, Colum was one of the only people in the society who didn't have to obey the fleet admiral's orders. Right now, that meant Colum was ignoring calls and messages.

Time to shower. Eric headed for the hallway at the far end of the living space. Off the hall were several smaller rooms that had been set up as offices, and one massive bedroom with three separate walk-in closets and a huge bathroom with three separate vanities. A bedroom fit for a trinity. He and his wives hadn't had anything that nice, not even when Dahlia had been thrust into the position of admiral of Kalmar. Then again, they'd had to hide their relationship, with him playing the dutiful politician's husband.

Eric had the sweatshirt half off when he heard the quick triple beep alert that meant someone was on the stairs.

The stairs to the fleet admiral quarters were stone, one of the castle's original spiral stairwells. No one could stumble up here by accident, especially since at this time of day, there shouldn't be anyone else in the building, and the entrance to the stairs was deliberately inaccessible.

The captain of the guard traditionally lived in the castle proper, along with the fleet admiral and their trinity. After that clusterfuck with the former captain, Mateo, and the traitor guard Derrick, Eric had declared that it was necessary for the captain of the guard to live and work with the other Spartan Guard to keep an eye on them. It had been a great excuse for Eric to have the castle to himself so the damned guards weren't always *hovering*.

He was far more comfortable as the one doing the guarding rather than being guarded.

He hadn't gotten a message from the Spartan Guard about anyone coming. Which meant either one of them was on the stairs and had gone rogue and was about to assassinate him, or they were under attack, and the state-of-the-art comms system had gone down. Maybe an EMP cannon, followed by a stealth attack. Or their system had been infiltrated, so the comm system wasn't reliable, and the only safe way to communicate was in person.

All those possibilities raced through his head in the space of a single heartbeat.

Eric ripped off his sweatshirt, the tank top coming with it. At the same time, he whirled, taking three steps toward the kitchen. He kept going, rounding the counter to put it between himself and the doorway.

That itchy feeling had morphed into a more familiar tingle of danger-heightened awareness.

He slapped his hand against the underside of one of the overhead cabinets. A hidden compartment popped down, revealing a SIG Sauer resting on a rubberized grip mat, a single loaded magazine resting beside it. He grabbed the gun in his right hand, magazine in his left, and slapped it in even as he raised it, aiming for the door, as it swung open.

Nikolett Varda sucked in a shocked breath when she saw him, the quick inhalation paired with too-wide eyes. There was fear in her face. She was afraid of him.

Eric's insides twisted, his heart or his stomach, he wasn't sure which, and it didn't matter. He jerked his arm to the side and down, no longer aiming at her.

For a tense moment, they simply looked at one another, and Eric remembered the last time he'd seen her. When her voice had been the only thing that stopped him from killing a woman with his bare hands.

Then, like a branch too heavy with snow, the silence broke, and they both started talking at once.

"What the fuck are you doing here?"

"Is this how you always greet guests, Fleet Admiral?"

There was a beat of silence as they absorbed what the other

one was saying, and then they both started up again, voices a little louder than before.

"Guests are usually invited, *Admiral*. And how did you get past the Spartan Guard?"

"I'm here to talk to you about some of my concerns and to propose changes."

Another moment of silence, and they eyed one another like gunslingers from a bygone era.

Then Nikolett's lips twitched. The smile blossomed, spreading across her face, lighting up her expression.

Eric's insides twisted again.

She chuckled—almost a giggle—and walked into his home, letting the door close behind her. She had a simple canvas overnight bag on one shoulder and a battered laptop case in her hand. She dropped the duffel and looked around with unabashed curiosity as she made her way over to him.

He put his gun back into the hidden compartment, slipped out of the kitchen, meeting her halfway.

Toe to toe, they eyed one another. Nikolett was like a force of nature, or maybe it was more accurate to say she was a force to be reckoned with. The other admirals had accepted his impromptu sabbatical, listened to Sophia, and generally behaved with the obedient deference that befitted the hierarchy of Europe's most powerful secret society.

Nikolett was different. She'd baited a trap to draw him out, to force him to take up the role of fleet admiral once again. As far as he could tell, she'd done it for no other reason than she expected him to do his job, expected him to do, and be, better. And when he'd nearly tipped into the darkness of his own rage, she'd talked him back into the light.

His first instinct, that whoever was coming through his door was dangerous, was spot-on. Just dangerous in a different way.

Nikolett's gaze slid from his face down his bare chest. She

took a deep breath, held it. When she exhaled, she turned to look away, and there was a faint flush across the pale skin of her upper chest, exposed by the modest V neck of the white dress shirt she wore. He didn't think she was embarrassed. No, that was a different kind of flush.

Light from the windows touched her hair, the curve of her cheek. *My God, this woman is beautiful.* It wasn't the first time he'd thought that, but right now, with her standing so close, her presence was like a punch in the gut.

She felt it too, this sparking attraction between them. The evidence was there in her slow breaths, the way her fingers twisted, and the fact that she snuck another glance at his bare chest.

Spark was a good word, because what lay between them was dangerous, the way a live electrical wire was.

He'd never been one to turn away from danger. And Niko-lett...well, she went where angels feared to tread, and was, as he'd just noted, dangerous herself. Not in the same deadly way he was, but danger was danger.

He liked danger.

Eric raised his hand, ready and willing to give in to this reckless desire he hadn't let himself acknowledge until this moment.

Nikolett looked up at him, holding his gaze in a way that seemed both fearless and shocked. Her gaze slid down to his lips, and she exhaled, her lips parting.

He was going to kiss Nikolett.

Eric saw it all, planned it in his mind so that when his own desire took over, he wouldn't have to think too hard.

He would slide his hand into Nikolett's hair and tip her face up. He'd hold her there, see if she pulled away, and if she didn't, he'd ask her if he could kiss her. He'd ask first, because consent, and because when he finally did kiss her, he wasn't going to be gentle. He was going to take her mouth, claim her. Demand that she submit to his kiss the way she had refused to submit to *him*, obey him.

Thinking of the word "obey" and Nikolett in the same sentence made his brain nearly short circuit.

That caused another momentary hesitation, and it was in that moment that his fucking phone rang.

The sound was loud, piercing. It was less a "ring" than an alarm. His phone had been set up so that for those few who had the number, they could enter a special code, just after they dialed the number. The code triggered the "alarm" ring, which sounded even if his phone was on silent or set to "Do Not Disturb."

He and Nikolett sprang apart, the fragile moment shattered. Eric turned for his weights area, snatching up the phone from atop the free weight rack where he'd left it. He glanced at the screen, then answered the admiral of Castile's call.

"De Leon?"

"Fleet Admiral. We believe Gabriella Torres is now in mortal danger."

"There was no ransom demand?" Damn it, he should have read the updated report on the kidnapping earlier.

"Not in the traditional sense. We believe she was taken by the mafia, by the Camorra. They wanted Emiliano Ortiz to—"

Nikolett was frowning, her head cocked as she listened, obviously able to pick up bits and pieces. Nosy woman.

When De Leon said "Camorra," she leapt over and grabbed his arm, yanking his hand away from his ear. Eric bared his teeth and shot his hand up, high above his head, but he wasn't fast enough. Nikolett clung to his arm with one hand, the other reaching out and hitting the speaker button on his phone screen before he was able to fully get it out of her reach.

Because she was holding his arm, when he raised it, she was

pulled forward, stumbling into him so that for a glorious moment, they pressed against one another. He felt her unsteady breath against his bare chest. He shivered in reaction. God damn it all to hell. When did an accidental touch make him feel more fucking alive than he had in...a long fucking time?

The Castile admiral was still talking. "—given the publicity, we doubt they will risk a ransom to her parents. The Camorra operations in Italy are primarily drugs and human trafficking, but in Morocco and Sardinia—"

Nikolett jerked back, running for the door. Eric blinked, then looked at the ceiling. No divine intervention explained what the hell she was doing now, so he ignored her as best he could, focusing on what De Leon was saying. He'd have to rip her a new one for butting into a private conversation once this was over, and it was definitely problematic that he was looking forward to a rage-filled reaction to his giving her a dressing down.

Nikolett rushed back, grabbing him by the elbow as she passed, dragging him toward the long dining table that was apparently her destination. She threw herself into a chair, jerked her laptop out of the bag she'd gone to retrieve, and within a second was typing, her brow furrowed.

He slid around to look at the screen, morbidly fascinated by whatever she was doing. Everything on her computer screen was in Hungarian, but he recognized some of the words...and more than that, he recognized the hollow-eyed look of some of the young women in the files she'd opened.

Eric brought his attention back to the conversation, asking De Leon a few more questions and listening to the plan of action. The life of a member was on the line, and De Leon was right to call him, because to save Gabriella, Eric would bring the full force of the Masters' Admiralty to bear on the Camorra.

He didn't want to go to war with the mafia, but if they had to, he would.

Nikolett waved to get his attention, pointing at her screen. She'd typed up a note in a blank document.

Eric read it, glanced at her. She added a few more words.

He nodded to her, and into the phone he said, "I have a human trafficking expert here. Give us a few hours to work that angle and see if we can find Gabriella that way."

Eric ended the call and looked at Nikolett. "You think you can find her?"

"When I heard him say Camorra, I had a feeling either arms dealing or human trafficking was going to come up." Her expression hardened. "Those are two things I know all too well."

"Any information you could get to help Castile find her?"

"I saw the news stories about the kidnapping. I didn't know she was one of us."

Quickly, Eric read her in, any thoughts of berating her for eavesdropping forgotten. Nikolett listened, taking notes a few times, and then turned to her computer, fingers flying furiously.

"I was thinking I could generate a list of names—people who do business with the Camorra, people who might have heard or know something that could help, but..."

She paused, frowning.

"Nikolett. Talk."

She frowned at *him*. "Pretend I'm the bad guy."

"You would make an utterly terrifying criminal," he assured her.

"Thank you. I kidnap someone. I need to keep her somewhere while she serves as hostage, to get the senator to do what I want."

"Right."

"He does what I ask, and..." She shook her head. "Why not just let her go?"

"Never leave money on the table," Eric said immediately.

"Right. The ransom. You said they think the kidnapping was a last-minute decision. If that's the case, maybe they didn't realize who they had until the news reported it. They didn't realize they could ransom her until they found out that's what everyone assumed they were doing."

"Possible, but since they planted a bomb at her family's house, wouldn't they know what she looked like?"

"Good point." Nikolett tapped her fingers on the table but then shook her head. "But back to the kidnapping. Keeping someone prisoner isn't easy."

"No, it's not." He saw where she was going with this. "You can't just throw them in a hotel room, not unless you have a lot of manpower to watch them."

"Which they might."

"True."

"Or," she said, "they have existing facilities. Places where they keep prisoners. They saw her, decided to kidnap her, and knew they could do it because they could keep her wherever they keep their human trafficking victims."

"Don't look for people, look for places," he said.

"Exactly." She turned to her computer. "If my contacts don't have information about any Camorra human trafficking facilities and properties in Spain, maybe they'll know who to ask. I also may be able to find women who were trafficked through there."

Eric looked at her, and for a moment felt helpless. "What can I do to help?"

"Coffee?" She didn't look up from her computer.

"I'm...the fleet admiral," he sputtered. "Your superior."

She made a humming noise of agreement.

"Your boss." He was fighting not to smile, to maintain the disgruntled tone.

"Yes, yes, you're right." Nikolett looked at him and smiled. "Coffee, *please*."

Eric's eye twitched, but he was grinning when he went to make coffee.

GABRIELLA LAY AWAKE, refusing to open her eyes, silently praying that she'd simply been having a nightmare. Perhaps her closed-eyes pretense would have been easier if she wasn't shivering on a rancid mattress with a spring digging into her lower back.

Denial was futile.

Lifting her eyelids, she was greeted by the same thing that she awoke to the last time she'd fallen asleep. Like Talya, she was beginning to lose track of time, uncertain if it was truly morning—like her body was telling her—or if it was still the middle of the night or day. Without the benefit of a window to the outside world, her internal clock was failing her.

She pushed herself upright, wincing at the stiffness in her joints. Her entire body ached, from the injuries of the attack as well as being forced to sleep on the threadbare mattress on the hard concrete floor.

Gabriella rubbed her arms, briefly wondering if she'd ever truly feel warm again. The chill that had settled over her went bone-deep.

Glancing toward the doorway, she saw that room service had delivered her breakfast as she slept. She would have to call to complain because they forgot the sugar for her coffee again. And her coffee. And anything even slightly resembling edible food.

Not that she wouldn't clean off the tray. Her hunger was finally winning out over her fear of consuming questionable food. At this point, she'd welcome food poisoning if only to fill the gnawing emptiness in her stomach.

Groaning slightly, she rose from the floor like a ninety-year-old woman with arthritis. Talya had suggested that she begin doing exercises in her cell, claiming it helped with the aches and pains that accompanied inactivity and too much time spent sitting on a hard floor.

"Are you awake, Gabriella?" Talya whispered.

"I am." Gabriella walked over to the tray, dropping down on the chilly floor rather than returning to her bed. Sitting here allowed her to talk to Talya more easily. The conversation was a welcome distraction. Without Talya, Gabriella suspected she would have succumbed to the mother of all panic attacks by now.

She'd always prided herself on being a strong woman, witnessing things in Morocco that would have frightened others. She realized she'd never experienced true terror until now, constantly wondering if each minute she spent down here would be her last.

"Did you not hear the two men come down with the trays of food earlier? The things they were saying?" Talya asked.

"I didn't." Gabriella's sleep had been restless since her arrival, something that had apparently caught up with her. If she'd missed the arrival of food—as well as the men talking—she must have finally managed a deep sleep. That should be comforting to her, especially considering this was the first time she'd actually felt like herself since the kidnapping. Instead, it bothered her to know that she could sleep through danger coming so close to her.

"I wondered—worried—that perhaps you'd gone quiet like the other women because of...what they said."

Gabriella trembled, an icy chill racking her frame. She wanted to blame it on the cold, but she knew it was fear. "What did they say?" she forced herself to ask, uncertain if she wanted to know.

"They stood outside your cell. One of them spit on the floor —I think it was the floor. Maybe you shouldn't eat the food they left for you."

Gabriella pushed the tray away, her stomach protesting despite the probable contamination.

"They spoke quickly," Talya said. "And quietly. My Spanish is weak, as you know. I heard a name. Ortiz."

"Emiliano," Gabriella said. "My husband."

"I see. Two other words I recognized. *Asta.*"

"Auction," Gabriella whispered.

"*Ja.* And *erede.* That one is confusing. I must not have heard them correctly."

Heiress.

Had the men been talking about auctioning her off?

"It means heiress," Gabriella said.

She and Talya had spoken a few times, those conversations followed by long silences. When they did speak, both of them seemed—by tacit agreement—to talk of happy things, childhood memories, favorite movies, songs, books. They'd used their discussions as escapes, distractions, sharing very little about their lives now, who they were.

"That is what I thought, but who—"

"Me. They were talking about me."

Talya fell silent for several moments. "Oh," she breathed at last. "Who...who are you?"

Gabriella grinned despite the panic slowly overtaking her. "Gabriella Torres. And you?"

"Talya Maes. I am a chemist."

"If we get out—" Gabriella started.

"If we get out," Talya whispered so quietly, Gabriella almost didn't hear her. It was apparent like the other women trapped down here, Talya's hope was fading as well.

This woman—a stranger—had come to mean more to Gabriella than friends she'd known for years.

"When we get out," Gabriella amended. "Let us make a pact. If one of us escapes, we will find the other. No matter what."

Talya laughed softly, sadly. "I wish I could see your face, Gabriella. Could see the fierceness I know to be there. It is a pact. It...it would be nice to know for sure that someone was looking for me."

CHAPTER FIFTEEN

No one had ever accused him of being indolent, but Nikolett made him feel lazy. Eric hovered behind her until she flapped a hand at him to go away. It wasn't the first time she'd done that in the past day she'd been here. Her other hand was typing, and she was also on the phone, speaking in rapid-fire Bulgarian.

He backed up, giving her space, and lacking anything better to do, he went into the kitchen and grabbed an egg and a bag of coffee. He rarely made Swedish-style coffee—he was a Dane at heart, and liked his coffee simple and elegant, preferring a perfect pour over—but preparing egg coffee gave him something to do.

Apparently, right now what he was good for was mostly preparing coffee, and he was okay with that.

The cynic in him, the rage and violence inside that had ruled him for so many years after his wives' deaths, was certain Gabriella Torres was already dead. He hadn't said that to her parents when he'd talked to them. He'd reassured them, promised them that he had and would continue to give De Leon whatever resources the admiral needed.

Being all but trapped on a tiny island in the middle of the Irish Sea, spouting platitudes at panicked parents and waiting around for status updates and after-action reports, went against his nature. He would be far happier on the streets of Madrid helping with the search and planning a raid and rescue.

He listened to the sound of Nikolett's voice and ignored the odd feeling of contentment it gave him to have her in his space. She'd spent the night in one of the second-floor guest rooms and showed back up at his door this morning, wearing casual clothes, her hair held back from her face in a low ponytail, ready to work.

Whatever she'd come to talk about had been set aside. She was now wholly focused on helping find Gabriella by working her contacts and connections in the black market businesses that the Camorra made their money from. She was the admiral of a territory, her time and resources both finite and precious, yet she'd immediately jumped in to help Castile. She hadn't demanded that De Leon formally request her help, which would have set an expectation of tit for tat, should she ever need help from him in turn.

She was up and moving now, pacing as she talked on the phone. He turned back to the pan on the stove, pulling it off at just the right time and adding the ice water, watching as the egg and grounds sank to the bottom.

"What did you do to that coffee?" Her voice came from right behind him, startling him.

Eric cursed and nearly bobbled the pan. "Damn it, Nikolett."

"You put...scrambled eggs in coffee?" She sounded horrified.

"Egg coffee. It's Swedish. My wife Trina liked it."

He poured the liquid out of the saucepan through an empty filter on top of his pour-over carafe.

"I forgot you were married before," she said quietly.

Eric waited for the creamy coffee to filter through, then took out two mugs, pouring one for each of them.

Nikolett eyed the coffee suspiciously before taking a sip. Then her brows rose and she looked up. "It's delicious."

"If you have nice beans, maybe a Norwegian roast, making it this way is unnecessary. This was the only kind of coffee she'd drink without putting a lump of sugar in her mouth."

Nikolett blinked. "I don't know that expression."

He chuckled. "I mean it literally. Some of the Swedes do it. Put a lump of sugar in their mouth, or hold it between their teeth, as they drink their coffee."

Nikolett took another long sip, then pulled her phone headset out of her ears, tucking it into her pocket.

He wanted to take the phone from her and force her to turn it off if only for a few minutes. She was going to work herself to death.

Eric clenched his teeth, heard his jawbone creaking. Nikolett was not his to take care of, except in an awkward fleet admiral to admiral way. If anything, he should be trying to put distance between them. After all, of the nine admirals, she was the only one who thought his orders were actually opening salvos in negotiations.

He set his cup down with a snap. "Why are you here, Nikolett?"

She jerked in surprise, and he could see the transition of emotions on her face, from relaxed and enjoying a good cup of coffee to defensive and confrontational.

He was an asshole.

Instead of helping her relax and take the break she probably needed, he'd forced her to put her armor back on, marshal her defenses.

"Fleet Admiral." She purred the words, and he was man enough to admit that the hairs on the back of his neck stood on end in alarm. She was pissed.

He widened his stance, crossed his arms, and looked down at her. She wasn't petite, but he towered over her, and he wasn't above using that.

Her eyes narrowed. He smiled because at this point, why not go all the way and really piss her off?

Nikolett's phone rang.

He stared accusingly at the pocket of her loose pants, the phone a visible weight.

She yanked the device out, looked at it, and then turned to pace away, answering as she slipped the earbud back into her ear. She spoke for several minutes, and Eric found himself wondering how hard it was to learn Hungarian.

Everything changed when Nikolett whipped around to face him. Her expression told him everything he needed to know. Three quick steps and he was out of the kitchen beside her, keeping pace as she zipped back to the dining table where she'd set up a workspace.

He watched her type, but she was typing in the same language she was speaking, leaving him to once more hover and wait. She ended the call, and as he inhaled to ask what was going on, she held up a finger, stopping him. She tapped out a number with her thumb and made another quick call. This time she was the one doing most of the speaking.

Eric was ready to shake information out of her when she ended the second call, but he didn't have to, because Nikolett swiveled to face him. He'd taken the chair beside her and when she turned, her knee touched his. It wasn't intimate, shouldn't have been intimate. He had more contact with strangers on airplanes.

But he felt the contact like the shock of a live wire.

Her face was calm, cold, but there was something in her eyes that made him want to burn down the world for her. Nikolett looked...afraid.

"One of my people has an alias, Szabó Olivér, an arms dealer who occasionally dabbles in human trafficking—buying not selling."

He nodded, waiting, while inside he wanted to break things, kill people. Do whatever it took to wipe that look off her face.

"He just got an invitation to a 'special' auction. In Spain."

Eric tensed but forced himself to be calm. Calm wasn't his natural state, but he was getting better. And besides, he was stuck on this fucking island. "What...who...are they auctioning?"

"The language used was that they were auctioning off some*thing* everyone was looking for." Nikolett tapped her screen, bringing up a website. The main picture was a still from the eyewitness video showing Gabriella half laying on stone steps, a man leaning over her menacingly, while up on the landing outside the door, Emiliano was getting worked over.

They'd blurred out Yurena's dead body.

Below that was a picture of Gabriella posing with her mother at a Torres fashion show.

"Something everyone is looking for," Eric repeated.

"And there was a mention of conditions on the sale."

"What kind of conditions?"

"There weren't any specifics."

"Wait. I want you to work directly with Vicente."

Eric reached out and grabbed his own computer from the

far side of the table. He had a perfectly good office he could have gone to, but he'd chosen to work out here. Near Nikolett.

He tapped a few keys, and a moment later the video window opened. The security minister of Castile looked calm and dangerous. And haunted. His wife was gone, and they were calling with news that was either bad or good, depending on whether or not Vicente assumed Gabriella was already dead.

"Fleet Admiral?"

Nikolett leaned forward, peering at Vicente's face. Then she straightened up with a snap, turning to her computer.

"Nikolett," Eric said. "Please tell Security Minister Coval—"

"I have an idea. Hold on." She flapped a hand at him.

Eric's eye twitched with irritation, but he trusted her...

He trusted her.

...and so he focused on Vicente.

"This is Admiral Varda of Hungary. She's been working the human trafficking angle because she has contacts in that world, and the assumption was that the Camorra would need somewhere to hold her, and they might have existing human trafficking facilities."

Vicente nodded once. "Please thank her for me."

"You're welcome," Nikolett said absently from just out of video range.

Vicente nodded again and stayed silent. Eric had known men like him, back in the early years of being a widower when he'd taken mercenary contracts with low survival odds. Men who were exactly as dangerous as they seemed. Who would do anything to get the job done, because they already considered their own souls forfeit.

"Vicente, there's no good way to say this. We think Gabriella is going to be sold at a human trafficking auction."

For a moment, Vicente's calm broke, and his expression twisted with grief and rage. Behind him another man started to curse. Vicente turned, and Eric saw Senator Ortiz leaning on a table, his head bowed between his hunched shoulders, fear lacing every syllable out of his mouth.

"Eric, look." Nikolett turned her computer, showing him an image. In it, a dark-haired, dark-eyed man with a medium skin tone and thick eyebrows stood talking to another man with a shaved head.

"This," she tapped the man with dark hair, "is what Miksa looks like when he's Szabó Olivér."

Eric looked at the video call, at the two men who were desperately searching for their wife.

"Nikolett might have a way for you to be at that auction," Eric said.

Vicente's face snapped back to the calm, tight mask. "I'll do anything."

Eric angled the computer so Vicente could see Nikolett. She glanced at him and there was something like surprise in her face for a moment, before she focused on Vicente, giving him the whole of her attention in that intense way she had.

"One of my security officers has an arms-dealer alias. He was invited to this auction," she told Vicente. "The two of you look enough alike that if you dyed your hair all black, you'd pass. This assumes that the few Camorra men who've done business with Szabó—that's the alias—aren't present at the auction in Spain."

"Your man has never been to Spain before under that name?"

"No, Szabó has taken meetings in Eastern Europe and once in Italy." Nikolett consulted her notes. "Do you speak Italian?" she asked Vicente.

"Passable. It is very similar to Castellano," he replied.

"The Szabó alias doesn't speak either. You'll need to take a translator. If Szabó doesn't say he'll bring his own when he accepts the invitation, they might provide someone who will translate from Italian to Hungarian for you. The invitation is in Italian, so we're assuming the auction will be in that language too."

"I speak no Hungarian," Vicente said grimly. "If they had a translator, it would blow the cover."

"I'll go. I'll go as the translator," Emiliano insisted, walking up to stand beside Vicente. "I can pretend to translate into Hungarian."

"You speak fluent Italian?" Nikolett asked.

Emiliano's jaw muscle flexed. "No. We don't need a translator. Castellano is similar to Italian."

"It would be better to take someone who is truly fluent as a translator. To capture subtleties." Nikolett turned to Eric. "Perhaps Rome could help?"

Eric held up his phone. "Milo, one of the security officers, is already on his way to Spain."

"She's my *wife*." Emiliano's snarled words snapped everyone's attention to him. His battered face was twisted with emotion, a toxic, panicked mix of anger and grief.

Eric watched as Vicente carefully put his arm around his husband, pulling the other man in to place a gentle kiss on his temple.

"I need to be there," Emiliano said much more softly. "I couldn't protect her before. Let me help rescue her."

Vicente looked at them—well, at the computer camera. "Perhaps this security officer from Rome could be our translator, while posing as a bodyguard."

It was risky, sending in Emiliano, who had no experience with anything like this, but fuck if Eric couldn't sympathize with that desperate need to protect someone.

"They know his face," Eric warned, pointing at Emiliano.

"I can make sure he looks nothing like Senator Ortiz," Vicente assured.

"You know the risks?" Eric asked.

Taking Emiliano in with him meant Vicente would not only be going undercover for a rescue mission, which was already dangerous, but he'd have to do all that while protecting Emiliano, with his only backup Milo, a man who was just as dangerous and capable as Vicente himself, but with whom Vicente had never worked before.

Vicente nodded.

"It's not a guarantee," Nikolett warned. "They might not be talking about Gabriella. And, since this is an existing auction, there are probably women from either Southeast Asia or Eastern Europe who were the original subjects of the auction."

"We'll do it," Emiliano insisted. "If Gabriella is there, if they're going to...to..."

Nikolett shared a worried look with Eric. "I can't guarantee your wife will be there. Can't guarantee that someone won't be there who might realize you're not Szabó."

Vicente nodded. "I don't need a guarantee, Admiral." Vicente looked at Emiliano. "I, we, need our wife back."

GABRIELLA STARED at the ceiling of her cell, her mind playing over the words Talya had heard.

Ortiz, auction, heiress.

They beat in her brain, a drumbeat pattern.

Ortiz, auction, heiress.

Her thoughts drifted to Emiliano and Vicente, and now, like always, when she saw her husbands' faces in her mind, her chest grew tight, her throat closing with tears she refused to shed.

She missed them. It was the only word she could think of to describe her feelings. She'd been married to them for mere days, and they'd spent the majority of those either fighting or fucking, but none of that mattered.

She ached for them, wished she could see them again. She would give them holy hell for being stubborn fools, then she would tell them exactly how their trinity marriage was going to work, and then she would seduce the socks off of them. Or maybe the seduction would come first.

It felt as if she'd been in this horrid place for weeks, though realistically she knew it had only been days. How many days, she couldn't begin to guess. As Talya said, time passed without anything to mark it. Without daylight or night, her time here had begun to feel like one long day that never ended.

She heard the loud creak of the door at the end of the hall. Food had been delivered to them already, so it was too soon for someone to come back.

Gabriella rose from the mattress, moving away from it until she stood in the center of the cell. She refused to cower, but there was no denying there was a part of her—one she wasn't proud of—that silently prayed the men had come for someone other than her.

Footsteps continued down the hallway. One person. Only one, who stopped just outside the bars to her cell. She didn't recognize him, and she briefly wondered if he was one of the men who'd kidnapped her and beaten Emiliano.

The only people to come down to the cells since the attack had been the men who delivered the food. She and Talya dubbed the one who served them Igor because he was a giant, menacing, silent creature, who stumbled in and leered at them before dropping their trays on the floor and fetching the empty ones. They hadn't seen the other man, the one who carried food down for the Eastern European women. She'd only heard him taunt the women, calling them whores—and worse—his cruel, frightening insults making them whimper and cry long after he'd gone.

This man had a swarthy complexion, marred by a thin scar along his right cheek that started at the end of his brow and went all the way to the edge of his jaw. His lecherous gaze traveled the length of her, mentally undressing her, assessing her worth. Never before had she felt so debased, humiliated. The man looked at her as if she were nothing more than an animal he planned to sell to the highest bidder, the word auction flashing through her mind again.

His gaze lingered on her breasts. She resisted the urge to lift her arms and cover herself when he licked his chapped lips salaciously.

She stiffened her spine, faking a fearlessness she didn't possess. Inside, she was quivering like a frightened kitten cornered by a Rottweiler, but there was no way she'd ever let this man see that. She knew who she was. Knew her worth. And it wasn't measured in female body parts or dollar signs.

"You have become a liability. A well-publicized problem, heiress." She recognized his voice as the other man, the cruel one. Rage radiated from him, as if the *gilipollas* actually believed that was her fault.

"I didn't ask to be brought here."

"Silence!" the man roared, slamming his hands against the bars so hard, the entire hallway seemed to reverberate in echo.

Gabriella could just make out the sound of whimpering farther down the hall, the Eastern European women unable to hide their terror. Gabriella sympathized with them when the man pulled out a key and unlocked the door to her cell. He stepped inside, slamming the bars behind him.

She took a step back, instantly hating herself for the act of cowardice.

The man moved forward. It only took three steps for him to reach her. Gabriella looked down, behind her, aware of the mattress brushing the back of her heels. It would take very little for this man to shove her down onto it.

But that didn't seem to be his intent.

"Ortiz is useless. A pawn in a game where he will never control the board."

Gabriella swallowed heavily, trying to dislodge the lump in her throat. The man had asked Emiliano for something. Something he hadn't been able to deliver?

Where the hell did that leave her?

"My parents," she said quickly. "As you know, they are very wealthy. They will pay whatever you ask for my safe return."

"I know who you are," the man said with disgust, spittle flying from his mouth, landing on her cheek. Bile gathered in her throat as she raised her hand and wiped it away. "But ransoming you to your parents is not an option either."

What the hell did that mean? Gabriella recalled the bombing at her family's estate. "Did you...are they..." She couldn't form the words, couldn't ask the question.

"Your parents are alive. And anxious for your return. Something the entire world knows, thanks to the media."

"I have money," she said, grasping at any straw.

The man shook his head. "No."

Gabriella wished she'd thought to move toward the wall. Her knees were perilously close to giving out on her, something that would drive her down to the mattress. She needed something to lean against because right now, the only thing keeping her upright was pride.

But how strong was that in the face of imminent death?

If Emiliano couldn't help her...

If they wouldn't ransom her to her parents...

If she couldn't be free...

What else was left for her?

Auction.

With that thought, a choked sob fell from her lips. One she couldn't hold back if she'd tried.

The sound of it captured the man's attention, his rage morphing to pleasure as he stroked the side of her face with his fat fingers. The fucking sadist enjoyed her fear.

"You are very beautiful, Gabriella," he said, as his oily gaze slid down her body, undressing her in his mind as he did so.

Her eyes narrowed in disgust. "And you are a filthy pig. One who will die a horrible death," she taunted, despite her better judgment.

The man slapped her, hard enough to wrench her neck in a way that hurt as much as the blow itself. Then, he threw his head back and laughed loudly, dismissing her words, treating them as little more than a joke. "You have spirit, my spoiled heiress. Do you know how much men would pay for the privilege of owning you, taming you, crushing you beneath their heel? You need a firm hand, a powerful master. There is nothing wrong with you a good rape or twenty wouldn't cure."

Gabriella stared at the man's face, blinking back the tears of pain, refusing to let them cloud her vision as she memorized every line, every blemish, every greasy inch of him.

Because she would be free one day. And when she was, she would find him and she would kill him with her bare hands.

Clenching her jaw, she held her words of hate inside, swallowing her own fury while silently plotting her revenge.

"You may still have some value yet," he said as he reached out and roughly took one of her breasts in his hand, squeezing it until she was helpless to hold back her gasp of pain. "Oh yes. You will make us rich men." Lowering his hand, he cupped her mound, her thin linen pants the only barrier as he used his touch to belittle, to humiliate her. "I bet this pussy tastes sweet."

She forced herself to stand silent as he manhandled her, refusing to show him any more fear. He fed on it, and she intended to see that—like her—he went hungry.

"Tomorrow," he grunted at last. "We will sell you to the highest bidder tomorrow. And I promise you, heiress, within a week, you'll be wishing you had this *filthy pig's* hands on you."

With that, he turned and left her cell, slamming the bars as he went. Gabriella stood still as a statue until his footsteps receded, the creaking of the door at the end of the hall closing. Even then, she remained where she was.

It wasn't until she heard Talya whisper her name that she crumpled into a heap on the mattress, her fear escaping in a flood of tears.

CHAPTER SIXTEEN

Gabriella struggled against the rough-hewn ropes binding her hands behind her back, the action only serving to painfully scratch her wrists, the tight knots refusing to give way.

She and Talya had been forced to stand together in the doorway of a small room off to the left of the makeshift stage, to watch as the first woman was paraded around in front of the crowd. She couldn't see the audience, her vision blocked by a flimsy decorative partition.

Igor and Pig—as she'd begun to call the man who'd manhandled her as he told her about the auction—had escorted each of them out of the cells, one at a time, earlier in the day. They'd been hooded and handcuffed, and then shoved into the back of a van. None of them had been drugged for the journey, the Eastern European women whimpering in fear during the ride, which wasn't more than an hour.

Upon arrival, they were all escorted inside, the hoods and cuffs only removed once they were secured in a large, window-less bedroom that looked like the dressing room of a brothel, lined with clothing racks that contained skimpy lingerie, bondage wear, corsets, and bustiers. The only other door in the bedroom led to an attached bathroom filled with makeup, hair products, and perfumes.

Gabriella had nearly cried the first time she'd seen Talya's face, the woman—her friend—a beautiful dark-skinned woman with black eyes, high cheekbones, and thick, long hair that hung to the small of her back. Talya's clothing hung on her, little more than rags at this point, ripped and stained with dried blood. There were scabbed cuts and fading bruises on her face and arms, obviously put there from her time in the box and the beating she'd endured. Despite the horror surrounding them, Talya's face had lit up when she'd seen her, smiling as if they were old friends being reunited after years apart.

The men had chosen outfits for everyone but Talya, who was cuffed to a chair, forced to watch as Gabriella and the other women got ready. When it was Gabriella's turn in the bathroom, they forced her to strip, then shower while they observed. Pig had made it clear that if she didn't prepare herself for the auction in an acceptable manner, he and Igor would wash her themselves.

Gabriella swallowed down the bile in her throat as she recalled the horrible men's eyes on her as she showered and dressed as quickly as humanly possible in the silky nightgown she'd been provided. While she'd been in the shower, they'd taken away her old clothes, and as much as she hated the dirty, stained garments, she would rather be wearing those—particularly the bra and panties—than the clean but thin chemise-style lingerie.

While she did her makeup, Igor behind her, watching every move, Gabriella had heard Pig asking Talya if she was ready to give them what they wanted. When she refused, Pig had dragged her into the bathroom by her hair.

Gabriella had half risen from the stool, wanting to help Talya, protect her.

Igor had forced her to sit, while Pig ripped Talya's clothes off and shoved her into the shower.

For a moment, it seemed like Talya had refused one time too many, and now she too was going to be auctioned, but Pig said this was practice, a preview of what would happen to her if she didn't give them what they wanted.

Once they'd all finished dressing, Pig had held up a bag and told them it was time to "accessorize." Gabriella and Talya had stiffened, but the other women hadn't reacted, and Gabriella realized they didn't understand. Everything about this was terrifying, but Gabriella couldn't imagine how much worse being in this situation would be while also having no idea what was being said.

Pig started with the Eastern European woman wearing a vinyl mini-skirt and under-bust corset, her breasts bare. Igor held her immobile, arms behind her back, as Pig put nipple clamps on her, tightening them as tears of pain slid down her cheeks.

The other woman had darker blonde hair, a lovely honey color. They'd put her in a brown leather corset and nothing else, so though her breasts were covered, her sex and ass were bare.

Gabriella had started to shake as the brown-corseted woman was bent over the bed. She'd gasped when Pig took a butt plug with a horse's tail out of the bag. He passed it to Igor, who shoved it in the woman's ass, using only spit as lube.

Gabriella had forced herself not to scream or run when they approached her, though she couldn't stop herself from shaking.

The relief she felt when they pulled out a white leather collar and leash made her light-headed.

Talya was last, and she too got a collar, but hers was a woven nylon dog collar. Igor attached leashes so he could lead them around like dogs. Then Pig cuffed Talya again, opting instead to use the rope to bind Gabriella.

Gabriella fought back tears as the first woman was sold, and the second pushed onstage for her time under the spotlight. The entire thing felt unreal. Where were Vicente and Emiliano? How would they ever find her now?

"Gabriella," Talya whispered, her voice tight with terror.

Gabriella looked over at her friend, who was visibly shaking. Despite the shower and makeup, Talya's time in the cell was taking its toll on her. Fear radiated from her dark eyes, her body little more than skin and bones after too many days subsisting on only bread and cheese.

"I...it..." Gabriella fought to reassure Talya, to tell her she was all right, but the words got lodged, stuck.

Instead, it was Talya who found the strength to tell the lie. *"Het is oke."*

VICENTE TAPPED his fingers against the glass of prosecco sitting on the table in front of him. Emiliano was seated beside him, looking nothing like himself, thanks to a blond wig, prosthetic nose, and black framed glasses. The makeup hid the bruises on his face.

Milo Moretti stood in the shadows behind him, near a wall. The Italian wore the ill-fitting suit of a thug, the loose lines of the jacket meant to disguise-but-not-really the double shoulder holster. Their guns had been confiscated at the door and placed in a lockbox, which they'd expected. Milo had carried two cheap guns with empty magazines. If they had to leave the weapons behind, it wouldn't be a loss, and with no bullets, the guns couldn't be turned against them.

If they needed guns to get out of this situation, the mission had failed. The plan was to go in, buy Gabriella, and leave, all while maintaining their cover identities.

That was going to be a tall order, and so much of their success depended on Gabriella's reaction when she saw them. And, Vicente admitted in the quiet of his own mind, on his reaction to her. If she was beaten and bloody, if their beautiful, fierce wife had been broken...

He'd mentally mapped the path he'd take through the room. Both he and Milo had ceramic blades concealed in their clothing. He figured in the first minute, he could slit the throats of at least two of the guards. Hopefully Milo would have his own weapon out and would be engaged by then.

By minute three, one of the guards at the front would have his gun up, and he and Milo would both be dead on the floor, Emiliano and Gabriella left to the mercy of these men. He had to hold on to that, remember it, so that no matter what condition she was in, he'd maintain the op plan.

Rufino Nori, looking exactly like his picture from the briefing, stepped up onstage. He welcomed them in Italian. Vicente looked at Emiliano, who gave a little start, then leaned over, covering his mouth with his hand as he pretended to translate.

When the first woman appeared onstage, Vicente's blood chilled. Beside him, Emiliano started to pray. Vicente wasn't a religious man, and he knew Emiliano wasn't either, but he understood the impulse.

The first woman being auctioned was bare-chested, the chain between the nipple clamps swinging. She moaned in pain as Rufino tugged on it but didn't react when he yanked the front of the skirt up, showing the audience her sex.

The second woman wore a corset and a butt plug, and struggled a little when Rufino turned her around and tried to bend her over. One of the guards jumped up onstage, forcing her arms behind her back, elbows locked so that she was forced to bend or have her shoulders dislocated.

Once she was in the position he wanted, Rufino spread her ass, showing off the plug. The crowd laughed, and Vicente forced his lips into a smile.

Emiliano had stopped praying, and somehow, that was worse.

Whatever they'd done to Gabriella, they'd find a way to fix it. To help her. The first two women were auctioned off in a matter of fifteen minutes each, the auctioneer working hard to drum up interest.

They were sold to the same person, a woman seated at a table near the front of the elegant great room in the large estate outside of Madrid. There were only ten tables, and of those, seven were filled. Tactically it would have been better for there to be a larger crowd because the Camorra would have less time to focus on each individual bidder. Vicente hated that he was relying on someone else's intel, and someone else's alias, but so far, the admiral of Hungary had delivered.

With no basis for comparison, he had no idea if this crowd was the typical size, or if the presence of "something everyone was looking for" had drawn an extra crowd. Gabriella's kidnapping was still commanding the lead in every news broadcast and on every front page.

Rufino stepped back up onto the small stage after delivering the second blonde woman with haunted eyes to the bidder in the front. He smiled, a genuine, excited expression, and started to speak.

Emiliano leaned toward him, ostensibly to start translating. He cupped his hand around his mouth again, to hide the fact that his lips weren't moving.

It was Milo's voice that came through the state-of-the-art comm hidden in Vicente's ear, the Italian security officer's voice a low murmur as he translated what the auctioneer was saying.

"Now it is time to meet the woman you came here for. This is a rare opportunity. But, obviously, there are some restrictions with this particular purchase."

Beside him, Emiliano jerked, whipping his head to face the small stage. Vicente dropped his hand below the tabletop, grabbed Emiliano's knee, and squeezed. Hard.

Emiliano leaned in once more, his hand cupped to hide his mouth. "If they've hurt her—"

"Gabriella *will* be hurt." Vicente didn't bother to soften the words but kept them low, mindful that he couldn't be heard speaking Castellano when the borrowed alias didn't know the language.

They'd been over this. Emiliano and Gabriella both had to hide their reactions, but neither had any experience controlling their reactions in dangerous situations. He'd been able to prep Emiliano, to some degree, but these next few minutes were going to be hard.

"The buyer must agree to keep her for a period of six months. No selling her...or ransoming her back to her loving mother. Tempting as it may be." He chuckled as if he'd made a good joke. "After six months, if you choose to try to recoup what you've spent, you have our blessing."

"How would you enforce this?" the man seated closest to them asked in Castellano. "You cannot tell me what to do with my property."

Rufino, who'd been all gentlemanly smiles, scowled, his eyes narrowed, dark and deadly. He responded in Italian, as if making a point. "We will enforce it the way we enforce anything."

The threat was pure menace and hung in the air. The man who asked the question nodded once.

"To ensure that you're buying her for the right reason, we expect her new owner to use her before leaving."

Vicente's body flushed cold.

Emiliano inhaled sharply. "Do they mean...?"

"You expect us to put on a show for you?" another bidder scoffed.

"If you would prefer not to expose yourself, we can provide you with a wine or beer bottle." Rufino shrugged negligently, as if offering up glass bottles to be used to rape someone was normal rather than horrific.

Emiliano was breathing hard. Under the cover of the tablecloth, his hand found Vicente's, squeezing tightly.

"She is strong," Vicente murmured, but inside he was cold. He'd been prepared to hit Gabriella, even beat her if necessary to ensure no one suspected this was a rescue. Bruises healed.

If he had to...

"And now," Milo's murmured translation cut through his inner turmoil. "Let us see her."

"NOW IT IS time to meet the woman you came here for." The man on the stage was speaking Italian, but Gabriella understood most of what he was saying.

"Come on, slut. Your turn. Time to get you ready." Pig yanked on the leash, and Gabriella choked, falling back a few steps. Beside her, Talya too was pulled back into the small side room. Igor swung the door closed, blocking out the auctioneer's voice. He was saying something about conditions.

Her turn.

This isn't real.

Even now, with fear thick at the back of her throat, she was having trouble believing this was really happening. Vicente and Emiliano would find her, would save her. She was, had been, so sure of that. Sure that it wouldn't actually get this far, that her suffering was finite and would end.

They were selling her. This was happening.

Talya struggled and Gabriella watched, oddly numb, as Pig placed a ball gag in Talya's mouth, fastening it behind her head. "Watch what happens to her. It will be you next time if you don't give the boss what he wants."

Gabriella started when Igor grabbed her upper arm. Her mind was screaming at her to run, to fight. She remembered reading once that, despite popular opinion, there weren't just two reactions to danger—fight and flight—but a third. Freeze. That's how she felt. Cold. Frozen.

Pig cursed. "Hold still, you stupid fucking whore." She'd begun to tremble so badly that he couldn't untie the rope.

The moment her hands were free, she sprang forward, her reaction flipping to "flight" without conscious decision. If she'd been thinking, she wouldn't have tried to run right then, not when Igor was holding her, his grip on her arm implacable. Reaching for the leash still attached to the collar around her neck, he jerked her toward him, his breath rancid, stinking of cigarettes and onions.

She closed her eyes, fighting back a wave of dizziness. She had to find a way to get through this, to push the panic clawing its way out from down deep.

I am Gabriella Torres.

She let those words play in her mind.

Vicente will find me. He'd told her so, said it back at the safe house. She held onto the memory, to the look in his eyes. Vicente, Emiliano, her parents, the Masters' Admiralty...they wouldn't stop looking. They would find her. She just had to survive.

And Gabriella Torres could survive anything.

She was calm inside, though still trembling and cold, as the door opened and Igor yanked on the leash, tugging her toward the stage.

Igor guided her up, then turned her toward the crowd. There were two spotlights, one on either side of the stage, shining so bright, they blinded her to everything behind them. Unfortunately, her hearing was fine. There was a murmur of voices and she felt the weight of too many eyes on her thinly clad body.

Rage welled in her, and she let it burn away the cold that kept her calm. She opened her eyes, and though she couldn't see them clearly, she scanned the shadowy shapes of the crowd. She let her disdain for the type of people who would buy and sell women like chattel show on her face. Her blood heated with fury and in her mind's eye, she imagined chaining the door to this place and setting it on fire with everyone trapped inside. She would see every single one of them burn in hell.

I am Gabriella Torres.

She repeated those words like a mantra, a prayer, even as the auctioneer began the sale. When the price reached two million dollars, she refused to listen, refusing to believe that her worth could be determined by dollar signs.

Closing her eyes once more, she focused solely on her breathing. Air flowed in. Air flowed out. In. And out.

She'd just about calmed the painful racing of her heart when she was pulled out of her head by a single word.

"*Venduta!*"

That word sounded like *vendido.*

Sold.

"For ten million dollars."

Her eyes flew open, and some small part of her was dispassionately impressed by how much she'd gone for.

The auctioneer grabbed her arm. She knocked his hand away. He grinned, then snatched up the dangling leash.

A man stepped onto the stage, blocking the spotlights with his massive shoulders, the harsh lighting cast him in shadow. The auctioneer passed him the leash. He took it with one hand, and the rage that had insulated her disappeared, leaving nothing but breathless fear. A huge hand gripped her upper arm, and the stasis that had held her broke.

She scrambled back, trying to break his hold on her arm, to pull the leash from his other hand. He squeezed her arm, and she lashed out, fighting him. Hopelessly. Foolishly.

"No," she whispered. This wasn't happening. She gave up trying to tug the leash from his grip and instead balled her hand. She punched him, but he leaned to the side, avoiding the blow.

"No!" she yelled louder, refusing it. All of it. "No!"

HIS WIFE WAS TERRIFIED, fighting for her life. Halfway across the room, Gabriella was dropping to her knees, and he realized she was still fighting, using the move to slide out of Milo's hold for a moment. Emiliano heard her sob of rage and terror. He stayed seated, forcing himself to watch casually as Milo once more grabbed her by one arm and this time got a fistful of her hair, yanking her to her feet and then off the stage. Milo bent her arm up behind her back before giving her a little shove, forcing her toward their table.

She was closer now, and he could see the tears on her face, the blind panic in her eyes. He'd nearly cheered when she sneered in regal disdain, and had a sense that everything was going to be okay when he saw that she looked relatively unharmed and was calm. She'd been calm right up until the end. Until Rufino said sold and she saw Milo.

Now she was scared and hurting. He should have gone up

there to get her. She probably would have recognized him, even with the makeup. She would have known this was a rescue.

That was precisely why Vicente had sent Milo to get her.

Vicente cleared his throat as Rufino approached with a tablet. Emiliano jumped up and, in his role as assistant/translator, he handled the payment. He keyed in the bank account number and routing information on the screen Rufino held out, answering Rufino's questions with nods and shakes of his head.

When Rufino's phone beeped, signaling the transaction had gone through, the man grinned and went over to shake Vicente's hand. When Rufino tried to start up a conversation, Vicente stared him down without saying a word.

Rufino stopped, looking awkward, and maybe a little intimidated.

A fierce pride at his husband's ability to be terrifying filled Emiliano.

He went back to the table, noticing that while they'd been dealing with the payment, some of the other buyers had cleared out, including the woman who'd bought the first two victims. And Milo had kept Gabriella back. Smart. Vicente had explained multiple times that one of the most dangerous points in this "operation" was when Gabriella got close enough to recognize them. Her reaction might give them away.

And to keep that from happening, Vicente might have to hit her. Hurt her. During planning, that had seemed nasty but understandable.

But as Milo brought her to the table, as he got a close-up view of her terrified, tear-stained face, Emiliano's heart broke.

"Please don't do this," Gabriella sobbed.

No, this was too much. He had to go to her, to show her that—

"If you react like her husband, you kill her." Vicente's

words were a mere breath of sound as he rose calmly to his feet, as if to greet a guest.

Emiliano reached down, grabbing the edges of his chair so hard, his fingers turned white. He remembered what Vicente had said, about doing immoral things for moral reasons. And he remembered his own words to Vicente, that after this was over, Gabriella would need him, because Vicente would understand what she'd been through.

Milo released her arm and instead grabbed her neck, holding her by neck and hair. Vicente stepped to the side so he was standing next to rather than behind the table.

Gabriella was a meter away, and Emiliano willed her to look up, to recognize Vicente, who didn't look that different from normal. He knew that the moment she realized this was a rescue might be the same moment this all went to fuck, but he didn't want her to be afraid even one minute longer than she had to be.

Her gaze darted over them, but her eyes were glassy with fear. She wasn't really seeing either of them.

Look up. Look up. It's us.

Milo brought her forward and forced her to her knees at Vicente's feet. Gabriella's lovely dark hair fell forward around her face, and a heartbroken sob seemed to echo through the room.

Vicente grabbed Emiliano's arm, pulling him in, his lips almost touching Emiliano's ear. "Milo, Emiliano needs to demand that everyone leaves. We need fewer witnesses."

His back to the room as he held Gabriella down, Milo translated the words into Italian, speaking slowly. Emiliano straightened away from Vicente, looking at Rufino. He repeated what Milo had said with the half of his brain that was rationally processing what was going on rather than the half that was horrified and heartbroken about what they were doing to their wife...and what they, Vicente, still had to do.

Whatever he said was right because over the next five minutes, the remaining bidders filed out, some casting longing glances at Gabriella's kneeling form.

While the guests all filed out, the guards remained, two standing sentry at each doorway and armed to the teeth. There were too many for them to fight, especially without their guns. Resigned, Vicente nodded to Milo, who started to release Gabriella's neck and hair.

"Hold, please," Rufino said. "There is someone else I'd like to see this."

Vicente grabbed Emiliano. "Say no. One word."

"No," Emiliano said aloud, not needing Milo's translation for that one.

Rufino's expression hardened. "This is one of the conditions of the sale."

Emiliano pretended to translate to Vicente as Milo spoke through their earpieces. Vicente nodded once, looking irritated.

One of the guards disappeared through a door at the back.

Milo was speaking again, the only one free to do so since no one could see his mouth. "Depending on who comes through that door, we might need to run for it."

Vicente grunted in acknowledgement.

Emiliano wondered if Gabriella could hear Milo's whispered words, but she was whimpering softly with each exhale, so he didn't think so.

The door at the back opened, and the guard appeared with...another woman. She was dressed like the first two victims had been, in a corset, and there was a thick gag in her mouth. Another victim. One they hadn't auctioned off. Why? Rufino had said he wanted the new person to see this. All those thoughts passed through Emiliano's mind and were quickly forgotten.

Clearly she wasn't a threat, so he ignored the woman as the guard forced her into a chair at the nearby table so she could watch.

Vicente gestured to Milo, who finally let go of Gabriella.

Vicente bent, reaching for their wife. Gabriella lashed out, slapping Vicente's hand away and then lunging forward, not trying to get away but to attack Vicente.

A fierce pride was followed by a desire to yell at her not to fight back, because if she fought back...

Vicente slapped her, a short shock of sound, followed by Gabriella's hard inhale.

Emiliano closed his eyes for a moment, fighting his own instincts. All their lives depended on them seeing this through.

Vicente grabbed Gabriella by the neck, fingers on top of the collar, jerking her up so she was still on her knees but no longer huddled in on herself. She raised her hand to fight, just as Vicente forced her chin up.

Gabriella's eyes went wide.

CHAPTER SEVENTEEN

Vicente.

The man holding her by the throat. The man who'd bought her...it was Vicente.

His hair was missing the silver at the temples, and he had a dark goatee, but it was Vicente.

The hand she'd raised to lash out, futile as fighting was, started to fall. Vicente caught her wrist with his free hand. The fingers around her throat tightened. A warning.

His eyes were hard, giving nothing away, but his fingers at her neck loosened, and the tip of his index fingers, hidden under her hair, stroked the side of her neck. A caress.

Vicente was here. They'd found her, were rescuing her, except...they were surrounded by guards with guns, and clearly Vicente wasn't here as himself.

She needed to play along. Pretend she didn't know them. Pretend that she was still terrified.

She needed to be scared or angry, but the sweet flood of relief was nearly as overwhelming as her fear had been, and she was having trouble thinking past it.

Vicente scanned her features and then he hauled her up by her throat. It hurt, and she grabbed his wrist, her bare feet scrambling on the floor as she tried to get her legs under her. He jerked on the buckle of the collar, undoing it and tossing it aside. Vicente looked her up and down, his expression first dispassionate, and then his lips quirked in a cold smile.

He snapped his fingers and hands grabbed her from behind. She jumped in surprise, and at the feel of unfamiliar hands, she didn't have to pretend to be scared. The big man who'd dragged her across the room jerked her back against his body, his fingers digging into her arms.

Vicente ran the backs of his fingers down her body, pressing the slick satin of the chemise against her.

What...what was he doing? Why weren't they leaving? Gabriella's stomach twisted, and for a horrible moment, she thought maybe Vicente wasn't who he said he was. Or the reverse, he was exactly as dark and amoral as he'd claimed to be. Maybe he was some sort of traitor to the society, and he really had just bought her.

Tears filled her eyes, and she let out a hard sob. "Vi—"

He pinched her nipple, which was hard, thanks to the cool air, all too visible through the thin fabric. He pinched her hard enough to send a shockwave of pain through her, and she let out a sob. He didn't let go, either, twisting to increase the pain until she cried out a second time.

This couldn't be happening. Oh God, if Vicente was evil, if he'd orchestrated all of this, Emiliano was dead. He'd probably been dead since the day of the kidnapping.

Through watery eyes, Gabriella watched as Vicente motioned to a blond man seated at the table. The blond rose and leaned in so Vicente could whisper in his ear, nodding in response to whatever Vicente was saying.

They broke apart, and the blond man came the long way around the table to stand beside her. He cleared his throat.

"My name is David Gorin. I'm Mr. Olivér's translator."

That voice.

Gabriella whipped her head to look at the blond man, realizing as she did, he'd positioned himself so that when she looked at him, the mafiosos wouldn't be able to see her face.

Emiliano. This time, her sob was one of relief. He was alive. He was here. He was...blond. And his nose was wrong. But it was him. That meant Vicente wasn't some evil double agent. Her husbands were here to rescue her.

"My employer wants you to know that he is not unreasonable, but you must understand that you are his property."

Gabriella let a small smile slip free and saw the relief in Emiliano's eyes.

The hands on her arms tightened. A warning. Whoever the man holding her was, he was with them, which meant he too was playing a part.

She took a breath, prepared to play along for however long it took them to get out of here. "I am not his property. Tell him to go fuck himself."

Behind the glasses, Emiliano's eyes were haunted but out loud he said, "Actually, my employer will be fucking *you*. Here and now."

Gabriella's eyes went wide. Emiliano couldn't mean that literally. His eyes closed, and he swallowed hard, looking like he was going to be sick. When he opened his eyes, he met her gaze, holding it.

He was serious. Gabriella whipped her head to Vicente, heart slapping against her ribs. His assessing gaze slid over her, and he played cold and cruel so well, that fear returned, edging out her relief.

Vicente snapped again, and the man behind her slid his

hands up to her shoulders, grabbing the straps of the chemise and yanking them down her arms.

The slick fabric slithered down her body, leaving her naked from the waist up. She grabbed the fabric, tried to yank it back up.

Under the guise of adjusting his hold on her as she struggled, the man behind her bent low enough to whisper, "I'm Milo. And I'm sorry."

Vicente tsked at her struggles and grabbed one bare breast, his fingers closing over her possessively. She jerked back, but there was nowhere to go; the man at her back was as solid as a wall.

"Normally my employer doesn't let others watch him, but using his property before leaving was a condition of the sale." Emiliano spoke loud enough to be heard by Rufino, Pig, Igor, and Talya, who were all seated at a nearby table. His expression was tortured.

Talya. They'd set this up so Talya could watch her being raped. They were hoping to scare her into giving them whatever it was they wanted.

She sobbed, and Vicente chuckled. Rage flashed through her and she brought up one leg, kicking out, aiming for Vicente's dick.

He had to let go of her tit to dance out of the way, but before she'd recovered her balance—having leaned heavily on the man with the Italian accent behind her—Vicente grabbed her arm, yanking her out of the other man's grip. Her upper arms were going to be black and blue.

Vicente shoved her, hard, so she fell back against the table, her arms braced on either side of her, the straps of the dress digging into her elbows, her breasts exposed and vulnerable. She scanned the room, looking at her husbands, their accomplice Milo, and then at the auctioneer, Igor, Pig, the guards, and finally Talya.

Her friend's eyes were wide and filled with tears.

Talya had no way of knowing that this was all an act. That this was a rescue.

Vicente snapped, and Milo reached for her. She reacted without thinking, raising one arm, the strap of the chemise ripping as she did, and slapped Milo hard.

Milo held perfectly still for several long breaths, then slowly turned to face her.

Fresh fear slid through her, and she didn't have to fake her panicked scramble away from him.

She was so focused on Milo that she didn't see Vicente move to intercept her. The world spun dizzyingly as one arm came around her waist, the other tangling in her hair. He pulled her body flush against his but forced her head back so she was looking at the ceiling.

His lips touched her neck, slid up to her ear.

"Fight me. You have to fight me."

She thrashed in his hold, tried to stomp on his toes, which was comically useless.

"I will have to hurt you, *mi esposa*. I am sorry."

"Let me go, you son of a bitch," she snarled, the words slightly strangled by the awkward position of her head and neck.

Vicente bit her earlobe, hard enough that her shriek of pain wasn't pretend.

"The fastest way out of here is for me to rape you while they watch."

Gabriella heard the desolation in his words, below the grim determination to do whatever it took to get them all out of this alive.

He released her, stepping back. The move, combined with

the emotional impact from that staggering statement, had her stumbling.

Vicente laughed, a cruel sound, and then stepped in front of her, blocking the audience's view, before he grabbed her gown, yanking it down so that it cleared her hips, sliding to the floor.

Gabriella wrapped her arms around her nakedness. She wanted to run. Why couldn't they just run and get away and be safe? She wanted to be back in control of her body and her life.

Vicente met her gaze, held it. He seemed to be willing her strength. His mouth moved, but the words were silent, forcing her to read his lips.

"Cry. Scream."

It was far too easy to start crying, a quiet sobbing that was a mixture of pent-up emotion, fresh fear for whatever was about to happen, and relief.

Somewhere behind her, Emiliano made a soft sound, a low moan of suppressed rage and fear.

Arms gathered her, pulling her close. Vicente's lips brushed her hair, and he whispered softly to her. How beautiful she was, how brave she was. Gabriella turned into him, huddling against her husband.

For a brief, wonderful moment, she felt safe. Totally and completely safe.

But she wasn't. She couldn't be.

She stiffened in Vicente's embrace, realizing what she, what they, had just done. Vicente's hand pressed hard against the small of her back.

"We are still playing our parts." Vicente breathed the words into her hair, so low she had to strain to hear. "It is a very human reaction to seek and accept comfort, even if it's from the one who hurts you."

That was a heartbreaking truth, and for a moment she

thought of Talya. Talya who was right there. Maybe they could take her with them. Maybe they could rescue her too.

"I have to touch you. Intimately," he continued. "But I cannot...I cannot bring myself..." He ran his hands up and down her naked back. She shivered in reaction to the touch and heard a cruel chuckle come from across the room. She wondered what it looked like from the outside. Did it look like she'd given up, that she'd accepted her fate, this stranger's ownership of her? She realized her breathing was still uneven from crying, and maybe that, and the shiver, looked like she was trembling with fear.

And she was afraid. She was afraid and wished, desperately, for this to be over. To somehow fast-forward.

"I hope they will allow me to use my hands. If not, I might have to use a wine bottle."

It took a moment for his words to penetrate. "N-no. Please. No." She wasn't pretending now.

Vicente's hands slid down her bare back and he dug his fingers into her ass, the touch cruel in comparison to his words.

"My love, my wife, I am so sorry, so sorry."

Irritation sparked to life, eclipsing fear and horror both. She didn't want Vicente apologizing. She wanted him to be cold and commanding and to get them all the hell out of here.

"Don't apologize," she whispered back. "Just get it over with." To make sure he got the point, she pinched him.

One of her arms was folded and squished between them, and she had enough wiggle room to pinch his pectoral hard enough that he grunted.

Vicente released her butt, and she started to step back, prepared to go back to fighting. The brief interlude with him had been enough to, hopefully, get her through the rest of this.

Vicente banded one arm around her waist, and the other

hand came down on her ass in a punishing slap. The sound echoed, and again either Igor or Pig laughed.

Gabriella pushed against his chest, but Vicente held her to him. Spanked her again.

And again.

"Ouch!" She wiggled and yelped. The spanking reminded her of that scene in the kitchen, and she met Vicente's gaze. Something sparked in the depths of his eyes.

He grabbed her by the hair, jerking her forward so he could whisper in her ear.

"Can you play along, little girl?" Vicente purred for only her to hear.

Gabriella's breath caught and heat slid through her body. There were a million reasons why she shouldn't respond to his teasing, to his challenge the same way she would have if they were safe and home. This was a thousand kinds of fucked up, and she was still, at her core, terrified. Yet her body, and her mind, jumped at the opportunity to handle this nightmare situation in a very...very...different way.

Vicente spun her around and forced her facedown over the table. She screamed, more from surprise than fear, but it worked. She heard laughs and a whimper of distress—the men and Talya.

He kicked her feet wide, and she whimpered with embarrassment at being exposed, but it didn't last long. Vicente was there behind her, his thighs against hers, hiding her exposed sex even as he gathered her wrists at her back, pinning them there.

With her head turned to the side, she could see Vicente motion for Emiliano to lean closer. She was close enough she could hear what they were saying and thought maybe it was for her benefit.

"We're going to play a game," Vicente murmured. "A little role play."

"No," Emiliano muttered. "Just get it over with and—"

"I'd like to avoid raping our wife." Vicente paused and pinched her ass. Hard. "Don't forget to scream, *mi luz.*"

Gabriella inhaled, then shrieked, loud enough that Emiliano winced. Ha!

"Role play," Vicente repeated, still leaning in as if discussing something with his translator. "Virgin concubine."

Gabriella suppressed the urge to break into gales of—possibly hysterical—laughter.

"Milo, cover," Vicente ordered.

The big man moved up next to Vicente, and for a moment they had privacy, Vicente and Milo's backs blocking the view of her, Emiliano, and hiding anything they might say, as long as they were quiet.

"No, virgin doesn't fit her," Vicente mused. "Scream, *mi luz.*"

"You asshole," she shrieked, "don't touch me!"

The corner of his lips twitched. Emiliano was looking back and forth between them, eyes wide with what might have been horror.

"Better this than a bottle," Vicente murmured.

Emiliano's eyes closed, and when he opened them, he seemed resolved. "You be the barbarian warlord. She's the kidnapped Spanish princess."

Gabriella froze, felt Vicente do the same.

Huh.

Emiliano had that all right on the tip of his tongue?

Well, well, well.

When they got out of here, after she had some intense therapy, they were going to block out some time to listen to Emiliano's role-play scenarios.

"Time's up," Milo murmured. He stepped back, the moment of privacy finished.

Vicente shifted to the side so he could slap her ass again. Damn it, the man had big, heavy hands. She didn't have to fake the yelp of pain, but that pain spread through her ass in a wave of liquid heat.

Emiliano leaned back, then dropped into one of the chairs. He tipped his head to look at her, where her face was pressed to the table. When he spoke, it was loudly enough for the audience to hear.

"My employer wants to know if you've been spanked before."

"Go to fucking hell," Gabriella snarled. Terrified, angry captive was a role all too easy to play right now. She kicked out, managing to get Vicente's shin.

Her reward was a series of ten vicious spanks. She squeezed her knees together, shrieking as each blow landed right after the previous, giving her no time to recover. But he'd been careful never to hit the same spot twice.

When the only sound was her panting breaths, Emiliano cleared his throat and said again, "My employer wants to know if you've been spanked before."

"Go. To. Hell."

Vicente hauled her up. The world spun, and then she was shoved back against someone. She hoped it was Emiliano, but it was Milo again.

"He wants her arms up," Emiliano said. "Behind her head."

Under the guise of translating, Emiliano was giving direction.

Milo grabbed her wrists, easily forcing her arms into place even as she cursed and struggled.

Vicente stood calm and relaxed, one hand in his pocket as his gaze traveled lazily up and down her body. Gabriella looked to the side, to where the men who'd kidnapped her watched, to where Talya sat gagged and bound, tears streaming down her face.

For a moment, reality crashed over her, and she started to huddle in on herself, whimpering as she tried in vain to twist her body in such a way as to hide her nakedness.

Milo squeezed her wrists gently.

A reminder that they were in this together, that everything that happened was another step toward the exit.

"Shall I ask the question again?" Emiliano asked her.

Gabriella took a deep breath. She couldn't make words come, so instead she raised her chin, a silent defiance.

Vicente smiled as he came closer. He touched her chin with one finger, then bent as if...as if he were going to kiss her.

Then he pulled back and slapped her breast.

Gabriella screamed in shock, in fear, but not in pain. Weirdly, that hurt less than the spanking, though it sounded just as loud.

He slapped the other breast, chuckled when she screamed again.

Again and again, he spanked her tits, making them bounce and sway, and as he did it, Vicente held her gaze, a dark, forbidden desire shining in the depths. When he bent to take her nipple in his mouth, she fought because she needed to, because she had to do something to make sure she didn't arch up into his mouth.

Vicente's warm, wet mouth encompassed her nipple. His tongue swept over her, and it felt so damned good, her knees went weak. Then his teeth closed on her hard, harder, biting down. She screamed, the sound breaking on a sob...of need.

She fought as he released her pink, aching nipple and switched to the other breast. She fought because she wanted her hands free to grab Vicente's head and hurry him up. To reach out and drag Emiliano into this.

He sucked her other nipple, teeth holding the very tip so his tongue could flick her. With each flick, her hips jerked, and somewhere in the back of her mind, she worried that if Vicente kept it up, her thighs would soon be slick with the proof of her depraved enjoyment.

"Scream," Milo reminded her.

She screamed, but it was breathy, as Vicente chose that moment to suck her nipple in a way that sent sparks of pleasure straight to her pussy.

Emiliano cleared his throat, shifting in his chair. She felt Vicente's lips curve against her, and then his teeth bit down, one quick, hard clamp that made her scream in real pain, before he released her.

Vicente straightened, looming over her, leaning into her so she was trapped between him and Milo.

Vicente's eyes were hot, his breathing labored, and where his hips pressed against hers, she could feel his cock, long and hard, and inside his pants instead of inside her where she wanted it.

This was going to happen. He was going to fuck her in front of all these people. The guards, the men who'd hurt her, the woman who was still trapped. He'd aroused her despite all that, and she hated him for it, just a little bit. Enough that when he bent to kiss her—and she didn't know if the kiss was a mistake, if he was momentarily overcome by desire—she bit him, hard enough to draw blood.

Vicente jerked back, snarling. He wiped the blood from his lip with the back of his hand, examined the streak of red.

Then he crooked a finger at Emiliano, who leaned in to listen.

Emiliano nodded, expression revealing nothing. When he leaned back, he first looked at Gabriella. "That was a mistake you will regret." Then he turned to Milo and said, "Put her on her back on the table. Our employer wants to get this over with so we can leave and he can punish her properly."

A LONG SOB drew Emiliano's attention, as he and Milo both looked across the room. The bound woman was crying, genuinely fighting against her bindings, despite the fact the man they'd identified as Denis Carnicero had his hand on her shoulder. The asshole was grinning, enjoying the woman's distress. It was obvious that if she were able, she would run across the room to save Gabriella.

Emiliano didn't know who she was, but it was clear she and Gabriella had formed a bond. Milo's eyes narrowed briefly when Denis' hand slid from the woman's shoulder down to her breast, reaching beneath the black corset to fondle her. He shifted, angling his body toward the audience, as if he were going to intervene.

It was the first time he'd seen Milo break character, though only for a second. Then Milo turned away from the woman, back to Gabriella, forcing her down onto the table as commanded. She put up a good fight, managed to kick Milo in the stomach, and did it all while cursing and crying.

Milo forced her arms down on either side of her head. It made sense for Milo to be the one who held Gabriella down, but...

Emiliano leaned toward Vicente, who quickly leaned in, the now familiar pretense of talking to his translator. Their eyes met, a grim understanding passing between them.

Emiliano leaned back, having pretended to get orders, and looked down at Gabriella. "My employer says that he will allow me and his bodyguard to use your mouth if you continue to misbehave."

Silence gripped the room, and Gabriella's eyes were wide,

uncertainty flashing over her features. He instantly regretted what he'd just said, but she went still, and that allowed him to wave Milo away. It had taken every ounce of patience he had to sit to the side while another man held his wife. If they wanted to get out of here alive, they were going to have to do this. But it would be the three of them—together.

Milo glanced at Vicente, who nodded his assent, before narrowing his eyes at Emiliano. He read the warning in the glare.

Emiliano grasped Gabriella's wrists, keeping them pinned to the table, holding her in place as Vicente roughly pushed her thighs apart and stepped between.

Gabriella whimpered and twisted but didn't fight the way she had with Milo. Her back arched and twisted as she tried to slide from his hold. Tears streamed down her red cheeks. She stilled at the sound of a zipper, her gaze flying to Vicente, who was indeed prepared to take their wife—right here, right now.

Vicente hesitated, his expression grim. Emiliano glanced at Vicente's crotch and realized that he wasn't hard. Gabriella's distress was real, and nothing about that was arousing.

Shit. Emiliano bent over her, leaning far enough forward that she could see his face, though upside down.

"You may be a princess—"

Her eyes widened, and her breath caught, held. Vicente stilled, then lay one hand on her bare thigh.

Their audience hadn't heard his role-play suggestion, so there was no way for them to know that calling her princess was a reminder to block out reality and pretend this was a game.

"—but now you belong to him," Emiliano finished.

And to me. He hoped she could hear the words he didn't dare say.

It took her a moment, but she exhaled and seemed to relax,

just a little. Vicente must have seen it too, because his hand slid up from her thigh across her stomach.

She narrowed her eyes. "I don't belong to him," she snapped. "I'm not his—"

"You are his slave," Emiliano assured her. "And he will do whatever he wants to your body."

Milo shifted his weight, enough to draw Emiliano's attention, a warning not to take this too far.

Vicente's hand palmed her breast, and Gabriella raised her head, fire in her eyes. "I don't belong to you," she snarled at Vicente.

Vicente raised one brow, then pinched her nipple. She screamed, and he twisted it, so she screamed again.

And when he released her breast, she was panting, her cheeks flushed, eyes hot. Emiliano knew that look. Their wife was turned on.

Vicente pinched the other nipple, and she cursed, thrashing a little.

Milo had moved to the side of the table, facing them. The clever man had positioned himself in such a way that he blocked the view of several of the guards. Emiliano could see them trying to covertly crane their necks, hoping to catch the show. The fuckers.

Unlike the guards, Milo ignored what was happening between Vicente and Gabriella, his gaze instead locked on the gagged but determined woman across the room. Despite being outnumbered and bound, she refused to assume the role of bystander, fighting hard to find some way to get to Gabriella.

Vicente switched Gabriella's attention from her tits to her pussy. He ran his fingers along her slit, chuckling darkly before bidding Emiliano to lean closer, whispering in his ear. Emiliano smirked at Vicente's suggestion.

"You are dry," Emiliano said for the enjoyment of the bastards in the room. "He says this will hurt."

The words were a lie. His close proximity gave Emiliano a bird's-eye view of the slickness on Vicente's fingers.

Even with the role play, even knowing she was physically aroused, Emiliano felt sick to his stomach as Vicente pulled his cock free and then grabbed her thighs, hitched them up around his hips.

"Stop!" Gabriella cried out. "Please don't. No. No!"

Every word went through Emiliano like a knife. If this was all an act, Gabriella should win an Oscar. Doubts assailed him. If it wasn't an act...God...what were they doing?

He lowered his face to hers, intent on kissing her shoulder, feeling the need to reassure her, to comfort her.

A slap to the side of his head twisted his face to the side. Vicente had slapped him. It hadn't been that hard, but his face started to throb, thanks to the preexisting bruises from the beating he'd taken. The fact that Vicente would slap him when Vicente knew he had a concussion, was bruised and battered under the makeup...

Vicente's eyes were dark with anger and warning.

Fuck. Emiliano realized his tender action nearly gave them away.

Vicente pushed on his shoulder, the action hard enough that Emiliano almost lost his grip on Gabriella.

Milo grabbed him by the arm and forced him back, away from the table. Milo's expression was thunderous, and Emiliano looked away, not because he was afraid of the other man but from shame at what he'd almost done.

In the split second Gabriella wasn't held down, she reared up and slapped Vicente. She raised her hand for a second blow, but Vicente released her legs, catching her wrist in one hand, the other fisting in her hair, forcing her head back. She was sitting on the edge of the table, her legs splayed, Vicente between them, her throat an elegant line of vulnerable flesh, and in this position, her breasts and sex were hidden from view by Vicente's body.

He chuckled, cruelly, tugging her hair as he forced her hand to the small of her back.

Her free hand raked across Vicente's back, and if he wasn't wearing a shirt and jacket, there would have been blood.

Vicente used the hand holding her wrist at the small of her back to drag her closer to the edge of the table. He bent his knees, his cock sliding against her pussy.

From where Emiliano stood, he, and only he, could see Vicente's mouth, read his lips as he whispered into their wife's ear. One word.

"Scream."

Vicente thrust, his cock disappearing inside her, and Gabriella obeyed, her screams broken by gasping sobs.

Emiliano's nerves were shattered, his heart racing. He clenched his hands into white-knuckled fists. Vicente was hurting her. He was going to—

Gabriella's scream faded into a moan. Of pleasure.

Vicente fucked her hard, the table squeaking as the force of his thrusts scooted the wooden legs across the hard floor. She struggled in his hold, scratching, slapping, cursing, but her hips were rocking, matching the rhythm of his thrust.

Vicente released her hair to grab her other wrist, forcing it behind her back too so he held both her arms in place with one hand.

Now free to use a hand, he palmed her breast, rolling her nipple.

She screamed again, and this time it was a thin, high shriek that he'd heard before. It was a sound of pleasure.

Vicente wrapped his hand around her throat, a warning

and reminder that they were in danger, though Emiliano doubted she'd forgotten that.

Vicente came loudly—or faked it—then released her, only to force her to lie back down on the table.

Rufino stood from his seat, walking closer.

Emiliano's blood froze in his veins. Had he figured out Gabriella was enjoying this? Had something they'd done or said made him suspect? He had the money; shouldn't that have been enough? Panic made Emiliano's stomach churn.

Vicente's gaze darted to the side, but he didn't turn to look as Rufino approached. Instead, he covertly wiped Gabriella's arousal-damp pussy with the tail of his dress shirt, and then stepped back, leaving Gabriella splayed on the tabletop, her panting, hoarse breathing easily mistaken for gasping coughs.

Rufino glanced over as Vicente tucked his semihard cock back into his pants, then turned his attention to the table where Gabriella lay. She gasped and started to roll to the side, closing her legs, but Vicente slapped her thigh, grabbed her knees, forcing them apart again.

Gabriella gasped, scrambling and struggling, but Vicente didn't let go. She sobbed and covered her face with her hands. Rufino laughed and, with a nod, went back to the other table.

Vicente let go of Gabriella, who curled up into a ball, whimpering. The only other sound was muffled shouts and protests from the other woman.

Vicente snapped, breaking the horrified trance that had gripped Emiliano.

Milo, clearly impatient to get them the hell out of here, grabbed Gabriella's shoulders and pulled her upright. Emiliano snatched up the torn, silky gown, and handed it to her. She fumbled it on, shaking. Milo gripped her upper arm, drawing her off the table and onto unsteady legs.

Vicente grabbed Emiliano, pulling him in. "Play the part. Get us out of here."

Emiliano nodded, forcing himself not to think too much about what had just happened. He turned to Rufino. "My employer says the requirement has been satisfied. He's taking his slave now." He grabbed Gabriella's wrist so Milo could let go of her, aware that they needed Milo's hands free if it came to a fight. Forcing himself to smirk, he said to her, "He wants me to remind you there's still the issue of your punishment."

Vicente turned toward the door, leaving them to follow.

Emiliano tugged Gabriella toward the door, but she twisted, resisting his grip. For a moment, he thought she was continuing the protest to make this look real all the way out the door.

He was surprised when she genuinely turned back toward the room.

"Talya!" she called out to the woman, starting toward her. Emiliano held her back. They'd risked all their lives to rescue Gabriella tonight, and they weren't out of the woods yet. There was no way they could save her new friend as well, though from the way Milo shifted, squaring his shoulders, it looked like their Italian man was willing to make the attempt.

Emiliano tried not to run, but when his hand touched the door, he felt faint with relief. He hauled Gabriella out into the night. There were guards just outside the door who glanced over, one of them smirking at Gabriella.

Behind them, Vicente and Milo were having a hushed conversation. Vicente crooked a finger at Emiliano.

Gabriella whimpered when Emiliano hauled her back toward the door.

He leaned in, listening, understanding why they'd stopped. He then released Gabriella, Vicente taking hold of her instead.

Emiliano and Milo ducked back in, and he pointed to the

gagged woman—Talya—as Milo whispered the Italian translation in his ear. "My boss wants to know when you auction that one. He'll be back for her."

The guard with Talya grinned evilly, removing his hand from her corset to pull her long, black hair hard enough that she had no choice but to look up at him. "You hear that?" he taunted. "You're next."

The look she gave them was one of absolute terror, her gaze focused on Milo. They'd played their roles convincingly enough that Talya believed she'd just witnessed Gabriella's brutal rape.

They'd saved Gabriella.

And become Talya's nightmare.

CHAPTER EIGHTEEN

Gabriella sat in the windowless room Emiliano had referred to as Vicente's "lair," rubbing her eyes wearily. She couldn't remember the last time she'd slept. After leaving the estate where the auction had been held, she'd believed Emiliano and Vicente would take her home—to either of their homes—and tuck her into bed. What she hadn't expected was to be brought straight from the auction to the territory headquarters.

After the insane mix of emotions she'd been through, now she felt oddly numb. Even the physical pain was muted, but that was thanks to a few tablets of painkillers.

She needed a shower—preferably a twenty-four hour, steaming-hot one. Part of her feared she'd never be able to wash off the dank smell, the clammy feeling of that horrible cell. The worst part was knowing Talya had most likely been returned there, and Gabriella couldn't do a damn thing to help her friend because she didn't know where that basement was.

A small sobbing breath escaped, breaking through her

numb feeling. Emiliano's head whipped her direction, and the hand he hadn't let go of since leading her into the room squeezed hers gently. Vicente glanced in their direction, but he was on a call, speaking quietly into a headset.

They'd gotten her out, but the situation wasn't resolved. The other two women, the ones who'd been auctioned off first, were out there somewhere, and Talya...

Vicente had explained in quick, urgent tones that they needed to debrief as soon as possible. Emiliano hadn't left her side and had been taking care of her as best he could, given that they were sitting in a room that looked like a supervillain's command center.

The assholes who'd auctioned her off also had a truly obscene amount of money. She hadn't had the heart to ask yet how they'd managed to pay for her—had her parents fronted the cash? Did the territory itself have that much cash on hand? She knew Emiliano didn't have that kind of money and suspected Vicente didn't either.

She was vaguely aware that focusing on the inconsequential issue of where they'd gotten ten million dollars was a coping mechanism, a stalling tactic that was helping her hold it together until she got someplace private.

The murmur of Vicente's deep voice stopped. A moment later, he was crouching in front of her, laying his hand over hers and Emiliano's. "Gabriella, are you ready?"

"To...debrief?" She used his word. It was easier to think of what they were about to do in those terms. If he'd said "are you ready to tell us what happened?" she might have broken down.

"Yes." His gaze searched her face.

She nodded.

Vicente rose and went to the door, opening it. At the same time, Emiliano urged her up out of the chair in the corner and led her to one of the chairs pulled up to a long metal table. She sat, facing the massive set of screens.

Milo slid into the room but paused when he saw her.

Gabriella looked away, not sure if the feeling that gripped her was embarrassment or anger, though she knew she had no real reason to be angry with the man who'd played bodyguard.

Milo walked across the room and placed a small slip of paper on the table in front of her. Emiliano, who'd taken a seat on her right-hand side, reached for it, but Milo put one finger on the paper and pushed it toward her.

Curiosity overrode the unnamed other feeling and she picked it up.

If you would be more comfortable without me in the room, hold up two fingers.

It was incredibly considerate of Milo to ask her directly if she was okay with him being here. Vicente had told her that the debrief wouldn't be just the three of them, so Milo's presence hadn't been unexpected, but the note was. Tears threatened, but she forced them back, breathing slow and steady as she swallowed past the lump in her throat. She looked up at Milo and then stacked her hands on top of the note, palms flat, fingers relaxed.

He nodded to her, then took a seat on the other side of Emiliano.

Vicente tapped a tablet he held balanced on one hand, and the screens came to life.

He glanced at her, then at the other two. "The four of us were there, meaning none of us are in a position to lead the after-action debrief."

"Who else is coming?" Gabriella knew she had no reason to feel ashamed. Nothing that had happened was her fault, and yet...

"Nikolett Varda," Emiliano replied. "The admiral of Hungary."

Gabriella blinked in surprise. "The admiral of Hungary?"

The screens went from gray to blue, and then a woman's face appeared. Gabriella wasn't sure what she expected, but in her mind's eye, she assumed the admiral of Hungary would be much older. Instead, this attractive woman appeared to be in her mid to late thirties, with long brown hair pinned up in a loose chignon and dark, piercing eyes that felt as if they could look straight into a person's soul.

"Gabriella? Hello, my name is Nikolett." She spoke in English, with a lovely Eastern European accent.

Gabriella wasn't sure where the camera was, so she just looked at the screens, into the other woman's face, which was larger than life size. Her throat tight, she nodded in acknowledgement.

"Admiral Varda is the reason we found you," Vicente said quietly.

"Before I became the admiral, I was a politician, and before that, I was a human rights advocate, trying to stop human trafficking out of my homeland."

Gabriella relaxed. This, this was something she knew and understood. "I'm an immigration advocate for people coming from North Africa. Morocco." An unexpected but wry smile touched her lips. "They actually accused me of human trafficking to try to stop me. Ironic, then, that I was trafficked." She laughed, and it wasn't totally forced.

Nikolett smiled, but her eyes stayed soft, sympathetic without being pitying. "I've continued that work, with considerably more resources at my disposal, as a politician and now as admiral." Her smile dropped, but she didn't seem angry or cold, merely businesslike. "One of my people had an alias who was invited to the auction."

Gabriella's mouth went dry, her chest tight with shame. "How...how many people were invited?"

"Not many," Nikolett assured her. "The alias is for an arms dealer who has done business with the Camorra. He's bought women from their auctions in the past, who we then help relocate or return home, depending on their needs."

Gabriella closed her eyes in relief.

"I'd like to ask you some questions," Nikolett went on, "but you can stop at any time, and—"

"The debrief needs—" A low, rumbling voice began through the speakers.

Nikolett's hand shot out, off-screen, cutting off the speaker's words.

Gabriella jerked in surprise. She hadn't realized there was someone else there with Nikolett. Maybe there was a whole room of people who were about to listen to her story.

"I'm sorry about that," Nikolett said. "I was about to say that I have one person here in the room with me, and we are going to record this. No one but the six of us will see or hear the recording. We do that so we can double-check our notes or review the discussion in light of any new information. If you would rather I not record, that is fine too."

Nikolett's words had the calm, measured pace of something oft repeated. Nikolett knew how to talk to sex-trafficking victims. That's why she was conducting this interview.

Victim. That's what Gabriella was.

No, that's what she had been. Now she was a survivor.

"Recording is fine." Gabriella straightened her shoulders and reminded herself she was safe.

It was easy to remember when, in tandem, her husbands put their hands on her, Vicente touching her thigh, Emiliano taking one of her hands in his, tangling their fingers together.

The questioning started slowly with what she remembered

of the attack outside Emiliano's house. She took them through everything she remembered about that, and then waking, describing the cell.

"You said there was another woman in the basement with you," Nikolett said.

"Three other women, all in different cells. Two Eastern Europeans. They didn't speak Castellano or English or French. I never learned their names. But then there was Talya." Gabriella's voice broke on the name. "She was in the cell next to mine. Tonight was the first time I'd seen her face."

"Did she tell you her family name?" Nikolett asked.

"Maes, Talya Maes."

The man in the room with Nikolett said something in a language that had hard consonants. There was a flash of motion on screen as a big man—visible only from mid-chest down— walked behind Nikolett, and then the sound of receding footsteps.

"She's Belgian," Gabriella added. "They kidnapped her in Belgium, transported to Spain. In a box."

Milo shifted, and she wasn't sure, but she sort of thought he growled, a low rumbling sound emanating from his chest.

Gabriella took a deep breath, struggling to get through this, to answer their questions and go home. She'd crawl into bed and remain there for...ever. She would never stop being tired. It just didn't seem possible.

"She was the only one not being auctioned. Do you know why?" Nikolett asked.

"I don't know specifics," Gabriella replied. "I only know that Talya is a chemist and she has something they want, something she created. The other two women, I think they were more traditional trafficking victims. Talya was some kind of hostage. She said they hurt her—"

Milo cursed.

"—but she still didn't give them whatever it is they want, and so they used the auction as...as a threat. If she doesn't give them what they asked for, she'll be sold just as I was. I think tonight..."

Gabriella had seen the horror in Talya's eyes as she'd been forced to watch what she had believed was Gabriella's rape, and she recalled worrying about Talya's breaking point. Had tonight been it?

Gabriella was struggling to come to grips with her own feelings about everything that had happened, the horror of it muted by the fact she'd known throughout it all that she was safe. They'd enjoyed rough, kinky sex before, and her husbands had tried to find a way they could all pretend it was nothing more than that. Given her a way to divorce herself from the reality, and live in that fantasy for a moment.

Gabriella had helped fake her own rape, and she'd managed it because she was with men she trusted, men she cared for...deeply.

What Talya saw was her friend being abused and tortured.

"Igor, or whatever his name was—" she began.

"We believe the man Gabriella named Igor was Borja Labrador. The man she called Pig is Denis Carnicero," Vicente interjected.

She'd been slightly delirious in the vehicle, constantly looking behind her, asking Vicente if Pig or Igor was following them. He'd asked her to clarify who those men were and where they'd been standing in the room, so she had.

Gabriella continued, "Igor told Talya before I was pushed onstage that she would be sold at the next auction if she didn't give the boss what he wanted. I...don't know who the boss is. I never saw him."

Vicente again explained. "Rufino Nori. He was the man who ran the auction tonight, who served as the auctioneer."

"Oh," Gabriella said, searching in her mind for some recollection of the man's face. There was nothing. "I didn't...see him." She'd been too blinded by terror, staring down the pinprick of a tunnel, everything on the perimeter lost in her sheer panic.

"The man who walked over at the end," Vicente said quietly.

She had a vivid flash of the stranger looking at her, Vicente holding her legs open. She squeezed her knees together, bile rising in her throat.

Nikolett asked her more mundane questions—what she remembered about the cell, about the amount of time it took to get to the estate where the auction was. Gabriella's stomach settled and she focused on the days she'd spent as a prisoner, not on what had happened tonight.

"Is there anything else you can tell us, Gabriella?" Nikolett asked gently.

"No," she whispered. "There's nothing. I...wish there was."

Nikolett nodded, her expression the perfect balance of calm and compassion that made it easy for Gabriella to talk to her without breaking down and crying.

Vicente cleared his throat and stood, his fingers brushing her shoulder in a featherlight gesture. He walked around the table so he stood where he was able to address everyone at once.

"The people in this meeting, and Admiral De Leon, know that Gabriella is safe. No one else."

Gabriella's head jerked up. "My parents."

"They can't know. Not yet." Vicente's calm was suddenly infuriating, and she wanted to leap over the table and slap him.

"My parents need to know I'm alive." She whipped around to Emiliano. "Give me your phone."

"Your rescue needs to be kept a secret," Nikolett said softly. "And your parents might not be able to hide their relief. Given the amount of media attention on them, it's too high a risk."

"Why does it have to be secret at all?!" She was on the verge of screaming, her muscles tight with anger and panic.

"If your abductors realize you were rescued, they'll know there was a breach." Vicente kept the same flat tone, but now she was glad for it. He was being reasonable and logical, and she needed that. Needed to hear the calm, dangerously cold calculation in each word.

"Even going in, we knew we'd have to keep you hidden when we got you out," Emiliano said softly. "That's even more true now, since we know they have another hostage."

Gabriella closed her eyes. "If they think I'm free, and telling the authorities everything I know, they might kill her."

"As a precaution," Vicente agreed. "Though it depends on what it is they want from her. How valuable she is to them."

"I'll stay hidden as long as it takes, if it means keeping Talya safe." Her throat tightened. "But is there a way we could tell my parents?"

"I'll talk to the admiral. If he went in person to explain, it may mitigate the risk."

"Thank you, Vicente."

Her husband's expression cracked, and for a moment the security minister was gone. Instead, the man standing alone in the middle of the room was one whose heart was broken, breaking still.

The silence went on a beat too long, and Emiliano started to scoot back, as if he were going to get up and go to Vicente.

Vicente looked at him, shaking his head once, and Emiliano settled back into his chair.

A map of Barcelona appeared on the screens, side by side with the video call feed. Vicente cleared his throat before speaking. "Milo was able to place trackers on several vehicles in the parking lot. We are monitoring all of them. Hopefully we will identify the detention location."

Detention location. What a polite way of saying prison.

"And where the other victims were taken, the identity of the buyer," Vicente finished.

"When we find it, we go back for Talya." Milo's voice was tight. "And the ones who were sold first."

Gabriella leaned forward to look down the table at Milo. One arm rested on the cold metal table, his fist clenched. Leaving Talya behind had clearly affected him.

"We weren't in a position to take action to rescue any of the others," Vicente said softly. "We didn't have a choice."

"I know we had to maintain our cover until Gabriella was brought out, but after, for Talya, we could have—" Milo started.

"No." Vicente's word cracked in the room. "There is no scenario in which we managed to rescue both women and make it out alive."

Milo looked away, jaw muscle working.

"We're...we're going to stop them though, right?" Gabriella asked. "We're going to find the other women. Rescue Talya. And stop them from ever doing this again."

Vicente's gaze met hers. "The men who touched you will die."

Gabriella's breath caught, the weight of Vicente's words heavy on her chest, and yet she felt a nearly gleeful satisfaction that they would die by her husband's hand.

"Milo," the unseen man's voice cracked through the speakers, barking out the name like a command.

"Yes, Fleet Admiral?"

Gabriella jerked. The man with Nikolett was the fleet

admiral? She'd met the former Masters' Admiralty leader, Kacper, several times prior to his death, but didn't know Eric Ericsson well enough to have recognized his voice.

He came into view, ducking to get his head level with Nikolett's and therefore in frame, a giant of a blond man. His nickname, the Viking, was fitting.

"As of right now, you're reassigned from your territory duties."

"To do what?" Milo asked.

"Find Rufino Nori."

"He will pay for what he did to Emiliano and Gabriella," Vicente vowed.

"And he'll lead us to Talya Maes. She's one of us."

The pregnant silence that followed Eric's words was brief but heavy.

Milo exploded up out of his chair, which toppled over with a clatter. He was speaking Italian so fast that Gabriella's exhausted brain couldn't translate any of it, despite how similar it was to Castellano.

Eric and Nikolett were talking, and Vicente now had a phone to his ear. A second later, the door opened and a tall man with dark hair and dangerous eyes slid into the room.

"Stop." The fleet admiral's words echoed through the room, against the concrete walls. "Talya Maes was reported missing by a coworker to the Belgian police. But the territory border runs right through Belgium, and because there were no indications she'd been kidnapped, neither France nor Germany had dispatched knights yet."

"She's been with those monsters for weeks," Gabriella snapped. She wasn't actually sure how long Talya had been with them, but it was at least a week. No, it was definitely more.

If she'd known Talya was also Masters' Admiralty, she

would have...well, she wasn't sure what she would have done. "She should have already been rescued."

The fleet admiral's expression was thunderous, and he nodded.

"Rodrigo," Vicente said to the newcomer. "Work with Milo. Find Rufino."

Rodrigo nodded his acknowledgement of the order from his commander and walked over to Milo, planting his hands on the table and bending low to speak to Milo, who'd resumed his seat.

"Gabriella?" Nikolett said.

She looked back at the screen, still emotionally reeling from the shock of learning Talya was Masters' Admiralty.

"Gabriella, we've arranged for you to talk to someone," Nikolett said. "Emiliano made sure there is a counselor onsite."

Emiliano nodded. "We'll go there now. Thank you for suggesting it, Admiral."

She smiled softly, then turned her attention to Eric, her expression going from compassionate to focused.

Emiliano stood, drawing Gabriella to her feet.

"If I said I didn't want to talk any more tonight..." Gabriella leaned into him but quickly straightened when he grunted. He'd removed some of the stage makeup, and the bruises from the beating were visible. He undoubtedly had more bruises hidden by his clothes. "I'm sorry."

"Don't apologize," he murmured. "And I wish I could take you someplace far away from here. But I trust the Hungary admiral. She said we needed to have a crisis counselor waiting. I think if you don't want to talk to her, she can talk to you. Tell you what to expect, as far as...as..."

"As far as the aftermath of being kidnapped, sold into sex slavery, bought by my husbands, and then fake raped in front of strangers while mentally role-playing?"

Emiliano let out a surprised laugh but quickly shut it down.

They were at the door, but she put a hand on his shoulder before he could open it. "It's okay, Emiliano. I'm okay. Well, I will be. *We* will be."

He nodded, but his gaze slid from her to Vicente, who was deep in conversation with Rodrigo and Milo.

"We'll be okay," he agreed.

But Emiliano didn't sound as if he believed it.

CHAPTER NINETEEN

"We're here," Emiliano said softly, kissing Gabriella's forehead. She slowly lifted her head, blinking a few times to try to bring the world into focus, to wake up.

They'd spent the past forty hours in the territory headquarters. After the debriefing, she'd seen the counselor, then a doctor, and the counselor again. She'd been scared and angry during the first counseling session, but the second...that's when the shame had come. Shame that she'd been aroused. Shame that she'd played along. Then shame that she was ashamed, because she'd survived, and intellectually she knew she had nothing to be ashamed about. The counselor had explained that what she was feeling was normal, that there was no shame in having felt physical pleasure, and that those feelings, and more would come in waves.

After that session, after she'd cried out the immediate aftermath of the trauma, her focus became getting out of headquarters. She wanted to be somewhere normal, feel normal again.

By midafternoon, two days after her rescue, she'd had

enough and calmly informed everyone they could leave with her, or she was walking out on her own, but either way, she was going somewhere with a good shower, proper bed, and far fewer people hovering.

Her husbands had made the smart decision and packed up to leave with her.

She glanced curiously out the car window at the house in front of them.

"It's my home," Vicente responded from beside her. "We didn't think you'd be comfortable..." He rubbed his jaw wearily, the next words sounding as if he regretted them the moment he spoke them. "At Emiliano's."

"It's still surrounded by the media," Emiliano added, allowing them all the chance to pretend that was the reason she'd be uncomfortable there, and not the fact they'd witnessed two murders and been attacked just outside his front door.

She nodded mutely. She must have fallen back to sleep the second they got in the car, using Emiliano's shoulder as a pillow. It was another of Vicente's large, armored limos. A *caballero*—she thought she'd heard Vicente call him Javier— drove them from the headquarters to here. She had no idea if this place was meant to be home or not.

"Come, Gabriella. Let's get you inside," Vicente said, opening the door and reaching for her hand. She hesitated as she looked at it, a sudden wave of...awareness coming over her.

For most of the debrief, she'd felt as if she were slogging through quicksand, her mind foggy, her body lethargic. Even afterwards, alone with the therapist, she'd been unable to do more than listen to the woman talk and assure her things would get better. Yesterday, she'd managed to share bits and pieces with the counselor, but not much. She was still struggling to adjust, to accept that she was truly free. Every time she closed her eyes, she was terrified she'd wake up to discover she was still in the cell.

Now, as Vicente tried to touch her, too many of the things he'd done to her at the auction came back to her, vividly. And she wasn't sure how to feel about any of it.

She forced herself to take the proffered hand, and if Vicente noticed her reticence, he didn't let on. Instead, he thanked Javier for driving them. Two figures hovered near the front entrance and she jerked back, dropping Vicente's hand so that she could reach for his gun.

Vicente grabbed her hand, halting her panicked response. "They're security operatives from *Seguretat Rodeleros*," Vicente reassured her. "They are here to protect us."

Gabriella hated this new fear inside her. She'd done truly dangerous things in Morocco without blinking an eye. But now? Now, she was afraid of every shadow, every little thing that went bump in the night. "I...oh."

Emiliano placed his hand on the small of her back. "It's okay, Gabriella. We're all okay. At least you reached for a weapon. My gut instinct told me to run."

She looked up at his face and took comfort in his self-depre-cating smile, appreciating his attempt at humor and that he didn't hesitate to share his own fears so she didn't feel so damn alone.

"We need to get inside," Vicente urged.

She was wearing black tactical attire that was far too large for her, a ball cap, and large sunglasses. Beside her, Emiliano was back in the blond wig to ensure he wouldn't be recognized either.

The disguises were a reminder that as far as the world knew, she was still missing. The media were watching both her parents and Emiliano—whom she had, apparently, been dating in secret for years.

Before they left, the admiral assured her he would go to her parents and they would be informed of her rescue, that she was safe. Knowing they'd be spared further worry was all she cared about. She'd hide for as long as it took for Milo and that other man to find Talya. Besides, there was no way she could handle the deluge of paparazzi that would descend on her once her rescue was revealed. At least not right now.

Vicente started to reclaim her hand but seemed to change his mind, lowering his arm. Instead, he nodded to Emiliano, who quickly guided her inside.

The Gabriella she'd been a week ago would have asked for a tour, would have taken her time exploring every room in the house, as she'd done with Emiliano's place before...

She wasn't that Gabriella. Not today. Maybe not ever again.

"Are you hungry?" Vicente asked. "I could make us a late dinner."

She was. She was starving actually, but her stomach was another thing that had turned against her. Every time she tried to eat something, she was overwhelmed by nausea. She shook her head. "Bed?" she asked, weariness sinking deep.

Vicente gestured to the stairs. "This way."

When they reached the top, Emiliano continued to lead her until they were in Vicente's bedroom, and it occurred to her, Emiliano had obviously been here before. For the first time, she studied her husbands, not just their faces—Emiliano had taken off the prosthetic nose back at headquarters and now stripped off the wig—but the way they acted with each other.

Something had changed between them while she was gone. The anger and resentment had vanished, replaced with, well, she wasn't sure what. But it was peaceful and cooperative and exactly what she'd wanted for them, even if it was just a momentary truce.

Gabriella no longer worried about their future. God. She'd lost sight of it completely, the past week obliterating her ability to feel anything akin to hope at the moment. All she could see when she closed her eyes was that cell, then being held down on that table by her husbands, taken in front of the men who'd tormented her.

The counselor had quietly and calmly told her that yes, what she'd experienced was rape because she hadn't had a choice.

Gabriella had initially protested, had insisted that even if the guys had said they planned to fight their way out rather than put on that terrible show, she would have insisted on going through with it to protect Talya.

She felt tears gathering, but they weren't sadness, or not just sadness. She was angry again, and she wasn't sure with whom.

She stopped, looking at her husbands. "I need to call the counselor."

Vicente walked out of the bedroom, returning a moment later with a phone. "This is a secure line."

She didn't think she needed a secure line, but the fact that he got her one made her smile. "Thank you."

They left her in the bedroom, and Gabriella sank down on the edge of the bed, dialing the number on the card she had in her pocket.

"Gabriella." The counselor picked up right away. Her voice was calm and soothing.

"I'm angry again," she said, voice thick with tears. "But I'm also...also so happy. So relieved to be here, with them." She didn't realize that was the other reason for the tears, not until the words were out of her mouth.

"Remember, there is no wrong way to feel," the counselor said. "You've been through a traumatic experience."

Gabriella closed her eyes, felt the tears tracing down her face. They spoke for an hour and a half, sometimes going back over what she'd already talked about--fear and shame--and now her relief at being "home" even if it wasn't her home. And the guilt. Guilt that she felt happy, that she was safe at home when Talya wasn't.

And there was one more thing, a desire that felt wrong. She wanted her husbands to touch her. Wanted their hands on her naked skin. Surely that wasn't right. She shouldn't feel that way.

"Nothing you feel is wrong," the counselor told her. "But you need to understand that your feelings might change, and that's okay too."

An hour later, Gabriella came out of the bedroom, feeling if not better, lighter for having unburdened some of her emotions. They must have been listening for the sound of the door opening because Vicente appeared on the steps.

"I'd like to take a bath," she said. "Will you help me?"

Emiliano appeared beside Vicente, then started up the stairs. When Vicente didn't move, Emiliano reached back, grabbed him, and urged him to follow. Gabriella stepped back into the bedroom and they joined her.

She'd showered a few times at headquarters, but she'd been too numb to feel the water hitting her skin.

Gabriella wondered if they'd let her sleep in the steaming-hot water. Even now, even days away from that dank cell, the chill of it still rested in her bones. Warmth felt like an illusion, something she'd never feel again.

Vicente left her briefly, walking into the en suite bathroom. She heard the sound of water running, saw steam begin to fill the room, and caught the slightest whiff of lavender before he rejoined them. Neither she nor Emiliano had moved during that time.

"Lavender?" she asked, fixated on why the scent was in Vicente's bathroom. It was an innocuous thing but easier to focus on than anything else.

He gave her a crooked grin. "My *abuela's* house always smelled like lavender. She said it was calming."

He stopped speaking, and Gabriella watched the quick play of emotions over his face. Vicente cleared his throat, then kept going. "Every year for my birthday, she gave me lavender bath oils, teasing me, telling me that of all her grandchildren, I was the one who needed to relax the most. She's been gone nearly thirty years, but I still keep buying the lavender bath oil." He shook his head but was smiling. "I don't even take baths... But she was right about it calming me, though I don't know if it's the smell or the memories attached to it. The scent reminds me of happier, more carefree times."

"For me, it's the smell of orange blossoms," Emiliano said. "It reminds me of home, of Seville."

Gabriella's gaze drifted from Vicente to Emiliano and back again. Emiliano had been more open about his childhood, his personal life, before her kidnapping, but Vicente had been buttoned up, aloof, determined to hold them at arm's length. None of that was present right now and it sparked her curiosity once more.

What exactly had happened between Vicente and Emiliano while she was gone?

She wanted to join the conversation, so grateful to both of them for trying to help her forget what she'd gone through by sharing happier memories. She bit her lower lip, fighting to think of her own story to tell. All she could smell in her mind's eye was the mustiness of the cell, the dank earthiness of the mold.

"I..." she started. Nothing else would come. She shook her head, lifting one shoulder, feeling like an outsider—in this room, in this marriage. She couldn't make herself fit anymore. Not here. Maybe not anywhere. Her chest tightened painfully.

It's the trauma making you feel that way. The internal voice sounded a lot like the counselor. *You are not broken or damaged. You survived.*

"Give yourself some time, Gabriella." Emiliano, ever the politician, was watching her, studying the situation, being careful with her. "The counselor said it will take time for you to process, and that you shouldn't be afraid to ask for what you want or need." She'd never wanted to be treated with kid gloves, but right now...

She jumped when Emiliano reached over and touched the tear she didn't know she'd shed, sliding down her cheek. He cupped her face, his gaze compassionate.

"We're here, Gabriella. You're safe," he whispered.

Those words should have brought her comfort, but simply hearing them didn't make her feel that way. "I know. I just..." She didn't finish her thought, didn't want to. It wouldn't be kind. These men had risked their lives for her. Had done difficult things that probably cost them both. All for her. To save her, to help her escape, to bring her back to them, to her parents, to her life, and yet, she didn't feel safe.

Vicente reached out for her, and again, his hand dropped before he touched her. She hated seeing the uncertainty in his eyes. Though she hadn't known him long, she'd counted on him to be strong, certain, to have a vision and follow through with it —right or wrong. Vicente was the man who got things done, but right now, he looked as lost as she felt.

"Come," he said at last.

She followed him into the bathroom, silently willing the sweet, soft scent of his lavender to soothe her. But it didn't calm her, rather it pushed her emotions even closer to the surface.

"Dammit," she muttered, swiping at her eyes as another

tear fell. She didn't want to cry.

Or was it that she didn't want to cry in front of them?

Vicente stepped closer to her, intent on embracing her. She reacted without thought, backing away—one step, then another, as visions of him grabbing her, stripping her, slapping her, flashed through her mind.

Vicente stopped in his tracks, quickly moving in the opposite direction due to her response. This was an awkward, uncomfortable dance, but she couldn't leave the floor, couldn't find the right steps.

She took one more backward step and found herself pressed against Emiliano, her back to his chest. She froze but didn't seek to separate. Instead, she let herself feel his body molded to hers. Emiliano kept his arms at his sides, allowing her the right to accept or reject the closeness.

She took a deep breath, then remained, glancing back at Vicente. What she saw went through her like a blade. The abject misery in his expression nearly killed her.

He'd saved her life.

But he'd hurt her, scared her, to do it.

And now she was afraid of him, and he knew it.

"I'm sorry," she said thickly, unable to stop the war raging inside her. She couldn't land on a side, couldn't find her way back to them.

Vicente shook his head, almost angrily, though she knew that rage wasn't directed at her. "Don't apologize. I gave you reasons to fear me."

"Tell us what you need, Gabriella," Emiliano soothed. "We'll give it to you. Whatever it is."

She barked out a loud, miserable laugh. "Can't you see? I don't know. God. I don't know!" Her hands began to tremble, unsure if she wanted to stay or run.

She'd thought she knew what she wanted. It had been so

clear and seemed so easy when she'd been on the phone with the counselor, but now her emotions were a tangled mess.

"Do you want me to leave?" Vicente's voice was hoarse, as if his throat—like hers—was closed tight. And while she knew he'd go if she demanded it, there was no denying it would hurt him to do so.

"No," she said hastily.

"You're saying that to spare me." Vicente edged to the side, toward the door, all while keeping his distance from her.

"I don't want to be alone," she insisted.

Vicente's expression was unreadable. "Emiliano will stay with you."

"Please," she whispered. "Please don't—" She took a breath, tried to sort through her words. "I want you both here."

"We're not going anywhere," Emiliano said. "We'll stay with you as long as you want."

Vicente glanced down at the bathtub and turned off the water, the steam rising enough to create a sauna-like atmosphere. Gabriella was still cold.

"Do you want us to help you undress?" Emiliano asked.

She looked down at herself, her eyes cloudy with tears. She beat them back once more. She was allowed to be sad and scared and also want them here with her. She could be nearly trembling with fear and also want their hands on her. For a while she was going to have to be okay with not being totally okay. She looked at her husbands. "Yes. I want...need...your help. Need you."

EMILIANO'S HEART RACED, his hands trembling. It felt as if he was walking through a minefield, every step fraught with peril. Vicente continued to remain apart from them, keeping his distance. It was hard to look at his stoic husband and not see the cracks forming. Vicente—like Gabriella—was fighting with everything he had to hold it together, but Emiliano feared neither of them would win that battle.

More importantly, he wasn't sure they should.

He reached out and slowly eased the tactical jacket off her shoulders. He waited to see if she wanted to take it from there, but Gabriella didn't move. He slid the black, logoed T-shirt over her head, giving her time to change her mind if she wanted to. She remained silent as he gently removed every piece of clothing. He caught sight of Vicente's slight wince when he spotted the bruises on her breasts, a result of him slapping them during their staged rape.

Gabriella hadn't lifted her gaze from the floor, so she'd missed the brief flash of pain on their husband's face before Vicente, as always, shuttered the emotion away.

Once she was completely naked, Gabriella raised her hands, crossing them over her body. He hated that she felt the need to do so. He would bet his entire life's savings that she had never shielded her naked body in front of lovers before, but there seemed to be no way she could keep her arms down. Just as she couldn't face them, her eyes still downcast.

Her vulnerability was flashing like a neon sign. While she hadn't been naked on that stage at the auction, he could imagine it must have felt that way, to be forced to stand before so many people, viewing her as if her only worth was her body, her face, what rested between her legs.

Emiliano wanted to level the playing field, to ensure that no one in this room was able to hide or claim a more powerful role.

"Would you like us to undress as well?" Emiliano asked.

"Please," she whispered, nodding.

Emiliano shifted behind her and untucked his shirt from his pants. Like her, he'd been given tactical gear to wear home, a black T-shirt, cargo pants that were a size or two too big.

Gabriella twisted, finally looking at him as he pulled off the shirt. His pants and boxer briefs went next. She never looked away as he stripped, though he knew that she—like he—could hear Vicente's clothing hitting the floor as well. Her gaze took in his body, but there was no fear in her eyes. He'd been worried, afraid they'd destroyed the connection they'd all shared at the safe house.

Once Emiliano was naked, he glanced across the room to Vicente, who'd undressed as well.

Lifting his hand to the large Jacuzzi tub, Emiliano encouraged Gabriella to step in. He was careful not to touch her.

Gabriella climbed in, then looked back at both of them...expectantly?

"Do you want us to get in as well?" Emiliano asked, taking them through all of this piece by piece, allowing her to call the shots as they went.

She nodded. "Yes."

Vicente had bought this house with his trinity in mind. The tub was the perfect size for three bodies, the bed large, the double vanities perfect for a wife and two husbands. It was curious, considering Vicente's original plan to live apart, but Emiliano didn't question it for fear it would remind their husband of the way he'd initially believed their marriage should work. Vicente had confided to him that he'd been wrong, but Gabriella hadn't been there. And given what had happened last night, what Vicente had been forced to do...he feared his husband would backtrack out of misplaced guilt.

Emiliano stepped into the tub first, pleased when Gabriella slid closer. He lifted his arms and she came to him, accepting his embrace, resting her bare back against his naked chest, nestling close.

Baby step.

Vicente climbed in next, taking a seat across the tub, facing them. He was careful to keep space between himself and Gabriella.

Emiliano placed a soft kiss on the side of her head. "Now what, *tesoro?*"

Gabriella didn't look at him as she shrugged, her posture one of absolute exhaustion...or perhaps something worse, defeat.

He couldn't stand it. It was time to wash away everything that happened between them, time to find their way back.

Emiliano reached for the body wash sitting on a shelf next to the tub and squeezed some into a washcloth. Lifting her left arm, he guided the cloth downward from her wrist to just under her arm, then he changed direction, moving back up. He moved at a snail's pace, giving her time to adjust and, if she chose, to reject, being gentle with the fading bruises as well as the fresh ones.

"You're going to smell like Vicente," he murmured in her ear, keeping his tone light, almost playful. The three of them had run the gamut of emotions since their wedding day, too many of them the bad ones. He wanted to show his lovers—his spouses—another way. He would share their pain, their anxiety with them, but by God, more than that, he wanted to share their joy, to revel in their happiness, their laughter.

"It smells good." Gabriella lifted her gaze to Vicente, who sat still as a stone across from them. Their eyes met, held as Emiliano continued his ministrations.

One more baby step.

Gently, he smoothed more of the body wash into her soft skin, keeping his motions gentle, slow, as he rubbed the cloth along her arms, her back, her chest. Then he urged her to twist, shifting her to the middle of the tub, closer to Vicente, so that he could draw the cloth lower, along her thighs. She giggled just a bit when he scrubbed her feet, obviously ticklish. He reveled in the sound—so grateful for that tiny bit of happiness from her.

He carefully avoided the spot between her legs, even though she drew in a quiet intake of breath when his fingers accidentally grazed her nipples. They tightened and her body flushed. He moved away from them, not wanting to spook her.

"Does anything hurt?" Emiliano asked, unable to ignore the crack in Vicente's armor, the look of anguish that flashed, then held.

She shook her head, responding to Emiliano even though she was looking at Vicente. "No. You didn't...I liked the pain." Once again, a tear slid down her cheek, and once more, she batted it away, refusing to let another fall.

"Stop that," Vicente said sharply, his deep voice booming, destroying the previous calm. They were the first words he'd said in several minutes.

"What?" Gabriella asked.

"Stop pushing the tears away; don't hide them from us. From me. I need to...I..."

Vicente was searching for a way to pay penance. Emiliano knew what Gabriella's tears would do to their husband. They would flay him more painfully than a bullwhip, yet he asked to see them, felt he deserved to know just exactly how much he'd scared her, hurt her.

Gabriella remained silent and still for several long minutes. Her fear morphing to something that looked like regret. "I don't blame you," she said at last. "You saved me."

"I know what I did to you, Gabriella," Vicente said woodenly.

"Stop." This time Emiliano issued the demand. He slid the body wash over to Vicente. "Your turn."

Vicente gave him a confused look, but Emiliano insisted.

"It's time to wash all of this away."

Vicente took the body wash, squirting some on his palm, absentmindedly scrubbing it along his arms, his chest. He slid lower in the water after a moment to sluice off the suds. Once he was done, Vicente resumed his previous statue-like impersonation, remaining so still, Emiliano suspected his husband would shatter into a million tiny pieces with just one touch.

Gabriella must have noticed the same. She slid across the tub, and for the first time, she didn't hesitate to touch him. However, there was no missing the way her hand trembled. She was trying to bridge the gap between herself and Vicente, but she was still struggling. "I know why you did it. You did it to save me," she repeated.

It felt as if she was saying those things to convince herself as much as Vicente.

Vicente shuddered when she feathered her fingers along his cheek, his own hands clenched around the rim of the tub. Emiliano knew their husband well enough to know he wouldn't touch her without permission, and he wondered how long it would take before Vicente would come to her freely, without that moment of hesitation where he sought her consent.

Watching the two of them together nearly broke his heart.

If they couldn't get past this...

No, Emiliano thought. They would get past it. They had to. They were his. And he would fight to the bitter end to save this marriage, even if it meant he was fighting *them*.

VICENTE SWALLOWED DEEPLY, fighting against his natural impulse, the part of him who wanted to pull his beautiful wife into his arms and hold her until the pain subsided.

But he didn't have that right. Because he was the one who'd hurt her, who'd put the fear in her eyes.

"Gabriella," he said, his voice thick. He'd slept very little the past few days, managing nothing more than restless catnaps. The reasonable security minister part of him knew she'd been perfectly safe at headquarters, that no one could get to her in the fortress he'd helped to ensure was impenetrable. However, the husband inside of him hated the closed door between them each time she went to lie down. So he'd placed himself right against the barrier, listening intently for the slightest sound of distress.

He glanced across the tub, and for a moment, a slight grin crossed his lips when Emiliano lifted his chin, giving him the same silent gesture Vicente had employed several times since their wedding. His husband was telling him to get it together and get on with it.

The smile faded when he looked down at Gabriella's despondent face, her expression a blend of uncertainty and... expectation? Hope?

He recalled their time together in the safe house. He'd been the one to take the lead, to call the shots more often than not. Gabriella seemed to need that from him now. Perhaps all of this would be easier if they'd been married longer than just a few days, if he hadn't made such a mess of their fucked-up honeymoon.

"Please," she whispered, and his arms lifted almost of their own accord as he pulled her onto his lap and wrapped her up in his embrace. She buried her face in the crook of his neck. He might have let her remain hidden that way, so grateful to have her in his arms, finally, after a long night of work and worry and guilt.

However, she shuddered slightly, and he realized why she was hiding. He lifted her face with two firm fingers beneath her chin and spotted the tears she didn't want him to see.

Now, as before, she swallowed them down.

He shook his head, even as the sight of them tore something

loose in him. He was a man who did whatever it took to get the job done. This should have been the same, but...

"I'm sorry. I'm so, so sorry."

"I know." Gabriella held his gaze, no longer bothering to hide her tears, to stop them. They flowed freely down her cheeks. However, it wasn't until she lifted her hand, drawing her fingers down the side of his face, that he realized he was crying too.

Vicente hadn't cried since he was a child. Yet somehow, someway, this woman had snuck under his defenses—with her passion, her fiery temper, her beautiful heart—and claimed him body and soul. There was nothing he wouldn't do, wouldn't give to keep her safe, to make her happy.

He'd failed her—failed Emiliano—but he silently vowed that would never happen again.

Seeing his tears seemed to free her, and Gabriella gave up any semblance of control, sobbing out all her fears, her pain. Vicente held her in his arms, softly swaying as he cried as well.

He wasn't certain how long they remained that way, but he realized the water had begun to go cold when Emiliano rose and stepped out of the tub. He reached for a towel and then said, "Gabriella, come to me."

Gabriella stirred at the sound of her name. She'd been quiet for several minutes, all her tears cried out, and he'd wondered if she'd drifted off to sleep. Vicente helped her stand, then guided her into Emiliano's arms, watching as he dried her with the soft towel.

She wrapped it around herself and stepped away when Emiliano reached for another. Vicente expected Emiliano to dry himself, so he was surprised when his husband gestured for him to come closer.

Emiliano dried Vicente off as well, the caring action

catching him off guard. The last person to do this had been his mother when he was just a child.

In a short time, both his spouses had broken through barriers that had been erected and fortified for decades. They'd slipped past what had felt like impenetrable walls and found a part of him Vicente thought had died a long time ago.

Once Vicente was dry, Emiliano finally dried himself, loosely wrapping the towel around his hips and guiding them both back to the bedroom. Vicente was grateful for Emiliano's presence, for his strength. Tonight, he was the guiding force, the steady hand, the one with enough wits left to get them all where they needed to be.

He'd drawn the curtains the night he and Emiliano had slept here together, before Gabriella's rescue. They remained closed, blocking out the night sky. It was relatively early, eight p.m. Vicente suspected he'd be wide awake at midnight. It would take them a few days to sort out their sleep schedules as Gabriella had mentioned her internal clock being screwed up, due to the windowless cell.

The moment the thought of her locked in such a terrible place crossed his mind, Vicente pushed it away.

Emiliano pulled down the duvet, then walked over to a dresser, pulling open a couple of drawers before finding what he sought. He brought back one of Vicente's T-shirts and pulled it over Gabriella's head before helping her onto the bed.

Neither of them moved, waiting.

"Don't leave me," she said assertively. "I don't want to be alone anymore."

Vicente's heart soared. Her voice was pure Gabriella. Gone was the fear, the sadness, the brokenness.

He climbed in, lying next to her, pulling her into his arms, and kissing her brow. "No more sleeping alone. From now on, it's the three of us."

CHAPTER TWENTY

For once, a call in the middle of the night was a good thing. Vicente wasn't actually asleep when it rang but was instead dozing. He'd gotten even less sleep than normal in the four days since Gabriella's rescue.

He answered the phone as he slid out of bed so he wouldn't wake his spouses.

"We've got Rufino," Rodrigo said. "How soon can you be here, sir?"

Cold anticipation cleared the last vestiges of sleep from his mind. "Where?" His phone pinged, and he looked at the screen. The location was about an hour away.

"Are you in a secure, defensible position?" Vicente pulled on his pants with one hand, the other still holding the phone.

"Yes, sir."

"Then you wait. How many with him?"

"Him and one guard."

"The girl?"

Faintly, Vicente heard Milo cursing.

"No sign of her here," Rodrigo said quietly.

Vicente mentally added some different tools to the list of things he needed to gather. "I will give an ETA after I've geared up."

They discussed a few logistics as Vicente finished getting dressed. When he hung up and turned for the door, Gabriella and Emiliano were waiting for him.

"You found them?" Emiliano asked.

"The boss. Rufino."

"Talya?" Gabriella leaned into Emiliano, who put an arm around her.

Vicente looked at them, both battered but brave. "He'll tell me where she is."

Emiliano's mouth compressed into a grim line, while Gabriella started to shake her head slowly. "Vicente, you don't have to do this."

He raised a brow as he finished getting ready to go.

"You don't have to...have to kill anyone" she said.

His lips twitched in a sad smile. "It's too late to save my soul, *mi luz.*"

"It's not," she said hotly, letting out that fiery core that she normally kept tightly reined in. A fire he'd worried he might have helped extinguish. She stepped into his personal space. "You're honorable and brave and yes, dangerous, but sometimes we need dangerous men."

Vicente took her in his arms, pressing a kiss to her forehead, and then to Emiliano's temple as he joined them. Their arms came around him, anchoring him, and maybe...just maybe... they were enough to bring him out of the dark.

"Death might be too easy for them," he said by way of agreement. "But this man gave the orders that killed Yurena and Thiago. He's caused suffering and misery."

That statement left enough room for them, if they wanted, to interpret it as his saying he wouldn't kill. Vicente was going to end Rufino's life because anything else was too risky, but he didn't want her worrying about it while he was gone. When it was done, he'd tell them.

Gabriella made a noise low in her throat, a weak protest.

"But his greatest crime," Vicente said softly, "was hurting the people I love."

Gabriella's lips trembled and tears slid down her cheeks. Vicente eased her away from his own chest, pressing her into Emiliano's arms.

Emiliano looked like he wanted to argue, to suggest the man be arrested and tried, but in the end, he only nodded. Vicente would not call what he did justice because justice required balance, required the fairness of the scales, and he had no intention of making this a fair fight. Ideally it would be no fight at all, but a quick infiltration followed by an interrogation.

Vicente hesitated at the door, realizing that he wanted to turn around. To get in bed with them and ignore the outside world. Ignore his duties, this job that had defined him for so long.

Maybe it was time to pull back, take a more administrative approach the way other security ministers did.

"I love you," he murmured, not sure if they heard. If they didn't, it was okay, he'd tell them when he returned.

Right now, he had a job to do.

MILO AND RODRIGO handled the breach. Despite being from different territories, they'd worked together as part of the MPF and were a seamless two-man team. They'd assessed the house and identified the best entry point as a ground-floor window on the east side of the large private home, where tall shrubs had been planted for privacy. They had an approximate house layout, thanks to cached photos off a real estate site, from when the house had been sold six years prior. It was an expensive piece of real estate but not outrageously so, not the type of property that was architecturally or culturally interesting enough to be noteworthy.

Milo, pressed against the wall, used a circular glass cutter on the bottom corner of the window, lifting out the round section of glass with the aid of the suction cup in the center of the cutting device. The instant he had the glass out, he shifted to the side, moving carefully but quickly. Rodrigo, wearing a tactical helmet and face shield, slid up to the window. Unlike Milo, he had to get in front of the window to do his job, hence the heavy tactical gear, which would offer some protection if their recon was incorrect and someone reacted to their break-in and burst into the room shooting.

Rodrigo reached through the window, disconnecting the wireless half of the magnetic alarm panel from the window frame with a tiny screwdriver. Leaving it in place, he carefully withdrew, taking the piece of tape Milo had waiting, and then inserted his arm once more. He taped a now-loose magnetic sensor to the small receptor, which was hardwired into the home's security system. With that done, he stretched, arm contorted, and flicked the window latch with gloved fingers.

The security was a simple residential system—as evidenced by screw-mounted window sensors—which most likely spoke to arrogance rather than stupidity. The only upgrades were cameras, but even those weren't high quality.

Milo had taken out the cameras with a laser, while Rodrigo had braced the front and side doors closed from the outside with simple brace bars, large planks of thick, rigid metal with a small U-shaped dip two-thirds of the way down the meter-and-a-half-long boards. The bars had been laced through the ornamental handles on each of the two doors, the handle fitting snugly into the dip. The ends of the bars were braced against the doorframes. Anyone trying to open the door from inside would be pulling against the frame. The only way to get out would be to disassemble the door handle from the inside, which could be done but took time.

They could have stopped there, but Vicente had given the order to ensure there would be no escape, so they'd made sure the cars were inaccessible too.

The side door let out onto a narrow, tiled patio bordered by the house, a gate, a small section of fence, and the side of the garage—a separate building and luxury feature that told anyone who saw it that the home had been built in the last twenty years. They'd filled the garage-door lock with quick-drying, expanding glue.

Rufino and his guard were trapped inside, though they didn't know it yet.

If they were desperate, and Vicente intended to make them very, very desperate to escape, the house's occupants would, after finding the doors useless, be forced to try to get out through the windows. But opening or breaking a window took far more time than opening a door. Time that would give Milo and Rodrigo a chance to bring them back in-line.

With this window open, Rodrigo pulled back and stripped off the helmet, which was heavy and restrictive, stuffing it into the small black duffel at his feet.

Vicente nodded his go-ahead when Rodrigo turned to look at him.

Rodrigo gripped the frame with gloved fingers and lifted. The alarm sensors remained in contact, and the window slid open, smooth and silent.

Milo dropped to one knee, and Rodrigo used his thigh as a step to climb into the now open window, which was over a meter off the ground, thanks to the house's raised foundation.

Once Rodrigo had checked the room, confirming what they

could all see—it was empty—he passed out a wooden chair. It was one of two that went with a small table pushed against one wall. Milo used the chair as a step, hauling the small bag of supplies in with him. They had to avoid kicking or thunking the wall as they entered, since that sound or the vibrations might be audible elsewhere in the house.

Vicente climbed in last, pulling the chair in with him and then easing the window down as the men geared up.

He took a moment to look around the room, examining everything in the ambient light filtering in from outside. Besides the table and chairs, the room seemed to be used for storage, with two heavy wooden crates the size of old steamer trunks and a dozen large plastic storage bins. Wearing gloves, he took the lid off one of the bins, clicking on a penlight to see the interior.

Unsurprisingly it was filled with plastic and tape-wrapped packages of white pills. He looked at the wooden crate, easing the hinged lid up. He'd expected guns or weapons of some kind. Instead, the bottom of the box was lined with a rubber mat. Vicente swept the light over the interior, even his jaded, dark soul recoiling in horror.

There were large O-ring bolts set into the short ends of the box, with heavy metal hand and ankle cuffs threaded through them. The box wasn't human-sized by any means, and anyone who'd been inside would have been curled up in the fetal position.

Milo had paused in the middle of his prep to look into the box as Vicente opened it.

The Italian man's breath caught, and he reached out, one gloved finger touching the bloody splats and scratches. The kind of marks left when someone pounded their fists and heels against the wood until their skin bled, or scratched at the wood in a desperate attempt to get free until their nails were torn off, bleeding fingertips painting tracks.

They'd found the box Talya was transported in.

"Open the second," Milo breathed, his tone an uneasy mix of hope and horror.

Moving quickly, quietly, they took the top crate off, set it aside, and carefully opened the second one.

This time, it was full of guns.

Vicente took one packet of drugs out of the plastic bin, tucking it into the equipment bag, which, now that the others were geared up, he would be carrying until the situation was secured.

Silently, Milo and Rodrigo got into position, and Rodrigo eased the interior door open. They wore tactical helmets and face shields as well as lightweight combat armor. Neither would stop a large-caliber bullet, and a headshot could be deadly, even if the bullet didn't pierce the helmet. The armor, which Vicente had picked up for them on his way here, was not their best protection anyway. It was a precaution, but also turned the two men, both physically imposing in street clothes, into massive, anonymous dark figures.

Their best offense was surprise. The element of surprise could win almost any battle.

Vicente waited in the dark silence of the small room while Rodrigo and Milo swept through the house. He listened to the shouts of surprise, then mingled fear and anger, as he pulled a ski mask on. Heard fists hitting flesh. Running feet that didn't make it more than a dozen steps before they stopped short at the same time as the small "pop" and crackling of sound that signaled a stun gun had been fired.

Less than eight minutes after Milo cut the window glass, Vicente walked out into a brightly lit hall and up the stairs to the second story. There were random blood droplets here and there.

As he'd instructed, Milo had Rufino in the master bathroom. He was bound to a black office chair—his forearms strapped to the chair arms, his feet taped to two of the five chair legs that extended like spokes from the central post. The chair was on wheels, and as he mumbled into the tape gag and thrashed, the chair wiggled side to side, spinning a little as it did.

Rufino couldn't talk, but his expression spoke volumes— rage and shock. He wasn't afraid.

He should be.

"The other one?" Vicente asked Milo.

"Secured in the hall bathroom." His voice was slightly muffled by the helmet he still wore but understandable.

Rodrigo would be taking the man's ID, and if he didn't have one, Rodrigo would get photos and fingerprints, sending all that information in. It wasn't likely, but depending on exactly who the man was, he might survive the night, might be on his way to spend the rest of his life in prison.

Rufino, however, was a dead man.

"Sweep the house," Vicente ordered Milo.

With a nod, he stepped out of the bathroom.

Vicente dropped the bag, which he had slung across his back, then leaned against the wall, studying the other man. "I should give you a chance to give me the information I want before I start hurting you."

Rufino sneered.

Vicente smiled, the expression obscured by the ski mask. From where he was standing, he could see his reflection in the bathroom mirror, could see that the smile made it look like he was baring his teeth.

There were the first flickers of uncertainty in Rufino's eyes.

Vicente crouched, reached into his bag. When he stood up, he held a syringe.

Rufino went perfectly still.

It was possible that Rufino would recognize him. It didn't matter, but if it happened, it would change the plan for this interrogation. Most people saw what they expected to see, and Rufino was no different. He didn't expect to see the Hungarian arms dealer Szabó Olivér, so he didn't see him.

Vicente pulled off the syringe cap, then almost casually stabbed it into Rufino's thigh. The man was wiggling again, and Vicente felt the tip of the needle shifting inside his thigh muscle.

"That pain is your fault," he said quietly. "You should hold still." Vicente looked up and applied a tiny bit of pressure to the plunger. "This pain? This is my gift to you."

He jerked the needle free as Rufino screamed into the tape. The syringe was filled with pure potassium chloride. At the amount he'd given—and into a muscle, not a vein—it wouldn't stop his heart, but it would burn.

Rufino's thigh muscle visibly twitched, his breathing labored.

Vicente raised the syringe again, paused, just to test. Rufino shook his head, eyes wide.

"That is all the pain you want?" Vicente crouched and patted the man's knee. "We could talk, but you hurt—"

The words "someone I love" were there on the tip of his tongue. But if Vicente told him who Gabriella was to him, the man might realize his own status as dead man walking and refuse to speak.

"—women. I find that unacceptable."

Rufino shook his head faster, mumbled words making their way through the gag.

Vicente gently eased the tip of the needle into Rufino's leg as the man whimpered and begged. He'd picked a spot mere centimeters from the first injection site, which was visible as a small black spot of blood on Rufino's dark blue pants. This time Rufino didn't thrash, and the needle was small enough that the spot wouldn't bleed when Vicente pulled it out.

Vicente held the syringe still, his thumb conspicuously off the plunger.

"I have questions. About your organization. About your operation." Vicente put his thumb on the plunger. "I am giving you the power to decide how much pain you need."

Vicente pushed another milligram into Rufino's thigh muscle. His scream was high and thin.

"After this one," Vicente amended. "You can stop me, but for now…"

Suffer.

Suffer for what you did to Emiliano and Gabriella. What you made me do to her. What you did to us.

He took his time, letting Rufino's breathing steady from shuddering sobs to something that was almost normal. Vicente had suffered this particular form of torture before, and it was horrible. A burning that felt like being stabbed over and over, the chemical interrupting cell processes. Injected into a vein, potassium chloride would interrupt the electrical signals in the heart. It was why it was one of the drugs in the lethal injection cocktail used by the Americans, China, and other countries for capital punishment.

When Rufino was calm, Vicente removed the tape from his mouth.

"Whatever you want," the man whimpered. "I will tell you. Then I will go. Never come back." He was speaking a jumbled mix of Castellano and Italian, using the bare minimum number of words needed, as if each one cost him.

Vicente made a show of capping the syringe, putting it back

in his bag. Then he stepped into the bedroom, grabbing an armless upholstered chair that had clearly been placed in the room by a decorator. Before he hauled it into the large bathroom, he turned on the recording app on his phone. It would both record and transfer the recording, in real time, to headquarters, so any actionable intelligence could be used immediately.

After taking a seat, Vicente crossed his legs, smiling. Out of the corner of his eye, he could see the specter of his own reflection, a dangerous, cruel man.

Rufino closed his eyes and swallowed.

"Who bought them?" Vicente asked after an appreciably tense silence.

Rufino's eyes opened. "You're here about the auction?" He'd regained some control, the pain clearly having ebbed.

Vicente raised a brow at the other man's apparent shock. "You hurt women," he repeated.

Rufino shook his head, but it was more in disbelief. "The auction is..."

Vicente knew, beyond a shadow of a doubt, that Rufino was surprised because he'd done much worse things to women than kidnap them and sell them to the highest bidder.

"Their names, and who bought them," Vicente repeated.

He rattled off two women's names, then gave the purchaser's name and information. Vicente expected the other man to lie or hesitate, but he barely even paused before saying, "The third one you know. The heiress. We had her. Sold her to Szabó Olivér. Hungarian."

"Why sell her instead of ransom?" Vicente asked.

Rufino's eyes narrowed. "She's the reason you're here, isn't she? I don't know where Szabó took her. I don't. He's an arms dealer." Rufino's eyes darted side to side, as if searching for something more to say, some way to push attention away from himself. "He works in Albania too, I think."

Vicente raised a brow. "You didn't answer my question."

"Ransom was...too much attention. And we weren't supposed to take her. Didn't know she'd be there."

So far, Rufino was confirming everything they knew, but Vicente frowned, as if considering this information.

"The man you sold her to, he'll ransom her, if he's smart."

"He had to promise to wait six months. Six months to enjoy her, and then he can get his money back, plus some. It's a good deal." Rufino's eyes widened, as if only now remembering the man who held him captive was—supposedly—looking for her. "It means she'll be alive!"

Vicente tapped his thumb against his knee, then plucked a nonexistent bit of fluff from his pant leg. "And your superior?"

Now, Rufino hesitated. Interesting. He was more afraid of Armani Capello than he was of the pain Vicente could cause.

Vicente let the silence stretch, then sighed, uncrossing his legs. "Do I need to—"

"Sir?" Rodrigo stood in the door of the bathroom. His voice was muffled by the face shield. He held up a phone, wiggled it.

Vicente reached for his own phone, scanning the message there. His brows went up at the suggestions that were coming through, but after a moment's consideration, he turned to Rodrigo and nodded.

Rodrigo pulled off his helmet, running a hand through sweaty hair.

Rufino jerked, the chair clattering and rolling. Eyes wide, he started talking so fast, and in Italian, that it took Vicente a moment to catch the meaning of what he was saying.

It sounded like, "I was never going to tell them anything. You can see I wouldn't, can't you? I wasn't. Was this a test? I'm loyal."

Vicente glanced at Rodrigo, then to Rufino and back. "Get Milo."

Rodrigo disappeared, only to reappear again a moment later with the other man, who'd removed his helmet as well. Vicente waited to see if Rufino would recognize Milo from the auction, but he was focused on Rodrigo.

Rufino spoke again, and this time Milo translated. "Tell your father that I'm loyal. I haven't done anything to merit being tested like this."

Vicente sat forward. "Who is it you think this is?" He pointed back at Rodrigo.

"Ah, you are not Capello's son? His nephew?" Rufino glanced at Milo, who continued translating.

"You think I'm Capello's son." Rodrigo's voice was hoarse.

"You're not?" This time Rufino spoke Castellano. "You must be."

"I'm not," Rodrigo ground out.

Rufino laughed then, and it was slightly hysterical. "If you are not his son, you should be. You move like him."

Vicente remembered the photograph. Rodrigo's statement that he didn't know who his biological father was. Vicente's instincts were screaming at him that Rufino was speaking the truth, not only as he saw it but a factual truth.

Vicente hid his grim certainty from his officer. Rodrigo was going to have to deal with this, whatever it was, but that was a concern for later.

"What about the other woman?" Vicente asked.

Rufino wouldn't stop looking at Rodrigo, and he chuckled again.

Vicente picked up the syringe.

Rufino's attention switched to him. "No, no, no. I will tell you, I will!"

Vicente injected a few milligrams into his other thigh.

When the screaming stopped, Vicente asked again.

"There was another woman. One you didn't sell. Why?"

"I can't sell her yet," Rufino mumbled. There was spit and snot running down his face, and his eyes were glassy.

"Why not?" Milo demanded.

Vicente slid a sharp glance his way.

Milo retreated into the bedroom, his face set in stony lines.

"They need something from her. Something to do with her job."

"What?"

"I don't know—"

Vicente raised his hand, and Rufino whimpered. "A formula. A drug formula."

That was unexpected, and Vicente paused to think. Eric had said Talya was reported missing by her co-worker. Where did she work? He was sure that information had been in the reports generated since the briefing, but he'd been so focused on caring for Gabriella and his trinity, he hadn't yet read all of them.

"What drug?" Vicente asked.

"D-don't know the name."

"What does it do?"

"Pain. It stops pain." Rufino whimpered. "That's all I was told." His head dropped. "Stops pain."

"Where are you keeping her?" Vicente asked

Rufino shook his head. "I'm not. Moved on. She didn't break when she saw the rape."

Vicente swallowed hard, Gabriella's face flashing behind his eyes as he and Emiliano held her down on that table. Then he recalled her face that night in the bath. His wife was a fighter. These men tried to break her and they failed.

"Wasn't supposed to take the heiress, but when we did, we realized we could use her. Two birds with one stone." Rufino took a heavy breath and sat up. "That's why I made sure the Torres girl was raped while Talya watched. That should have made her talk. She didn't. So they passed her on."

"Passed her on how?" Vicente demanded.

"Another auction. Not here in Spain. I don't know. I don't. They're going to keep trying to get her to give it to them. They need it."

He was babbling now, and it wasn't just from the pain. Some of the chemical might have made it to his bloodstream.

"Eventually they will make her talk. Somehow. Torture. Gang rape. Sell her." He shrugged as if it didn't matter.

In the bedroom, Milo made a sound of pain. He'd fixated on the woman Talya. Maybe she'd been the first person he hadn't been able to save. Maybe some unspoken thing had passed between them.

If Vicente were a better person, he would feel the same horror and anxiety to find her that Milo did, but all he felt was relief that Gabriella was safe.

He went through all the questions again two more times, having to use the needle only once more to get Rufino's attention. Vicente was satisfied that he had all the information he was going to get. In that last round of questioning, it was clear that Rufino was making things up simply to have something to say, which was one of the main reasons torture for information gathering didn't work when done by amateurs who couldn't tell when the subject was desperate and babbling.

"Pack it up," Vicente said.

"The other one is already in the car," Rodrigo replied.

That meant whatever Rodrigo had learned hadn't been enough for an execution onsite. The bodyguard would be leaving the house alive and become part of the coverup Admiral Varga had suggested.

"Good." Vicente stood, reaching into the bag.

"Sir, do you want me to..." Rodrigo jerked his chin at Rufino.

"No."

With a nod, Rodrigo left.

Vicente pulled the garrote from the bag. Rufino's eyes went wide.

"No, no, no. Please! I told you everything. I can—I can tell you more, and—"

Vicente spun the office chair around so Rufino was looking in the mirror. So the man could see Vicente's face as he stood behind him.

Vicente bent forward, the syringe in one hand.

"Emiliano Ortiz? The man you had beaten? He is my husband."

Rufino's brows drew together in confusion before his eyes widened.

"Gabriella Torres?" He met Rufino's gaze in the mirror. "The woman you kidnapped and terrified. The woman you made me hurt—"

"You? You! No, wait. I don't—"

"—is my wife."

Vicente stabbed the syringe down into Rufino's thigh, depressing the plunger.

He screamed through clenched teeth, body arching up so hard that the tape creaked.

With a practiced motion, Vicente slid the steel wire around Rufino's neck, crossing it at the back, and yanked it tight.

The body thrashed, either in pain or a desperate need for air. Vicente held the pressure, arms straining, until the body went limp.

He stepped back, avoiding his reflection in the mirror, as he packed away the murder weapon and walked out of the bathroom.

CHAPTER TWENTY-ONE

"It's done," Vicente said as he entered the bedroom, those two words seeming to weigh a thousand pounds.

Gabriella nodded, unwilling to ask for any of the details. For one thing, she wasn't sure he would tell her. For another, and more importantly, she really didn't want to know.

If Vicente said it was done, then that was it. He'd dealt with the auctioneer in such a way that she was safe—at least from him.

One down, but how many more to go? Pig's and Igor's faces flashed in her mind.

"Oh," she said.

Vicente had left them over nineteen hours ago, yet it felt like a lifetime had passed since then as she feared something bad would happen to him. While they'd made inroads toward healing their broken parts in the bath, she would have lived a lifetime of regret over the things left unsaid if he hadn't returned.

Emiliano, who'd been attempting to distract himself by reading, closed the book and laid it on the nightstand. They'd only come to bed an hour or so earlier, when Emiliano joked that Gabriella had hit her steps for the next year and a half with her pacing and suggested they move their worrying to the bedroom.

"Talya?" That was the only question Gabriella wanted—needed—answered.

Vicente shook his head. "We didn't find out where she is, but Milo will continue the search. He won't rest until he finds her."

Gabriella tried to take comfort in that, but she'd been in that cell, and she understood exactly how long a single minute in that cold, dreadful place could feel, especially with an ax poised right above your head. She recalled Talya's terrified face in those few moments, just before Gabriella was saved and taken away from the auction...and her friend was led straight back down to hell.

Weariness was written in every line on Vicente's face, but there was more than that—dark emotions that sent a sharp pain through her heart. Desolation. Resignation. Shame?

Emiliano must have seen it too. "You did what you felt needed to be done."

Vicente didn't reply to that, didn't even give any indication that he'd heard him.

Gabriella recalled the bath they'd taken together. The way Emiliano had gently attempted to wash away not only the stench and the clamminess that had settled over her skin but the fear, the confusion, the numbness.

The warmth of the water, combined with the way he'd cared for her, had slowly drawn her out of the darkness, brought her back to them.

She wanted to do the same for Vicente.

He called her *mi luz*, my light. He needed the light now.

She rose from the bed, reaching out her hand to him.

Vicente stared at it for a moment before shaking his head. She knew him well enough to know he didn't want to touch her with the same hands that had just...

She swallowed heavily.

He'd killed a man tonight. She could see it in his troubled eyes, in his stiff posture. He'd taken a life. To keep her safe. And to ensure that other women wouldn't suffer as she had.

For the first time, she let herself consider that truth, let her feelings reveal themselves. And what she discovered shocked her.

She was glad he'd killed that man.

Gabriella didn't give him the chance to refuse her hand, grasping his, and using that grip to pull him closer.

"Come with me," she whispered, drawing her lips softly over his cheek, his beard scratching her. She led him into the en suite bathroom and Emiliano followed them.

Gabriella dropped his hand, stepping to the shower to turn on the water, adjusting the temperature.

As she twisted back to her husbands, she watched as Emiliano gripped the back of Vicente's neck, drawing their heads together. "You did what needed to be done," he repeated quietly but with a confidence that said if Vicente dared to disagree with him, he wouldn't win.

This time, Vicente nodded. The stoic was back, and Gabriella hated it.

"I'm glad you did it," she said.

Vicente reared back slightly, his gaze flying to her face as if to confirm she'd really said what he thought he heard.

"He sells women to be used, abused, tortured, and he feels no remorse for it, doesn't even understand it's wrong. How many women did you save by extinguishing his life?" Her voice grew stronger, angrier with each word. "You did. What needed. To be done."

She and Emiliano could—would—say those words as many times as needed until they finally sank in.

Vicente didn't respond, but he'd listened, and she could tell her words had penetrated the defenses he kept in place, that allowed him to compartmentalize, to separate his emotions from his actions. Her brave husband had too much experience dealing with the worst humanity had to offer. He'd faced pure evil time and again, all to keep the Masters' Admiralty's secrets, to keep them safe.

But was the society asking too much of him? Putting too much on him, forcing him to carry their heavy burdens so that the rest of them could live in their little bubbles, believing that the world was fair and just? How many times could they push Vicente into the dark before he failed to find his way back?

No. Gabriella refused to allow that to happen. No matter how many times he went there, she would always bring him back. Always.

"Take off your clothes," she said, as she began to pull off her own lounge pants and T-shirt. "Both of you."

None of them spoke as they disrobed. Unlike earlier, Gabriella held her husbands' gazes, wanting them to see, to know, that no matter what life threw at them—and sweet Jesus had it tossed some shit at them—they would get to the other side together.

They were hers.

She stepped into the shower, beckoning them to join her by crooking her finger. Vicente got there first, shifting under the hot spray, grabbing body wash and scrubbing it into his skin with a vengeance.

"Do you think this will wash away my sins?" he asked, his tone equal parts humor and sincerity.

"Don't," Gabriella said. "Don't go there."

"Gabriella," he started, but she shook her head, held up her hand to ward off any denial he might offer.

"Stay here. With us. In this moment."

"I'm here," he said.

She tilted her head. "You know what I mean."

Emiliano stood behind her and he wrapped his arm around her waist, his hand lightly touching her stomach. It was intimate without being sexual, something she was grateful for.

For now.

Soon, that wouldn't be enough.

"There's more we need to say to each other," Emiliano mused. "So much has happened in a short time. The past few days...it's all felt too raw, we needed time to come to grips with our own feelings. But I don't want to let another night pass without saying things that need to be said."

Gabriella looked at Emiliano over her shoulders and smiled, feeling not for the first time as if he could read her mind. "Our master of diplomacy," she teased.

He tickled her sides and she giggled, feeling for just a moment like a carefree young girl, one who was experiencing love for the first time.

Love.

Gabriella let the word play in her mind. She liked it. It felt right.

Vicente sluiced off the soap but made no move to touch her or Emiliano. He might be able to clean his body, but his soul was going to take more work. She reached around him to turn off the water before stepping out. She handed both her husbands towels, then dried herself off.

She wrapped it around her body, not bothering to put her pajamas back on. Vicente and Emiliano followed suit, covering themselves only with the towels.

They returned to the bedroom as a unit. Gabriella climbed

onto the mattress, resting her back against the headboard, her legs straight out in front of her. Vicente sat on the edge of the bed next to her thigh, facing her, and Emiliano crossed to claim the opposite side, a bit farther away, her foot brushing his hip.

"Where should we begin, Senator?" she prompted.

Emiliano grinned and then, the courageous, wonderful man opened up a vein for them. "I know that we all came to this marriage with different expectations, different hopes. For me, my desire was to be a part of a true marriage, to experience something I'd never seen but had always wanted. I watched my mother struggle to raise me and my brother on her own. I witnessed her loneliness. Recognized it in her because I felt it myself. I longed for more. So when I was invited to join the Masters' Admiralty, when I was told I would be part of a trinity, I knew I'd found my place, my future."

He reached out, running a lone finger along her calf. "What I didn't expect was...this. This overwhelming, all-encompassing feeling of not only happiness but of truly belonging. I'm grateful to be here, and I promise to never take what we have together for granted."

Gabriella scooted down the bed, kissing Emiliano. "I promise the same," she whispered. "The entire time I was in that cell, the one thing that kept me going, that gave me the strength to hold on, was the knowledge that the two of you were looking for me. That you wouldn't stop until you found me. And then you did. You risked your lives to save me."

"Gabriella," Vicente started, the self-recrimination back in his voice. They weren't going back there.

"You were faced with an impossible task, and yet, you found a way to help me through it. You got me out of that horrible place in one piece."

She said the last bit with conviction, desperate for them to understand that she was okay. They'd turned the corner, and she had no intention of looking back over her shoulder.

"I think we all came to our marriage with expectations, so certain that the future we'd imagined for ourselves would be the one we got. Emiliano expected an instant family, no more loneliness. I was certain my marriage would be just like the one my parents share. But I think...I feel like ours can be even better than theirs. I'm going to fall madly, wildly, passionately in love with you. I might already be there."

Emiliano ran his hands through her hair, grasping it so that he could pull her close enough to steal another kiss. Then he drew his lips over her cheek to her ear, where he whispered, "You are amazing, a gift."

She gave him a wobbly smile, touched by his words. Then as one, she and Emiliano both looked toward Vicente. Despite the fact he was with them, he was still holding himself apart. "You had expectations too," she whispered to him.

"Cente," Emiliano murmured, his nickname for their husband taking her by surprise.

Part of her was afraid that, now that the immediate danger had passed, he would return to his previous stance on how their marriage should be.

Vicente blew out a long, heavy breath, deflating like a balloon slowly losing air. "I've done everything wrong since the day of our wedding."

Gabriella shook her head, but Vicente raised his hand.

"No. It's true, Gabriella. I have spent the majority of my life focusing on my career, dedicating my life to the Masters' Admiralty and my role within it. That focus...it blinded me to other things, important things I pretended I didn't want or need. I was angry with the admiral for putting me in this trinity. In any trinity. I'd always planned to do my duty, to accept the spouses chosen for me, but in my mind, I also knew my job would come first."

Gabriella's chest tightened painfully. If he pushed them away again...well...the temper she'd only partially managed to rein in around them would be completely unleashed.

"Then the two of you appeared in my life. And a bomb blew my well-ordered, unentangled plans for the future to hell. Literally. I didn't expect to feel like this. *Joder!* I didn't expect to feel anything at all. I'm a master of controlling my emotions, but all of that control fades away when I'm with you. In this, I am truly powerless. Just know that I would lay down my life for you, and I will love you both until the day I die."

Gabriella lifted her arms to him, drawing him across the bed to them, Emiliano reaching out as well, the three of them laying the final plank down, bridging the distance at last.

Vicente broke the embrace first, only to solidify his own vow with a kiss. He took her lips gently, worshipping them. Then he twisted and offered Emiliano the same kiss.

When they parted, Emiliano claimed her lips as well, and like Vicente, he kept it soft, caressing.

After the bath their first night here, they'd climbed into bed together, exhaustion and stress winning out as they fell asleep in each other's arms. She'd needed them close physically, even as she'd remained emotionally distant. It had been the same each time they went to bed, but tonight, she longed for something more.

She shifted higher on the bed, slowly dragging the towel away from her body, tossing it to the floor. Neither Vicente nor Emiliano moved, waiting for her consent, their expressions well-schooled so they didn't frighten her. She felt another piece of her heart slip away, lost to them forever.

"I want you to touch me," she whispered. "Please."

The moment the last word passed her lips, her husbands

shifted as one, both dropping their towels, looking at her as if she was the most beautiful woman they'd ever seen.

"Lay down, *mi luz*," Vicente said. "On your back. Let us take care of you."

Gabriella slid down, hating the way her hands suddenly shook. She wanted this. She did.

They were too observant, too focused on her for her to hide anything.

Vicente ran his finger along her lower lip. "Trust us to take care of you. To give you what you need. If it is too much, if you become frightened, all you have to say is stop."

She nodded, hating that her body and mind were betraying her, ganging up on her.

"You went through a traumatic event, Gabriella." Emiliano ran the back of his hand along her cheek, soothing her even as he looked at her as if she hung the moon. "Give yourself time."

"I don't want to be afraid of this," she admitted, hoping those words wouldn't set them back.

Vicente kissed her. "I love you. We will find our way together, *si?*" Before she could respond, his lips traveled south along her neck. "Close your eyes, beautiful wife. Try to shut down that clever brain and let yourself feel how much we care for you. How much we love you."

She closed her eyes, tilting her head to the side to provide Vicente better access to her neck. She smiled when she felt his tongue brush her collarbone, but it faded, morphing to a gasp when she felt Emiliano's hot breath on her breast. He paused for just a moment, giving her time to say yes or no.

"Please," she whispered, aware that with these two men, her vocabulary seemed to shrink whenever they touched her like this.

Emiliano laved his tongue over her tight nipple before

sucking it inside his mouth. Her back arched as she tried to lift herself closer toward him, silently asking for more.

Vicente cupped her other breast, rubbing his thumb over her nipple.

She lifted her hands, grasping their heads, trying to hold them to her, but Vicente had other things in mind. He gently pried her fingers loose, kissing the palm of her hand before placing it on the mattress.

Her eyes flew open and her pussy clenched when he slowly pressed her legs apart, settling between. He looked up, winking when his gaze found hers. The gesture was so surprising, so charming, she laughed.

"You're peeking."

Any fear she felt fled after his playful words, his actions the opposite of the man who'd bluffed his way into a sex auction, playing the cruel, abusive slave owner to get her out.

This man...well, he was one she couldn't wait to spend the rest of her life with.

"I don't want to miss a second of this," she admitted, her words ending on a gasp when Emiliano increased his suction on her nipple before releasing it with a pop.

"Didn't want you to forget I was here," Emiliano joked.

The entire interlude was so different from everything that had come before—lighthearted, fun, the three of them revealing previously unseen silly sides.

Gabriella sucked in a harsh breath when Vicente used his thumbs to open her, drawing his tongue along her slit before using the tip of it to tease and play with her clit in a way that had her toes curling.

Over and over, he used his tongue, then his fingers, driving her closer to her orgasm. His efforts, combined with Emiliano's, were too much. At this rate, she wouldn't last long.

"Come for us, wife," Emiliano said, lifting his head from

her breast for just a moment. "Show us how beautiful you are when you fly apart."

The moment he finished his request, he lowered his head, taking her nipple back into his mouth the exact same second Vicente thrust his tongue inside her. She came roughly, crying out Emiliano's name, then mindlessly, she called out Cente, who groaned, lifting his head, his beard wet from her arousal.

"Call me that again," he demanded, hungrily.

"Cente," she whispered, as her orgasm began to wane. "My Cente. Mine."

"Yours," he vowed to her. Then he pulled Emiliano close, giving him a kiss, sharing her taste. "And yours."

She lifted her arms. "Need you."

He shifted upwards, caging her beneath him, sliding inside her slowly, with a gentleness she didn't believe him capable of. He kissed her and she tasted herself. He rocked inside her gently, every stroke a promise and an apology rolled into one. When he reached the peak, she was right there with him, the two of them flying apart together.

Vicente kissed her one more time before shifting to her side. Emiliano remained where he'd been, their voyeuristic husband, smiling widely, his eyes filled with something that looked a lot like awe.

"Come inside me, love," she said, reaching out to draw him to her. He didn't need to be asked twice. Like Vicente, he treated her with care, running his lips over her cheeks softly.

"So beautiful," he murmured, his cock thrusting in deeply, then holding for a moment, her inner muscles fluttering around him. Neither of them was in a hurry to reach the end, enjoying every single second, separating and appreciating every pulse, every thrust, every spark.

"Gabriella," he whispered, and she knew he was there.

"Me too," she said. They came together, Emiliano pushing

deep, then stilling, filling her. She shook with her own orgasm, let it wash through her, over her, sweeping away everything that had happened.

They'd known. Known exactly what she needed.

And they'd given it to her.

Tenderness. Closeness.

Love.

CHAPTER TWENTY-TWO

Eric laughed, his head thrown back in amusement, eyes crinkled at the corners. Nikolett forced her attention back to her notes, hoping that the flush she felt wasn't evident on her face. The sound of Eric's laugh made her feel warm but also sad. Sad because she'd so rarely heard it.

There was absolutely no reason why she would or should have heard the fleet admiral laugh. They were not friends. He was her superior in a hierarchical, nondemocratic governing system.

And she treated him the way she'd treated every authority figure in her life—she questioned his orders and confronted him when she didn't agree.

Her attempt to draw the fleet admiral out—or back in, depending on the point of view—had resulted in a tense, dangerous scene at her nearly complete residence not long ago. Most nights, she still thought about the way he'd looked, holding a killer against the wall, an all-consuming rage twisting his features. They called him the Viking, and she'd believed it was because of his height, his coloring. After that day, she understood that the nickname was also, in part, due to the nearly mindless violence that could overtake him. She wouldn't have believed the stories about his berserker rage if she hadn't seen it herself.

Since then, researching Scandinavian berserkers had become a hobby. She'd read modern academic accounts, from medical hypotheses about the "mushroom theory" to literary analyses of the Volsunga Saga.

Every time she read a description of the berserkers—elite, dangerous warriors who went into battle in nothing more than a loincloth, except for maybe a wolf skin, depending on whether the author of the text believed "berserker" and "wolf skin" warriors were the same thing—she thought of Eric. It was far too easy to picture him in a loincloth, draped in the pelt of a wolf, making his already massive shoulders broader, adding to his two-meter-plus height.

Imagining him like that did not leave her feeling concerned about the potential ramifications of the society having a leader who might not think clearly during a battle.

No, imagining him mostly naked and dangerous made Nikolett want to bite him, just to see if he would bite her back.

Szar. Nikolett looked down at herself, saw the pink flush that was spread across the pale skin of her chest exposed by the loose neck of her soft long-sleeved shirt. She'd been on the Isle of Man nearly a week, and she'd been sink-washing underwear and wearing her comfortable evening lounge clothes as daywear, out of necessity. She adjusted the neckline to hide her reaction to him. If it were only the physical reaction, she could deal with it. It was simply a normal biological response to a man she found attractive.

But it was more than that. She didn't just want the fleet admiral sexually. She wanted to be near him. Talk to him. Spend time with him.

Her reason for coming to the Isle of Man in person rather than just calling had been flimsy. She tried to be brutally honest with herself, so she'd acknowledged and accepted that she'd just been looking for an excuse. She wanted to see him. Needed to check on him after everything that had happened the day he'd nearly killed someone in her home.

The situation in Spain had given her a far better reason to be here, and she'd stayed, doing everything she could to help bring Gabriella Torres home. Talya Maes was still out there, suffering at the hands of the Camorra human traffickers, and a horrible little part of her was glad there was an ongoing reason for her to remain here.

Eric smiled as he spoke to the woman on the screen. Leila Virtanen, formerly of Kalmar—the territory that encompassed Scandinavia—was now married to the admiral of Rome. The meeting hadn't started yet, since they were waiting for Castile to join, so Eric was taking a moment to talk to Leila, the hard consonants of the Scandinavian language unfamiliar and interesting.

Nikolett had also, in her scarce spare time, started trying to learn Danish, which was Eric's first language.

Bolond vagyok.

She was, without question, a fool.

Eric's computer beeped quietly, a small box appearing at the bottom corner of the large wall-mounted monitor. They'd moved from his dining table into his office, which was sparse except for the large white desk, a filing cabinet, gun safe, and the TV-sized monitor mounted on the wall.

She'd set up at one end of the desk, joining the conference call from her own computer. Her computer and arms were visible in the edge of Eric's camera feed.

He answered, and then adjusted the display so each of the five video feeds was displayed equal-sized on the screen.

In the upper right was Eric's, the image being captured by a camera mounted into the top of the screen, showing a wide swath of the office. Eric dropped into his chair behind his desk, the smile from talking to Leila gone.

The center top video was briefly empty, Leila having stepped back. A dark-haired man took her place, settling into the chair. He was looking off to the side, and briefly, hands appeared, one on his shoulder, another one squeezing his fingers. His spouses checking in with him, in an emotional, physical moment of connection. Then they were gone, and there was the faint sound of a door closing.

Antonio Starabba, admiral of Rome, put on a sleek headset, his expression blank as he looked toward his camera, nodding once to acknowledge that he was here and ready to begin.

The third video feed was Nikolett's own, the side wall of Eric's office behind her a nondescript white. If not for her computer and arms being visible in Eric's feed, it wouldn't have been obvious they were in the same place.

Left of the two video windows in the bottom row was a chic-looking woman, her head bent as she listened to the man beside her. Their mics were muted. The admiral and vice admiral of France, Victoire Dubois and Louis Girard.

The final screen was the new arrivals—Admiral Santiago De Leon of Castile, with security officer Rodrigo Alvarez at his side. They were sitting behind a metal table in a windowless concrete room, weapon cabinets at their backs.

"Admirals," Eric said in greeting. "Vice Admiral," he added with a nod to Louis on the French territory screen.

"Fleet Admiral," they each murmured in turn. They were speaking English. Usually they spoke French at these meetings —French being the long-standing *lingua franca* of the society— but Nikolett's English was better than her French, so they'd opted for that language. She really should be focusing on improving her French rather than learning Danish.

But forcing the meeting into English was really an excuse to make sure no one was speaking their native language. Nikolett had been fighting her whole life and always looked for ways to level the playing field.

It wasn't that she didn't trust the French admiral or vice admiral. It was that she didn't trust anyone until they gave her reason to trust them.

"Santiago, introduce Rodrigo," Eric ordered.

The Castile admiral tipped his head to the side, indicating the man beside him. "This is Security Officer Rodrigo Alvarez. He was part of the Rufino takedown team, along with my security minister, Vicente Coval, and the officer from Rome, Milo Moretti."

Antonio nodded in acknowledgement of Milo's involvement.

Santiago's brow furrowed. "But it's possible Rodrigo has previously unknown ties to the Camorra."

Antonio's brows rose. "That explains why you asked for that report."

Nikolett frowned. Had more information come in? She looked at Eric, who didn't meet her gaze. This wasn't a surprise. He'd gotten a report from Castile that he hadn't shared with her.

Anger tightened her gut, but she reminded herself that he had no obligation to share anything with her. It still felt like a slap in the face, given all she'd done so far. She held onto her anger, let it straighten her shoulders.

"The Camorra are a problem," Eric declared. "Castile has successfully covered up their actions so far. We don't think the Camorra know they have a problem, not yet."

"Covering up what?" Victoire demanded but then shook her head. "Our focus should be on finding Talya."

"You didn't know she was gone until we told you," Nikolett pointed out.

Victoire's mouth tightened. "We were aware Talya hadn't been seen in several days. We were unaware it was an emergency situation."

Nikolett shrugged one shoulder, letting her body language say that she thought the distinction was meaningless. Maybe in the French territory, missing people weren't automatically considered to be in mortal danger. In Hungary, anytime someone was missing, she assumed the worst. It was much better to be pleasantly surprised when it turned out they went on a spur-of-the-moment vacation or lost a phone, than to assume they were okay and later find the body.

Nikolett felt Eric watching her and glanced at him. He had one brow raised. Maybe he thought she was being rude or confrontational. She'd been called both many times before. If Eric thought that, said that, it shouldn't hurt. But it would. It did.

She had a crush on the fleet admiral, and it had to stop.

"We weren't able to get any specifics as to Talya's current whereabouts from Rufino, the man in charge of the Camorra's operations in Spain," Santiago said.

"The man formerly in charge," Rodrigo added.

They took a minute to absorb that tacit acknowledgement of murder.

"What we do know is that the auction of Gabriella Torres, along with the sale stipulation that she be raped while still at the site of the auction, was, in part, to scare Talya Maes into giving them information on a drug she was developing." Santiago's words were crisp and unemotional, stripping some of the horror out of them.

But Nikolett saw Victoire flinch, and her own insides were cold with fear. Both her own fear and fear for Talya, who was still captive and suffering. Fear for Gabriella and the healing she would need to do from what had happened to her. Vicente's report on what had happened at the auction had been clinical, while Milo's had held more detail, brief hints about the men's attempts to shield Gabriella emotionally, if not physically, while also doing what was needed.

"We have preliminary reports from the pharmaceutical company she worked for," Vice Admiral Louis said. "Reports, plural. She's worked on several pain drugs, and any one of them could be what they are after, plus for in-process research, the notes are minimal."

"Do we own the company?" Eric asked.

"No, it's publicly traded, and none of the leadership or board are Masters' Admiralty," Victoire said.

"Buy it. Get controlling interest," Eric commanded. "There are records they have that they're not giving us."

"We got the information via—"

"Pharmaceutical companies employ the equivalent of private armies and intelligence agencies," Eric interrupted. "No matter how much political or financial pressure you used to get the information, there's something they didn't tell you."

Victoire nodded once, a hard jerk. "Yes, Fleet Admiral."

Nikolett tried not to let jealousy overwhelm her. Damn it, no one fell in line like that when she gave orders. Her vice admiral rarely obeyed without questioning and analyzing, which was annoying, but also exactly why Nikolett had chosen Nyx.

"Antonio, where did the Camorra take her?" Eric demanded.

The admiral of Rome raised an eyebrow. "You think I know because I'm Italian?"

"I think you should know because the Camorra are still rooted in northern Italy, in your territory." Eric grinned. "And also because your father is as close to a mafia Don as we have. What would he do?"

Antonio let out a single laughing huff, but the amusement didn't reach his eyes. Instead, his video feed disappeared, a map in its place.

"We monitor the Camorra's activities, as do the Italian authorities, but in the past twenty years, thanks to legislation and interagency efforts, their ability to operate has been hindered. Armani Capello, current head of the Camorra, has several properties in northern Italy." A circle appeared on top of the map, encircling the area just east of Genoa, along the coast.

"Traditionally the mafia has used Sicily as a stronghold, but it's the Cosa Nostra, not the Camorra, who have a strong presence there."

"Alliance?" Nikolett asked as she took notes.

"No. A hands-off truce, but in the past, there was a rivalry."

"You think they took Talya to Italy?" Victoire asked.

Antonio raised a brow. "It's what my father would do. Assuming Armani has a property that serves as his stronghold."

"Strongholds can be blown up," Eric reminded him.

Antonio nodded grimly. "They can, but if we were to have holding cells at *Villa Degli Dei*, they would have been in the basement, and the bombing would not have freed anyone, only given an opportunity for possible retrieval."

Eric grinned. "You holding out on me?"

"Fleet Admiral?"

"Did you make a fun secret prison and not invite me?"

Antonio snorted in surprised amusement. "If I told you, it would hardly be a secret, Fleet Admiral."

"Fair enough." Eric sat up, elbows on his desk. "Until we

have definitive intel otherwise, we assume Talya is at a property owned by Armani Capello somewhere in Italy. Which means we need a way in."

On screen, Rodrigo clenched his jaw, turning his face to the side.

"Rodrigo," Santiago said. "Would you prefer..."

"No, Admiral." Rodrigo faced forward and reached for a keyboard on the table in front of him. A moment later, a pair of images replaced the video feed from Castile.

Nikolett had seen them already, so she watched and listened for the reaction from the others. Antonio went perfectly still. Victoire's eyebrows rose. Louis leaned closer, as if studying the side-by-side images of Rodrigo and Armani.

"The resemblance was noted in the pre-op meeting before the auction." Rodrigo's voice was calm and level. "At that time, it seemed to be a coincidence." The images disappeared so they could once more see the video feed. "Also at that time, I let it be known that I don't know who my biological father is."

"You think we can use this resemblance?" Victoire asked. "To get Talya back?"

Eric nodded once. "There's more."

"During the interrogation of Rufino, he seemed to recognize me," Rodrigo went on. "When he saw me, he thought we were there as some sort of test by Armani."

"What do we know about the Capello family?" Nikolett asked.

"Armani has several cousins but no living siblings or children," Eric said. "However, Antonio was able to uncover some old rumors."

Antonio looked down, as if at notes. "And now I see why you wanted this information. Thirty-four years ago, Armani was offering a reward for information on a woman. They were in a relationship until shortly before she disappeared. I can confirm that she spoke with the Italian anti-corruption authorities, and was planning to testify against the Capello family, and the Camorra."

"They got to her first?" Nikolett asked. This was the information Eric had gotten before the meeting and hadn't shared with her. It shouldn't hurt as much as it did.

"The reward was still offered—actually the reward amount was raised—even after the authorities lost contact with her."

"A cover story," Nikolett proposed. "To help the Camorra conceal the fact that they got to her and killed her?"

"Or she went on the run from both the authorities and the mob," Eric countered.

Nikolett was watching Rodrigo, saw the way his shoulders were hunched. "Rodrigo," she asked. "How old are you?"

"Thirty-three...I'll be thirty-four in a few months."

The timing was right. Nikolett sat back, thinking.

"Your mother, is she still living?" Louis asked.

"No. And her name was Martina Alvarez. Not Benedetta Brabilla. That was the name of the Italian woman." Rodrigo's voice had gone hard and harsh. He took a breath, returning to a measured neutral tone for his next words. "She died when I was young. I was raised by my aunt, her sister, and my uncle."

"Do we have photos of Benedetta and Martina?" Nikolett asked.

"Benedetta has no digital footprint," Antonio said. "Someone scrubbed it. We have people doing analog searches."

"Can we find out who?" Eric asked.

"We're working on it," Antonio assured them.

Nikolett was tired of talking around the issue. "Thirty-four years ago, an Italian woman, Benedetta, was in a relationship with a dangerous man. She got pregnant, and realized it was too dangerous to stay with Armani, to let her child become a part of the family." She paused, waited, but no one disagreed or stopped her, though Rodrigo's jaw was clenched. "She tried first to turn against the Camorra, to testify, perhaps in exchange for protection. Something happened that made her change her mind and she ran. Ended up in Spain, where she changed her name to Martina, and had her baby, Armani's child, in secret."

"My aunt is Spanish," Rodrigo snapped. "I'm Spanish.

"Perhaps she *is* your aunt, and Benedetta hid the existence of her sister from her lover and his family. If they were born in different countries, that might have helped keep the secret." Personally, she thought it unlikely, so she went on. "Perhaps the people you know as aunt and uncle are no blood relation. Can you talk to them?"

"This story—" Rodrigo started again.

"This story is what you will use to infiltrate the Camorra." Nikolett looked at each screen. "True or not, your resemblance to Armani Capello and the timing of Benedetta's disappearance are an opportunity. Can you talk to your aunt and uncle?"

"Yes," Rodrigo said shortly.

Once more, Nikolett felt Eric looking at her, and when she glanced his way—in person, and not at his image on the screen—there was a look in his eyes she couldn't decipher.

Eric leaned back. "The admiral of Hungary is correct. What we're proposing is to have Rodrigo infiltrate the Camorra as Armani's long-lost son."

"Here is where I must object," Santiago said. "The risk to Rodrigo is too great. Any attempt to insert him would raise suspicion."

"Then we make Armani come to him," Nikolett countered. Eric slanted another glance her way, and she realized how cold she sounded. "Rodrigo, my apologies. I didn't mean to say your safety wasn't a priority."

"I know my job," Rodrigo said, and it seemed to be addressed to all of them, his own admiral included.

"This might not help us find and rescue Talya," Victoire said. "We are assuming she is in Italy, but we have no proof of that."

"No, so you keep searching for her," Eric said. "Work with Castile. But if she's not there, Rodrigo being on the inside might mean he can find out where she is."

"The resemblance isn't going to be enough to make Armani trust Rodrigo, not if he shows up trying to ingratiate himself," Santiago countered.

"We make sure Armani comes to him," Nikolett said again, a plan forming.

"Admiral?" Eric said to her. "What's your suggestion?"

Nikolett stared at the far wall, examining and refining what had been an amorphous idea but which now had shape and mass.

"We combine two needs—bringing Rodrigo to Armani's attention, and staging Gabriella's public rescue."

"Make him the hero?" Antonio asked.

Nikolett shook her head. "Not quite." Quickly she outlined what she was thinking, which involved using the cover-ups Castile already had underway to hide the murder of Rufino. Together they hashed out the details, conferencing in Vicente, Gabriella, and Emiliano, the latter two having major parts to play.

Rodrigo's expression had gone stony as she talked.

When plans and contingencies had been formulated, everyone given their assignments, Eric sat back. "We need to make this work. We need a man on the inside."

"To rescue Talya," Victoire said.

Eric nodded. "First, we rescue our person, then, we prepare."

"Prepare for what?" Nikolett asked, feeling the tension coming off the fleet admiral.

Eric looked at each of them in turn. "The Masters' Admiralty is about to go to war with the mafia."

NEARLY SEVEN HOURS LATER, eyes gritty from looking too long at her computer, Nikolett walked into Eric's office, her notebook in hand. "I can't give him concrete human-trafficking ties with what I have. Not if we're going to kill off the Szabó Olivér alias."

Eric looked up. His hair was standing on end, and he seemed to have melted into the chair, his big body hunched uncomfortably.

"Straight arms dealing?" Eric asked.

"Better drugs than arms dealing if we can't do human trafficking," she countered.

"Right. They want Talya for some drug." Eric propped his elbows on his desk, his thumbs pressed to the corners of his eyes.

Their job was to create a secret criminal activity record for Rodrigo, something just hidden enough that it would be believable for the media to "uncover" his illegal activities. She'd hoped she could implant his name within existing networks and aliases who worked in human trafficking, but since part of the plan involved Rodrigo "killing" Szabó, she hadn't been able to make it work. She could create an arms dealing paper trail for Rodrigo, but they wanted Armani to think Rodrigo had experience either with trafficking or drugs, both subjects that might put him in a position, once he was embedded, to see or hear about Talya.

They were both tired and mentally worn out. Gabriella's rescue should have been the end of this issue; instead, with the revelation of Talya's identity, it was the beginning of a much more complex rescue.

Eric sat up. "The Americans. What if we give him a background of human trafficking in the U.S.?"

"Can you get the passport data manipulated?" she asked. "And you have ties there?"

"Yes."

"That would...that would work." Nikolett sat on the corner of his desk as Eric picked up the phone.

He held it to his ear, but after several silent minutes, he snarled, "Pick up the phone, Juliette," then slammed it down.

"No answer?"

"It's still daytime there. She should answer my fucking calls."

She knew why he was snapping—exhaustion. Exhaustion and worry were why she wasn't watching what she said. Even as she spoke, she knew this was a bad idea, but her mouth was moving faster than her common sense. "The same way you always answer my calls?"

Our calls. She should have said "our calls." Meaning herself and the other admirals.

Eric rose from his chair, towering over her. "Have something to say, Admiral?"

"I do. You disappeared for months." *Shut up, self. Shut up.* "I'm sure that the Grand Master will do the responsible thing and call you back in a timely manner."

Eric kicked his chair back so hard, it hit the wall. The sound made her jump, which only pissed her off more.

"You want to watch how you talk to me?" Eric purred, his blue eyes bright and flashing with anger.

"No. I don't."

"Good," Eric snarled. "Don't. I'm fucking sick of being treated like, like..."

"Like you have responsibilities?"

His eyes narrowed. "Like I'm fucking trapped."

Nikolett's heart hurt for him. But her mouth kept going. "You have restrictions placed on your time and actions." She pushed off of the desk, standing toe to toe with him, though her head was tipped back in order to meet his gaze. "That is not trapped."

"You think you know trapped?" He took a step, his big body bumping hers. The contact set her skin alight, and she tingled everywhere he'd touched, even through her clothes. If he ever put his bare hands on her...

"Better than you do."

When he took another step, she retreated. She had to. It was either that or fall onto her ass. No, she couldn't counter the sheer mass of him...

...but she could stop him.

Nikolett raised her hands and put her palms flat on his chest. "Stop."

His slow advance halted. His chest rose and fell under her hands.

Need slammed into her, laced with a heady power. Hands still on his chest, she pushed, just a little nudge. He backed up, let her back him up until he was against the wall.

"You're not trapped, Eric."

His gaze searched her face. "I can't do what I want. What is that if not trapped?"

Her stomach muscles clenched, and she looked into those blue, blue eyes. "And what do you want?"

The corner of his mouth kicked up, a quick smile that faded back to a serious, intent expression that made the rest of the world fall away. "You know what I want."

She did. It was all right there. Unsaid but finally acknowledged.

Nikolett took a breath, held it as she balanced on a point, knowing that whichever way she fell, after this moment, nothing would be the same.

"Then take it," she whispered. "Take what you want."

Eric's eyes widened for a moment, and then the world spun around her. He'd grabbed her, reversing their positions so now she was the one against the wall. His hands found her hips, hitching her up, his knee braced under her ass to keep her in place.

She could see his desire for her, shimmering like heat rising off pavement, and knowing that he wanted her, feeling it, only made her own arousal flare brighter.

Still, he hesitated, long enough that her patience broke. Nikolett looped one arm over his shoulders, holding tight. And with the other, she touched his lips, a brush of her fingertips over his soft, warm skin.

That was all it took.

Eric lifted one hand to cup her head, fingers tight in her hair, pulling her head back, her face up.

He kissed her.

His lips were hot and soft at the same time, but she had only a moment to relish that sensation before his tongue swept across and between her lips, demanding she open. She yielded because he demanded it, because she wanted to. He tasted her, and she tasted him. Every part of her body was alive with arousal, her nipples tight in her bra, her sex slick with need. When she tried to adjust the angle of the kiss, he tightened his hand in her hair, holding her still, controlling her, and she whimpered in desperate desire.

He bit her lip, reward or punishment, she wasn't sure, and then his tongue was tasting her again, sliding along the inside of her lower lip, touching the corner of her mouth. She thought she knew what a good kiss was, but Eric's kiss proved how wrong she was, how pale the passion she'd felt before was compared to the neon glow of what he could make her feel.

She smoothed down his mussed hair, then slid a hand under the collar of his shirt, fingers spread on the broad, warm expanse of his back. His hand slid up from her hip, under her shirt. At the first touch of his fingers on her bare skin, she gasped, her stomach muscles quivering in reaction.

They broke the kiss for a moment, both panting, sharing one another's air.

Their gazes met, their faces so close together it was hard to focus. In that moment, they acknowledged what they were about to do, let the anticipation build. It was a delicious kind of stalemate, to see who would break first, who would be so overcome with need that they bridged the small distance and initiated the next kiss.

His phone rang, playing the American national anthem.

Eric jerked back so suddenly that when Nikolett's feet hit the floor, she nearly fell over. She looked up, grinning in wry amusement at herself.

Eric was looking at her as if she were a stranger.

"Eric?"

He turned away, snatching up the phone. "Juliette."

Nikolett felt sick to her stomach. She stumbled around to look at his face. He laughed at something the Grand Master said, but the amusement was forced, his eyes still hard, distant. He looked at her, then pointedly at the door.

Nikolett stilled, her body brittle and cold where she'd been tight and hot only moments before. She picked up her notes, turned on a heel, and walked out of his office.

The last thing she heard was him speaking with what she knew was forced, false joviality. "Can I interest you in going into business with me? Just a little human trafficking."

CHAPTER TWENTY-THREE

Gabriella's dramatic rescue dominated the news cycle across Europe the night of the staged rescue, ten full days after her true rescue. Emiliano appreciated the fact that the story had all the elements that made it perfect. There was footage shot by a witness—Milo—of Rodrigo emerging from a burning building, a seemingly unconscious Gabriella in his arms. Rodrigo's military background, good looks, and heroic actions made him an instant romantic hero.

There was also a video of Emiliano, looking frantic as he raced into the hospital. However, a battered senator going to be reunited with his before-now secret girlfriend wasn't as good as the footage of a heroic veteran pulling her from a burning building, so Emiliano's got far less airplay.

The next morning, when Gabriella left the hospital, it had been with Emiliano holding her arm, Rodrigo behind them, as if guarding her.

The identity of the four bodies found in the burned-down house—Rufino Nori, Szabó Olivér, and the men Gabriella had dubbed Igor and Pig—was treated as a footnote, the men's ties to organized crime apparently all the explanation anyone needed as to why they'd kidnapped Gabriella. The arrest of half a dozen other people with financial ties to Rufino was mentioned only in the written articles, not important enough to be part of the video news reports.

The burning home had been staged to make sure that Rufino, Pig, and Igor's bodies would be nothing but bone, needing dental records to identify them. Without the flesh, the strangulation marks from the garrote Vicente had used on each of them wouldn't be evident. The body they used for Szabó was Rufino's guard.

Vicente hadn't talked about what he did, those nights he disappeared after getting phone calls, but Emiliano had asked Vicente if they suffered before they died, and Vicente had only looked at him with the low, unblinking regard of an apex predator.

It took the media a day longer than expected to uncover the trail of crimes they had fabricated for Rodrigo. A news station in Madrid, the same one who'd managed to corner a taciturn Rodrigo for an interview, broke the story.

Rodrigo Alvarez had been fired from *Seguretat Rodeleros* a month ago, and the company's oddly worded press releases as to why he'd been let go was just enough to whet the appetites of the curious.

One of the fire-destroyed house's neighbors—played by Vice Admiral Natalia—told the first curious reporter who showed up that she'd seen Rodrigo at the house before, many times, long before Gabriella was kidnapped. She planted the seed that Rodrigo and Rufino were associates.

Next, they discovered that Hungarian authorities were looking for someone who matched Rodrigo's description for questioning in conjunction with the disappearance of a dozen young women who'd been recruited for "modeling jobs."

Then Rodrigo's secret social media profile, crafted by one of the French security officers who was a cyber expert, had been "uncovered." The profile was full of pictures of him with beautiful young women. The photos showed them smiling, the captions talking about how he bought them drinks and was going to take them on trips, get them modeling and singing jobs. Predatory grooming behavior.

They'd been prepared to leak travel information, but some intrepid hacker managed to obtain Rodrigo's passport records, which showed repeated trips to the United States, to Washington, D.C., which, along with being the U.S. capital, was a hotbed of sex crimes and sex trafficking.

Financial records in the U.S. showed multiple large-cash deposits, some from "escort" services, into a U.S.-based bank account under Rodrigo's name, the money all having been quickly transferred out to a bank in the Cayman Islands.

The people who'd swooned and lauded Rodrigo turned on him, betrayal making them savage. Rodrigo was no longer the heroic veteran who'd found and rescued Gabriella, but a vile criminal who'd been in business with Rufino, Szabó, or both, transporting women and guns from Eastern Europe to the U.S. via Spain. His supposed rescue of Gabriella now looked like it had actually been a second kidnapping—that he was planning to do what the others had not and ransom her back to her parents. It was widely agreed that he killed Rufino, Szabó, and the others and set the house on fire.

The public howled for his blood, reporters filming with glee as he was brought into the Madrid central police station in cuffs, only for the outrage to grow when he was released the next day citing lack of evidence for any of the crimes he'd supposedly committed.

It had been a delicate balance, making sure there was

enough information to paint the picture they wanted, while not actually putting Rodrigo in jail.

Four days after Gabriella's "rescue," Rodrigo Alvarez went on the run.

"YES, YOU." Emiliano randomly pointed to one of the reporters in the third row amidst the sea of raised hands at the special press conference called in lieu of the media frenzy surrounding Gabriella, Rodrigo, and him. Countless video cameras were pointed in his direction, in addition to the endless flashing from the newspaper photographers snapping pictures. Rodrigo's highly publicized "rescue" of Gabriella as well as his immediate "fall from grace" ensured that every news franchise in Europe had reporters here, covering what would likely remain on the front pages for days to come. Emiliano had been answering questions for fifteen minutes already, but the press showed no signs of slowing down.

He'd been given strict instructions from the fleet admiral to keep the press conference going until all the necessary talking points had been covered.

"You previously withdrew your support of the anti-corruption bill. Given recent events, has your stance on that changed?"

Emiliano nodded. "It absolutely has. I am firmly committed to seeing the anti-corruption bill passed through Parliament during this session. We cannot allow organized crime to continue to run rampant in our country. The new laws this bill will create as well as the task forces that can be formed to root out these criminals—these drug and sex traffickers—and bring them to justice will ensure a safer life for all Spaniards."

Hands flew in the air again, everyone yelling out his name

in hopes of being called upon. Yes," he said, pointing to a reporter toward the back.

"Will you be working with Senator Juan Alonzo on the bill going forward?"

Emiliano was well-versed in fielding questions with a rock-solid poker face. Simply hearing Juan's name had him seeing red, but he ensured none of his anger toward his colleague showed, his calm, cool smile firmly in place. Alonzo, the arrogant blowhard, had hopped on the bill, vowing to spearhead it after Emiliano withdrew it not because he believed in it but because the bill was basically written and his entire career had been made by riding on the backs of smarter, harder-working men.

The problem was that by stepping up to support a bill he couldn't give two shits about, Juan could have gotten Gabriella killed. Something Emiliano would never forget, nor forgive.

"Senator Alonzo is now on the anti-corruption bill committee. There is still much work to be done to see this bill passed. I'm sure Senator Alonzo relishes the opportunity to put in those long hours with me and the other committee members."

Alonzo had a reputation amongst their peers for eschewing committee work, opting instead to make big statements to the press about the work done by others. By calling him out, Emiliano was holding Alonzo's feet to the fire. If he wanted to share the credit, then by God, he was going to do the damn work. And if he didn't, well, Emiliano would find a way to make certain that information was brought to light to his constituents during the next election.

"Senator Ortiz!" several voices shouted at once, hands waving again.

"Yes," he said to a female reporter he recognized from *El País*. "Griselda."

"This is a two-part question, Senator."

Emiliano gave the reporter a charming smile. "Of course it is."

"Is there any truth to the reports that Rodrigo Alvarez is tied to organized crime, that he was, in fact, working with Rufino Nori?"

Emiliano took a deep breath, pausing for dramatic effect. "You've read the same reports I have, Griselda. All I will say is that I trust law enforcement and the justice system, with the help of the anti-corruption bill," he slid in smoothly, "to punish Rodrigo Alvarez if he is found guilty of the crimes of which he's accused."

Hands flew in the air, but Emiliano nodded at Griselda. "I believe your question was two parts."

Griselda grinned. "When can we expect to hear wedding bells between you and Gabriella Torres?"

Emiliano chuckled, then raised his hand. "I'm afraid that's all we have time for today." He stepped away from the microphone as the room continued to erupt with reporters calling his name, trying to entice him into answering just one more question.

He left the stage, escorted to the exit by one of the non-Masters' Admiralty members employed by *Seguretat Rodeleros*. Bruno was serving as bodyguard and driver for him until Vicente was certain the Camorra's attention had been turned elsewhere, preferably toward Rodrigo. Vicente had wanted to come, but Emiliano had put his foot down, insisting his husband remain at home with Gabriella, who wasn't comfortable with the paparazzi surrounding her every time she stepped out in public.

Bruno muscled him through the crowd of reporters and onlookers outside, opening the back door to the bulletproof limo. Emiliano pondered how long it would take before Vicente would feel comfortable allowing him and Gabriella out of his sight. While they'd talked out their feelings about the attack and Gabriella's kidnapping, Emiliano was wise enough to know it would take more than words for Vicente to overcome the guilt he felt about it. Only time would heal that wound.

When he arrived back at Vicente's house, Vicente and Gabriella met him at the door.

Gabriella gave him a kiss, grinning widely as she teased him. "Ah, the clever politician. Two words I never thought I'd put side by side."

"Minx," Emiliano said, tickling her playfully.

"We watched you on television," Vicente said. "You handled the questions well. Immediately after the press conference ended, they began flashing up photographs of Rodrigo Alvarez, recapping everything once more. If Armani Capello is who we believe he is, chances are good that he will contact Rodrigo."

"I can't imagine what Rodrigo must be going through. To never know his father, then to discover there's a chance he's..." Gabriella paused.

In her mind, like Emiliano's, Armani Capello could only be pure evil. To sell human beings—women, children. To sell dangerous drugs that led to addiction, to death.

"Rodrigo is a good officer," Vicente said with a confidence no doubt meant to bolster Gabriella, to reassure her that Talya would be found. "He has a job to do."

"I hope this plan works, that Talya is found quickly. I hate thinking of her still being held prisoner."

"We'll find her," Vicente said.

"You know I suspect a lot of the reason Rodrigo is still front-page news is because he has that dangerous bad boy thing going for him," Gabriella said matter-of-factly.

"Dangerous bad boy?" Vicente asked, amused. "I'm not sure Rodrigo would consider that a compliment."

Emiliano chuckled. "Why do I get the feeling you and I don't qualify as dangerous bad boys, Vicente?"

Gabriella cupped his cheeks and kissed him, softly. "You have nothing to worry about, husband. You and Vicente are exactly my type."

Vicente reached over to claim his own kiss. "I love you, Gabriella."

Once those words had been spoken, the three of them shared them frequently, whispering them every night after they made love.

Gabriella deepened the kiss, her hand drifting down to cup Vicente's ass. "I want you," she murmured to Vicente. "And you," she purred, turning toward Emiliano.

"I want you too, *tesoro*," he confessed.

Vicente pointed toward the top of the stairs. "Then it's unanimous. Bedroom. Now."

AS SOON AS they were upstairs, they lay her down between them. Gentle, solicitous. The way they had been in the two weeks since the auction. Gabriella lay back, eyes closed, enjoying the soft stroke of their fingers, the gentle flutter of lips.

Vicente spread her legs so Emiliano could slide between them, his tongue soft but firm, just the right amount of pressure. She relaxed into the sensations. The soft, gentle sensations.

Emiliano's gentle pussy licking.

Vicente's soft kisses on her shoulders and breasts.

Soft.

Gentle.

Gabriella's eyes popped open and she sighed.

She had two husbands, and by God that should mean that at least one cock was pounding into her at all times.

If they didn't stop being so fucking gentle, she was going to lose it. She knew—yay counseling—that her recovery was not a linear path, and that meant it was okay if, for tonight, she wanted something very different than the gentleness she'd needed before now. And that it would be okay for her to need nothing but gentle touches again.

But right now...she needed to *feel* them.

The key, as with all things, was communication.

Gabriella placed her hand on Vicente's face and pushed him back. He rolled away immediately, his expression closed. She glanced at him and raised one brow, smirking as he frowned in confusion.

Then she wrapped her legs around Emiliano's head, hearing his muffled sound of surprise, and rolled, forcing him onto his back so she was sitting on his face, her pussy grinding down on his mouth, chin, and nose.

His hands shot up, grabbing her waist but immediately loosened.

Reaching down between her legs, she grabbed his hair, tugging. "Stop being so gentle," she demanded. "And fuck me."

Vicente, posed uncertainly on the side of the bed, raised a brow.

Below her, Emiliano made muffled noises.

Vicente cocked his head to the side. "Can he breathe?"

"I don't know, but I'm willing to smother him if that's what it takes to get him to fuck me."

Vicente grinned. That wonderful, wide grin. "You want a bad boy?"

She nodded.

"I want a bad girl," he said.

Her pussy clenched in response.

Emiliano smacked her ass, hard enough to make her yelp, and then tossed her off him. She fell into Vicente, who wrapped a possessive arm around her.

Emiliano propped himself up on one elbow, panting. "If I have to die, smothered in your lovely pussy is the way to go, but I'm not quite ready for death."

"Then you have to fuck me," she reiterated.

"I'm not sure how much of that you heard..." Vicente nuzzled her hair, his breath hitting the soft skin behind her ear. "Our wife would like to be fucked."

"Really fucked. I want...I want to know that we can still have it rough." Dark thoughts, memories tinged by fear, skittered along the edge of her awareness, but desire punted them into the dark recesses of her mind.

Emiliano's eyes searched her face. "Whatever you want, but you have to promise you'll tell us if you want us to stop."

"But I don't want you to stop. I want..." Realization slammed into her. "I want us to do it now, while I'm still...still a little afraid. I'm worried if we wait, then I'll never be able to have sex this way again."

"And if that's what happens, it's okay—" Emiliano started.

"No," Vicente interrupted. "It's not." The way he said it, she knew he'd followed her rather convoluted logic.

"Vicente—" Emiliano began.

Knowing Vicente understood emboldened her to ask for exactly what she wanted. "I liked rough sex before. Liked it kinky. Liked to be made to feel like...like your little fucktoy." The words felt dirty and right, and she was briefly distracted by the way Emiliano's eyes slid down her naked body and Vicente's cock twitched against her ass. "If we stop doing that, because of what happened, then I've lost something I like, something I want, because of them."

Emiliano squeezed his eyes closed. "To help you get over your kidnapping and the fact that we borderline raped you in public...you want us to treat you like our little fucktoy?" He opened one eye.

Gabriella felt the grin spread across her face. At her back, Vicente's chest was vibrating with suppressed laughter.

Emiliano sat up and reached for her, tugging her out of Vicente's hold. "You two are mutually assured destruction without me. You know that, right?"

"Absolutely."

"Yes."

Emiliano's chuckle lit up the room. She knee-walked across the bed as he drew her in, and Gabriella leaned close, expecting a kiss.

Instead, Emiliano pulled her face down across his lap and spanked her, ten hard slaps that made her squeal and jerk. She panted against the covers, letting the emotions come one after another. Little spurts of fear, followed by masochistic desire, followed again by an urge to fight. Not fight to get away but fight to make them take her, put their hands on her in ways she would feel in the morning.

Relaxing into the spanking—softening and submitting— would be good but not exactly what she wanted right now, so when Emiliano's hand rose again, she rolled off his lap, bumping into Vicente.

Emiliano's eyes were wide and uncertain, his hand poised in the air. She could feel his doubt, his worry he'd gone too far, radiating off of him.

She was done with words, at least for now, so she popped up onto all fours, leaned over, and bit Emiliano's soft bottom lip.

He yelped in surprise, and Vicente grabbed her by the hair, tugging hard enough to make her scalp prickle with sweet pain. When she still didn't stop biting their husband, Vicente reached between her legs and pinched her clit.

Gabriella reared up with a shocked gasp. She was wet, so he hadn't gotten a good hold on the small nub of flesh, but it had been enough to make a spiky ball of sensation—so acute she wasn't sure if it was pleasure or pain—roll through her.

It was almost enough to make her come then and there.

Still holding her by the hair, Vicente forced her down on her back on the bed. When her head hit the pillow, he switched his grip to her neck, holding her with just enough pressure to make her feel...safe.

"Do you want her pussy or ass?" Vicente asked Emiliano without looking at him.

"Ass." Emiliano touched his lip, then looked at his fingers, checking for blood. "You should fuck her mouth. Leave her pussy empty. Like we did in the kitchen of the safe house."

Vicente's eyes crinkled at the corners. "How sadistic of you."

Gabriella moaned in pleasure as her legs were forced apart, knees bent. She heard Emiliano putting on gloves, and then his lube-slick fingers were sliding between her butt cheeks. He toyed with her rear entrance for only a moment, a few teasing circles to spread the lube, and then his finger was in her.

She reared up off the bed, only her head and heels touching the mattress while her fingers kneaded the covers like a cat's claws. Arousal thrummed through her, leaving no room for anything else, and that was exactly what she needed.

Vicente released her neck and slid off the mattress, standing and leaning over the bed so he could watch as Emiliano worked a finger into her ass. Apparently unable to see, Vicente grabbed her knees, forcing them up and out. She wrapped her arms around her legs, holding them in place, not caring how wanton she seemed.

Vicente rewarded her by reaching down and grabbing one breast. Holding it tightly, he used the fingers of the other hand to slap her, directly on the nipple.

They all froze, thoughts going back to the night of the

auction, to the faded bruises that had colored her tits for the week afterward.

"Again," she begged.

Vicente did it again, slapping her nipple, just hard enough to make it sting, to make her pussy and ass clench, the fullness of one...no, now two...of Emiliano's fingers inside her, emphasizing how empty her pussy was.

Vicente repeated the controlled spanking on the other tit, her nipples throbbing gently when he was done. Their breathing was ragged in the quiet of the bedroom. The slick sound of Emiliano pumping into her ass the only other sound.

"Turn her so I can take her mouth," Vicente ordered.

She wanted to protest. To tell them she needed one of them in her pussy. But she'd asked them to use her, to treat her like a fucktoy, and they were.

It was infuriating.

It was also so fucking sexy, she thought she might come just from them finger-fucking her ass.

Emiliano grabbed her by one thigh, spinning her so that her head was at the side of the bed. He'd moved with her, keeping two fingers buried in her ass, which was stretched, burning just a little.

Vicente yanked her off the side of the bed, and her hair, caught under her, forced her head down, so she was looking at the far wall. But that view was quickly obstructed when Vicente stepped close. He was naked, and she liked that, needed that. She saw his strong thighs, his balls hanging between them, and then all she could see was his cock as it brushed her nose, cheeks. When she didn't open her mouth fast enough, he reached out and pinched her tender nipples. She licked her lips, then lifted her head, capturing the tip of his cock in her mouth.

The top of his cock felt distinctly different on her tongue

than the underside would have. When he pulled out, she was able to lick the head, the salty slit, and then he was shoving back in, fucking her face. The angle of her neck made it easy for him to slide deep, deeper, until the fat tip of his dick was in her throat, his balls resting on her nose and cheeks. He held his cock in place, not just thrusting and withdrawing. She fought the urge to gag and the panic because she temporarily couldn't breathe.

When he pulled out—and it couldn't have been longer than ten seconds, though it felt like so much more—he murmured, "good girl."

Her pussy clenched in response.

"She's so fucking wet," Emiliano panted. He pulled his fingers from her ass. She heard him strip off the glove, heard a condom wrapper and the bottle of lube, and then she felt his cock head centered to breach. Vicente had pulled out until only the velvety soft head of his cock was in her mouth, her tongue rubbing the slit at the tip.

Emiliano started to push, his cock blunt compared to the slender taper of his fingers. She panted around Vicente, who grabbed her breasts, thumbing her nipples almost absently.

Emiliano braced his hands on the back of her thighs, forcing her legs down, her body bent in half. She released her knees, reaching up and around to dig her nails into Vicente's ass.

She felt Emiliano reposition himself, the mattress shifting, and then he thrust, his cockhead forcing open her ass. She yelped around Vicente's cock, her pussy clenching in time with the beats of her heart.

"Do we have something I could—" Emiliano started.

Vicente growled. "Just use your hand."

"We need one of those clit vibrators."

"With a remote control. We'll make her wear it under her clothes."

Emiliano groaned. "Fuck, don't say anything else or I'm going to come."

She listened to them plan how to use her, and it was as sexy as anything that had come before. Unable to see them, or respond verbally, she dug her fingers into Vicente's ass and wiggled her hips.

"You want us to fuck you?" Vicente slowly pushed his cock deeper, making sure she felt each inch. Wantonly, she licked and sucked, so fucking turned on, she would have done anything they wanted.

Emiliano's cock slid into her ass. Slick with lube, it entered smoothly, caressing each nerve ending in her anus. Vicente's cock twitched, and she wondered if it was because he was watching Emiliano fuck her ass, if that was bringing him close to the edge of his own iron control.

She was enjoying the slow, dirty fucking, their cocks in her, Vicente's hands on her breasts, and the maddening emptiness of her pussy. Focused on all those sensations, on how the sum of them had her perilously close to the edge, she was unprepared for the tempo change.

In tandem, they withdrew, both cocks all the way out of her ass and mouth.

She worked her jaw, licked her lips, prepared to say something.

Vicente didn't give her the chance. He pressed his thumb past her lips, wedging it between her teeth to keep her mouth open.

"Now."

Emiliano rammed his dick into her ass, forcing her open wide with the thick head and sliding all the way in, his hands on her thighs, locking her in place.

Vicente yanked his thumb out of the way and thrust into her mouth, all the way in, his cock head in her throat.

Gabriella's back arched as her ass throbbed, and she gagged on Vicente's cock.

"You're our fucktoy, aren't you, little girl?" Vicente's words were dark ribbons sliding through the silence of their bedroom.

She couldn't even whimper her agreement.

They withdrew and thrust in again, moving together to fuck her, to use her.

It was coarse and crude, and if anyone but the men she loved had treated her like this, it would have been a horrific violation.

Context, context was everything. Even the night of the auction they'd tried to give her that, and she loved them for that and for so much more.

Vicente's hands squeezed her breasts. He plucked and pulled at her nipples. All she could do was accept what they gave her.

No. She could do more. She could take. Take what they gave her, but more than that, take them. Take them as her lovers, her husbands.

That sweet, romantic thought had no place in this fucktoy moment.

The stretching burn at her ass had faded, replaced by warm pleasure as she was fucked. Her jaw was starting to hurt, but she relished the feeling of Vicente's cock in her throat.

All good things must come to an end. Emiliano transferred one hand from her thigh to her pussy, the heel of his hand on her clit, rubbing it in hard little circles.

She screamed, nearly choking on Vicente's cock. He withdrew quickly, reaching down and supporting her neck, holding her head up, his thumb caressing the spot behind her ear. He was still rock hard, and she kissed and licked the side of his cock as Emiliano fucked her ass and rubbed her clit.

The orgasm ripped through her, shocking in its intensity. She whimpered, too breathless to scream, and held tight to Vicente.

Emiliano kept fucking her, kept up the pressure on her clit even after the orgasm was done and she was trembling. Residual pleasure pulsed through her as Emiliano's cock railed her ass. She heard grunts, and then Emiliano's rhythm changed, the smooth, measured thrusts gone. Now he was jackhammering into her, using her hard and rough. He groaned, cheeks flushed, as he too came.

They were still for a moment, the only movement Vicente's soft caress of the skin behind her ear.

Emiliano withdrew from her ass and slid off the bed. She started to close her legs, but Vicente slapped her inner thighs. She froze, remembering, shame trying to take root.

"I love looking at your pussy," Vicente murmured. "Soft and wet. Beautiful."

She gathered her courage and let her legs fall open wantonly. Her pussy was still pulsing in the aftermath of her orgasm, and she liked that Vicente was looking at her. She considered changing the tone of the moment, sitting up, laying back, keeping her legs spread, and then telling them they could look but not touch.

There was time for that later, for them to take a night during which she controlled everything they did. She'd tell them when and how to touch her, not allowing them to touch one another, or themselves, without her permission.

Vicente had iron control, so he wouldn't break, but maybe she could push Emiliano to the point that he was so turned on, he'd grab his dick, desperately stroking himself. She'd order Vicente to stop him, maybe spank him for disobeying...

Her body pulsed with fresh arousal at that fantasy, but it wasn't the right time. First, because right now she needed their hands on her. Second, because she knew that it was time to be soft again. She was ready, if slightly doleful, for this to switch back to the gentle cuddling they'd been doing before now.

Vicente helped her sit up, and she was briefly light-headed. She closed her eyes, and when Emiliano's arms came around her, she expected him to hold her close, tuck her against his chest.

Instead, he guided her onto all fours on the mattress. Her eyes popped open just as Vicente grabbed her hips, hauling her lower body off the bed. Her feet hit the floor, and he toed her ankles apart. Emiliano scooted with them, his hand tangled in her hair, and when she opened her mouth, he guided it to his cock, which smelled of soap and was damp from washing—when had he left the room?—between her lips.

A shiver of delight went through her when she realized they weren't done.

Of course they weren't. Vicente hadn't come yet.

"Keep your cock in her mouth," Vicente ordered Emiliano, "while I fuck her."

She played with Emiliano's dick with her tongue, breathing in the scent of his skin and sweat, feeling the hardness of his hand in her hair, holding her in place.

Vicente's thumbs spread her labia, and then his cock was there. That first thrust brought him balls deep, her slick body more than ready. Her pussy, which had felt ignored and empty, was now full, stretched by his rock-hard cock.

That was all she needed for the second orgasm. She was primed like a pump, and the velvet slide of his cock inside her, filling her, had a soft, throbbing climax rolling through her.

His curse sounded like a prayer, and he only thrust half a

dozen times before he too was coming, his dick hot and hard inside her.

She was shaking when they finally laid her in the middle of the bed. Her stomach and thigh muscles trembled. They lay on either side of her, Emiliano's head on her chest, his lips close enough to one nipple that he could kiss and lick it at his leisure. Vicente pulled her leg over his, keeping her thighs spread, and then rested his hand on her pussy, his long middle finger between her labia.

Their touch was possessive and intimate. Despite her recent earth-shattering orgasms, desire stirred low in her belly.

"If you don't move your mouth and hand..." she warned.

Vicente casually slid his finger up to her clit, and Emiliano shifted, his bent arm laying across her middle so he could play with the nipple not near his mouth.

She moaned low in her throat.

"You're ours," Emiliano said.

They played with her. Random, soft touches that kept her just on the edge of orgasm, for what felt like hours, letting her come only when they wanted her to. But this loss of control made her feel safe.

Loved.

GABRIELLA'S EYES were closed in bliss, moments away from sleep, when Emiliano's voice cut through her pleasure-induced fog.

"The reporter asked when we were getting married."

Gabriella's exhaustion evaporated and she realized that in the midst of all the talking they'd done this past week, there was one major thing they hadn't settled. Not yet.

Vicente sighed. "You want to talk about this right now? After...that?"

Gabriella couldn't restrain her giggle. Because *that*...had been fucking hot, amazing, brutal, beautiful.

But she could also understand why that question from the reporter bothered Emiliano, why it still lingered in his mind, even after the most mind-blowing sexual experience of her life.

Because their marriage, their commitment to each other, the way they moved forward from here, really mattered to him, and he wouldn't be able to truly relax until he had the answer to that one question. He'd mentioned his lonely childhood, but Gabriella wasn't sure she'd really understood how deep that loneliness had sunk.

"You didn't answer the reporter's question," Gabriella pointed out.

"I wasn't sure...I didn't want to speak...for all of us. Until..."

Vicente shifted to his side, propping his head up on his hand. "Neither of you is going to like what I'm about to say. But I want you to listen."

Gabriella's stomach clenched. "Don't," she said firmly. "Don't spout all that foolishness again."

Vicente reached out, stroking his thumb over her lower lip. He gave her a look, the perfect blend of reproach and pleading. "Let me say this."

Her tongue darted out, teasing the pad of his thumb. "Fine. But if I don't like what I hear, I reserve the right to smother *you* with my pussy."

Vicente chuckled. "As far as death threats go, I think that might be my favorite yet."

She purposely ignored the fact that he had probably been on the receiving end of too many death threats.

"You both heard what I said at the safe house about our marriage."

Emiliano scowled. "Vicente. We talked about this. You said you were wrong."

Gabriella turned her attention to Emiliano. "When?"

Emiliano hesitated, unwilling to respond, which was answer enough.

"And what did the two of you decide? Without me?" she asked, not bothering to shield her growing anger.

"We agreed that I'd been a fool to think I could be married to the two of you and remain apart. I'd sooner attempt to live without air," Vicente replied.

"Oh." His words instantly soothed the tiny part of her that was still hurt by his initial dismissal of them, of their marriage.

"However, I wasn't wrong about how we go on from here."

Gabriella sat straight up in the bed, ready to go to battle with Vicente.

She was surprised when Emiliano placed a firm hand on her shoulder, drawing her back down to lie between them.

She shot daggers at him, daggers Emiliano ignored, his focus solely on Vicente. He shifted her so that he could spoon her, the two of them looking at their husband. Then Emiliano said, "Explain."

"I was wrong about staying apart from you. But, the two of you should be a married couple legally and in public. The relationship was established with the kidnapping."

"Vicente," Gabriella started. "You're a part of this. You can't ask us—"

"There's no way in hell I'll let the two of you live without me."

The tight knot in Gabriella's stomach loosened. "You won't?"

"You're mine. Both of you. Nothing is going to change that. In our private lives, I will be every bit a part of this marriage as the two of you. Given what's happened the past couple of weeks, I don't think anyone will blink twice if you bring extra security into your home, in the form of a dashing, dangerous older man—"

"You aren't old," Gabriella interjected, reminded of her first night with Vicente.

Vicente chuckled. "Perhaps not, but I'm at least a decade away from dangerous bad boy."

Gabriella laughed. "Guess it's a good thing I have a daddy kink then."

Emiliano didn't share their humor. "And children?" he persisted, clearly determined to clear all the hurdles tonight.

"Will be ours," Vicente replied easily. "Yours, mine, and Gabriella's. We will raise them together. All of us. They'll only know love, Emil. Never loneliness."

"Emil," Gabriella mused, glancing over her shoulder at Emiliano, then back at Vicente. "And Cente? I feel like I missed a conversation or twenty."

"Don't worry. We will catch you up, Gabby." Emiliano used the nickname gingerly, shifting slightly to—wisely so—protect the crown jewels.

She narrowed her eyes. "Hell no."

Vicente chuckled. "It would seem we guessed correctly, Emiliano. But it doesn't matter. She will always be *mi luz*."

"Our light," Emiliano corrected, then placed a soft kiss on her shoulder, before reaching out to cup Vicente's face. "Good answers, by the way."

Gabriella shifted to her back, between her beloved husbands. "Can we go to sleep now? Because I fully intend to wake you both up in a few hours so that the three of us can begin exploring some of those sexy role-play scenarios of Emiliano's. I never got my honeymoon."

EPILOGUE

Rodrigo threw down the kickstand of his motorcycle and pulled off his helmet, taking in the budget hotel in front of him. He'd been on the run over a week, completely cut off from any semblance of his real life.

It wasn't his first time out in the field, living in places most sane people would never step foot in—though Monaco's idea of a seedy hotel would be three-star in most of the rest of the world. Still, it reeked of desperation and neglect—the kind of place people ended up after they'd lost everything at the casinos. He'd stayed in worse, but this time when he returned home, everything would be different. His role within the society would change and he didn't know how.

So, regardless of his past experience, this time...he was struggling.

They'd blown up his life. His face and his real name splashed across the front of newspapers all over Europe and beyond. At the end of this, it would be impossible for him to return to the job he loved. Security officers operated in the shadows, not in the spotlight, blending in, hiding in plain sight. Returning to his previous life was no longer an option.

Maybe losing all of that would be worth it to save the woman and to get the answers about his real father that he'd been seeking his entire life. He wanted—needed—to know who he was, where he was from.

Whenever he asked Tia or Tio about his father, about who he was, they would shoo him away, telling him only that his papa had died and that no good ever came from looking backwards.

Eventually, he stopped asking, though the questions never left him. And he'd fought to ignore the constant telltale heartbeat that had pounded inside him his entire life.

Headlights flashed over him as a car pulled into the parking lot, and he stiffened, quickly assessing the vehicle, the threat level. He'd been released from jail due to lack of evidence, but given the public's hatred of him, the authorities probably would have found something to charge him with.

Of course, it didn't matter. The Masters' Admiralty would get him out of it—their plan hinged on him being a villain but also free.

The Rolls-Royce that slowed wasn't a model he recognized, which meant it was probably a custom or one-off coach model. Those cost tens of millions of dollars, which was expensive even for Monaco.

Rodrigo unzipped his leather jacket and wrapped his hand around his 3D-printed plastic gun that Vicente had given him before he left Spain. The velvet blue Rolls-Royce slid into the parking spot next to his Rieju Jaca 125 motorcycle. The bike had been provided by his admiral, and in a pinch, he could sell it for quick cash.

The motorcycle was almost the same blue as the car.

The windows of the car were tinted, making it impossible for him to see inside. The well-trained security officer part of him told him to move, to find cover. No, it screamed at him to get the fuck out of there.

However, his gut told him to stay put.

The front window of the Rolls-Royce slowly slid down, only halfway, the driver just a shadowy figure, hidden within the depths of the luxury vehicle.

"Rodrigo Alvarez?" a deep voice asked.

"Who wants to know?" he replied in French.

"You won't need that weapon," the voice said in the same language.

"Oh?" His hand tightened on the gun. "I have no interest in you, and you should have no interest in me."

"My man will kill you, if you don't move your hand." The second voice came from the backseat, and it was smooth. He spoke Castellano with almost no trace of accent. "You are Rodrigo...Alvarez."

It hadn't been a question, but Rodrigo replied, speaking Castellano as the second man had. "I'll ask only one more time, who wants to know?"

The second man chuckled, a deep, throaty sound, more rumble than laugh. Then the rear window slid down.

Rodrigo reared back at the face looking out at him—the one that was so much like his own.

"I want to know," Armani Capello replied.

Rodrigo knew his role, knew what was expected of him, but at this point, none of this was playacting. His heart was racing, his palms sweaty as he stared back at his future...his past...and the answer to questions he probably shouldn't have asked.

Regardless, he said, "And who the fuck are you?"

"I'm your father."

. . .

IF YOU'RE interested in reading more about Eric, Nikolett, Rodrigo, and Milo, be sure to check out the entire Masters' Admiralty series.

Treachery's Devotion
Loyalty's Betrayal
Pleasure's Fury
Honor's Revenge
Bravery's Sin
Wrath's Storm
Suspicion's Fire
Desire's Addiction

AND SEE where it all began! Be sure to read the entire Trinity Masters series as well.

Elemental Pleasure
Primal Passion
Scorching Desire
Forbidden Legacy
Hidden Devotion
Elegant Seduction
Secret Scandal
Delicate Ties
Beloved Sacrifice
Masterful Truth
Fiery Surrender
Necessary Pursuit

JOIN THE SOCIETY! Hey fans of Facebook! Did you know there's a Trinity Masters/Masters' Admiralty fan group? Come join the fun—behind the scenes news, exclusive sneak peeks, cover reveals and (gasp) too many screenshots of texts between Mari and Lila.

SUGGESTED READING ORDER

Because there is some crisscrossing between the Trinity Masters and Masters' Admiralty series, Mari and Lila are always asked about the reading order. Well...ta da! Here it is.

Elemental Pleasure

Primal Passion

Scorching Desire

After Burn - Free short story

Forbidden Legacy

Hidden Devotion

A Very Trinity Christmas - Free short story

Elegant Seduction

A Grand Master Christmas - Free short story

Secret Scandal

Delicate Ties

Beloved Sacrifice

Treachery's Devotion

Masterful Truth

Wildly Inappropriate - a Trinity Masters, BDSM Checklist, Wild Irish crossover short story (because Lila is insane).

World's Collide - Free short story. Crossover with Lexi Blake.

Loyalty's Betrayal
Pleasure's Fury
Honor's Revenge
Bravery's Sin
Fiery Surrender
Hollywood Lies
Necessary Pursuit
Joyful Engagement
Wrath's Storm
Suspicion's Fire
Desire's Addiction

ABOUT THE AUTHORS

Virginia native Mari Carr is a *New York Times* and *USA TODAY* bestseller of contemporary sexy romance novels. With over two million copies of her books sold, Mari was the winner of the Romance Writers of America's Passionate Plume for her novella, *Erotic Research*.

Join her newsletter so you don't miss new releases and for exclusive subscriber-only content. Find Mari on the web on Facebook | Twitter | BookBub | Email: mari@maricarr.com.

Lila Dubois is a top selling author of contemporary erotic romance. Having spent extensive time in France, Egypt, Turkey, England and Ireland Lila speaks five languages, none of them (including English) fluently. She now lives in California with a cute Irishman.

You can visit Lila's website at www.liladubois.net. She loves to hear from fans! Send an email to author@liladubois.net or join her newsletter.

Made in the USA
Las Vegas, NV
24 April 2026

45882105R00208